Ellen Archer

Hill's
Gold

Hill's Gold

A NOVEL

Ellen Kingman Fisher

CLIO MUSE PRESS
Denver

Hill's Gold, by Ellen Kingman Fisher
Copyright © 2018 Ellen Kingman Fisher
All rights reserved

Published by Clio Muse Press
Denver, Colorado

ISBN: 978-0-9994950-0-1
LCCN: 2017916026

Front-cover image from the Library of Congress Prints and Photographs Division, Brady-Handy Photograph Collection. call number: lc-bh826-265a.

Back-cover image © Scott Rothstein/Shutterstock.

Cover and interior design by Pratt Brothers Composition
Maps by Jay P. K. Kenney
Editing by Melanie Mulhall, Dragonheart Editing and Writing
Marketing plan by Mary Walewski, Buy the Book Marketing

This book is printed in the United States of America

Quantity purchases: Schools, companies, professional groups, clubs, and other organizations may qualify for special terms when ordering quantities of this title.
For information, email: ClioMusePress@gmail.com

To Hank, Greg, and Jeni,
and especially to Fred

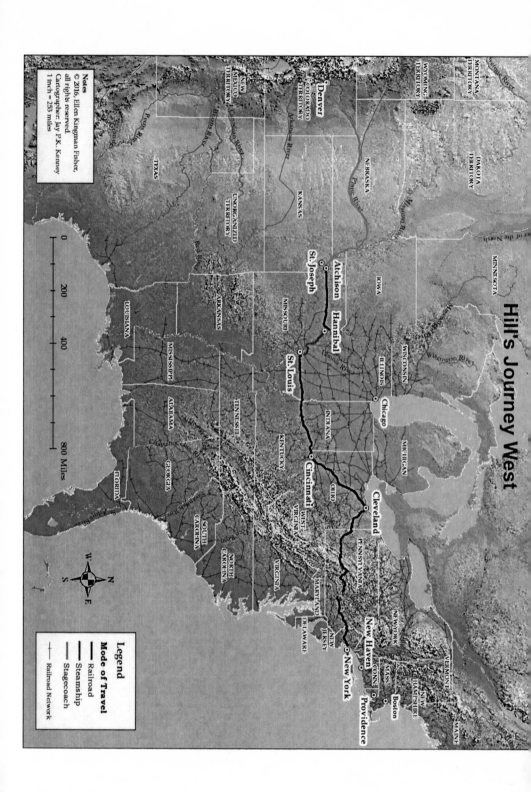

Hill's Journey West

Notes
© 2016, Ellen Kingman Fisher,
all rights reserved.
Cartographer: Jay P.K. Kenney
1 inch = 253 miles

Legend
Mode of Travel
— Railroad
— Steamship
— Stagecoach
+ Railroad Network

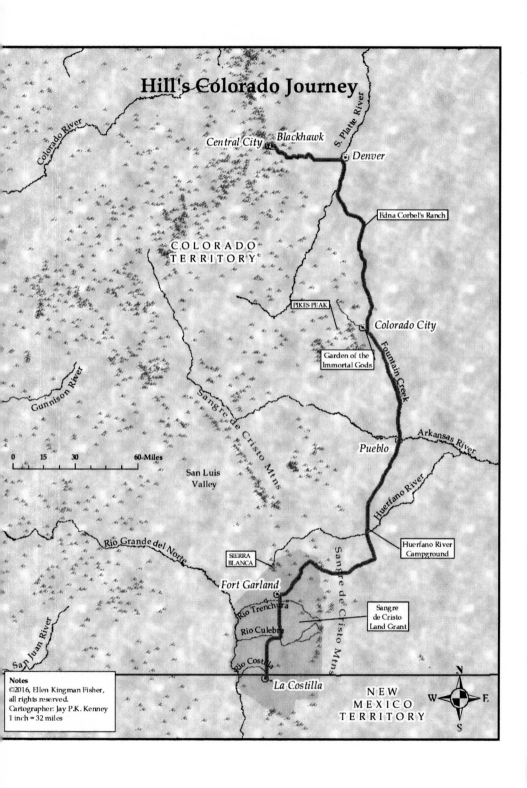

Hill's Colorado Journey

Colorado River

S. Plate River

Central City • Blackhawk

Denver

Edna Corbel's Ranch

COLORADO
TERRITORY

PIKES PEAK

Colorado City

Garden of the
Immortal Gods

Fountain Creek

Gunnison River

Sangre de Cristo Mtns

Arkansas River

Pueblo

0 15 30 60 Miles

San Luis
Valley

Huerfano River

Rio Grande del Norte

Huerfano River
Campground

SIERRA
BLANCA

Sangre de Cristo Mtns

Fort Garland

Rio Trenchura

Sangre
de Cristo
Land Grant

Rio Culebra

San Juan River

Rio Costilla

La Costilla

NEW
MEXICO
TERRITORY

N
W E
S

Hill's Gold

ONE

The knock jolted Nathaniel from his reading. Leaving his students' lab reports on his desk, he hurried to open the front door and found a breathless boy on the stoop of his Rhode Island home.

"Is this . . . thirty-seven Angell . . . Street, sir?" the boy asked, his tousled blond hair drifting into his eyes.

"It is," Nathaniel confirmed with a nod to the numbers above the door.

"Sorry to disturb you, sir, but they asked me to deliver this letter." The boy thrust a small folded document toward him. "It came all the way from Colorado Territory."

Nathaniel took the letter to read the inscription. Then he remembered the boy and pulled out a coin from his trouser pocket.

"Very kind of you, sir." A wide, gap-toothed smile lit the boy's face as he slipped the coin into his own breeches and bounded away.

Nathaniel returned to his study and sat down in his swivel chair. The letter had no envelope. Instead, a thin sheet of paper was folded, the address on the outside fold and the contents on the inside. Postage from the West was based on weight, and this document was as light as possible. He carefully put the tip of a letter opener against the seal to slit it open without damaging the contents.

Denver
October 10, 1863
Dear Professor Hill:

I am writing on behalf of William Gilpin, former governor of Colorado Territory, who, with other investors, has purchased a vast parcel of land, previously called the Beaubien Land Grant, in the Sangre de Cristo Mountains of southern Colorado. We believe this land may hold as much potential as Colorado's famous Clear Creek gold area.

Due to your knowledge of chemistry, several of our business contacts have recommended you to assess the mineral resources of the acquisition. Remuneration for analyzing the land would be $2,500 and ten percent of the holdings if valuable metal is found. Your part of the project is expected to take ninety days including travel beginning late spring 1864.

We hope for a positive response, which we will follow with more details. I am in Denver temporarily for the army and will start east in the next several days. In the meantime, the former governor will respond to you.

Yours sincerely in closing,
Colonel William H. Reynolds

Nathaniel put the delicate paper aside so he could open a drawer for a sheet of vellum. He swiveled in his desk chair, which sent the springs thrumming as he considered his answer. This proposal was the third he had received to investigate mining properties in the West. The others, quickly discarded, had been poorly thought out schemes of finding another California Gold Rush.

He reached for the letter and reread it, trying to remember recent reports about mining problems in Colorado. Apparently, the valuable minerals were trapped inside the ore. The difficulties had mildly piqued his interest, but he had not given them much thought since.

Dipping his pen in the inkwell, he began to compose a reply, thanking Colonel Reynolds for his generous offer with the intent of rejecting the assignment. But his hand balked. Here was a letter asking him to apply his knowledge of chemistry to a specific project and offering to pay him more than he earned in a year as a professor at Brown University. And if gold or silver were found, he would receive ten percent of the landholding.

Humbug! He did not like to admit it, but he knew why he was hesitating. This proposal was fanning the embers of the conflicting feelings he was already having about his university career. The exchange of ideas with his students often exhilarated him, but he missed the hands-on, practical application of his knowledge. He idly drummed his fingers on the desk, ruing the restlessness that had always been with him. Even as a child, he liked solving practical problems, taking things apart and putting them back together for an intellectual challenge. It was like an itch he could never quite scratch out.

Trying to think of words that would turn down the offer for the present yet still keep the matter open, he dipped his pen in the ink again and frowned. It was utter foolishness to give even momentary consideration to something that might jeopardize his academic career, but he vacillated. There had already been profitable strikes in Colorado. Was there any reason not to think that there might be more gold or silver? This was a chance to use his skills as a chemist, to do something tangible.

Then his mind went the other way. It seemed like an opportunity, but it was also a risk. The war had made for uncertainty. Was he willing to forfeit his job? He started to crumple the paper as if his gesture would crush the temptation it contained but released his hand and smoothed the tissue. It was more than a guaranteed stipend and share of the land that appealed to him. The allure of the West pulled at his imagination.

The newness there seemed to allow people to experiment—to shape things instead of living within the form that society had already molded in New England.

"Nat, was there someone at the door?" Alice asked, speaking quietly so her voice would not carry up the stairs and awaken their toddler, Crawford. Her floor-length skirt whispered with each step as she stepped into the room and crossed it to stand close to her husband. "I thought I heard knocking." Smoothing his jacket, she let her hand rest on his shoulder.

"It's another offer." He tipped back slightly to look up at her without removing her hand, pleased to share his thoughts. "This one is a little different."

"Is it the West again?"

"It is, but it's more specific." The information swirled in his mind as he spoke. "It's from Colonel William Reynolds, writing on behalf of the former governor of Colorado Territory."

Alice shifted slightly, letting her hand fall at her side. "To look for property with gold like the others wanted you to do?"

"Yes and no." He hesitated. "The former governor and his investors actually own the land, quite a bit of it, apparently. He wants me to assess the mineral resources."

"In the Colorado Territory?"

He nodded. "Uh huh. In the southern part. It's not quite like the other offers. This one comes with a stipend and part of the mineral wealth. Whether we find gold or not, I will get paid."

"We?" Her voice was slow and wary. "Are you using *we* as if you're thinking of going?" She drew away from him, her brow furrowing.

He kept his response breezy. "I'm only tempted to find out more. That's all at this point. I remember reading something that said it was not only difficult to find gold in Colorado, but once found, it was difficult getting it out of the rock. It's an interesting conundrum."

"Couldn't Colonel Reynolds just ship you samples to analyze?"

"He's an investor with former governor Gilpin." Nathaniel chose his words carefully. "It's not that easy. I would have to go there to look at the property. The governor is proposing I go for the summer." Nathaniel had not even reconciled all the issues that were flying around in his mind, and now he was trying to assuage Alice's worry.

"Three months? You're not really considering leaving Providence for that long?"

"I'm really not considering it, just rolling ideas around in my mind."

Alice looked at him imploringly. "How can you possibly think of crossing the Plains? You've read about attacks by Indians and bandits. It will be certain death."

Nathaniel's brown eyes linked with the blue of hers. "I'll ask Gilpin about the risks before I go any further with this. But remember, Alice, drama sells newspapers. The danger is probably overdone. I shouldn't have worried you."

She straightened up. "We're going to have another baby in the spring. How can I tend to a new baby when I can't be sure you're safe?"

"I haven't forgotten about the baby." Nathaniel reached out to wrap his arms around her expanding waist. He wanted to reassure her by holding her tight, but she pulled away in exasperation, escaping from the room with quick steps.

He watched her leave with regret. Their relationship had been close since they married in 1860. She was not only beautiful, with light brown hair clasped at the nape of her neck and alert blue eyes that seemed to shoot stars when she spoke, she was intelligent. An avid reader, she served as an indefatigable sounding board for his ideas, whether they were about his consulting jobs or academics at Brown. Her opinions were backed up with facts. They did not agree on everything, and they sometimes bristled when their views differed, but they always reconciled. Their love and their respect for each other were strong.

Nathaniel touched the letter again. He had to know more, even though he would reject the offer in the end.

→ ←

The infrequency of mail deliveries from the West tried his patience, but the former governor responded to all his questions, and with each answer, Nathaniel's interest heightened. He had asked who would make up the team of prospectors. Laborers and engineers was the answer. Money for a party of at least twenty prospectors, surveyors, and engineers had already been raised. What equipment would they take? Gilpin provided a detailed list of supplies. A caravan of mule-pulled wagons, called ambulances, would carry them down to the undefined southern border of the territory.

He used the time in the latter months of 1863 to check references. William Gilpin was known in military and political circles. He came from a Quaker family and had graduated from the University of Pennsylvania. Afterward, he went to West Point, but he quit to fight the Seminole Indians as a second lieutenant. Gilpin left the army in 1838 and moved to St. Louis where he opened a law office and edited an independent newspaper. There he became smitten with the western frontier and had been promoting it ever since. Appointed by President Lincoln, he served as Colorado's first territorial governor from 1861–1862.

The other two investors were well known in Providence. Reynolds was a cotton textile manufacturer. James Aborn, who would be in charge of organizing the prospectors and engineers, was a businessman who had left for Colorado with the Fifty-Niners. The credibility of Gilpin and his investors buoyed Nathaniel's spirits. Going west reminded him of the myth his mother had read to him as a child about Jason and the Argonauts and their perilous voyage across the Black Sea to search for the magical ram's fleece in an unknown land. Gilpin's expedition would be over dry land, but it would be just as daring.

"The stagecoaches crossing the Great Plains are always armed for protection from Indians and guerilla bushwhackers," Gilpin assured him in a letter. "I have also made contact with your acquaintance, Mr. Watson, in Central City." That same morning's mail brought him a letter from Joe Watson, enthusiastically inviting him to visit.

After reading both letters, Nathaniel wandered from his study into the warmth of the kitchen, where he found Alice in the rocking chair knitting a baby sweater. Crawford was nearby in his playpen, trying to squeeze a leather ball through the slatted rail. He pulled a chair from the kitchen table to sit across from his wife. "Alice, do you recall the young chap who worked at the dry goods store downtown?"

"I'm not sure. Are you referring to the owner's son?"

"Yes, that's the one. Joe Watson. Do you remember that he went to Colorado with the Fifty-Niners?"

She stopped knitting to think. "I had forgotten that. I guess I haven't seen him for quite a while." Alice pulled the soft yellow yarn from the tangled skein.

"I had lost track of him myself. I went down to the dry goods store and had a long chat with his father. He told me all about Joe and what is happening out West. After I spoke with him, I decided to write Joe. He left here to go to a place called Central City, near the big Clear Creek gold find. He had no luck in finding gold so he built a small dry goods store. It's somewhat like his father's, and much to his father's consternation, Joe has no desire to return to Providence to help with the family business."

"It seems to me that he was only a boy when he left," Alice replied without looking up from her knitting.

"He had just finished school, and I imagine he's grown up quite a bit in the four years he's been there. Leaving home and living in the West would give little choice." A touch of envy tinged his voice. "Let me read part of his letter."

His eyes darted across the page so he would not inadvertently read the words recounting the town's altercations and a description of almost everyone wearing a gun for defense. "My dry goods store has a large second floor that is my living quarters, and there are several beds available for visiting men. It is safe. I would welcome you when you come and welcome any recent news of Rhode Island you might bring with you. As you requested, I can arrange to have you meet some of the mine owners here." Nathaniel did not continue with the words, ". . . although many are returning as mining plays out."

Alice listened attentively as he read but said nothing. Nathaniel suspected that she was holding her tongue because she was uneasy about the possibility of his traveling to the West, despite what he was doing to erase her apprehensions. "Isn't that encouraging, Alice? I think young Mr. Watson could be quite helpful."

Alice kept her eyes on her knitting. "Hmm." She finally looked up as she changed the subject. "Tomorrow is the day I take Crawford to Mama's for the afternoon. I'm going to a meeting about improving sanitary conditions for the Union troops. Some of our soldiers don't even have fresh water or a dry place to sleep. The conditions are becoming abominable."

Nathaniel realized there was no further point in trying to persuade her. For her, the West was like falling off the edge of the world. The war was so close and dreadful, and the West so far away and intangible. "Give your mother my regards. I know your efforts will make a difference."

He got up, stuffed his hands in his pockets, and returned to his study. In a glum mood, he sat down to reply to Joe Watson. Alice's insecurity was disconcerting. In the past, she was eager to know all the details of his work at Brown and about his business consulting, but since the recent letter from Colorado, she avoided talking about the proposed trip that was now filling his thoughts. For the first time in their three-year marriage, they were not sharing their lives. He wished he could slow things down to let her catch up with his enthusiasm, but he needed to make a decision about the trip in time to be ready by spring.

Later that week, the aroma of beef stew greeted him when Nathaniel returned home from the university and hung his coat and hat on a hook in the foyer. He passed through his study to put down his valise before entering the kitchen and encircling Alice's shoulders from behind to kiss her neck as she leaned over the stove.

"How was your day, Nat?"

"Successful. The students are happy with the chemistry lab. You should see their faces when they are mixing chemicals instead of just listening to me lecture." He released her, and she turned to face him, her eyes sparkling.

"Are the other faculty members enthusiastic?" she asked.

"It's the usual. Some come up to John and me and ask questions about what we're doing in the laboratory. Others grumble in their beards about a new method of teaching." He laughed. "Change can be threatening."

"I'm really proud of you for sticking with your idea of a laboratory and getting it to work."

"Thanks, love. I like that coming from you." He leaned over and gave her cheek another peck.

She gave him a cheerful smile and turned back to her cooking.

Before returning to his study, he paused in the doorway. "I forgot to mention. The last letter I received from William Gilpin said the stagecoaches are all armed. He assured me I could travel safely."

Her cheer vanished. "Wouldn't he just say that because he wants you to come?"

"Over and over, I hear high regard for the former governor," he assured her. "Rumor has it that he has even met with President Lincoln. I think I can put stock in what he says."

Alice stopped her stirring to face him. "Why can't you be satisfied with routine? Everything is finally going so well at the university. A trip would upset everyone." A frown of frustration scrunched her brow. "Our family is growing. Aren't there challenges enough here?"

"But this one really is out of the ordinary."

"Out of the ordinary and so much risk! This was bad enough in the first place, but the timing makes it even worse. It's really too much to deal with right now." She leaned down to take out the loaves of bread from the oven and banged the door shut.

"I still have hurdles before I make a decision, but I wanted to talk to you first." He walked forward and put his arm around her, but she was stiff and mute. With a sigh, he finally pulled away and returned to his study to weigh all the facts of a trip that was becoming a fixation. In addition to persuading Alice, he would have to convince the university's executive board.

TWO

ϙ

Nathaniel was a popular figure at Brown University. He had the look of intensity to him, but was also warm and engaging. Students were attracted by his inspiring teaching and often gathered around him to discuss ideas. His dark hair was always neatly parted on the left side, reaching just over his ears to meet the fringe of whiskers that extended the length of his jaw. Typically, a starched white collar jutted up from wide lapels to frame his face in friendly formality.

His laboratory method appealed to students but made older faculty members wary. Some of them were sure to resent another out-of-the-ordinary proposal such as going to Colorado. Before asking the executive board for a meeting, Nathaniel decided he needed to consult with his favorite colleague, John Peirce. John had been an ally who supported Nathaniel's far-fetched idea of a chemistry laboratory. If he were going to take another risk—an even greater one this time—he had to test his rationale, so he had asked John to meet him at his office.

The morning's cold hung heavy in a leaden sky, forecasting a nor'easter by afternoon. More than likely, his return home from classes would be through sleet thrusting sideways across Narragansett Bay. Nathaniel carried work for his next class with him, but all he could think about was explaining to the Brown University executive board why a trip to Colorado Territory made sense. Reaching the second floor, he saw John leaning against the doorframe. The tweed jacket he wore was snug against his muscular body, and an overcoat was slung over his arm. His healthy physique gave him the appearance of an athlete, not an academic.

They greeted one another and Nathaniel ushered his friend into his office. "John, I need a good listening post and you're the wisest one I know."

"Flattery won't make my responses any more palatable."

"I know, I know. That's why I consult you. You always give me your opinion straight up. I enjoy listening to your reasoning about issues, no matter how bitter the pill you make me swallow."

Nathaniel's desk dominated the small college office. Bookcases lined one wall and a small fireplace sat at the end of the room. Shrugging out of his woolen coat, Nathaniel lit a fire while John hung up his coat. Then he pulled his chair from behind the desk to sit across from his colleague. "John, when I first told you about the letter from Governor Gilpin, I gave it little mind, but since then, I've given it more thought. I'm seriously considering taking him up on his offer to go to Colorado."

"Hmm, I'm not surprised." John took out his pipe, tobacco pouch, and container of matches before continuing. "I guess temptation outweighs what the university has recently given you." Wrinkles crinkled the edges of his thoughtful eyes. Brown University had lured John from Yale ten years earlier, and he was still regarded as a well-respected newcomer. "It concerns me," he said with a puff of smoke, "and I'm probably not the only one. What does Alice think?"

Nathaniel idly straightened a stack of papers before answering. "She's reluctant about it, scared more than anything, but I hope she'll come around." He looked up, beseeching approval.

"And what about the executive board? Have you broached the subject with them yet? It hasn't been long since you smoothed their ruffled feathers about the chemistry laboratory."

"You're opening all my old wounds." Nathaniel was no longer able to sit. He got up from his chair to pace the length of his small office, stopping to gaze out the window at the river flowing toward Narragansett Bay.

"The one thing you have in your favor is that they're happy with the way your last project turned out. That doesn't negate the fact that you challenged their authority. They haven't forgotten that part. It's as fresh as newly dropped manure," John grumbled.

Nathaniel turned from the view to face John. "I would hope that the success of the laboratory would be what they remember."

"No matter how successful the lab is, I'd be careful about pressing your luck."

The caution was met with momentary silence before Nathaniel's thoughts tumbled into words. "I'm trying to think through all my options before I make a decision. I'm not going into this rashly, which is why I'd like to ask you if you would be willing to fill in for me during the summer if I do decide to go. The students will be gone, but I'll have to reassure the executive board that my administrative work will be covered."

John looked at Nathaniel with a steady gaze. "You seem to be quite a ways down the road in your planning."

"No, just thinking ahead. And I'm not ungrateful for what you've already done for me."

"I've invested a lot of my own reputation in changes to the chemistry department. This is not going to sit well with the executive board, and that will be a reflection on me, Nathaniel." The tobacco in his pipe flared red as he inhaled deeply. "They just made you Brown's youngest full professor of chemistry. That's a rare distinction, and it's going to appear as if you are throwing that honor in their faces."

Nathaniel was frustrated that John's usual humor had been replaced with irritation. "Why wouldn't they think that consulting in Colorado will turn out as well as the lab?"

"The lab you created has value for the university."

"This might too," Nathaniel retorted.

"The offer to go to Colorado is just a private contract. *Some* members of the executive board may realize that Brown will benefit from your increasing reputation, but others will envy you and try to thwart you. Do you really want to risk that?"

"So you think I should give up the notion altogether? Cast off a once-in-a-lifetime opportunity?" Nathaniel asked as he walked from the window to sag into his chair.

"It's not my decision, but you've already been granted one special request. You're tempting fate. It's a dangerous game, and it's not only your life you're playing with. You are toying with your mortality by crossing the Plains, risking the possibility of leaving your family fatherless, and gambling with your career. You need to calculate what you have to gain against what you might lose."

"I know there are few jobs like this," Nathaniel admitted, twisting uncomfortably in his seat. "I'm at the top of my profession, yet there's something lacking. Something inside me wants to solve problems and see the results rather than only making explanations."

"Don't you see results in your students?" John asked with impatience. "I do understand the difference. *I do.* But not everyone on the executive board will. They hired you to be an academic. They may decide you're no longer interested in that profession."

Nathaniel let out his breath with a whistle. "I'll consider what you've said. I asked for your honesty and you've given it to me. Your friendship means as much as anything at Brown."

John stood and went to knock his burned pipe tobacco into the open fireplace.

Nathaniel's chair scudded backwards as he stood up too. "It may not seem it, but I appreciate your opinion and everything you've done for me."

John reached for his overcoat, ready to leave, before gripping Nathaniel's hand and shaking his head in skepticism. Then he turned away to go to his own office.

Nathaniel watched his wide-shouldered colleague disappear and then glanced back at the valise of papers next to his desk. He pulled his pocket watch from his vest. Class would not start for half an hour. Too distracted to review lab experiments, he walked out the door and turned right to go down the hall to the chemistry laboratory.

The lab was outfitted with a long, narrow center table lined with crystal beakers of chemicals ready for students' experimentation. This hands-on technique for teaching had come from Nathaniel's chafing at simply lecturing to students. His favorite childhood memories were of the experiments he'd conducted with his mechanically inclined father, whose inveterate love of tinkering, gadgetry, and invention had rubbed off on him. Nathaniel had known his students would benefit more from conducting experiments than from just receiving classroom lectures. John had supported him when Nathaniel first approached him with the idea, and that support had created a bond between the two men.

It had taken a full week for Nathaniel to get a meeting with the executive board about the issue of creating a chemistry lab. The dozen men on the Brown University executive board had earned their positions through long years of scholarship and teaching, and their esteem meant that they were rarely challenged. Nathaniel and John were seated at the end of the long mahogany table. The older men sat erect, their grizzled sideburns almost electric with tension while they listened to his plan. Turning to his ink-sketched diagrams, they whispered terse comments among themselves.

Finally, President Sears said, "Mr. Hill, you are free to raise money for a chemistry laboratory . . . outside of your teaching responsibilities. If you use university time, not only will we terminate the laboratory idea, but also your position."

The executive board's challenge had been laid down in 1860. Nathaniel barely had time to breathe as he kept up with his classes while trying to raise the $14,000 needed to build the laboratory, but it was completed for the beginning of the 1862–63 academic year. When fall classes began, the young men were quiet as they first entered the lab and saw the new layout. Then they burst into enthusiastic conversations about the chance to actually experiment with chemicals during class.

The chemistry lab was a success, and Nathaniel was promoted to full professor in the spring of 1863. Applications to Brown's chemistry program had multiplied, and Nathaniel's reputation for innovation and scholarship spread up and down East Coast. Columbia, Yale, Amherst, and Rensselaer Polytechnic Institute soon adopted Nathaniel's model, and businessmen approached him with contract proposals.

While Nathaniel had earned the board's goodwill with the creation of a chemistry laboratory, he knew he would need more than that to persuade them to allow him a leave, something typically reserved for the sabbaticals of aging professors. A little more than a year had passed since the lab had become operational. He knew John was right about risking his career again, and travel to the Rocky Mountains was life-threatening, no matter what assurance the former governor gave. It was not just about him. What would Alice and the children do without him? For a week he brooded. If he chose to go, it was against the advice of the two people closest to him: Alice and John. The risks of asking were obvious, but his heart also knew if he did not act soon, his dream to do something tangible would slip away and he would gradually sink into the prestigious but placid routine of his elders. He had to make a decision soon to be ready to leave in the spring. Fortunately, the executive board had scheduled a meeting before the winter recess.

A damp, blustery wind blew in from the bay the day the executive board met. Little light filtered through the leaded-glass windows, leaving the room as dim as the mood of the board members. The faculty members asked Nathaniel questions to satisfy their curiosity about the West. He optimistically sensed curiosity, maybe even envy, poking through the cloak of their annoyance. When he spoke, it was with passion about the project and the possibilities for new information for university students. He tactfully explained that fresh ideas inspired men to learn. Forward-thinking ideas, he believed, set Brown apart and above other institutions and attracted students.

After half an hour of discussion, the faculty tersely approved a leave with an ominous coolness. If he did not return in time for fall classes, his job was in jeopardy.

→ ←

Nathaniel trudged up the narrow oak stairs to his office, mulling over the varying reactions to his upcoming trip. Some of his friends hinted at irresponsibility, people he barely knew approached him with schemes for profit, and many faculty members resented it. Alice was panicked. He could hardly blame her. She was close to her time.

When he removed his coat, the room felt chilly. He pulled the iron ring to open the flue of his small, tiled fireplace. With a strike of a match, the kindling under the logs caught fire. He sat down at his desk, tilting back in his chair. The lab experiment results he promised to return to his students the next morning lay in a pile. Usually eager to see how the young men responded to his teaching, their answers now held little interest. He picked up the next student paper. If he did not finish them now, it would be another late night.

"Halloo, Professor Hill. Are you in there?" a disembodied voice asked from the hallway. The question was followed by a rat-a-tat-tat on the door. That kind of greeting did not suggest it was a student.

"I'm here. Please come in."

An official-looking man opened the door and stuck in his head. "Professor Hill?"

"Yes?" Nathaniel stood up from his chair.

"I'm here representing Elisha Dyer, the former governor of Rhode Island. He desires a meeting with you at your earliest convenience." The man reached forward to hand Nathaniel an envelope with a thick red seal.

"Governor Dyer?" Nathaniel opened it, and perused the formal request. "Why does he want to see me?"

"I really cannot say." The slender man's waxy face was so thin that his ears stood out like sugar bowl handles. "Governor Dyer requests an indication of the time you will see him."

Nathaniel rubbed his chin as he recreated his calendar in his mind. "Tomorrow at noon—that's the first time I have."

"Exchange Building. Noon." Giving a perfunctory nod, the messenger left Nathaniel alone with his papers. A frown crunched the bridge of his nose as he began to read. The next day he left his last morning class, begging off questions from the students clustered around him, and hastily walked eight blocks to the two-story Exchange Bank Building in Providence's city center. Nathaniel knew that Dyer was one of Brown's notable alumni in chemistry. He had served as governor in the late 1850s and had gone to Washington, DC, to serve with a Rhode Island volunteer regiment the year after the South seceded. Nathaniel was not sure, but he thought Dyer now worked for his family's mercantile business.

The small-statured assistant who had delivered the formal request greeted Nathaniel. His heels clicked together in salutation, a sign that he was a former military man. He helped Nathaniel off with his coat, hung it on a hook, and tapped on the heavy door before swinging it open. Elisha Dyer was a compact man dressed in a dark suit with black silk vest and striped trousers. A gray silk cravat lay against his starched shirtfront. His full hair progressed from white to grey as it extended into frizzled muttonchops. He came around his desk to shake Nathaniel's hand. "Please have a seat, Professor Hill."

"Thank you. I'm honored to meet you, Governor Dyer."

"It has come to my attention that you will be leaving for the Colorado Territory this spring." The governor's tone was brisk and confident.

"That's right, sir. I have a contract to investigate property there."

"In the Clear Creek area where gold has been found?"

"No, not close to Clear Creek at all," Nathaniel said firmly, stressing the distance. "This property is hundreds of miles south of the Clear Creek mining towns, at the border of New Mexico, where no gold has been found yet. I will spend most of my time there. If there is extra time, I will go for a short visit to Central City, forty miles west of Denver, to see a young man I knew in passing. He left Providence a number of years ago."

Nathaniel glanced around the well-appointed office. At the far corner the blue state flag with stars encircling an anchor stood. A portrait of George Washington hung on the wall behind the governor's polished mahogany desk. Dyer was out of office, but he had not given up the trappings of power.

"I've checked your reputation. We are, after all, both graduates in chemistry, and now you teach at Brown. You have also had a number of business consulting jobs."

And apparently you know even more than that, Nathaniel thought.

"You've accomplished a great deal. I commend you."

"Thank you." Nathaniel squirmed in his chair, knowing expectations usually followed a compliment.

"I've heard that you are honest as well as enterprising."

Nathaniel girded himself as Dyer reached over to pull out a prepared document from a cubbyhole.

"I want to give you a promissory note to purchase land in or around the mining territories—near Clear Creek. Like everyone, I'm intrigued by the riches of the West." He unfolded the documents as he spoke. "The US government's financing of the war is playing havoc with our money. It's becoming worthless. I'd rather have the hard currency of gold coins than bloated greenbacks."

Nathaniel nearly bolted from his chair, but he paused. "Governor Dyer, I'm flattered by your trust—"

"We're in the third year of this insufferable war. The government simply hasn't the money to meet the demand of the notes with the fancy green writing on the back," the governor interrupted.

"I have the same opinion about the value of coins over greenbacks, sir, but I'm not sure I can do you any good. I'm really under the hire of former Governor Gilpin. It's uncertain whether I can even take a side trip to Central City," Nathaniel said in feeble protest.

Dyer's face tightened, his eyes narrowed. "You just said you would be taking time to visit an acquaintance. I would think you could investigate other property while you are there."

"Sir, one of the reasons I would like to visit Central City is to learn more about mining problems. I'm hesitant—"

"I think you sell yourself short. I imagine your chemistry will hold you in good stead. I'll draw up the rest of the legal work for a potential seller and have it for you by week's end." The former governor rose and extended his hand as he said, "I know you have to return to the university."

Nathaniel gave an uncomfortable bow, apprehension knotting his stomach. "I'll be happy to see what I can find for you, sir."

"Thank you. I envy you your trip, and I'm sure you will be very careful in your travels. The dangers are well known."

"I appreciate your concern."

Nathaniel raced out of the bank building, his feet barely touching the marble stairs as he descended. At the corner, he saw a hack. The lounging driver straightened up and put on his hat as Nathaniel rushed toward him. "I'm almost late for class. Take me to Brown, my good fellow."

The carriage arrived at Brown's science building a few minutes before the tower clock struck one. He took the stairs two at a time and sprinted down the hall to the chemistry laboratory.

Foregoing the usual introduction of a new topic at the beginning of class, Nathaniel decided to give his students a task. Directing his hand to the right side of the room, he said, "All right, men, I want this half of the room to mix the chemicals I'm going to list in the first column, and the rest of you are to put together the ones in the second. You have the next twenty minutes to work, and then we will discuss the differing results."

Nathaniel quickly wrote two columns of symbols on the board with chalk. As the students went to work, he slumped on the stool he used as a desk chair. Anger began burning inside him. Elisha Dyer's desire to reap some reward was his only reason for caring if Nathaniel survived crossing the Plains. The insistence of power was inescapable.

Nathaniel pulled out his pocket watch. The twenty minutes he had given his class were over. Numbly, he rose and began probing his students for their responses. "Gentlemen, let's start with the left side of the blackboard. What was the reaction when you mixed the chemicals and why?"

His students responded tentatively to his mechanical interrogation. Usually, he asked rapid-fire questions randomly, keeping everyone alert as they anticipated being called on—a method to draw the answers out of students. His father had used this same technique with his sons—Socratic questioning he called it. Even as a young boy, Nathaniel realized that he understood things better if he figured them out for himself.

At last, the bell signaled the end of class. Nathaniel followed the students out of class but avoided walking among them. Back at his office, he bundled papers from his desk into his valise and wearily closed his office to go home.

Fifteen minutes later, he walked through the front door to find Alice in the parlor reading a book to Crawford. The blue fireplace tiles reflected the light from the fire.

"This is a welcome sight." He cupped his hands under Crawford's chubby arms to lift him. "Hello, little mischief. It looks like you're being a good little boy for Mama." He could feel the rapid heartbeat as he pressed his son to his chest. With a kiss, he handed Crawford back to Alice.

Alice rose heavily from the couch. "Whatever did Governor Dyer want?"

"What a day," Nathaniel muttered. "I thought I'd never make it through, and I still have papers to finish tonight."

Crawford began to wriggle in Alice's arms. "But I can barely stand the suspense."

"I'll hang up my coat," Nathaniel murmured before brushing his lips across her cheek. "We can talk in the kitchen."

Alice was already feeding Crawford mashed carrots when Nathaniel sat down at the table. "The former governor wants to write a promissory note for property in Colorado."

"What does that mean? He's going to pay you?"

"No, not me. He wants me to be the bearer of a note to pay the owner of a property he wants to buy."

"Why does he want to own land in Colorado Territory? For gold?" she asked quizzically.

Nathaniel massaged his temples with his thumbs to make his head stop aching. "That's right. He expects me to find land with gold."

"It isn't just lying around in plain sight ready to be taken, is it?"

"You understand that . . . and I'm sure he does too. He wants the jingle of gold coins in his pocket instead of the fluctuating value of greenbacks."

Alice wiped Crawford's face with a damp cloth and gave him a Graham cracker. "Greenbacks? That's what Congress is in a stew about, isn't it?"

"A stew? That's one way to put it. They're printing money to fund the war—notes with green ink on the back allowing the bearer to demand currency."

"Every time the government prints more greenbacks the value declines, right?" Alice asked.

"Yes, and it's affecting everyone, including us." He ran his fingers through his hair. "First it was the banker, and now Governor Dyer. I don't know how they have the nerve to ask me to shop for property . . . and then insinuate that I might not even make it to Colorado alive."

"Banker? You met with a banker?"

"George Lungren stopped me on the street corner on the way to campus today. I didn't even recognize him at first because it's been so long since I last saw him, but he asked me to find land for him." Nathaniel's eyes flashed with frustration. "I have no desire to find land for anyone, but especially not a former governor, and certainly not mere acquaintances like Lungren."

"What if you can't find what the former governor wants?"

"I don't think Governor Dyer has given failure a thought. For men of power, a desire and results are one in the same. I just wish I weren't in the middle of it."

"This trip was a bad idea from the start," Alice replied with a flash of irritation.

Nathaniel glared back at her. "I don't know why everyone's making my life so complicated."

Despite having tried to ward off other requests, two colleagues had also persuaded him to take their promissory notes. The stakes for the trip were getting higher. The thought of unintentionally spending other people's money on worthless land made him shudder.

In his study after dinner, Nathaniel sorted accumulated papers. He had designated the cubbyholes on the left for his consulting projects and the ones on the right side for academics. His life was just as divided. Each half was enough for one life, but he was not willing to give up either. The desk lamp flickered as he turned to finish his student papers. The hall clock chimed 11:30 before he was finished. It would be another short night of sleep. Extinguishing the gas lamp, he lit a candle and shuffled up the stairs to bed. He had slept only a few minutes when he felt something tugging at his nightshirt, but through his exhaustion, he could not figure out what it was. There was another tug and a voice.

"Nat, Nat, it's time," Alice whispered loudly.

"It's not morning yet. Let's get some sleep."

"Wake up. The baby is coming. You need to fetch Dr. Carpenter and Mama to take care of Crawford. Hurry! It's coming fast."

"What? Oh, of course!" Nathaniel jumped from the bed, struck a match to light the lamp, and looked at his wife. "Are you okay?"

She clutched her belly with a long moan. "I will be if you get Dr. Carpenter. But hurry."

In the circumference of light, Nathaniel could see the perspiration on her pale, round face. He pulled on the clothing he had just taken off and clambered down the stairs. "I'll be right back." He pumped water to fill the largest pot he could find, set the pot on the stove, and added firewood to the stove's embers before racing out of the house and down the four blocks to Dr. Carpenter's house.

He returned in half an hour with the doctor and his carriage. They had stopped to awaken Harriet Hale, who would come in her own carriage to help her daughter and watch Crawford. Dr. Carpenter had delivered

Alice, her brothers, and Crawford. He was a kindly man, tall with angular cheekbones and beetle brows above watery blue eyes.

Opening the front door for the doctor, Nathaniel handed him the lantern. "Water is heating on the stove. Do you need anything else?"

"Bring it to the bedroom. At the top of the stairs, isn't it?"

"Yes, yes, the first door." Nathaniel wanted to cover his ears against Alice's cries.

He stumbled to the kitchen to light another lantern. With two thick pads, he gingerly carried the water, trying not to slop it over and scald himself. He found he could not hold the pot and a lantern, so he adjusted his eyes to the dark between the lantern below and the light above and carefully ascended the stairs, setting the water to the right of where Dr. Carpenter was standing in the bedroom. Speaking to both Alice and the doctor he said, "Call out if you need anything else." Then he departed, knowing the bedroom would be off-limits to him, and went to check on Crawford. In the dark nursery, he listened to his son's peaceful breathing.

Downstairs he damped the lantern and flopped down on the parlor settee to close his eyes. Noise from the bedroom above rang in his ears.

Nathaniel's legs were bent uncomfortably on the settee, but he was too tired to care. He dozed intermittently until he felt a shake of his shoulder and pulled himself out of a restless dream to focus on Dr. Carpenter.

"Congratulations, Mr. Hill. You have a new daughter. April 10, 1864. The second baby doesn't take as long as the first. Alice is asleep, and from the looks of you, I think you could use some more yourself. The sun won't be up for another hour."

"Thank you, Dr. Carpenter." Nathaniel shook the doctor's hand with elation and accompanied him to the door, then wearily slumped back down to the settee. He knew that Alice would be pleased with a girl, but for the life of him, he could not remember the name they had chosen if the baby was a girl.

The name was Isabel, and in the weeks following her birth, he and Alice were so preoccupied with their separate duties, they scarcely had time for conversation. Meanwhile, the packages of supplies for the trip continued to stack up in his study, giving it the appearance of a warehouse. A carting company would pick them up.

It struck Nathaniel that his newborn daughter would not even notice his absence when he was gone. A sense of guilt washed over him. A second wave of guilt followed the first because he knew that even though Isabel would not miss him, Alice would.

THREE

⳺

On the day he left to go west, Nathaniel opened the front door to a spring mist and the scent of crabapple blossoms. He regretted that he had not said good-bye to everyone as he had intended. More time should have been spent on studying the vast land of Colorado Territory, and he wished he had spent more time with Alice, but the time had come, fully ready or not. Perhaps life was always like that. One was never fully prepared to leave what was known before going on to something new. He shook his head in remorse. His two pieces of personal luggage leaned against each other on the stoop. The equipment had already been taken away and would spend almost six weeks in transit.

Alice and Crawford were in tears. Only infant Isabel slept peacefully in her mother's arms, unconcerned about the impending separation. Nathaniel stopped at the door to embrace his wife, momentarily delaying the finality of leaving his family.

"Please write often, Alice," he implored, knowing letters would be an empty substitute for her nearness. He finally detached himself and pulled his bags down the front stairs toward the waiting hack. The door closed like the last chapter of a book.

Nathaniel opened the newspaper beside him and glanced at the war headlines, but energy to read eluded him. Instead, he looked through the windows at the familiar signposts of his life—ship masts with white sails on Narragansett Bay, church steeples, and plumes of dark factory smoke erupting into the overcast sky—receding with the train's quickening pace. The train fell into a rhythmic clickity-clack lullaby, and he fell into a fretful sleep.

He was jarred awake, almost catapulting into the aisle, and grabbed the seatback in front of him with the train whistle shrieking in his ear. Clothing and packages hurtled off the racks and onto the seats and floor below as the squealing brakes ground the train to a halt. The car erupted into a cacophony of babbling voices.

He tugged at his watch to check the time. A half hour had passed since the train left New Haven. A delay might mean a missed connection in New York. He only had an hour between the scheduled arrival in New York and the departure on the Cleveland-bound Erie Railroad. Stuffing his watch back in his pocket, he lamented his decision to continue on instead of staying overnight in New York and taking a morning train, but in his eagerness to be on his way, he had risked the close connection. Acid filled his stomach.

With a gust of cool air, the conductor strode through the door at the front. "Anyone hurt here?" He looked around at the belongings strewn throughout the car.

The confused passengers barraged him with questions. "What happened? Why did the train stop?"

"Cattle on the tracks," he replied as he picked his way down the aisle.

Nathaniel rose as the conductor went by. "Excuse me. How long do you expect to be delayed? I have a connection to make."

"As soon as we scatter the animals. It's a large herd, not eager to move. Consider yourself lucky that we didn't derail." Apparently satisfied there were no injuries, the conductor turned and returned to the front of the train.

Nathaniel retrieved his valise, which had shot forward. Nearby passengers were speculating about how much time it would take to get going again. He waited impatiently until he finally felt the vibration of the train rumbling to life. Forty-five minutes of precious time had been wasted.

Toward late afternoon, clustered buildings signaled the approach of New York. Nathaniel did not wait for the train to stop. After putting on his topcoat and hat, he grabbed his valise and went to the baggage car to search for his suitcase in the jumble of spilled trunks and boxes. Back at his seat, he wedged the suitcase into a space beside him. There was no time to wait for a baggage man to unload it and take it to his next train. He would have to haul it himself.

The train decelerated with a hiss of rising steam. Nathaniel took his watch from his pocket. The train bound for Cleveland was due to leave in a matter of minutes. He pulled his collar up against the drizzle. Dragging his luggage behind him, he scrutinized the signs on the confusing rows of platforms. Running down one corridor, he found a train—but it was the wrong one, and he had to backtrack. When he found the right train, he ran the last yards, gasping short breaths to hurl himself into the car just as the train began pulling out of the station. Towing his luggage behind him, he moved awkwardly down the aisle until he found his seat and collapsed onto it.

The passenger across from him looked up from his newspaper. "Close connection?"

"Way too close," Nathaniel replied as he mopped his forehead with his handkerchief and gave his large suitcase to the baggage handler. He took the receipt and tucked it in his valise.

It would be hours before a meal stop, and he had not eaten anything since breakfast. His heart was still racing from the dash between trains. He knew it would not be the last close call. The next three weeks his life would be controlled by transportation schedules and every variety of thing that might go wrong, from derailments and fires from defective engines to robbery by gun-toting bandits.

The west side of New York was squeezed with tenements, and as the train got on its way, he watched shabbily dressed people going about their business along the dirt streets, dodging heaps of manure, garbage, and clogged sewer drains. Dead dogs and rats lay on the piles of refuse. It was not until the next day that the scenery opened up to rolling fertile land, vast stretches of which were under cultivation. Sturdy farmhouses dotted the land, which was ringed with fences to protect livestock.

For the umpteenth time he went over in his mind whether assessing Governor Gilpin's land was reason enough to risk his life. In reality, the chances of dying were as great as fulfilling his contract. In the past, he had risked his career and his reputation, but never his life. The naysayers could end up being right. A chill shuddered up his spine with thoughts of leaving his children fatherless. In the idleness of the long train ride, his mind drifted back to his own father.

A workbench like his father's was what Nathaniel had wanted the summer he was ten. He had learned how to use a hammer, and he wanted to make things, as his father did. Peter, his father, had seen the value in it and had constructed one for him.

Peter had given him small jobs like sanding rough planks, building containers for supplies, or replacing leather fittings on harnesses. Compared to his father, his work had been rough and lopsided, but he felt his skill growing with practice. With each finished task, his father had rewarded him with a hand-me-down tool.

His parents' seven-hundred-acre farm in Montgomery, New York, was in the middle of the rich Appalachian Valley between the Hudson and Delaware Rivers at the south end of the state. The red brick Georgian house had been passed down for four generations of Hills.

As young boys, he and his brother James spent mornings milking cows and mucking barns, but their afternoons had been filled with free time to explore and dream. James was a reader while Nathaniel was a doer.

With the coming of fall, the leaves flamed red and orange and smelled the musky scent of mulch and bark. Nathaniel had regretted the change in seasons when the cherished companionship of his father was replaced with daily pony rides to the schoolhouse. He'd been an attentive student, excelling at math and reading, but at the end of the day, he would become fidgety, anxious to return home to his projects. When the final school bell rang, he slung his books across his pony's withers and trotted home to see what his father had put on the workbench for him. One afternoon in mid-September, he'd found the horizontal rake from the thrasher leaning against the bench, too large to fit on the plank.

The large, toothed implement was used to beat grain from the hay as the thrasher moved, but it had kept breaking away from the hay wagon. With harvesting done, his father had asked him to find a solution to keep the thrasher on the wagon, and he had felt proud to be given something important to do.

Following school each day, Nathaniel had run to the barn after watering and feeding his pony. Over a month's time, he tried one idea after another. At dusk, he would hitch the draft horses to the wagon and sigh in frustration as the thrasher fell off again. One evening he noticed metal rings for a pulley. He took two of the iron rings and attached them to the wagon, then riveted two heavier iron hooks on the thrasher. Finally, convinced that his invention would work, he walked in the darkening evening light from the barn to the house to ask his father to come test his device.

His father often spent time before dinner going over accounts or reading in the book-lined room designated as the family library, and that was where he was that evening. Nathaniel had found his father slumped over with his head on the desk, his arms dangling awkwardly beneath him.

The doctor had been summoned, but it had been too late. Nathaniel's father was already dead. He was thirty-nine.

The train's shrill whistle startled Nathaniel out of his daydream. He looked around to get his bearings. Again, he considered his situation. It was always possible to turn around at Cleveland and choose reason and embarrassment over adventure and danger, but he suspected that pride would prevent him from returning like a cowardly mongrel, tail curled between its legs. He gazed out the window, searching for an answer, and he realized this was really as much a journey about finding himself as it was a contract with Gilpin.

A lantern was lit at each end of the wooden coach, and he pulled his valise up to his lap to keep it close while he slept. Like the other passengers, he contorted his body to find a position to sleep against the seat's hard slats. Stops to get a meal, fuel, and water would be the only breaks.

For three nights, darkness swallowed the train as the lanterns flickered out. During the day, Nathaniel peered through the windows at the unfamiliar land. When his train arrived in St. Louis at ten in the morning, he had his baggage transferred to the steamship for the 120-mile boat ride to Hannibal. He would spend the night in St. Louis, so he asked the conductor for directions to the Mississippi River. Pushing through the crowded muddle, he set out. St. Louis was under martial law to keep the warring factions in order.

At the river landing, he stopped at an eatery, famished from having not eaten in some time. While he ate, he watched as Union soldiers and sailors lined up to board the gunboats for their portentous passage south. On the other side of the river, wounded men hobbled off boats or were carried on stretchers to merge with the throng of the city.

When he was finished with his meal, he turned toward the center of town to find his hotel. A new white tent with a sign, The Missouri Valley Sanitary Fair, caught his eye. He walked to the row of tables in front of it. "Are you raising funds for the war effort?"

"We're collecting money to help make conditions sanitary for our soldiers," answered the stocky woman in a tight black dress. "My son was in Vicksburg, so I know about the deplorable conditions."

"My wife is involved in the same thing in Providence," he said wistfully. "How much have you raised? I'd like to tell her when I write."

"We've been open a week and have raised over one hundred thousand dollars." Her satisfied smile quickly washed away. "Unfortunately, it will take so much more."

"I'd like to contribute." He slid six bits along his palm into the metal pot with a jingle and thanked her for her good work, somehow feeling closer to Alice by doing so.

The 120-mile trip on the Mississippi from St. Louis was a relief from train travel, but from Hannibal to St. Joseph he was again on rails. The car was old and low-structured without interior lamps. On Monday, June 2, he arrived in Atchison, Kansas, which was the terminus of the railroads west. With the other passengers, Nathaniel wearily crossed the dusty road to a peeling, log-framed combination eatery, saloon, stable, and hotel. Soot irritated his eyes and ground between his teeth, and his bladder was overly full. He was in great need of a washbowl and latrine.

"We heard the train. Come on in," the proprietor said, greeting him through a thick swirl of black mustache. "What's your drink?"

"Just water, but I could definitely use a hot meal after I wash up."

"There's a pitcher of water and towel on the washstand in the back hall. Keep on going and you'll see the privy. I'll get you a plate of food."

At the washbasin, the lye soap and cold water generated little lather, but the first layer of grime came off on the stiff, stained towel. He felt fresher, but his stomach was still in a tight knot with hunger. He found a table in the dining area.

Chewing on the leathery jerked beef on his plate made his jaw ache. The bland potatoes and bread were not much better, but he was too hungry to turn down the food. While eating his tasteless meal, he looked around at the stained log structure that served as a stage stop. The only decorations were worn signs tacked on the wall with warnings to passengers. His food stuck in his throat as he read. "In the event of runaway horses, remain calm. Leaping from the coach in panic will leave you injured and at the mercy of the elements, hostile Injuns, and hungry coyotes."

"Falling into a pack of coyotes—there's a danger I hadn't considered," he muttered, pushing his plate away. His head drooped in misery. This was not the glorious venture he had in mind!

As the sun poked slowly over the horizon the following morning, stablemen hitched four horses to a coach for the first leg of the six-day journey from Atchison to Denver. The stage would travel all day and much of each night, with only brief stops every twelve miles for food and to change horses.

Nathaniel took his seat on a cramped bench inside the coach, squeezed between three other men. There were four across from him, with so little space that their legs dovetailed his. "Pardon," he said as he banged his knee against another passenger. "Not much room." Bags of mail crammed under their seats crowded their feet, and robes of heavy brown buffalo hide were stuffed at the back for warmth at night. Travelers had to hold their smaller pieces of luggage on their laps, while their larger ones were strapped on top. Valuable material was kept in a strongbox in the front boot. Nathaniel sized up the seven other passengers as the stage began to rumble forward.

"Might as well get to know names," one of them said. "It's going to be tight for six hundred miles with fifteen inches for each of us to sit on. It's too cold at night for anyone on top this trip."

Everyone nodded weary assent.

"I'm Owen Mathers. Going west to make boots. They're in short supply and no one can do without 'em. I'll make a living that-a-way." The compact man with a ruddy complexion had a gleam in his hazel eyes as he talked about his future in the West, his ambition greater than his experience. Nathaniel guessed him to be in his early twenties.

The six other travelers introduced themselves in hesitant formality, none of them as forthcoming about their aspirations as Owen. They were various ages, some younger than Nathaniel and others graying. From their handshakes he could tell which of them worked the land and which sat at a desk.

Other than introductions, there was little conversation during the morning ride. The broad-rumped horses moved at a steady pace as they pulled the coach over the pockmarked road, jarring the men against each other with such force that hand luggage became flying obstacles. Nathaniel held tight to his valise and coughed back the dust that seeped inside through every crack. He had reached the end of his ability to sit when he felt the stagecoach slow at mid-morning to exchange horses at a makeshift stage stop next to a narrow stream. The leather-clad driver jumped down and opened the coach door. In minutes, the stable hands were grasping the steaming horses, preparing to harness in a fresh team.

"We'll be here for fifteen minutes. Do your business and get some food," the driver barked. "Don't go a wanderin'. If you're not here when it's time to go, that's more room for the others." He moved toward the rough-hewn stage stop.

The guard stepped down cautiously, his beard tangled from the wind and sweat leaking through the headband of his hat. While the others ate, he kept his rifle cocked and eyes alert.

Nathaniel stepped behind a tree to relieve himself before entering the stage stop to purchase jerked pork and hardtack. Outside, he washed food down with swallows of water from the stream and saved some of the meager fare for later.

The driver signaled to load up. Nathaniel was last. He already felt an ache in every bone of his rattled body. The rifleman hopped up next to the driver as the coach began to roll, causing the overweight man on Nathaniel's left to knock against him. The dark-bearded passenger with the tall hat uncorked a small glass container with a pop, took a swig of the transparent brown liquid, took another, and then offered it to the man on his left. Nathaniel had already noticed the sign tacked up above the forward seat: Share Bottles! In turn, each man tipped the bottle to his lips. When it came around to him, Nathaniel passed it back to its owner saying, "Thanks for the offer, but I don't indulge."

Liquor and nervousness soon loosened their tongues, and one by one, the passengers described their expectations of what would greet them in Denver. Liquor brightened the flame of their future to a full blaze. Anticipated wealth became so real that they could almost feel the jingle of coins from their expected success. Crushed in between the door and the man with the overhanging belly, Nathaniel tried to shut out the whiskey-laced conversation. For hours the swaying stagecoach banged their aching bones.

"You've been quiet so far. What brings you west, Hill?" Owen Mathers asked, cheeks flushed with spirits.

The boasting of his companions had made Nathaniel taciturn rather than infecting him with their enthusiasm. He began to question if anyone going west had a shred of credibility, including his employer. While he saw no reason to divulge his own mission, he finally gave in to Owen Mathers' badgering. "I have a three-month contract to investigate land for valuable minerals."

"You're going to make this trip and only stay for three months?"

"That's all the time I have. I left my university job and family behind in Providence." Nathaniel was now kicking himself for divulging anything.

Owen Mathers' eyes connected with Nathaniel's. "Must be an important contract."

"Maybe, maybe not. I'll get paid one way or another. I'm a chemist. I use science to solve problems."

The men gave him looks that said they thought his was a cockamamy gambit, requiring crossing the Plains in return for no more than a stipend for his effort. They gauged his foolishness the way he did theirs.

Nathaniel shrugged off their incredulity. "It's a chance to put science to a practical use."

The coach became silent as all eight passengers gazed out the small, hazy, isinglass windows, seemingly lost in individual thoughts. Nathaniel shivered as he questioned whether he was doing the right thing. Then his body relaxed. The only thing he would really regret was shrinking away from challenge and not following his passion.

His focus drifted from his companions to scan the featureless panorama. He longed for the sight of trees, yet he was relieved by their absence because they served as a screen for attackers. The only permanent signs of civilization were sporadic homesteads with knots of small buildings and bands of travelers clustered for mutual support. Some were in wagons, others on foot, wearily tugging handcarts heaped with scant belongings. Starvation and thirst were easy to read on their faces. Occasionally, an abandoned piece of bulky furniture lay by the wayside, once a treasure and now an unbearable burden.

Owen Mathers pointed to the window. "Ah, we're getting closer. See the blue peaks in the far distance?" He rubbed his handkerchief to clean the isinglass. "It's the beginning of the Rocky Mountains."

"We must be close to our destination then," exclaimed another passenger.

"Not quite so soon," Owen said. "The mountains are still a long way off—a day away is my guess."

"Ugh," moaned the overweight man. "Just when I thought this torment might be over."

The driver had told them that a painted windmill was the signpost for the last stop, where they would stay overnight before arriving in Denver. They finally caught sight of it at the road's slight turn, only to have it disappear at the next bend. Nathaniel craned to see more, but the view was obscured from his position, and he raised his arm to massage his neck and shoulders. Every muscle had tightened in the rocking stage. Finally, he clearly saw the radial blades of the windmill. Someone gave a cheerful whistle. Four Mile House was a low sod brick on the Cherokee Trail where sojourners stopped for a meal and to clean up before arriving in Denver the next day.

Nathaniel was the first to step off the stage. Gripping his valise, he stiffly walked to the building, followed by the other passengers who were jabbering in relief. When his eyes became accustomed to the dim light, he could see benches tucked under pine plank tables and buffalo robes in a pile to be scattered on the floor for sleeping.

"Howdy, men, make yourselves comfortable. I'm Mary Cawker, and I run this establishment with my sons, Lem and Harry. They'll be comin' in when they're done taking care of your horses." She was a wiry woman of short stature, clad in a checked dress and blue apron. Gray crept up her temples, but the rest of her hair was tawny gold. Her small feet were buried in scuffed leather boots, shapeless from wear. "Make yourselves at home. The washstand is in the corner and the privy is out back. I'll get you some grub shortly." Flies buzzed around the pork and potatoes simmering on the Franklin stove.

Nathaniel breathed in the aroma. "Either the food smells better because we're closer to civilization or I've just gotten used to traveler's fare," he said to Owen, who leaned against the wall waiting for his turn at the water pitcher and towel.

"Don't get your hopes too high," Owen scoffed. "We've been on the road so long we'd eat fried squirrel if she set it in front of us."

The men took their places on the hard benches around the table. Without speaking, Mary Cawker dipped her long ladle into the cast-iron pot and spooned hot stew into metal bowls that she passed down the table. A basket of steaming bread followed. Finished serving, she retreated into a chair at a slight distance from the others with her own bowl of hot food. The seat of leather and antlers enveloped her small body like a bony cocoon. They were the only visitors at Four Mile House that night, so they had her undivided attention, but there was little talk as the ravenous men slurped large spoonfuls.

"Now that you've et your dinner, there's something you need to know." She paused, heightening the suspense. "It's a grizzly tale, but best you know it before you get to Denver." She filled her spoon one more time before continuing. "Denver will be all in black crêpe when you get there tomorrow morning." The wavering candlelight licked shadows on the wall, sending an ill-omened chill under Nathaniel's skin. "They dug four graves and buried all the Hungate family yesterday."

"What happened?" blurted Owen Mathers, hands gripping the edge of the table.

"Murdered and mutilated—an innocent family!" she replied, her voice loud and high-pitched.

"Where?" Owen asked.

She paused and rubbed her arms with her hands as if to chase away a chill. "About thirty miles south of Denver." As if breaking a spell, their host pulled herself out of her chair, shuffled a few steps to put her bowl on the counter, grabbed a bottle of whiskey, which she then offered her guests, and returned to her chair.

Her face was knotted in anger. "Nathan and Cheryl Hungate were newcomers, hired by Isaac Van Wormer to look after his cow camp. She cooked for the five hired hands and kept up the house, and he oversaw the cattle—in trade for a place to live with their two young'uns." Mary's fingers toyed with strands of her hair, tucking them behind her ears. "The story was told to me by people riding east. Nathan and the hands left the missus and kids to go looking for strays. The redskins had been getting close and nicking off wanderers, so the hands wanted to keep the cattle nearby. All day they were gone a-looking for the lost ones, but didn't find hide nor hair. At the end of the day, they were bone tired and fit to be tied. The sun was already slipping behind the hills. Nathan Hungate rode ahead to see to his family. When he crossed the creek, what he saw was a twist of smoke in the sky. He dug in his spurs up the last hill."

All eyes were on Mary. The room had cooled, but Nathaniel's forehead was moist with sweat.

"The hired men said Nathan got there in time to find his wife lying in the dirt outside, her body next to their son's. The baby was rolled between them. All three had been sliced from ear to ear, their heads cut almost clean off." The speaker cleared her throat to send a big, thick glob to the adjacent spittoon before continuing. "The hired men had ridden up to the west side of the creek just in time to see the Indians skulk from the trees to surround Nathan and slit his neck to join his family. The hired hands were no match. Turning before they could be seen, they rode to Denver to tell of the uprising."

The shadows on the walls of the Four Mile House flickered in the candlelight. No one moved.

Owen finally broke the silence. "If the Indians had the cattle, why did they come back to the cabin? Why not just take their stolen beasts and go back to their own camp?"

She turned to him somberly. "Nathan was threatening the Indians. He had been going after the red rustlers when they tried to filch his strays. Guarding Isaac Van Wormer's cattle was how he made his living. He was paid by the number of head he protected."

"Were a few calves worth his life?" Nathaniel asked. "He sounds foolhardy."

"He had to do something to feed his family," Mary said. "If no one stands up to them, we all might as well turn tail and move back East."

"But in the end, was it worth it?" Nathaniel persisted.

"Not for the Hungates, but they're not the only ones. Sometimes they spare their victims' lives only to kidnap them into slavery. We need to protect ourselves, and the government's been spineless." She dabbed her eyes with a handkerchief. "Beg your pardon, gentlemen. I've kept you up. But it was right that you know what you're riding into tomorrow. You deserve not to be surprised." She stood up and sauntered to the stack of buffalo hides. "Push the tables to the wall and take a hide for your bed. Breakfast's at six, but you'll hear me rustle before then."

Nathaniel's skin prickled with horror as he pushed back from the table. "Wait. How old did you say they were . . . the Hungates?"

Mary looked over her shoulder. "I suspect Nathan had reached thirty, Elizabeth not that many years."

"And the children?"

"The son about two and the girl still suckling. They had their lives to live."

Nathaniel mumbled, "They're the age of Crawford and Isabel."

She turned. "Did you say something?"

"No, no. I was just talking to myself." Nathaniel's breath caught as he thought about the story. He pulled up a dark hide from the pile and moved it to the corner. Being only four miles from Denver gave him no reassurance for his safety. He only hoped word of the deaths did not reach Alice.

FOUR

A loud, deep "Whoa!" reverberated from the driver's box as he edged the stage close to the board walkway. Denver often tacked *City* on the end of its name in an attempt to convince the nation of its stature. The buildings, mostly made of wood, had false fronts to exaggerate their importance. A few brick buildings were mixed among them. Nathaniel felt little about the frontier town's appearance, only relief that they had arrived safely.

He straightened his cramped legs to step down onto firm ground, smoothing the wrinkles from his topcoat. A small crowd was waiting for the stage's arrival, but the eight travelers were too giddy with their safe arrival to notice at first. They disembarked and lingered on the board walkway, smiling and laughing, not quite ready to disperse. After their shared experience, the travelers were no longer strangers, and they wished each other success.

They were interrupted by a voice calling out from the crowd, "Which of you is Professor Hill?"

Nathaniel looked up in surprise. He had not expected to be met by anyone. Governor Gilpin had written that he would not see him until breakfast the next morning. The rumpled travelers paused in curiosity.

"Do you know anyone here?" Owen Mathers asked in a whisper.

"Not that I recall." Puzzled, Nathaniel held up his hand to identify himself. "I'm Professor Hill, from Providence, Rhode Island."

A skinny man in worn work clothes pushed toward the front. "I'm Amos Sprague. Happy to make your acquaintance. Any trouble on the road? Any Indian danger?"

Nathaniel took a step forward to answer. "We were fortunate. It was a clear passage—no attack, although we saw burned-out buildings and graves along the way."

"Others weren't so lucky, Professor Hill. We had a funeral here two days ago." His lips were thin and hard as he came close enough to shake hands.

Nathaniel grasped the extended hand, feeling the rough calluses of its workman's grip, and looked into Sprague's solemn eyes. "I'm sorry." He paused and turned with a sweep of his hand to include the seven other passengers. "My fellow travelers and I bring our condolences. We learned about the Hungates at the Four Mile House last night. We can only grieve with you about such a senseless tragedy."

Sprague shuffled uneasily. "An innocent family murdered. Denver can think of little else. Our lives are at risk."

The crowd murmured angry agreement.

"Our deep sympathy to you," Nathan said. "The death of a young family is a terrible loss."

"We appreciate your sentiments," Sprague acknowledged with a nod. "You're Governor Gilpin's man, but could you spare a minute to give us a piece of advice on some of our holdings? Most of us have sunk more than we can afford, with poor results. We need advice about how to get the gold out." He extracted a tattered gray handkerchief to blow his nose. "How long will you be around town before you leave for the Sangre de Cristos with the governor?"

Nathaniel's valise was dead weight, and more than anything, he wanted to go to the solitude of his hotel room. Instead, he stayed on the mud-speckled walk. "I'll know more about my schedule after I meet with Governor Gilpin tomorrow morning. Hopefully, there will be time before I leave." He gave a consoling glance at the despairing faces. "I want to hear about what's going on in the mines. Knowing more about your problems may benefit me too."

"Then we'll just tell you a little bit about ourselves today and save the rest for later," Sprague replied, sounding a bit dejected. "You've been on the road a long time. I'm sure you're about played out."

The seven other passengers went their way toward their lodging, leaving the reticent professor to deal with the crowd. The roughly dressed men formed an uneven line behind Amos to wait their turn to speak to Nathaniel. Squinting from the late-morning sun, Nathaniel listened more than replied, letting each man have his say. He respectfully concentrated on their worried faces, but the reminder of the Hungates made him edgy.

The last man held back until all the others were done. Then the slender, dark-haired young man dressed in a neat half-length frock coat stepped forward to introduce himself. "I'm Reverend Tom Potter." He looked at Nathaniel with intense azure eyes that twinkled when he spoke. "We don't get many experts from the East, mostly just hopefuls. You've just heard their worries—Indians and mining failures. Welcome to Denver. It's a city of dreams or, sometimes, nightmares. Let me show you to the Pioneer Hotel." He pointed down the street. "We knew about your arrival because one of the newspapers whipped up excitement by trumpeting your anticipated visit. Residents are interested in anyone who might have answers about the mining problems that are eating away at their scant fortunes."

Nathaniel nodded. "Ah, so that's how they knew. I wondered."

The two men ambled toward the Pioneer Hotel, mud collecting on their boots as they made their way. Indians and mines were not the only problems. In mid-May, spring storms and melting snow sent torrents of water into nearby Cherry Creek and the shallow, sprawling Platte River. The lower part of the town had almost washed downstream. Nine people had died in the flood, and the entire operation of the *Rocky Mountain News* was swept away.

"Reverend Potter, under normal circumstances I'd invite you to join me for a meal, but I've been traveling for weeks with little chance to wash up and change my clothes. That's my first order of business. Then I need to write my wife to ease her fears. It's going to take a long time for a letter to get to her. Alice is a worrier." His eyes softened. "She'll read my letter in relief, and then, in no time, her mind will form new fears. She can't imagine why I would risk life and limb to come here."

"Oh," Tom said as he unbuttoned his jacket. "Speaking of letters, I have two letters for you." He extracted them from an inner pocket and handed them to Nathaniel. "The postman entrusted them to me knowing I was going to meet the stage."

Nathaniel's heart lurched as he looked down at the letters, then he shook his head in disappointment. "Thank you, Reverend Potter. I know there hasn't been time for one from my family to arrive, but I was just hoping."

"Please call me Tom. I hope you'll be in town a few days before you leave with the governor. I want to hear news from New England, and I, too, have some curiosity about what made you risk your neck to come here. One of Governor G's schemes, I imagine?" Tom clasped Nathaniel's hand with a minister's assuring grasp as he turned to leave. "I look forward to a conversation if you can spare the time."

Nathaniel pushed the letters into his breast pocket with a gentle shove. Tom's comment about the governor's schemes made him want to ask more questions, but weariness propelled him through the hotel door. The clerk at the front desk was a balding man with muttonchop whiskers drifting down to blend with his long, curly beard. He stood at attention, sucking in his protruding belly, to greet the town's honored guest.

"You're the last of the stage passengers, sir. It's Professor Hill, isn't it?" The fleshy clerk leaned down to point to the opened register book.

Nathaniel set his valise on the floor with a puff of dust and reached over to dip the pen in the ink. "A very tired and dirty Professor Hill but pleased to be here." He inscribed *N. P. Hill, June 14, 1864*. "Could you tell me where the bathtub is and have my suitcase taken up to my room when it's delivered?"

"I'll ask to have the tub filled with hot water. When you're ready, go around behind the kitchen. You'll find it there." The clerk pulled a numbered key from a cubicle, gave it to Nathaniel, and pointed to the stairs with his ham-sized fist.

Nathaniel's feet were leaden as he walked wearily up the stairs and put his valise on the single chair. He then inspected the two letters—solicitations to buy land from acquaintances in Providence—and promptly discarded them. Without waiting for his suitcase and clean clothes, he stumbled tiredly downstairs and went through the lobby, down the hall, and behind the kitchen.

It was a small wood-planked room containing a zinc bathtub with a high back that he could sit in with his legs bent. He laid his towel on the bench and stepped in to submerge his body in the warm water. With a triangular hunk of lye soap, he methodically scrubbed every inch of his body until his flesh prickled. The warmth eased his sore joints, his muscles relaxed for the first time since leaving Providence, and he stayed until the water cooled.

By the time he returned to his room his suitcase had arrived. He extracted his nightshirt and slipped it on, settling against the lumpy pillow on the narrow bed. Too exhausted to do anything more, he pulled up the blanket and drifted into a fitful sleep. During the night, the covers knotted around him as images of shadowy men on the attack filled his dreams.

When the first rays of dawn filtered in through a curtained window, he sat bolt upright, his heart pounding, as he figured out where he was. His eyes inspected the room in confusion. Then he finally remembered that he was safe, at least for the time being, in Denver. He lay back down, not wanting to get out of the first real bed he had been in since leaving St. Louis. Half asleep, the minister's words about one of Gilpin's schemes jumbled in his consciousness. Weeks of fatigue and tenseness made his eyes close again until the aroma of coffee and sizzling frying bacon from the dining room below roused him. He retrieved his remaining set of clothes from his luggage and put it on, noting how loosely it hung on him. He had lost weight on the trip.

Descending the narrow staircase, he stopped to survey the big dining room with its long bar and unlit hearth. Most of the worn pine tables were occupied with men wearing collarless shirts, their slouch hats piled on empty chairs while they ate their breakfast. He gave a friendly nod to two of his fellow stage riders. At a nearby table sat a solitary, bearded man, head down, eating his meal while reading a thin newspaper. "Would you be Governor Gilpin?" he asked as he walked over to the man.

A crooked smile spread above the man's bushy brown beard when he nodded yes.

Nathaniel extended his hand. "I'm Nathaniel Hill from Providence."

"Ah, it's you, Professor." Gilpin stood up, inspecting Nathaniel with steely blue eyes while he shook his hand. "I thought you'd at least have some gray at the temples with the title you come with, but you're barely middle-aged. Have a seat. I was hungry, and I couldn't wait." He beckoned the proprietor with a wave of his hand as Nathaniel sat down.

"What's it for you?" The proprietor asked, reaching down to fill a cup from the steaming pot he was holding.

"No coffee, just water, but hot cakes, bacon, sausage, and eggs, once over easy." Nathaniel paused to think what else. "Fried potatoes, biscuits, and gravy." His stomach was pinched with hunger. He glanced at Gilpin, who was looking at him with a combination of amusement and astonishment. "I haven't had much to eat the last few weeks," he explained. He felt a wave of excitement about finally meeting the governor face-to-face. "I'm interested in hearing more about your land, Governor Gilpin."

"It's an interest we have in common, Professor." The governor's fork went from plate to mouth, only momentarily stopping his speech. "We're going to some of the best territory in the country, the Snowy Range. Most call it the Sangre de Cristos."

"Is some of it like what I've just come over? All I saw for the last three hundred miles was sagebrush and dead grass."

The proprietor brought him two plates heaped with food and set them on the table with a clank. Nathaniel reached for his fork and joined his employer in eating.

"The Great American Desert is what explorer Stephen Long called what you just crossed, and the name stuck. It is really high Plains with little timber or water, but full of wild critters. There's more dry land where we're going, but the Sangre de Cristo range has mountains over fourteen thousand feet high. The snowmelt sends the creeks and rivers running in the spring, just like here."

"Is that where you live when you're not in Denver?"

"I've lived there some, but now mostly in Denver. I've lived in a lot of places the last twenty years, but *this* is the place with opportunity."

Nathaniel looked at him skeptically. "That remains to be seen."

"Once you get to know it, you'll see that it's just beginning. It's here where convention doesn't rein you in or want to stop you."

"I hope you're right, because I am doubting my reasons for coming here."

"There shouldn't be any doubt at all. This land holds a man's soul. When my end comes, I'm going to be buried on the highest summit of the Snowy Range, laid on my back, with one eye turned toward the Atlantic, the other to the Pacific."

Nathaniel could not suppress a laugh, in spite of doubts.

The governor looked wounded. "I'm serious. I've lived among the Spanish and even the Indians." He pushed his finished plate to the edge of the table and continued sipping his coffee. "Some of what I've learned from the natives is more valuable than the education I received at the University of Pennsylvania and West Point."

"Frankly, after hearing about the Hungates, I don't trust Indians."

"I've both lived with Indians and fought against them, so I know them well. They won't be a problem where we're going."

"I'm beginning to doubt there's any place in the West that's really safe."

"The Indians you'll see on our trip are mostly broken-down wrecks who weren't successful in their past life and will be hard-pressed to survive the constant lines of settlers vying for the land." The governor folded his thin newspaper and put it on the extra chair next to his worn felt hat. "They won't bother us."

"I've heard almost everyone here wears a gun for protection. What makes where we're headed any different?"

"I'm not denying that there will be more bloody Indian wars on the Plains, but we shouldn't have any problems during our exploration. Anyway, I've taken precautions. I've ordered guns and supplies from the army." He dislodged a piece of food from between his front teeth with an uneven fingernail. "Then again, the army is part of the problem. It tangles them into treaties and then later changes its laws without a second thought. Just when the Indians get used to the new geography, they are told at gunpoint to go to another location. They are running out of time and space, and the army just exacerbates an already bad situation." Gilpin bristled with irritation. "It's not only Indians. There are outlaws of all description, spilling over from the Kansas-Nebraska wars, who are robbing stages and burning houses."

"What about the time it will take us to survey the land? I've allowed only ninety days in total." Both of Nathaniel's breakfast plates were now empty, and he pushed them aside. He looked at the man across the table, trying to gain an anchor of confidence in the former governor.

"Thirty days on site is what I'm planning."

"Colonel Reynolds wrote that it is a seven-day ride from Denver to your property. Exactly how far away is it? From the map he sent, I estimated two hundred miles."

"It will take about that much time, but it's probably more like two hundred fifty. There are at least a million acres stretching across southern Colorado Territory encroaching into New Mexico."

"A million acres!" Nathaniel leaned back in amazement. "I studied maps with various measurements, but not all of the boundaries were clear. It didn't quite seem like that much. That's bigger than the state of Rhode Island."

"With that much land, there's shiny stuff somewhere, most likely around the rivers." The former governor shifted his chair away from the table to casually stretch out his legs, although there was a constant military readiness about him.

"Have you had any specific signs of gold or silver?" Nathaniel asked.

"I have no conclusive idea what's there. That's why I've hired you as my chemist-mineralogist-geologist-etcetera." He ran the words together into one title with a smile on his lips but intensity in his eyes.

Nathaniel's eyebrows arched at the title, but he did not comment. "What makes you think we'll find anything?"

"Mountains and streams—just like the Clear Creek strike."

"How did you acquire the land?" Nathaniel had been told, but he had to test the veracity of it face-to-face.

"I needed a livelihood after I was replaced as governor. There's value in the land here, so I decided to raise money to buy the Sangre de Cristo grant. It's part of the Mexican land grant system. Reynolds and another Easterner, James Aborn, advanced me money to secure the title."

"Did you purchase it from Mexico?"

"No, we bought it from Don Carlos de Beaubien, or Charles as he called himself. His son, Narciso, owned the land, but he was killed during the Taos Rebellion in 1847 when the Mexicans rebelled against American ownership of land in northern Mexico. As you see, acquiring it was not without complications, but it's been confirmed by an act of Congress. Together, the three of us—Reynolds, Aborn, and I—own the whole tract. We paid Charles Beaubien $41,000."

Nathaniel was quiet in thought, wondering if this project might be beyond the scope of reality. Its connection to Mexico also made him uneasy. His breath came out in a deep exhale as he looked across the table to try to read his companion's eyes. "Was it legal?"

"I told you, Congress made it legal in a treaty in 1848." The former governor brushed aside Nathaniel's concern. "We will explore three rivers in the south—the Costilla, Culebra, and Trinchera. I've made my best guess about how long it will take. As the contract says, you will get one-tenth of the tract for your services if we come up with any valuable glitter, in addition to the stipend of twenty-five hundred dollars we've already paid you. It's all been spelled out." He idly pulled stray pieces of food from his beard as he talked. "But now we have a little spare time. You said you sent your instruments by oxcart before you left. They won't get here for a little while, so you can spend a few days in Denver. Then we'll travel west to Central City. I understand that you want to see Joe Watson, formerly of Providence, there." He began to stand up, ready to leave.

Nathaniel shoved his chair back and rose with him. "Yes, I want to make time for Central City. I'm a chemist, so I'm curious about the mining problems. My former acquaintance has been there since the gold rush. He may have useful knowledge."

"Learn all you can, Professor." Gilpin shook Nathaniel's hand. "I'll try to introduce you to some of the locals while you're here."

"That would be helpful. Do you have a specific day to leave, Governor Gilpin?"

"Call me Governor G, like the rest of the town." An unreadable smile flickered across his lips. "Nothing specific at the present. I have some things to take care of before we visit Central City. I'll let you know."

With that, he put the dusky black hat on and stepped through the entrance.

On his own now, Nathaniel went to the telegraph office to send telegrams to Alice and Joe Watson to tell them he had arrived safely and to let Joe know that he would see him soon. Joe Watson would no longer be the boy he remembered working after school and Saturdays at his father's dry goods store. Joe failed as a gold-seeker and was now a merchant. Nathaniel really had no relationship with him, but even a tenuous connection with Providence made Joe more credible than a mere stranger. Still, he wanted to meet Joe in person before he mentioned his dilemma of finding property for men in Rhode Island.

Back in his hotel room, Nathaniel turned to his correspondence. He first took care of business letters to his Brown colleagues and various investors, then he relaxed and lingered over a more personal letter to Alice. He gave her a leisurely description of the scenery on his stage ride and the many people he had seen traveling by wagon and on foot, but he omitted anything about the Hungates. Not wanting to alarm her with his doubts about the governor, he decided not to voice them. Instead, he gave his favorable impression of the minister, Tom Potter. He let the ink dry, sealed the letter, and addressed the outer flap, regretting that this was his only means to communicate.

Over the next several days, Nathaniel periodically tracked down the governor, attempting to set a date to leave. He was unsuccessful in getting the date, but Gilpin quickly found someone else he insisted Nathaniel meet. The topics of conversation were similar: the economy, the Indian terror, laments about the War of Secession. Even in this far outpost of Colorado Territory, the strain of the war was prevalent. General Grant and the Union troops were engaged in one of the bloodiest battles to date at Cold Harbor, ten miles north of Richmond, Virginia. So far, Grant seemed to be making little headway against General Robert E. Lee's Confederate fortifications, and there were reports of massive casualties on both sides. The war weighed heavily in Denver.

At first, Nathaniel was keenly interested in talking to residents to find out why they ended up in Colorado and how they were managing to survive. He had genuine interest in their stories and sometimes returned to his room to write quick notes about them, but his frustration was growing as Gilpin continued to delay. The days of his leave of absence were ticking away without anything to show for them.

In between meetings, he spent his time exploring Denver. The contrast between his current surroundings and Rhode Island were remarkable. There was no ocean and no bays for landmarks. The town was laid out parallel to the Platte River, with streets going from northeast to southwest. Cherry Creek ran through it, emptying into the wide, shallow Platte on the western edge.

There were grocery stores, meat markets, a bank, a billiards hall, and a plethora of saloons. Houses and businesses were mixed together. At the outskirts of town, the Arapaho Indians set up seasonal campgrounds. Their cone-shaped tipis rose to almost twenty-five feet, with three long poles at the center and other poles radiating out. They were covered in taut animal skins to give them their full circular shape. Nathaniel had seen their camp and the smoke rising from their tents in the distance, but had not ventured there. He found it surprising that Indians were allowed to camp so close to town.

Having become familiar with the main streets during his first two days in Denver, Nathaniel decided to walk farther afield his third day there. Looking down a small lane, Nathaniel noticed a man in rumpled trousers and a coarse wool jacket coming in the opposite direction.

Recognition glimmered across the man's wrinkled face as he approached and called out, "Professor Hill, I'm Amos Sprague. Do you remember me? I was there when your stage come in. I thought you'd be on your way by now. Are you heading someplace, or would you have time for some palaver about mining?"

Nathaniel tugged at his pocket watch and glanced at the time. He had no commitments, but he did not want to be tied up in case the governor took it into his head to leave. But one look into Sprague's forlorn eyes made him acquiesce. "I can spare a little time."

Putting his hand on the back of Nathaniel's arm to direct him, Amos said, "We can cut down this street to get there faster."

The café was quiet with only two other customers. A gaunt man with a wispy goatee came out from the kitchen to take their order. Once their orders were taken, Amos pulled out a pouch of loose tobacco and rolling paper and quickly crafted a small cigarette. After taking his first long draw and directing his exhalation of smoke away from Nathaniel's face, he sat back and relaxed. "Let me do some explaining. There's many men here in a similar bind as me. I have a mine near Clear Creek that gave some return, but that ended over a year ago. Since then, we've tried everything—hydraulic, and any other way we can think of to crush the rock—but we get little of the metal."

"You can see signs of gold or silver in the rock?"

"Yeah, that's what's so hard—seeing it glimmer but not able to get at it."

"Here's your food," the waiter interrupted sullenly. He took the plates and glasses from a worn metal tray and thumped them in front of each man before skulking back to the kitchen.

Amos reached for the sugar bowl and took two cubes to drop in his hot coffee, then continued. "When my claim first showed out with gold, I needed to get money for equipment. A few family members came up with cash for a chance at some profit. Now I've gone through their cash and any profits that came my way. My family's not a happy lot, and I'm scrounging to eat. What do you make of it, Professor . . . Nathaniel?"

Nathaniel took a bite of his buttered bread. It was freshly baked and still slightly warm from the oven. Eating gave him time to think about his answer. He had heard similar stories during the past three days. "My guess is that the gold and silver are being held in chemical combination with sulfur instead of being distinct elements that are mixed together and can break apart and separate."

"You lost me on that. Come down to my level." Amos used his stained fingers to swab up gravy with a biscuit and looked up at Nathaniel expectantly.

"I'm going to have to put a lot more thought into it before I can come up with something that makes better sense—if I ever can."

"You're a chemist. Can't you use some of your chemicals?"

"I wish there was a way, but there aren't any chemicals that do that." Nathaniel saw the small glint of optimism disappear from Amos's doleful brown eyes and felt helpless to come up with an answer for the desperate man. "I want to be honest and not raise your hopes. It doesn't bode well for Governor G either, and it's most likely a problem for me too."

"You? I thought you were only here for the summer. The rest of us have pulled up our roots, and our lives are at stake—even the governor. This is a big undertaking for him."

"Unfortunately, I have more than I wish wrapped up in all of this."

"I can provide more facts if you need 'em," Amos said, trying to rekindle a spark of hope. "Or I can get some men to meet with you that know more than me."

"Not yet. I need to learn more about the geology of this situation. From what I've heard, the answer isn't apparent." Nathaniel's torn bread lay unfinished on his plate by his emptied water glass.

Across the table, there was nothing but a brown stain of gravy on Amos's plate and disappointment in the air.

"I'm glad I heard what you had to say, Amos. I'll to try to find some answers, but if no one else has come up with anything, I'm not sure I can either."

Sprague threw his spent cigarette on the floor and snuffed it out with his heel, reluctant to leave without information. "I thought you would have some answers."

"I only wish I did. Right now, I think I should find the governor and see if he's ready to leave."

Nathaniel reached into his pocket for money to pay for their meal. "Let me get this. You've been generous with your information, and the least I can do is to buy you biscuits and coffee." He took coins from his pocket.

"Are you sure? Thanks. The next one's on me."

They both rose from the table and passed through the café's swinging doors, pausing outside to shake hands.

"Can we talk again later? After you thought about it? We need an expert like you."

Nathaniel's gut knotted with feelings of inadequacy. "You need more than an expert. I don't know of a solution, but I'll get in touch with you one way or another before I leave to return to Providence."

"Look in your books, Professor. There must be something there."

The two men turned and went in different directions down the dirt street. The intensity of expectations jangled Nathaniel's nerves.

অ

Nathaniel had not been to church since he had begun his journey. He had finally pinned the former governor down to a departure date, and this would be his only opportunity to hear Tom Potter in the pulpit before leaving. On Sunday he walked to the People's Theater on Larimer Street where Reverend Tom Potter held services for his small Baptist congregation. He was eager to see what inspiration the young minister might kindle in him. If nothing else, it would take his mind off his complete exasperation at Gilpin's delays.

The People's Theater was a long, whitewashed, clapboard two-story building. During the week, it provided space for meetings during the day and drama performances at night. The legislature occupied the second story to conduct its business. On Sundays, Tom held services in the main hall, hoping eventually to raise money for a church of his own. The room stretched the length of the building with a wide center aisle separating neat rows of straight-backed chairs. Light streamed in through a series of four-paneled windows along the wall.

Nathaniel stopped just inside the doorway to watch the other church-goers take their seats. The congregation was mostly men, all dressed in their Sunday best. The few women in the congregation wore finery too, with broad-brimmed hats trimmed in cascading flowers or feathers. Some of the churchgoers walked unhesitatingly to a particular row. Others sauntered to a middle section. As in Providence, there was a tacit seating order. Not wishing to intrude, he took an available seat halfway back. After he sat down, he studied his surroundings. The dark stage provided a simple setting for the altar, with a tall gold cross centered on a horizontal table draped in the same burgundy velvet as the draperies. A tall oak lectern to the left sufficed as a pulpit. At the opposite side of the stage was an unassuming upright piano.

As the clock struck nine, the piano player plunked the first chords of the hymn "A Charge to Keep I Have." The congregation rose and followed the out-of-tune piano, singing in long, drawn out nasal tones. From the back of the hall, Tom Potter started up the aisle, his black frock coat swaying with his measured strides timed to the rhythm of the music. Reaching the stage as the hymn ended, he put a leather portfolio with his written notes on the lectern and extended his arms to signal the congregation to sit down before speaking in a steady, confident tone.

"Today's sermon is about Jason and the Argonauts, a Greek myth." He moved away from the lectern toward the audience and continued. "As a young man, Jason discovered that he was the true heir to a nearby kingdom and traveled there to regain his dead father's rule. When he arrived, he met his power-hungry uncle, the usurper of the throne. Determined to have his due, Jason demanded his place as head of the kingdom. The wily uncle gave his fair-haired nephew an ultimatum. Only when Jason sailed beyond the known world to retrieve the Golden Fleece would his uncle relinquish the kingdom. The fleece, symbol of the kingdom, lay in a foreign land under the watch of a herd of fierce bulls, an army of warriors, and a never-sleeping dragon."

Tom paused, returned to the lectern, and turned several pages of his notes. "Jason was young, but not naïve. He knew that his cunning uncle's test was devised not only for failure but most likely also for death. Yet, he accepted the challenge without hesitation. Finding the Golden Fleece and taking his father's place on the throne was his destiny—not only a chance for adventure, but also an opportunity to prove himself.

"Plans for the trip immediately began to fill his mind. The danger was undeniable. No one had ever traveled to the far edge of the world and returned. He would have to use cleverness and strength to combat the obstacles ahead of him. Only hours after meeting with his uncle, he began to search for supplies and men. He would have to persuade the kingdom's strongest and bravest young men to accompany him."

As the preacher spoke, Nathaniel felt himself being drawn into the fable. It was a familiar myth his mother had read to his brother and him as children. Listening, he tried to fit his Colorado journey into the myth's story. Could he define his own golden fleece?

Tom rested his arms on the sides in a relaxed grip as he spoke. "Jason set sail in a magical boat named the Argo. For weeks the sea threw waves across the bow of the tiny boat, threatening to capsize Jason and his Argonauts in the roiling sea. The few islands they found were not places of refuge but chimerical deathtraps from which they barely escaped, yet their resolve for their goal never wavered. Finally, they arrived at the mythical land and anchored their boat at the shoreline.

"The journey and danger, however, were far from over. When the ruler of the faraway land came to the water's edge, he defiantly announced that he was the protector of the fleece, and he would only relinquish it to someone who overcame the never-sleeping dragon that guarded it. Both men knew that hazards awaited them if they attempted to reach the dragon, and even then, there was little chance of combating the ever-watchful beast."

The minister paused and slowly crossed the stage. Nathaniel thought it was to give his congregation time to think of the possibilities before he went on with his sermon. Nathaniel looked at the rest of the churchgoers. They were quietly expectant. When Tom began speaking again, his tone carried conviction.

"Exhausted with tension from the trip, Jason returned to his boat to consider what to do. The only imaginable outcome was catastrophe—his own death and the same for his valiant men. Yet, he had faith in his Argonauts, and his young heroes believed in him. His intrinsic nature would allow him to do no less than confront the obstacles between them and the fleece. With cleverness rather than strength, Jason yoked the guardian fire-breathing bulls, overcame an army of warriors, and defeated the always-vigilant dragon."

Again the pastor paused, then spoke slowly and deliberately. Nathaniel knew that he was doing so to emphasize a point.

"One after another, he had overcome the obstacles, and the goal he desired was his. When he finally held the curly, gold-flecked fleece in his hands, he realized that overcoming challenges was as great a reward as the sheepskin." The pastor stood silent for several minutes.

Tom Potter then turned and walked with slow, thoughtful steps back to the lectern. He picked up the notes he had scarcely glanced at and put them in the leather folder. The silent audience bent slightly forward, awaiting his concluding words.

"My brethren, I use this story because many of you can be considered Argonauts searching for your own Golden Fleece. I challenge each of you to define what you seek in the West. Consider whether it will give you true satisfaction or whether your desire is purely for fortune and fame." Tom Potter stopped, seemingly to let the words take effect before going on. "You will hear more about seekers next Sunday because, after all, Jason has met his goal of finding the fleece, but he still has a return journey over perilous seas before his mission is complete."

Nathaniel looked around him. Many of the parishioners had been leaning forward in their seats, as if the pastor's words could be both heard and understood better by the slight bend towards him. Now they sank back against their seats. At the front, two deacons silently moved on each side of the congregation, passing the soft velvet collection pouch down each row. As it was handed to him, Nathaniel slid a silver dollar into the pendulous cloth and passed it on. He knew the amount would surprise Tom, but it was small recompense for the inspiration he had just provided.

As the congregation stood in unison, Nathaniel rose with them to sing the closing hymn, "Nearer My God to Thee." Even though the words were drawn out, he stumbled to keep up with the tempo set by the piano. He wanted to keep Tom's words in his mind to test them against his perception of his own mission.

When the service was over, the parishioners began chatting as they gathered their hats and gloves. Nathaniel stood motionless, not wanting his thoughts to dissipate. Tom's sermon seemed somehow directed at him in particular, and from snippets of remarks he overheard around him, he was not alone. What a gift, Nathaniel thought, to come up with words that each hearer took personally. Joining other worshipers meandering to the back of the meeting hall, questions filled his mind. What was he pursuing in Colorado? Was it merely to fulfill an interesting contract to build his reputation, or did his soul need challenges? Had he risked the slow death of his spirit through the sameness of teaching, year after year?

The congregation lingered until Tom Potter arrived at the back of the theater to greet his parishioners and listen to their reactions to his words. When Nathaniel reached Tom, he grasped the preacher's hand in both of his. "I'm impressed, Tom. It was a powerful message."

The young preacher nodded appreciatively. "I'm glad my words meant something. Sometimes my ideas don't make the leap from pulpit to congregation. It's a reward when that happens." A smile spread across his face as he slowly retracted his hand. "Nathaniel, let me introduce you to some people you haven't met yet."

Nathaniel followed Tom from the theater out to the entryway where someone had propped open the door to let in the June breeze. He knew it was unlikely that he would see any of them again, but he shook their hands with words of respectful introduction. As the last parishioners trickled out, he again approached the minister. "Tom, will you be around before the noon meal? I'd like to drop by and talk to you about the ideas in your sermon."

"I promised to have Sunday dinner with some of the church elders. It's a tradition. But what about later this afternoon? I'll be working on my next sermon. Jason and his Argonauts have more challenges ahead." He smiled. "Come by my office at the back of my house."

Most people had retreated inside for their noon meal, leaving Denver's streets at peace from the usual percussion of clopping horses and clanging wagons. The fragrance of roasting fowl met him before he pushed open the double doors to the Pioneer Hotel.

"Professor Hill," the clerk called out as he went by the front desk on his way to the dining room. "There's a letter here for you." He reached behind him to pull out a packet, small in his oversized hand. "From Providence," he said with a knowing beam.

Alice's lacy writing made Nathaniel's heart jump. "Many thanks. This is a good day indeed." With a smile, he walked to his favorite table in the back corner, ordered his meal, and carefully broke the seal on the letter.

Providence

June 1, 1864

My dearest husband,

It has only been two days since you closed our front door for your journey. I no longer want to pass through your study for the emptiness of it.

I will cut out newspaper articles that might interest you and put them in a folder for your return. The war news is dire from Georgia. The Union forces are having great difficulty there. No one knows what the result will be, and the death rate continues to mount.

Kate and I went to hear a lecture on the Young Women's Christian Association. Mainly, the organization works to provide housing for the immigrant and rural girls who are pouring into the cities. But it does more than that. It gives them training and something to do other than being tempted by the streets. Desperation often brings them here, and they don't have the good fortune that I do of having a family nearby to turn to. Both Kate and I want to find out more about their situations so we can help.

The children are a comfort to me in your absence. Crawford has been sick with the grippe, but Isabel has resisted so far and is growing rapidly. I long to hear news from you, but I know I will have to wait for your word. My hope is that you are well and safe.

Your devoted wife (and children),
Alice

Reading the letter made him ache with loneliness. The meal the waiter set in front of him of roast chicken, green beans, mashed potatoes, gravy, and even fresh lettuce made him all the more nostalgic. The food was reminiscent of Sundays in Providence when he and Alice went to her family home for dinner. She was probably there now without him. Dinner at the Hales was always a lively occasion because of their interest in current events. Constant banter rang around the dinner table—always friendly but with an underlying testing of each other's ideas and a tacit demand to prove one's opinions. A wistful smile slid across his face as he remembered those spirited meals.

The roast chicken was a feast compared to the stringy meats of his cross-country travel. When he took his last warm bite of tart cherry pie, he complimented the proprietor, pulled a greenback from his money clip to pay the bill, added a coin as gratuity, and left the hotel for the two-block walk to Tom Potter's office.

It was only a few moments after knocking before Tom pulled open the door. "Come in, come in, Nathaniel. I'm already at work, as you can see." He closed the door and pointed to the papers spread on the small desk behind him. "I like to start preparing the next sermon while the momentum of the last one is still with me. Interaction with the parishioners feeds my desire to say more."

Nathaniel hesitated before stepping in. "Do you want me to come back another time?"

"No, not at all. I have a good train of thought, and I can continue later. Have a seat. The one with the cushions is the most comfortable."

Nathaniel was curious about how such a talented man had landed at such a rough outpost. "Tell me, Tom," he said as he got settled, "how did you end up in Denver? You could fill a large church in more settled areas."

"To tell you the truth," Tom replied with an easygoing laugh, "I came because I can contribute more here than I can in the East. There is something intriguing about seekers—more so than those who have already made up their minds about life."

"Does that mean you intend to stay? You sound as much a missionary as a preacher." He studied the slender minister, now in a simple waistcoat, his frock coat evident on a hook to the side. Shelves with neatly arranged books were on the wall next to the door leading into the kitchen, and a small wooden cross rested on an unfilled center shelf.

"I hope so. I'd like to build a church—really a meetinghouse—as a formal place of worship. People here have come to chase one dream or another, leaving behind the homes and lives that underpinned their values and morals. Most are without families, and whether they realize it or not, they are searching for some sort of social structure. I'd like to help them with that." Tom folded his hands on his lap, and his eyes met Nathaniel's. "As I said this morning, I think of them as Argonauts. Instead of ships, they use prairie schooners, their white canvas covers like sails at sea. Many are coming for gold, but not all of them. Some don't even know why they have come west. Hopefully, there is something more here than the material gain that so many think is essential to everything."

"You're right about the travelers. I saw hundreds of them riding or walking. Sometimes we had a brief conversation at a stage stop. Many had no more answer for being on the road than 'seeking something new.'"

"They may be seeking something different, but what these pilgrims find won't always be better," Tom said. "Some are escaping obligations and others are looking for opportunities. It's an unsatisfied crowd."

"Inventions are often the outcomes of dissatisfaction. It's not always bad," Nathaniel replied, raising his eyebrows, hoping for agreement.

"For some, the move will be positive. But some should have stayed put no matter how hard their lives. There's no doubt that the risk-takers are settling the West. Those who survive here have a different character than those who stay behind."

"Why did you use that word *pilgrims* instead of emigrants . . . or even Argonauts?" Nathaniel teased. He was probing the labyrinth of the minister's thoughts.

"No words from a preacher are accidental."

"I imagine not."

Tom smiled at Nathaniel, as if the two shared an unspoken understanding. "A pilgrimage is a journey with many layers, all of which aren't perceived. The Golden Fleece everyone is seeking should be more than material possessions. There is a spiritual layer if they allow themselves to tap into it. I would like to guide them there."

Nathaniel's posture straightened in interest. "Their attraction to the West intrigues me."

"The pilgrims, or Argonauts, are on a quest, but the fleece they find may surprise them."

"So when they come, you want to help them find answers—save their souls?"

"Saving souls is a complicated business."

"Not all gold seekers will be God seekers," Nathaniel pointed out. "I'm a churchgoer, but I know many souls that don't want to be saved."

"I understand, and I have given a great deal of thought to that." A broad smile spread on Tom's face. "I'm glad you've come to Denver, Nathaniel, and I look forward to future conversations."

"Meeting you has only added to my intrigue with the West." Nathaniel pushed himself up from his chair. "I'm supposed to leave with the governor the day after tomorrow, but, of course, deadlines are always problematic for Governor G."

"You expect to be gone for a month?"

"That's all the time I have. I need to leave immediately after the trip to return for Brown's first term. The higher-ups did not want me to leave to begin with, and I need to be back before classes start."

"Why do you think they object? Isn't what you're doing called a sabbatical?"

Nathaniel picked up his hat. "I think sabbaticals are usually spent in a library. This is really just a leave of absence. Maybe that's part of the problem. Most academics spend their time in the world of books."

"Can you take something of value back to Brown to placate them?"

Nathaniel shrugged. "That's uncertain. They seem to see this as a lark for enterprise, not scholarship. In their minds, it's almost a character flaw that I want to be away from their prestigious university."

"Will they be happy if you come back with new knowledge and information you can impart to students?"

"It depends." Nathaniel frowned. "If what I bring back suggests too much change, they won't embrace it. But if I learn something that will add to academic reputation, that will be altogether different."

"I think I'm beginning to see the problem. I wish you and Governor G luck, Nathaniel. I hope you both find what you're looking for."

"I'll be in touch before I go back." He reached for his coat hanging on the hook, put his arms through the sleeves, and bid Tom adieu.

Nathaniel's mind quickly turned to the letter Alice had sent him. He hurried back to his room to pen a reply, knowing that she was longing for word from him as much as he had been yearning for contact from her before her missive had arrived. He could be less guarded in this letter because he was in the relatively safety of Denver and did not need to be so reserved about telling her about his experiences. Being able to let his thoughts flow from pen to paper was a relief.

Denver
June 19, 1864
My Dearest Wife,

I just received your first letter. You cannot imagine what cheer it brought me.

I am finding Colorado Territory an extraordinary place in beauty and people. It's a land of extremes, water being one of them. For miles there can be too little water to grow anything, then the skies open up and there's too much. The skies are an endless blue from the time the sun comes up until regular afternoon showers, and sometimes even hail, make everyone take cover.

Most of the people have come here to make their fortune, but each story has a unique twist. I'm interested in their reasons for being out West and make it a habit to take my meals with someone living here. While we eat together, they describe their often outlandish ventures, many based on gold. I find myself regretting that I won't be here long enough to learn if their dreams are realized. Little of what they tell me benefits my business here, but listening to them is a way to find out more about what makes up the place that I inhabit briefly. When I am less distracted, I will write you vignettes about some of the characters I have met.

I told you in another letter about the Baptist preacher who met me the day I arrived. Tom Potter seems to have an exceptional way of reading the minds of people and putting to words their motivations and concerns. You aren't the churchgoer I am, but I think you would enjoy making his acquaintance. I wish you were here for me to discuss his sermon with because you always pick up points I miss.

The day after tomorrow, Governor G and I are finally leaving Denver for Central City. Denver is referred to with "City" and sometimes Central without the City. We will be on our way unless, of course, he postpones one more time. But if he does, I'll go on my own. He will go to pursue his everlasting business dealings and I for the purpose of becoming reacquainted with Joe Watson.

Then we leave for the Sangre de Cristos. Much to my consternation, I have learned what others already know: Governor G dillydallies. His habit is to set deadlines that he doesn't meet, despite his original intentions. I could pull out my hair in frustration. Time is of the essence, and I am powerless to control the man who controls my destiny.

War is a daily column on the front page of the newspaper, just as it is in the East. It has disheartened me to read of so many casualties at

the Battle of the Wilderness and Spotsylvania as Grant tries to defeat
Lee. It is a brutal business keeping the country intact and moral. I
dread thinking about my students who left to serve in the army on
one side or the other. Some must be among those killed or missing.

You are especially in my thoughts in the late afternoon and at
dinnertime. I miss our meals and hearing your reactions to what
I'm doing. Your opinions on current affairs are as valid as any man's.
Being apart makes me realize how much you mean to me.

Please tell a story to Isabel and Crawford about their Papa's adventures in the Wild West. It won't be long before I can spin yarns of my
own for them.

Pass this letter on to my mother for her comfort. My next letter
will relay what I find in Central City, if I indeed ever get there.

Your affectionate husband,
N. P. Hill

In Providence, Alice pulled open a drawer in Nathaniel's desk to find a
letter opener. She stuck the point carefully in the small seal to open his
latest missive. She was balancing Isabel on her arm, keeping her away
from the sharp instrument. The humid July heat dampened her brow
and made Isabel fussy. The outer flap would not lift up and she did not
want to rip the paper. When she heard Crawford crying in the next room,
she rested the envelope and opener on the blotter and walked down the
hall to find him.

"Just a minute, darling. I was going to open a letter from Papa."

Hearing the word, Crawford wailed, "Papa, Papa, Papa."

Alice reached down and smoothed his forehead with her hand. "Honey,
you feel so hot. It couldn't be just the weather making your skin burn."
She looked at him more carefully. "You have a rash. Oh, Crawford, I think
you're sick." She bent over with difficulty to pick him up for comfort,
squeezing Isabel as she did. Both children rested their unhappy heads on

either side of her neck, making her ears ring with their cries. "Let's go to the kitchen and have something to eat." She knew she had to send a message to the doctor right away. The milkman was at the end of the block. When he reached their house, she would ask him to fetch the doctor.

Two hours later, Dr. Carpenter tapped on the front door. He had taken care of Alice and her brothers when they were children. She met him, holding Crawford. Isabel was in her crib for her afternoon nap.

"Good afternoon, Mrs. Hill," he said in greeting as he placed his medical bag on the parlor floor. Then he turned his attention to Crawford. "Can we take a look at you, young man?"

Crawford clung to Alice, his lower lip quivering.

"Here, sweetheart. Let's lie on the divan," she said.

Crawford lay down but held tightly to Alice's hand as Dr. Carpenter opened his dark leather bag and pulled out his stethoscope.

"No," Crawford shrieked.

"It's okay, sweetie. Let Dr. Carpenter listen to your heart." Alice knelt on the floor to be close to her two-year-old.

With stethoscope ear tips in place, Dr. Carpenter placed the chestpiece in different places, then gently ran his knobby fingers along the rash on Crawford's face and neck. "Stick out your tongue, son."

Alice could see that Crawford's tongue was as red as a strawberry.

The doctor probed Crawford's neck. "His throat is swollen, as are his glands."

Crawford did what he was told, but did not stop crying. Alice tried to comfort him while she held her breath in fear.

Dr. Carpenter straightened up, his face somber.

"What it is, doctor?" Alice took Crawford in her arms and rose from her knees to meet the doctor's eyes.

The doctor put the stethoscope and metal tongue depressor back before responding. "It's an easy diagnosis with his rash and pink tongue. Your son has scarlet fever."

"Oh, no." Her hand flew to her mouth. "That can be fatal, can't it?" Tears welled in her eyes.

Dr. Carpenter put his hand on her shoulder to comfort her. "It's very serious, Mrs. Hill. I usually see the fever in children a little older, but Crawford is a strong little boy and has every chance of pulling through. There is nothing to do but keep him cool and comfortable."

"Will you come back to check on him?"

"Yes, I'll stop by tomorrow afternoon." Dr. Carpenter closed his medical bag with a snap and turned toward the door. "I will call on you tomorrow."

Alice tried to comfort Crawford, but his chubby hands clutched her in frantic discomfort. She could feel the heat of his body and began to cry, too, but then took a sharp breath and stopped. "Come on, Crawford," she said calmly. "Let's get a cool cloth to put on your forehead. That will make you feel better." She shifted him to her left hip and grasped the banister to go up the narrow stairway to the bedrooms. He was heavy to carry, and she sighed as she thought about how fast he had grown.

Crawford finally fell asleep, tucked under the starched and ironed cotton sheets, with Alice sitting on the bed beside him. The wet, white cloth was a stark contrast to his florid face. A fine, red-textured rash covered his chest and armpits. "Please get well again, little one," she whispered. "I couldn't stand to lose you." Recollections of her younger brothers' deaths plagued her.

Her head dropped into her hands. She was nervous and scared. Then she stood up with a start, remembering the letter from Nathaniel on the desk. She could not imagine what she could tell him without making him feel helpless to do anything, being so far away. Before she could go down to get Nathaniel's letter, Isabel began to cry from her crib. Alice stepped into the baby's room and quickly changed her diaper. Then she picked her up and began patting her back so she would not wake Crawford. "Oh, dear baby, your brother is very sick." She bent forward to kiss Isabel's small cheek as she carried her down to the kitchen rocking chair for her feeding.

→ ←

Alice was relieved to have her mother with her. Harriet had come quickly after receiving Alice's message. The support, both physical and emotional, was a comfort. Crawford was very hot and motionless. He refused to eat anything and struggled to swallow sips of water. His eyes were closed tight. The red rash now covered his neck and behind his ears. Mother and daughter stood by the narrow bed, hugging each other for moral support, not daring to speak of the frequent finality of scarlet fever.

Isabel started to cry in the next room.

"Here," Harriet said, "I'll sit with him. You take care of Isabel."

"I don't want to leave him, Mama. I'll see what Isabel needs and be right back. I'm so frightened." Alice almost tripped as she plunged through the door toward her daughter's hungry wailing.

She returned quickly with Isabel. "Oh, Mama, it's been two days. How much longer can his little body endure this?" She began crying.

Harriet patted her shoulder. "We have to be strong for Crawford's sake, Alice. Come. I'm going to get a little shaved ice with cherry juice. He seemed to favor that a bit."

Alice felt her mother's comforting arms wrap around both her and Isabel for a moment. She was sick with worry about Crawford, and she missed Nathaniel's strength. But he was thousands of miles away, and she needed to find the reserves to carry on within herself.

SIX

ϙ

The governor was busily loading a worn wagon while talking to someone Nathaniel could not see as he approached the Lawrence Street Livery Stable. Nathaniel paused several yards away, not wanting to interrupt a private conversation, and looked out at the distant mountains. Snow was still evident on them, even though it was late June. At this time of morning in Providence, the sun would still be trying to burn through a shroud of dampness.

They were finally leaving for Central City, and Nathaniel was anxious to get the trip underway. He took a hesitant step forward and saw through the stable door two gray-brown ponies, the recipients of Gilpin's banter.

"Morning, Governor G. I'm ready for the trip."

The governor turned and greeted him. "Morning, Nathaniel. I'll be set in a minute. My friends in Central City asked for supplies as long as I was coming, but it's going to be a trick to get it all in without overloading." He removed two tan canvas bundles to make space for a bigger metal box.

"Is this wagon what we're riding in to Central City?" Nathaniel asked, setting his valise inside the stable door.

"It's a horse cart, not a wagon, or you might even call it a buggy. Do you see any other conveyance?"

Nathaniel casually inspected it. "Will this cart make it to Central City? It looks a little worse for wear."

"Believe me, I've counted on it for years."

"I'll take your word for it."

Gilpin tried to squeeze a carton between two oddly wrapped parcels, muttering under his breath when it would not fit. "Look, I'm not quite finished. I think you should leave me to my work. If you keep distracting me, we'll never get on the road."

"I thought you said we had to leave first thing."

"I had some things come up that delayed me. Come back at ten. We'll get going then."

"Is there anything I can do to help?" Nathaniel asked as he removed his jacket. "I have a knack for fitting pieces together."

"Thanks for the offer. It's really a one-man job." Gilpin made a clucking sound to the ponies, making them look up from their eating.

"All right, have it your way. I'll be back in a couple of hours, but Joe Watson is expecting me tomorrow." Nathaniel watched in frustration as the governor began to remove each item to start the loading process all over again.

"We'll get there in due time."

Nathaniel pushed through the stable door to return to the hotel, his body rigid with irritation. He was beginning to wonder if Gilpin's plans were as unreliable as the decrepit cart he was loading. He thrust open the hotel door and headed for the dining room. Only one table was vacant—one with a discarded newspaper on top. Someone had left behind recent news.

"Flapjacks, sausage, and a glass of water," he said to the waiter as he unfolded the paper. The first pages were filled with details of the war. General Sherman's fight to best the Confederates under Johnston in

Atlanta was still at loggerheads. After finishing with the discouraging war news and his breakfast, he got out his most recent letter from Alice to reread.

Providence
June 12, 1864
My dearest husband,

Everything must be so different where you are in the West from life here. I envision you surrounded by mountains and people carrying guns. I wouldn't be surprised if you told me you had taken up target practice. I pray for your safety.

Crawford and Isabel change almost daily. Crawford somehow understands your absence and tries to carry on small conversations with me to take your place. They spend time at Mama's when Kate and I go to the lyceum or work on the war effort in town. The lectures at the lyceum, especially about English history, are enthralling, but it all seems ancient compared to the newness of your adventures.

John is kind to stop by with news of Brown, and I know you have written to him about what you are doing. I saw President Sears on the street. He inquired about you and tried to probe, rather obliquely, about whether you have found gold. I think it paints you in a bad light for people to think you are just another gold seeker.

We miss hearing your voice and tales of your day. I tell the children stories about you so they do not forget their papa. We send you three kisses.

Your loving wife,
Alice

Reading her news, even if it was two weeks old, intensified his longing for her. He took out his ink and pen to tell her how much he missed her. He tried to imagine what she might be doing. Most likely she was with their children. The thought of them amplified his melancholy.

After finishing the letter to Alice, he wrote to his Brown colleagues. Those done, he checked the time. Two hours had elapsed. Collecting his writing material, he left the hotel and walked back to the livery stable.

"Governor, you're all loaded. Did you get everything to fit?"

"Only the essentials. There will be some disappointment in Central City, but they'll have to make do with what we have for now." The governor was harnessing the two ponies, Oro and Silvy, their matted, uneven hides as unkempt as their rig. The wheels clung to the axles in different alignment, and the boards were cracked from weather. "You had a long breakfast, Nathaniel?"

"And wrote three letters, and read a newspaper," Nathaniel replied with unconcealed annoyance.

Gilpin looked away in distraction. "Just a minute." He hastily threw a tarp into the cart and dashed over to speak to a passerby. At the edge of the walkway, Gilpin's hands and shoulders gesticulated in animation as he stood talking.

There was nothing for Nathaniel to do except move to the shade and wait. From his observations, Gilpin thrived on flaunting his business ideas and former political position, even though his official influence had dissipated like steam from a cooling kettle. Conversation for Gilpin was apparently easier than action.

Nathaniel paced, watching the stable hands go about their business as he waited. The sun was nearing its apex when Governor Gilpin returned to complete the final hooking of his two ponies and to take his seat on the buckboard behind them. His hand thumped the seat next to him, indicating that Nathaniel should join him. The rusted springs groaned as Nathaniel hoisted himself up. Gilpin rattled the reins and rolled his tongue making a *brrt, brrt* sound to get the ponies in motion. The fully loaded cart lumbered west out of town. It was already eleven.

When the ponies fell into a steady trot, Gilpin loosened his hold on the reins. "What do you think of this territory so far, my chemist-mineralogist-geologist-etcetera?"

Nathaniel ignored the nickname and leaned comfortably against the backrest. "I haven't seen enough to have a qualified opinion, but so far, it surprises me. I gave little thought to what the surroundings would be like. I was more focused on assembling the right equipment and preparing to leave home."

"And now that you're here?"

"I thought everyone who came to the West came for gold. Now that I've spent a little time talking to people, I think it's the promise that pulls them here . . . that and the mountains. I'm beginning to understand the appeal."

"It's the lust for gold that brought most of them," Gilpin guffawed. "A hundred thousand came in 1859 when the rush started."

"And most of them returned home?"

"Ninety-six thousand have. It has been a pretty steady procession of people leaving, and it has not stopped altogether. The 'go-backs,' that's what they are called. For them, Pikes Peak turned out to be a bunch of hogwash. Most of them lost everything. It wasn't just their money but their spirit that was worn thin by their broken dreams."

"I saw a few of those on the way out here, walking in rags, looking half-starved. But not everybody left."

"Some couldn't. They were running away from troubles or trying to find answers when they didn't even know the questions." Gilpin laced the fingers of his free hand through his thick brown beard to smooth it. "And some, like me, just decided to wait for the next opportunity."

"People have been telling me their stories. So many came here on one quest or another, searching for their golden fleece as Revered Potter would say. The Argonauts of the myth were willing to face extraordinary obstacles to get their reward. The same seems true here."

Nathaniel gave the governor a sideways glance to see if he was scoffing or taking it in, and seeing him receptive, he continued. "In my brief time here, it seems the successful ones came for one reason but often stayed for another. It's the drugstore owners, boot makers, and those like them that are making a profit. They adapted. They slayed the sleeping dragon with cleverness."

"People here still live on the edge," the governor insisted. "Life is hard for most of them. But that's what I'm doing—adapting—from governor to land owner, and many things before that, always clawing at success any way I can." Gilpin's beard shook in sardonic laughter. Then he went quiet.

In the silence, Nathaniel wondered again about his own motivations. Was he adapting too? Consulting in Colorado was an unusual break from his academic routine and full of expectations. Gilpin expected him to find precious metals on his land. His Brown colleagues expected him to come back to Providence ready to focus on classes and give up the frivolous notion of business consulting. Alice expected Colorado to be just a lark, and once he'd finished, he would return home to a normal domestic routine. His investors expected him to bring back contracts for valuable, gold-bearing land for them. Nathaniel exhaled a deep breath. Others were sure about what he would do, but after time spent in the West, *he* was less clear about his future. Providence was supposed to hold his heart's compass, but undefined magnets were pulling his soul elsewhere.

The governor broke into his thoughts. "Well, Nathaniel, as for myself, I'm here for the promise you mentioned. So far it hasn't altogether panned out, but I'm counting on the riches of my new land. That's my quest. This one's got to work. I've bet everything on it." Gilpin rubbed his wide thumb along the darkened leather of the reins, and the two men fell into the silence of their own imaginings.

After an hour of plodding across dry grass plains, the road began to ascend. The ponies slowed their steps and then stopped. The governor rose to almost standing, imploring his ponies. "Oh, com'n now, Silvy. The hill's not so bad. Oro, get going." Gilpin swung down from the cart to the ground and began pulling on the collar across the withers while flailing a quirt in the direction of the ponies without ever striking them. He pulled again, but the ponies leaned down to chomp on the grass as their coarse tails flicked away flies. Looking up at Nathaniel he said, "I'm sorry. They think they're hungry, but I fed them this morning."

"Morning was quite a while ago. We got a late start . . . remember?" Nathaniel's teeth ground at the prospect of another delay.

Gilpin stepped up to return to his seat. When he snapped the quirt on Silvy's rump, the cart slowly began to move. Satisfied that they were on their way again, Gilpin started a monologue. In the rays of the sun, his beard was the color of burnt sienna, and it bobbed up and down as he spoke. At first, Nathaniel nodded at his comments, but then he shut out the sound. The road was narrowing as it steepened. On the high inclines, the ground fell away precipitously on the left into a narrow gorge, and on the right, the mountains almost scraped the cart.

The road became little more than a path of hacked-out rock, at places just wide enough for the overloaded cart. Below them, Clear Creek roared as it tumbled over the rocks, full of water from the spring runoff. Nathaniel clutched the back of his seat, leaning right in an instinctive effort to help balance the cart away from the ravine. He squeezed his eyes shut against the sensation of toppling down into the frothy creek. "Governor, are we going to fall in the water?"

"Calm down, Nathaniel. The ponies have a sense of balance. Trust them."

Gilpin's behavior belied his words. His right shoulder was brushing Nathaniel's as he, too, tilted away from the ravine side of the cart.

The intense sun that had struck their topless cart all day finally radiated red like glowing embers turning to ashes as it slid behind the highest peaks. Nathaniel struggled to control his annoyance. "How much more of this? I thought you said we shouldn't travel in the dark."

"We had to take this side road because the May floods wiped out the bridges on the main one. Don't worry. Oro and Silvy have never failed me." The cart came to a sudden stop, and Gilpin was silent. He stepped down carefully, threw the reins up to Nathaniel, and began walking in front of his ponies. "Come on you fat, lazy rats, we can't stop here," Gilpin shouted, trying to be heard over the rushing water.

Nathaniel clutched the reins. The sky began sprouting pinholes of twinkling stars as Gilpin walked in front of the ponies. The going was tedious. "It must be eight o'clock, governor. Weren't we supposed to arrive at the halfway point then?"

"We're getting closer." Gilpin stopped talking, making Nathaniel's heart pound harder.

"Governor, can you see the way?"

"We're feeling our way. Would you like a sip from my flask? It makes the trip less difficult."

Nathaniel's waving away of the offer was invisible in the dark.

At 9:30, they saw a few lights from Idaho Village twinkling in the distance. It was their midway point to Central City. When they approached a two-story log house, the cart slowed. The governor told him the house was owned by Eldora Conrad, a New Hampshire widow who, like many in the sparsely settled territory, tried to make ends meet by opening her spare bedrooms to travelers.

The cart stopped, and Nathaniel staggered off with his valise and satchel to go to the back door while Gilpin took his ponies to the barn to feed and groom them. When Nathaniel knocked and entered, the proprietress jumped up from the kitchen table where she had been dozing with her head on her arms. "Oh, my gracious," she said, rubbing her eyes. "For a minute, I thought you were an apparition. It's Professor Hill, I take it."

Mrs. Conrad bustled around the table to pull out a chair for him. "Have a seat, Professor. Governor G wrote that the two of you were coming, but I thought it would be earlier. Actually, I thought it might be two days ago. I'll have everything ready for you in a jiffy." A worn but clean apron covered her ample frame. She stretched to pull a glass and bottle from a long pine shelf. "Here. I expect you'd like some whiskey."

"No. No, thank you. But do you have anything for dinner? I haven't had a bite since breakfast. We thought we would be here before nightfall." He stepped toward the tall, narrow table that held a pitcher and bowl of water and began to scrub his hands.

The widow smiled. "Governor G always seems to run a little late." She turned to the cast-iron stove, kept warm in anticipation of their arrival, and continued to talk while she added kindling to the stove's embers. "How was your trip?"

"Treacherous. We almost slid down the mountain into the creek. I've never been at this high altitude before. Do you live up here by yourself?" he asked, conjuring up an image of Alice managing an inn so far away from civilization.

"I'm a bit of a rare bird to be a woman alone out here." She laughed as she ladled thick, brown broth with chunks of meat and potatoes into a bowl. The aroma filled his nostrils before the dish reached the table.

"Thank you, Mrs. Conrad. I'm famished." He dipped his spoon into the rich stew and tentatively let his lips touch the heat of the steaming liquid. "Isn't running a way station perilous for a woman?" He swallowed and realized how pleasant it was to be talking to a woman. She was one of the few he had spoken with since his arrival.

"It's not an easy life for man or woman. Idaho Village isn't very big, but we band together to protect each other and share what we can when supplies run out, which they often do. Danger is part of the West, Professor. You accept it." She brought a basket of warm bread and a dish of creamy butter to him. "In the two years I've been here, I've learned to take the bad with the good." She poured a glass of water for him, the metal pitcher reflecting the flickering lantern flame as she brought two glasses to the table and sat at the far end from Nathaniel. "There's no denying there's adversity, but I'll put up with a lot to have the freedom I didn't have back home. And anyway, there's nothing left for me in New Hampshire. My husband died, and we had no children. I wanted to get away from what my family expected of me. The newness of this place seemed like a good way to start over." She filled another bowl, knowing Gilpin would soon come in.

Nathaniel watched Eldora move through the kitchen. Her dark brown hair framed her unlined face. She looked not quite thirty years old. Her future was slipping away, and he hoped she would find the right kind of man to take care of her. Nathaniel dipped the crust of bread into the remaining broth. "You're an excellent cook . . . and a brave one. Since I've been in the West, it's been a rare day without some kind of danger—fear of Indian attacks or bandits, barroom brawls, and most recently, the danger of slipping off the road and into rushing water. I wonder what might come next."

Her cheeks dimpled as she sat down. "You've just nicked the surface. You didn't mention mountain lions, bears, blinding snowstorms, or lightning strikes. And I could add even more to that list."

Gilpin banged the door open. "Good evening, Eldora." He stopped and knocked his boots against the threshold to shake off the dirt before entering.

"Whiskey, Governor G?" she asked, rising.

"A glass and the bottle, if you don't mind. I'm mighty dry." Gilpin washed his hands at the washstand and went to the table, where a bowl of stew and a large chunk of fresh bread awaited him.

Eldora took Nathaniel's empty bowl and refilled it. He ate as Eldora and the governor talked about the people they both knew in Denver. She filled Nathaniel's bowl a third time.

Relaxed and finally satiated after the third bowl, he felt his eyes begin to droop. "Where do you want me to sleep?"

"Down that hall, second bedroom on the right," she replied, pointing the way.

Nathaniel located his valise and satchel under the table and went to the room. After splashing water on his face and brushing his teeth with a mixture of soda and salt, he slumped into the lone chair to pull off his boots. The chair then became the resting place for his clothes before he sank into bed. Conversation and laughter from the kitchen registered in his mind only briefly before he fell into an exhausted sleep.

The rising sun sliced through the mountain peaks to the east of Mrs. Conrad's lodge as they prepared to leave for the last part of their trip to Central City. Nathaniel was grateful for the early start. There would not be a repeat of navigating a narrow, precipitous road in the inky dark. Even in the daylight, travel was bone-jarring and slow. Gilpin let his ponies pick their way and, for once, kept his thoughts to himself. Thankful for the quiet, Nathaniel took in the mountain vista, finding beauty in its harshness.

Just after noon, Central City's buildings appeared on the hills above. Log cabins, some of them two stories tall, clung to the mountains along with tents, which were peppered about. The cart stopped at one of the few brick structures. Watson's Dry Goods was crowded in among a jumble of offices, stores, and saloons stacked on either side of the street. Nathaniel reached back for his luggage, then took the long step off the buggy. With a wave, he said good-bye to Governor Gilpin, who was going to stay with a business acquaintance for two nights. Gilpin nodded in response, snapping his quirt to make the ponies move on.

A bell jingled when Nathaniel pushed open the door, alerting the young proprietor. Joe Watson rushed from behind the cash register and clasped Nathaniel's hand in a strong grip. "Professor Hill, you've arrived at last. I got your telegram."

"It's good to see you, Joe. And please call me Nathaniel."

"Of course. But the last time I saw you I was just a lad." He smiled mischievously. "I'll have to get used to not calling you professor. It's good to see you, although I have to confess I don't remember you coming into the dry goods store very often."

"It's not surprising. Alice did most of the shopping."

"Anyway, my father had me back stocking shelves more often than not, so I didn't see all the customers. I've been hankering to have someone from Providence pay a visit and tell me the goings-on of my hometown. Your letter saying you were coming was good news to me."

"Likewise. I've been thinking about a conversation all the way across the Plains. I'll give you news about Providence if you can tell me more about the mining districts."

Joe reached out for Nathaniel's luggage. "Good enough. But you've been on the road since yesterday. Let's set your bags behind the counter where they're safe and go up the street for lunch. Is that agreeable?"

"Just what I need." Nathaniel handed over the satchel and leather valise that were beginning to show their wear from the trip.

Joe wedged them under the counter out of sight. "After lunch, I'll get you settled in our bachelor quarters above. I hope you're willing to stay with my friends and me. A rooming house is out of the question. We want to show you our western hospitality."

"If it's not a bother. Thank you. It will definitely make things easier."

Joe nodded. "Let's walk up the street. I'm eager for first-hand information. I never know what slant the newspapers are putting on things."

"And I want to know about your life in the mountains." Nathaniel looked around the small mercantile. It had a prominent position on the main street, convenient for everyone in town to get to. "You seem to have done pretty well."

"Well, I'm not rich, but I'm not going broke either, although it's often slim pickings around here."

Saloons, boarding houses, and cabins snaked up the steep incline, almost piled on top of each other. The modest structures were drab but still provided the only bit of color in their denuded surroundings. "What happened to all the trees?" Nathaniel asked.

"Used for construction or heating. Not very attractive," Joe admitted.

"Everything looks new. Central City seems all future and no past."

"You could say that. Everyone arrives by one means or another, a burning passion, stoked by the thought of getting rich. They cut down trees, throw up a building in no time at all, and then go search for gold. There's not as much planning out here as there is in the East. The West has its own brand. You'll see that the longer you're here."

"I'll have to see it fast. I won't be here long."

When they entered the Thunder Café, the dozen other customers gave Joe a nod of recognition. As the proprietor of the dry goods store, he was well known in town. He stopped at each table to introduce Nathaniel, a hint of nostalgia for Rhode Island mixed with pride for Colorado in his voice. The two men reached an empty table and sat down for their meal. Words spilled out before the waiter arrived, but they stopped their conversation long enough to give him their orders when he did.

"Catch me up, Joe. What's been keeping you occupied in Colorado Territory for four years?" Joe Watson was in his twenties. He had a chiseled face and muscular arms bronzed by the sun. His hair was longer, curling behind his ears, and even redder than Nathaniel remembered, but he still had the familiar spray of freckles across his cheeks. His light-blue eyes reflected restlessness.

Joe chuckled, resting his elbows on the table after they ordered their food. "Sometimes I'm more occupied than others. I left Providence on a whim when I heard about Pikes Peak gold. The thought of spending the rest of my life in a Providence dry goods store was beginning to rub on me anyway." An engaging smile lit his face. "Like many young—and not so young—men, I was itchy for a fast fortune."

"Yet here you are working in a store again!"

Laughing loudly, Joe tilted his chair back. "You just defined the West. You head out searching for one thing and end up doing something else. Men come here for all reasons. I was tired of doing my father's bidding and wanted freedom fast—a youth's unreal idea of fast. My father hissed and spit like a trapped cougar that his eldest son was abandoning the family business, but I wouldn't listen and left. Then, when I got here, I found the rumors were not quite true. Fast fortunes in gold are rare. I took a look around and decided there was money to be made in selling supplies to prospectors—clothes, bedding, utensils, and other dry goods. So here I am doing the same job I chafed against in the East. But at least I'm my own boss, and there's some satisfaction in providing what people need."

"Enterprising, I'd say."

Joe shrugged. "It's a good way to keep up on things. Everyone needs supplies." Joe laughed again, showing a row of even white teeth above a golden red beard. "Sometimes I'm the boss of nothing—when I can't get supplies or people run out of money to spend. We always live at the edge, and transportation complicates things."

"After our trip to get here, I can understand why that might be a problem."

"I'm always at the mercy of wagons to bring me goods. I've even considered starting a carting business on my own until the railroads arrive. Right now I don't have the spare cash to finance it, but I haven't given up on the idea. You starve here unless you're ready to seize an opportunity." He lifted his elbows off the table when he saw the waiter coming with their food. "What about you? Why were you willing to brave danger and come west? You only told me about Governor G's contract in your letters."

"You're not the first to ask that question."

Their plates were filled with dark, kidney-shaped beans and pork, and their talk slowed to accommodate their mouthfuls.

Nathaniel took another bite before continuing. "I keep discovering more reasons than I understood when this all began. At the moment, I'm not sure any of them will pan out enough to make the trip worth leaving home and the university."

Nathaniel drained his water glass and rotated it, the light making prisms as he idly turned it in his fingers. "The reason I first decided to come was the opportunity to use chemistry in the field to survey Gilpin's land—use what I know in a practical way. Maybe there was an underlying sense about testing my knowledge . . . maybe even testing myself. Money was an incentive too. The stipend Governor G has paid me is substantial. I think those are the things that induced me to come."

He looked up to gauge Joe's reaction. "Of course, all the talk about the West had something to do with my being here. I first saw the western landscape in an Albert Bierstadt painting exhibit in Boston. What he put on canvas, I wanted to see in person. The light and majesty seemed imaginary. Now I find the reality even greater than his art, and certainly more real. The scenery is astonishing—mountains more than a mile high. Look at the gulch we just walked up," Nathaniel said, pointing toward the window. "The houses are stacked up the side of the hill so closely that if you tripped on your own front porch, you would be in danger of falling down the chimney of the houses below. It's something."

Joe shook his head, frowning in mock disagreement. "I can't say what we're doing to Central City is all beautiful."

Nathaniel had a fleeting vision of the hillsides stripped of trees, but let it slip away to continue his train of thought. "Unexpectedly, there are a number of monetary reasons for me to be here. For better or worse, I'm dealing with not just one governor but two. Of course, Governor Gilpin is the principal reason. He wants me to find gold or silver on his property, whether it's there or not. But there are others. Before I left Providence, several people, including Rhode Island's former governor, gave me promissory notes to purchase land—land with mineral value, of course." Nathaniel shook his head in frustration.

Joe grinned. "Hobnobbing with another governor. I am impressed. I knew you were important, but not *that* important."

"I only met him once, but he's a man you don't want to get on the wrong side of. Like most powerful men, he expects people to produce what he wants. Unfortunately, he's not the only one. Alexis Casswell and Albert Harkness, two members of the senior faculty at Brown, also have high expectations about my finding them valuable land."

Nathaniel put his fork down. It was actually more complicated than what he was telling Joe Watson. How his career fared at Brown was likely tied to what he found for Casswell and Harkness. It was all about university politics and job longevity for him. The country's economy was weakening, and if the news he brought back from the West was not good, they could find subtle ways of inhibiting his career—or even push him out of the university. Then where would his family be?

"The more I hear reports about the difficulty of getting gold out of the rock, the more apprehensive I get," he said. "You know, their interest in property isn't just a game. They feel their wealth slipping away in greenbacks, and they want hard currency. They're under pressure and are putting that pressure on me. That's why I've asked you to show me around Central City. I'm being asked by important men to do things that may be impossible."

"I'm a merchant, not a mining expert, but I know men who are. Everyone has a burr under his saddle about what's going on, and it can be a cutthroat game here too. But after receiving your last letter, I've already set up some appointments for you. Watch what you say. They will be more interested in talking to you as a professor than someone who might be competing with them for valuable land. Unless, of course, they want to sell out. And they will only do that if they think their land is worthless. Be wary about what you spend money on."

Nathaniel frowned. "I need to figure out how to avoid being fooled. Men I can't afford to disappoint are counting on me."

He was impatient to get started. The sooner he began his work, the sooner he would have a sense of whether he was going to please or disappoint the men counting on him.

SEVEN

ᛏ

Nathaniel walked along uneven ground between heaps of rubble, called dump, from a mine shaft. Leading the way was one of the miners Joe had arranged to show Nathaniel his property. The short, wiry man wore canvas trousers with holes worn through the knees and broken-down leather boots.

"I don't know how much you know about mining, Professor Hill," Bill Stevens said as he shoved back his dark slouch hat, revealing a forehead that was white against his otherwise deeply tanned face, thanks to the hat's protection from the sun.

"Next to nothing," Nathaniel confessed.

"The rectangular troughs are sluice boxes. They're lined with carpet to trap any heavy minerals when water is sprayed down them." Stevens pointed to the long box-like structures hooked together, propped up on stilts, and pitching down the hillside. "We've gotten some results, but not enough."

"You divert water to wash the dirt down and then comb through for the heavy metal?"

"Yep. It's a pretty simple operation. Over there is stamping machinery where we crush the ore." Stevens retied his bandana to cover his bare neck. "Stamp milling has been pretty unfavorable. We can crush the ore, but it still doesn't release the gold." He turned to Nathaniel. "Come, follow me. I'll take you in the shaft."

The two ducked their heads as they entered the timber-framed tunnel. After a few yards, Nathaniel felt the temperature drop. Stevens took a candle and holder off a hook and struck a match to light it. The flame flickered tentatively before igniting the wick and sending shadowy light over the irregular, rocky walls.

"That's a hoist, isn't it?" Nathaniel asked, looking at a cylindrical spool with wire cable.

"It's what we use to haul ore out to the surface to crush and wash down the sluice boxes." He started walking, and Nathaniel, eyes adjusting to the dark, followed the circle of light wavering in front of him, Stevens' voice trailed behind him. "There's about a mile of tunnels only one level down." Nathaniel's feet stumbled along tracks. After a few minutes, Stevens turned, opened a gate, and balanced the candleholder in one hand while grabbing the ladder rungs with the other. At the bottom, he held up the light. "Okay, come on down."

Nathaniel clung to the ladder rungs and worked his way down. It was damp, and he felt the temperature drop with each step. A drop of frigid water hit the back of his neck and slid down his skin under his shirt. At the bottom, he could see the forged iron bucket used to haul things up and out.

"Here's more trouble," Stevens said. "We can't get the metal out of anything this deep."

"It's because of sulfides. They bind up the metal. That's about all I know at this point." Nathaniel looked around at the timbering running across and at the sides for support. "It feels confining down here."

"It's hard work down here, and we'd be grateful for any information on how to get the ore to release its metal. Working with no rewards is no kind of life."

"I'm going to look into the problem, but don't get your hopes up. I can't promise anything at this point."

"Well, if you've seen enough, let's go out." Stevens stepped on the lowest rung of the ladder to ascend.

Nathaniel met with more miners Joe had recommended, but like Stevens, they were seeking answers themselves and gave him no new information. Each, at the end of his rope, tried to put on a brave face. It wasn't just the miners' emotions Nathaniel was trying to keep in check, it was also his own worry.

He went back to his room above Joe Watson's store and started giving context to his thoughts by listing the problems on the left-hand side of a page. The right side was for solutions. It remained blank. He felt a mixture of intrigue and frustration as he tried to formulate answers.

Nathaniel had taken an immediate liking to Joe's quick wit and insider's knowledge of a mining town. At the end of his two-day stay, the two men had agreed to have a last meeting over breakfast at the Thunder Café before Gilpin was to pick him up.

Joe took a scrap of paper from his jacket. "Now that we've done the business part of your trip, let me ask you about some people I remember in Providence. When I got your letter saying you were coming, I started jotting down names so I wouldn't forget. Let me ask you about them, one by one."

Nathaniel recounted details and stories about each individual. Sometimes he had to think a while before remembering a name Joe mentioned. They talked and laughed for an hour as they ate flapjacks and bacon. Finally, Joe mentioned a last name: Claire Foster.

"I wondered if you were going to ask about her. Wasn't there some disappointment when you left for Colorado?"

"Hmm. I'm afraid there probably was. When I left, she might have thought that my intent was to leave her, but that had nothing to do with it." Joe idly fingered the strip of cloth folded into a tie at his neck. "I probably dashed her hopes by coming west, but I was anxious for opportunity and still too wet behind the ears to commit to anything forever. I can't say I've figured out all my life even now. I'll keep trying to make my livelihood as a merchant, but maybe inside I'm still sheltering hope of finding gold."

Joe shifted restlessly in his chair. "Claire still writes, even after four years." He shook his head. "I never made any promises, but I know there were expectations. My feelings for her are still there, but not enough to reel me back East to a conventional lifestyle. And I don't want to have a wife behind wondering what I'm doing in this part of the country—worrying about whether I'll ever come back."

A shadow of guilt darkened Nathaniel's expression. "You've touched a raw nerve. I've left Alice behind in a constant state of worry. I think she lives in fear that every letter coming to her door—if any have even arrived yet—is an announcement of my death. The newspapers do nothing but fuel the flames of danger, whether it is the war or rampages in the West." He took a swallow of water and continued. "She expected to live the life of a faculty wife in New England, with a growing family of sons and daughters. I've put her life in a bit of turmoil. I'm sorry for that because I can't imagine life without her."

"Would you ever consider moving west?" Joe asked. "And would she come too?"

Nathaniel shook his head. "Alice and I are comfortably settled in Providence. There's no reason not to stay there."

"I ask because there have been times when I have been tempted to ask Claire to join me."

"I don't know Claire. I only know that she is a schoolteacher. I can't say how she would do in the West."

"I can't either. If you ever do meet her, give her my regards."

"It will be my pleasure."

Joe smiled and changed the subject. "What do you think Governor G has been up to while you've been here? Believe me, if there's an arm available, he's going to twist it. I suspect he has been trying to persuade someone about something. The trouble is, in his world, commitments and rules are meant for other people."

Nathaniel nodded in agreement. "I'm learning more about that by being around him. I wish I could say I have full confidence in him." Nathaniel took out his pocket watch. "Time means nothing to him either. Coming to fetch me this morning is just an example. He should have been here by now."

In Providence, Alice's straight-back chair was pushed close to Crawford's bed. Harriet sat next to her in a rocking chair. Alice turned to her mother, teary-eyed. "I just can't bear the uncertainty about my son and my husband. There hasn't been a word since the telegram saying he was in Denver."

"It takes a long time for letters to travel. We shouldn't worry yet," Harriet replied as she wound a loop of soft pink baby yarn around her needle and knitted another row.

"I need to write him tonight just in case the mail is getting through, but I can't tell him about Crawford's scarlet fever—not until I know that he'll get well."

Harriet looked up from her knitting. "Wouldn't you want to know if the situation were reversed?"

"I'm sure I would, but there isn't any point in sending him into an agony of worry when there's nothing he can do." Alice twisted her linen handkerchief as she spoke. "My conscience aches, but I just can't do it."

Crawford lay in his narrow bed, pale and motionless. After five days, his fever had broken, but he kept his eyes closed and resisted food, his throat still sore and inflamed. The chubby little boy had melted to a bony frame with ribs showing through his skin. Dr. Carpenter told Alice and Harriet that the next days would be critical for his survival.

Hearing rustling in the next room, Alice reluctantly turned from Crawford's bed to walk down the hallway into the small, sunny bedroom where her daughter had been sleeping. So far, the baby showed no signs of flushed cheeks or a rash. Alice bent over the crib to pick up Isabel, gathering the pink blanket around her. "Shush. Don't wake your brother. He needs to sleep to get better. Let him sleep a little longer." Nestling into Alice's shoulder, the baby cooed contentedly. "You're such a comfort, little girl."

She kissed Isabel's warm, silky head as she walked downstairs to the kitchen to nurse her, leaving Harriett to watch Crawford. Usually, nursing was the most peaceful time of her day, but thoughts of Nathaniel intruded on her calm. Her decision not to write him about Crawford's illness was firm, yet she despaired at the betrayal it carried. She and Nathaniel had an unspoken commitment to honesty in their marriage. But if she wrote, she would have to admit to herself that Crawford might die.

EIGHT

ꯆ

Nathaniel and Governor G rode the last two hours from Central City to Denver in a late afternoon rainstorm. Electric spears of lightning forked the sky, followed by ear-splitting claps of thunder. Rain turned to hail, making a relentless thwack against the oilcloth they had wrapped themselves in. They were hunched over and miserable when they finally arrived at the Pioneer Hotel. Barely saying good-bye, Nathaniel grabbed his wet valise and satchel and tossed his oilcloth behind him as he dashed for the front door.

In his room, he had to light a lantern to see what he was doing, even though it was only mid-afternoon. He changed his soaked clothing and sat at the narrow table to go over the lists he had made about all the difficulties of extracting valuable metals. The miners had described the methods they had already tried: crushing, hydraulic power, heating, as well as far-fetched ideas like soaking rocks in Epsom salts. He considered combining some of those methods, but the benefit of doing so eluded him. The side of the paper waiting for viable solutions remained blank, and the reality of not having answers made his stomach churn with acid.

Not wanting to deal with mining problems any longer, he turned to real estate—another problem. Nathaniel had toured properties in Central City and Black Hawk, which was a mile to the southeast of Central City. There were ten in all. After listing them, he graded them for suitability, based on what the owners described and what he could see with his own eyes. Of the ten, he marked three—the Calamity, North Star, and Windswept— with the grade of A for having the most promise. He gave a B to three others: Hesperus, Fairfield, and Bobtail. The remaining four had little potential. He marked those with an X. He did not want to jeopardize his reputation by promoting anything that he thought had little promise.

Absentmindedly, he leaned back against the spindles of his wobbly chair and almost toppled over, forgetting that he was not sitting in his familiar swivel chair at home. Jerking the chair upright, he settled down to review his conclusions one more time. His priorities seemed logical, but he decided to test them with Joe. Then an intriguing idea entered his mind. With six reasonable holdings, the three best properties could satisfy his obligation to Dyer, Harkness, and Casswell in Providence. That left three more—secondary, but still plausible.

He pondered whether it would make sense to use some of his stipend from the governor to purchase property for himself. It was an odd thought to consider buying land in Colorado, but if the mining problems could be solved, real estate values would soar. The decision to purchase mines did not have to be made right away. He could mull it over for a few weeks until he finished investigating Gilpin's property in the Sangre de Cristos. There was more property for sale in Central City and Black Hawk than desire for it, so the mines in question were unlikely to be snapped up by someone else before he returned. Nathaniel stacked the lists neatly on the corner of the table to put them in his valise once the soaked leather was completely dry.

→ ←

His equipment finally arrived in Denver. It had come first by railroad from Providence and then by oxcart from St. Louis. When it came, Nathaniel went to the stable, where he checked and rechecked every package. Everything was there, undamaged. He repacked it for storage in a covered cart referred to as an ambulance. It would be pulled by four mules when the prospectors traveled to southern Colorado. Until then, it would remain safely in storage at the stable.

Gilpin had said he would send word when he was ready to leave, but there had been nothing. Edgy by the second day of inaction, Nathaniel decided to check to see how the governor was proceeding with his own packing. Time was slipping away. He had to leave for Providence by the end of summer to get back for fall classes.

He took his usual route to the Lawrence Livery Stable, walking by the familiar commercial storefronts: a bank, an ambrotype and photography gallery, a billiards hall, saloons, and other enterprises. At the stable he found the governor, his back to the street, under the sloping overhang, surrounded by stacks of equipment, engaging in his usual banter with his ponies. "I won't load you down too heavy, but we've got to take it all. I'll pack careful, girls," Nathaniel heard as he came closer. The odor of urine-saturated hay and manure stung his nostrils.

"Good morning, Governor G. Looks like you're almost ready to go."

Gilpin gave a start and turned toward Nathaniel, his lips pulled into a pinched smile. "Ah, it's my chemist-mineralogist-geologist-etcetera." He gave a thin laugh at his usual goading. "I'm planning to be on the road tomorrow. We will start on the second of July, an auspicious day to leave."

"At first you said we would leave June thirtieth, and now it's July second. We seem to be falling behind again, Governor."

"This is a big job, Nathaniel. We can't take the chance of forgetting something. The survey depends on careful preparation."

"I've already seen to my own equipment. It's ready to go." Nathaniel stepped into the stable corridor, carefully avoiding tripping over the jumble of boxes. "What are all these bottles?"

A rumbling laugh came from beneath Gilpin's heavy beard. "It's medicine."

"It looks like whiskey to me." Nathaniel stuffed his hands in his pockets.

"One in the same . . . one in the same. It's part of the equipment."

"Take none for me."

Nathaniel turned and stepped away from the stable's shadows into the sunlight.

"We leave tomorrow," the governor called after him, shoving a box with his boot.

"Believe me, I'll be happy to be on our way."

"The gods will give us their blessings by traveling over July Fourth."

In the morning, Nathaniel came down from his room a few minutes after the hotel dining room opened its doors for breakfast. He barely noticed what he was eating because his mind was fixed on the promise of the territory's southern mountains. The room was just beginning to fill when Nathaniel finished. The kitchen had prepared the extra food he requested and wrapped it in beeswax-coated paper to protect it. He would have something to eat at noon the first day.

When he left the hotel, his step was brisk with eagerness to finally start on his long-planned journey. Carrying his personal belongings, he rapidly covered the distance to the livery stable. He could hear prospectors' voices bickering and laughing a block away.

At the stable, he found the twenty explorers jovially razzing each other as they loaded the last crates and equipment for the journey. Two wagons, each led by a four-mule team, would carry the heavier instruments and equipment. The cooking provisions and rifles would be transported on a lighter cart pulled by two horses. They would pass few places for provisions, so food would often depend on their ability to hunt. Each of the mounted men had a shotgun strapped behind his saddle and wore a pistol. The party expected to find only the peaceful Utes on the journey, but Gilpin had assured him that he was prepared for the unforeseen.

The prospectors had been gathering in Denver for days. Nathaniel had already met all of them and moved among them with friendly greetings. Within half an hour of Nathaniel's arrival, the caravan was ready to go.

Nathaniel stood at the edge of the hard-packed street to watch the teamsters mount and flick their long whips across the mules' backsides. They made a tight turn on Larimer Street to pull out of town. Other squads of men followed the first wagon, their procession disappearing to the south. All that remained of the cavalcade were settling clouds of dust and expectations of what the prospectors might find.

"Governor, they will get ahead of us if we don't get going." Annoyance erased Nathaniel's ebullience.

"Just a few more things to do. We will meet them at a ranch thirty-eight miles to the south. They'll set up camp, but you and I will stay inside."

"What about our safety?" He was now grim-faced as he stood beneath the overhang of the stable entrance. "They have the arms."

"Get over your paranoia. I told you the route is quite safe—"

"Like the Hungates? Was that paranoia?"

"No, just a rarity." Gilpin's body was rigid with displeasure at being interrogated. "It was in a different location . . . and anyway, I have my own pistol and rifle."

"I like the safety of numbers. And traveling alone and in the dark raises all the risks unnecessarily."

"I'm almost ready," Gilpin snapped. "We'll leave soon." He gave a loud slap to a horsefly on his neck and retreated to the stable's interior.

The morning air was heating up, the ground hard. Nathaniel walked back and forth, passing from the front to the back of Gilpin's worn horse cart, squinting in the intense sunlight while he watched other customers come in and out of the livery with horses and wagons. He pulled at his hat to shade his eyes.

Gilpin finally rolled back both sides of the stable door. "Come on, you scruffy ponies," he said, cajoling them out of the dark interior to the head of the wagon. He hitched them and picked up the reins as he swung onto the driver's seat. "Okay, we're on our way. Put your baggage behind you under the oilcloth."

Nathaniel shoved his satchel and valise securely under the cover and stepped up to sit beside Gilpin.

"Settled?"

Nathaniel nodded, bracing against the backrest, his feet on the buckboard. "After so much time planning, we've finally managed to leave." It was noon, but they were finally on their way.

"*Brrt, Brrt,*" Gilpin chirped, slapping the straps against his ponies' rumps. "Move on out, girls."

Nathaniel was surprised that even after hours of traveling, Pikes Peak, the symbol of the gold rush that drew thousands, remained illusively in the distance. When the sun began to slide behind the horizon, Nathaniel leaned back to tug at the gold chain across his vest to retrieve his pocket watch, then struck a match in his cupped hand to check the time before the dimness turned to dark. 7:30. "How much longer to the ranch, Governor?"

"We're about three quarters of the way, maybe a little farther."

"Three quarters!" Nathaniel groaned. "That will get us there about ten. I'm hungry. I finished my lunch hours ago, and now we'll have to pick out the road in the dark again."

"Have a drink, Nathaniel. It makes you forget about your stomach. We'll get there in due time."

"Thanks, but I'm not interested." Nathaniel pulled a gray wool blanket around his shoulders to ward off the chill of the blackening sky and muttered under his breath.

The rough road was barely discernible by moonlight, but Oro and Silvy moved instinctually, their hooves making percussion music like a rhythmic tattoo. They occasionally stopped to inspect the route. Apart from that, Gilpin continued his daylong talk about half-thought-out schemes for making a fortune: finding gold, investing in stock, inventing machinery. Nathaniel wondered if Gilpin's mind ever stopped dreaming up unrealistic ways to manipulate every system.

When the buggy came to a flat stretch in the road, Nathaniel exhaled and struck another match to look at his watch. It was nearly ten o'clock.

When the flame blew out, he looked up to see a glow in the distance. "What's making the light, Governor?"

"It's our way station." He chuckled, showing a flicker of white teeth through his thick beard. "You've managed not to die yet, Nathaniel."

Nathaniel glared at Gilpin, but his look was lost like a candle in the wind, and they continued on to the ranch. "Do you want any help with the ponies?"

"I'll take care of them. It won't take me long. Let the household know we're here. I'm sure they've been waiting for us." Gilpin continued around to the two-story barn to feed and water Oro and Silvy.

Nathaniel walked toward the back, gave a loud knock, and pushed open the timbered door to step into the warm, well-lit kitchen. The lively chatter and laughter stopped abruptly as the residents stood up, embarrassed by their gaiety.

"Ah, welcome. You're here at last. You must be the professor that Governor G wrote about. We thought you were coming much earlier, but we're up in celebration. The Fourth is Monday, and we are making merry all weekend. I'm Edna Corbel. My husband, Harry, would greet you, but he's already gone to bed. He has to get up with the sun. The rest of your party is camped outside. Did you see the tents?" She finally stopped to take a breath.

"Sorry, I didn't notice. There weren't any visible fires."

"They turned in hours ago. These are my two daughters, Agnes and Margaret, and their friends Clara, Tom, Bill, and Henry." She nodded her head in sunny acknowledgment to each of them. A gingham apron with deep pockets incongruously protected an iridescent blue dress trimmed in lace with a flounced bow in the back. They had all remained standing.

They were interrupted by Gilpin opening the door and banging the dirt off his boots. "Edna, we're famished. I know it's late, but do you have anything left to eat?" he asked.

"Don't worry, I've cooked up a storm," she said with a chuckle. "I've fed the young people and your crew, and I still have plenty left. I've even managed to stay awake." She laughed again. "There's a bowl and pitcher of water for washing. I'll get the food. Take a seat everyone."

"We wish you could have come earlier," Margaret, the elder sister, said.

The two daughters' words overlapped each other as they began to regale the travelers with stories about the ball from which they had just returned. "The Abernathys cleared both their parlor and kitchen to make space for dancing. Mr. Smith played the fiddle, and everyone joined in. There was hardly room to move. You should have seen Grandma Hoffenbeck do the jig."

They all began giggling.

"We moved here from Missouri to farm," Edna Corbel explained. "It's been a hardscrabble life trying to grow things and make ends meet. Most of the time we work from dawn to dusk, but despite the hardships, you can see that we can still have fun."

Finished with his second helping, Nathaniel stood up, his entire body drained. He waved away the offer of more food. "Thank you. I can't remember when I needed a meal more. It was very satisfying." Turning to the six young people, he said, "Excuse me. I wish I could stay and hear more about your festivities, but I'm tired, and we depart early in the morning."

Leaving Gilpin, who was tilted back in his chair, happy to have an audience for his storytelling, Nathaniel walked down the hall to the room they pointed him to. Entering it, he found three beds. One was disheveled and apparently spoken for, by whom he was too tired to ask. He fell into bed, putting a wadded feather pillow over his head to muffle the sounds from the kitchen, and quickly fell asleep.

In the morning, Nathaniel and Gilpin joined the prospecting party where it was camped by a stream adjacent to the Corbels' outbuildings. They had a full day of travel ahead of them. Of the twenty prospectors Gilpin had paid to come with him, there was a handful of professionals—engineers, geologists, and surveyors—but no chemist. Most of the others were ragtag men including muleteers, laborers, and a cook. All had a hard-edged craving for a share in an ever-elusive fortune.

Together they continued their route due south from Denver toward the border of the New Mexico Territory, a border that was often in dispute. The distance they traveled each day depended on a source of water. The second day's campground was at the foot of Pikes Peak in a grassy area surrounded by red sandstone rocks stretching toward the sky in wind-shaped configurations. Nathaniel quickly set up their tent so he could explore while Gilpin unharnessed Oro and Silvy and gave them their nosebags of oats. Nathaniel walked through the rocks marveling at their shapes and colors and scrambled up a high butte to get a panoramic view. Only the sound of the cook ringing the iron triangle for dinner brought him back from the spellbinding vistas.

"What are these red rocks?" He asked Gilpin. "I've never seen such towers. And the grass, it looks like a lawn. The view is even more beautiful than in a Bierstadt painting."

"Some people call this the Immortal Garden of the Gods. Indians consider it a sacred place, and it is full of game. Our men have already found enough deer for dinner and plenty to jerk for tomorrow. We will let the horses and mules graze a bit. From here on out, the grass will get scarce as we go along."

The next day was blistering hot. Gilpin and Nathaniel fell behind the others and found a stream with muddy banks to let the ponies drink. "We'll stop here to noon for an hour or so," the governor decided. When Gilpin dozed off, Nathaniel got up to retrieve pen, ink, and paper to describe to Alice where he was spending the fourth of July. The letter could not be sent for days, but writing was a way to feel close to her.

Alice was finally getting back into a routine after Crawford's close call with death by scarlet fever. Rippling like a washboard, his ribs showed through his skin, but he was full of laughter, like the happy boy he had been before his nearly fatal fever. This Tuesday would be the first time she would take the children to visit her mother since Crawford's illness.

Her free time on Tuesday and Thursday afternoons was carefully scheduled. She would spend a little time with her mother before the children fell asleep for their naps, attend a meeting, and then do errands.

After lunch, a punctual knock at the front door signaled that her parents' Concord buggy had arrived. George, the longtime liveryman, carefully guided them down the walkway from the house to the carriage. How she longed for Nathaniel to be home with her and the children. Judging from the date, she knew that Nathaniel was on his way to southern Colorado, where he had warned her there would be no mail delivery. With Crawford on the mend, she had finally written to him about their little boy's scarlet fever. In the same letter, she had described Providence's muted celebration of Independence Day, thanks to the war. She tried to imagine how Nathaniel had spent his Independence Day.

When the buggy rounded the corner, her family home came into view. Most of her memories of growing up there were about trying to keep up with the daytime rough-and-tumble games of her older brothers, Wendell and Jessie, and the conversation and reading as a family around the fireside at night. She admired her brothers' intellectual curiosity. She found the same traits in Nathaniel. His similarity to her brothers had appealed to her from their first meeting.

The trio clambered from the carriage and stepped up the stairs to the back door just as Harriet opened it and reached out to pick up Crawford. "Come in, come in."

"Grandmama, I snap the whip," Crawford chortled.

Harriet wrapped her daughter and baby in her free arm as she ushered them into her house.

The welcoming familiarity of the kitchen spread over Alice like a soothing balm. The stress of taking care of her ill son and baby daughter slipped from her shoulders as she unconsciously let care transfer to her mother. She smiled at how easily she abdicated responsibility when she entered her parents' home as she bent down to put Crawford in his playpen with a stack of wooden blocks.

Harriet tucked Isabel into a wicker bassinet. "Alice, are you and Kate going to another meeting this afternoon?"

"Yes, Mama. It's another one about getting the Young Women's Christian Association started. Kate and I want to be of help." Alice sat down at the nearby kitchen table.

Harriet paused on her way to the stove. "Explain it to me again. I still don't understand the purpose."

"Young women, girls really, keep coming to Providence from other countries, mostly Ireland."

"Why are they coming?"

"To better themselves. They mostly come from the countryside and don't know the ways of the city. They don't know where to live, how to get a job, or take care of their health . . . and really so much more. There are people who are just waiting to take advantage of them, and they are so vulnerable. Instead of giving them a job, men can put them into bondage, almost as slaves. The girls don't know who to believe, and dishonest people weave stories full of lies to lure them. It's easy to be gullible when you don't know anyone and you have no means."

"Alice, where have you gotten information like this? It sounds so coarse. Are their lives really your business, dear?"

"But if it isn't my business, whose is it?" Alice asked, trying to keep the impatience out of her voice. "It just seems so unfair that I have a family to support me and they have nowhere to turn."

"Are you just going to help with organization? Surely you won't mix with these unfortunates, Alice." She paused briefly before changing subjects. "Do you want some tea?"

"Not yet. I just had a cup at home. Thank you. These girls are coming with so little and hoping for so much. Those I have met are just young girls from families that are losing everything from famine. If I can help them train to get a job, I would like to."

"Train them for what? Are you going to teach them how to be housemaids?" Her mother stood erect as she waited for the teapot to boil for her own tea.

"Maybe there are new opportunities in factories. The YWCA has a program to instruct young women about their new surroundings. It gives them a safe place to stay and help with contacts, but it needs volunteers."

"Can't someone else do it, someone without children?"

"Kate plans to volunteer, Mama, but more women are needed. It's only a couple of hours a week. It won't be more than that."

"Are you sure you're not taking advantage of the fact that Nathaniel is away?"

"Mama, I've always volunteered. You encouraged me."

"But you were with your own kind before," Harriet reminded her.

Bored with his blocks, Crawford puckered his lower lip, started crying, and held out his arms to Alice. She stood up, put her hands under his small arms, and drew him toward her, patting his back consolingly. But the noise had disturbed Isabel, and she began to cry too. Harriet gathered up the baby from the bassinet, putting her cheek against her small head. Mother and daughter walked back and forth in opposite directions, skirts swooshing, each rocking a sobbing child and not making eye contact as they passed.

On the sixth day of their journey to Colorado's Sangre de Cristo Mountains, Nathaniel and the governor could see the dust of the main exploration party ahead. Oro and Silvy were laboring up a long, inclined stretch of the road. Piñon trees replaced the scrub oaks of the lower plateau.

Gilpin turned to Nathaniel. "This is La Veta Pass. It's about nine thousand feet in altitude. Did you know that the War of Rebellion briefly came to Colorado and that soldiers passed by here?"

Nathaniel looked at Gilpin in surprise. "I thought this bloody war only corrupted my part of the world with its deplorable cost in money and lives. Sometimes I can't bear to open the newspaper."

"It's a high-stakes gambit the South has undertaken."

"More than that," Nathaniel said in exasperation. "The Confederates are acting illegally by trying to break away from the country, and their insistence on keeping the Negro in servitude is just plain immoral. President Lincoln is right in trying to keep the country together."

Nodding, Gilpin said, "I'm a Lincoln man myself. I went to Washington to meet him early in his presidency. There's no question that the job is more burden than pleasure. In person, you could see the deep lines on his face. The weight of his decisions was in his eyes, yet he was cordial. We sat in his private study across from each other and talked about his dreams for the West. It's part of the opportunity and destiny of this country, Nathaniel. He believes it as much as I do. He was worried about the ambitions of the rebs in this part of the world. The President and I talked about that too."

Nathaniel raised an eyebrow. "I guess I was too preoccupied with teaching and the events of war on the eastern coast to know what happened in Colorado. I can't remember ever reading about it."

Gilpin shifted in his seat and began to explain the Southwest's involvement in the war. "The South was organizing in Confederate Arizona in March two years ago. Their targets were north and west—north to Colorado's gold and silver mines and west to California for gold and its ports. The South was running out of money and thoughts logically turned toward the mines.

"Anyway, the Confederates sent two or three hundred mounted troops north toward Glorietta Pass. It's on the Santa Fe Trail in New Mexico at the southern tip of the Rocky Mountains. Confederate Major Pyron intended to mass his Texas-mounted artillery at the pass to assault Fort Union, about a hundred miles north of Santa Fe. Glorietta was a pivotal position. If they controlled it, the rebs could defend against Union force and break the Union's possession of the West. And that, they believed, would be the decisive coup of their secession."

The former governor stopped the horse cart at the top of La Veta Pass to let Oro and Silvy gulp air. Their velvety gray nostrils flared with the labor of climbing the hill.

Ahead of them, far below, lay the arid San Luis Valley. It was dotted with low brush and greasewood and flanked to the right by a mountain peak rising fourteen thousand feet with traces of snow still evident in the couloirs, even in July. Nathaniel gasped at the contrast. Even the smell of piñon accentuated the difference between this land and the one he had come from. It was even different from Denver.

Taking another swig of his "medicine," Gilpin clucked at Oro and Silvy and started the decline down the hill toward the San Luis Valley. They planned to stop at Fort Garland, which was one day away from their destination.

Gilpin continued talking. "The Union forces were under the command of John Slough and John Chivington—the two Johns." Gilpin sniggered at the reference to the two Johns and muttered, barely audibly, "That worthless peacock, Chivington, always taking credit for everything." He took another swig before continuing. "They led a forced march of four hundred Colorado militia south from Denver on the road we just covered, over La Veta Pass. They reached Fort Union and went on to Glorietta Pass, all in fourteen days. Fourteen days! The men and their mounts were almost consumed by exhaustion. Fortunately, the New Mexican volunteers, led by Manuel Chaves, informed Chivington that they had learned of a large Confederate supply train nearby. Tired as they were, they were able to block the Confederates in the narrow pass, burn eighty wagons, and scatter or kill five hundred horses and mules."

"Was it just a skirmish or did it really matter?" asked Nathaniel.

"It mattered, by damn! There wasn't much bloodshed, but that was the end of the western war. The rebs stuck their tails between their legs and went home. They even gave up their plans to build a railroad through Southern New Mexico to California's gold fields." Gilpin gazed down at the rutted dirt on which they were plodding, silently shaking his head. "Yes, it mattered from a lot of different directions. It cost me my job," he added bitterly.

Nathaniel was interested in Gilpin's version of the story and let his travel companion continue.

"Politics, Nathaniel, it's a nasty business. Lincoln named me the first governor of the new Colorado Territory at the outset of the war in 1861. It was his predecessor, James Buchanan, who had signed the territory into law. There were as many problems in the West as the East, just different ones.

"Even Colorado had some Confederate sympathizers seething against the Union and Lincoln. They were cheering for a reb invasion, and some were secretly plotting for it. I had to take things into my own hands for the sake of Colorado, but really for the sake of the country. I made up a regiment. It was protection against the Confederates, but also against the raging Arapaho and Cheyenne. The government had reassigned US Army troops for other duties because the Union was having massive numbers of casualties. Well, I had both their grand war and war with the Indians. I asked local men to step up for a military regiment.

"As I said, Lincoln and I had talked about this, but no one believed me afterward. The men weren't going to *volunteer*. I had to pay them. I issued drafts, and the First Colorado Regiment began to train at Camp Weld on the outskirts of Denver City. The First Colorado was a success, but it was expensive."

The many lines in Gilpin's worn face deepened as his saga continued. "The drafts against the federal treasury totaled three hundred seventy-five thousand dollars. I admit it was difficult for the government. They were, and still are, printing greenbacks. It took a lot to finally get those men paid. In the summer and fall of 1861, no one knew just how valuable the men of the First Colorado Regiment would be. My detractors called them 'Gilpin's pet lambs.' Pet lambs! Without them, the war would have been over the following spring, and the other side cheering.

"I fought for my job. I tried to reason with the soldiers who were mad when they learned that the drafts might not be paid. I pleaded with the government to pay them. I went all the way back to Washington to argue. The people of Colorado needed protection against Indian threats and Confederate intentions. Eventually, the government settled up after endless paperwork was submitted by each man to document his expenses. But by then, it was too late for me.

"So now I'm putting my past behind me. The land is my future. It will release me from my debts and uncertainty." Gilpin tipped his hat down further, as if to shield his eyes from the sun, but Nathaniel suspected it was for more than that.

NINE

🜚

Nathaniel shifted his weight to relieve the soreness from seven days of constant bumping along in the cart. They were at the southern end of the broad San Luis Valley. Cottonwoods stood like lonely fences along narrow streams. Otherwise, only scrubby brushes mottled the tan, flat land. In the distance, there was a subtle change in the unrelieved barrenness. He blinked, not sure if he was really seeing square, earth-colored structures coming into focus. He straightened but did not say anything until he could clearly discern the patterns of low, squat buildings. "It looks like we're entering a foreign country, Governor G. What odd looking buildings, all light brown and without a roof. Is this La Costilla?

"And its twenty-five hundred inhabitants. You might say we're the foreigners. Did you ever consider that?" Gilpin scoffed.

"Not until now. I assumed all of us are Americans." Nathaniel shielded his eyes from the sun. "What's the construction material? It looks somewhat similar to that of the fort we just overnighted at, Fort Garland."

"Adobe. Very practical." Gilpin tightened his hold on the straps as Oro and Silvy picked up the pace, sensing that buildings meant hay and oats. "Builders mix fine soil with water to make a stiff paste and add straw. They pour the mixture into wooden molds for bricks, which are baked in the sun for a few days. They're about three times the size of bricks you're used to and make very thick walls. The buildings are usually one or two stories high. Inexpensive and efficient—pretty ingenious, wouldn't you say?"

"It seems so, but how do they make a living here?"

Gilpin pointed east. "Look over in the distance. There are small farms with plots of beans and potatoes. They irrigate them by redirecting small streams that flow to the valley from the surrounding mountains."

Nathaniel shaded his eyes with his cupped hand. "I think I see animals too."

"They raise sheep, goats, and pigs in their pastures, and they gather wood in the uplands. Hunt and fish there too. They expect little from life and make the best of what they get from the land."

The features of the inhabitants came clearer as the pair in the ramshackle cart hurried closer to the village. "They look like Mexicans with their dark complexions," Nathaniel murmured.

"There are a mixture of Spanish, Mexicans, and Indios living there."

"They own the land?"

"No, most of them are renters or squatters, even though they've been here longer than any of us. The treaty I told you about, Guadalupe Hidalgo, settled title to land grants here in 1848. It also gave the former Spanish the right to choose between Mexican and American citizenship. Almost all became Americans. The treaty stipulated that they could use the land."

"What will happen to them if your land becomes valuable? Do they worry that you'll be taking something away from them now that you and your partners own a million acres of the land they live on?"

"Our grant doesn't include La Costilla, but it's very close."

"They still must be wondering about what might change."

Gilpin redirected the ponies and did not look at Nathaniel when he answered. "We still let them hunt on the land and keep a few of their structures on it. But you're right. I think there is some suspicion that things might change. The gold rush I am hoping for would bring many outsiders here with little regard for the past, only their own stake in the future. It will be a boon for some and a calamity for others."

"Do you worry about *the others?*" Nathaniel asked, his eyes squinting suspiciously.

"It's life in the West. Everyone accepts it," Gilpin replied with a self-assured shrug.

"That seems unlikely," Nathaniel muttered under his breath. "Do the people here speak English?"

"There's one family that does. Otherwise, it's all Spanish or Indian dialects. And one person who speaks German."

"What!" Nathaniel pounded the seat in exasperation. "You and the crew are going up into the mountain streams prospecting and will leave me behind in La Costilla with no one who speaks English?"

"You'll make do, Nathaniel. I've done it for years." Gilpin looked amused rather than guilty.

"This is absurd, Governor. It would be better if I came with you."

"We've had this conversation before. There's nothing for you to do until we look at everything," he said. "I will return as fast as I can, and until then, you'll be safe at the German's trading post. He's a good man—Frederick Posthoff."

"Safe from what? You keep saying there's no danger."

"There isn't any. It's a walled compound."

Looking in the distance, Nathaniel could see the adobe walls of the combination fort and trading post. Most of it was a story-and-a-half high with taller rectangular towers at the northeast and southwest corners. In another ten minutes, they had reached the structure. Gilpin proceeded along the west side of the wall for half a mile, passing the entry gate, until they came to an attached corral and stable enclosed by a six-foot wall, half covered with a sloping roof for shade. It was at the far end of the fort with its own entrance to keep the odors, flies, and vermin apart from the sleeping rooms, general store, and café in the interior compound.

Gilpin stopped the horse cart, got down, and opened the gate. He was greeted by a stable hand who held Oro and Silvy while Nathaniel stepped down.

"Get your luggage and I'll show you where we'll stay," Gilpin said.

Nathaniel retrieved his valise and satchel from under the oilcloth and followed Gilpin's rapid pace out of the corral. They turned to the right, past the tower on the southwest corner, and continued on to the main entrance of the walled fort. That took them into a courtyard lined with doors and overhangs propped up with poles. At the open expanse across from the entrance, Nathaniel saw their exploration party beginning to set up canvas tents and moving their necessaries into them.

To Nathaniel, the fort's interior looked confined and foreign. "Look, governor, there's no reason I should stay here."

"You're too valuable to risk out there. Nathaniel, it's really manual labor to examine the source of the streams. They are the most likely place to find gold, and they are high in the mountains. We won't be gone more than a month."

"A month? You know I only have two weeks," Nathaniel reminded him acidly. "It makes better sense if I go with you to the rivers."

"It's safer here. You would have nothing to do there," Gilpin said matter-of-factly as he began walking past the campground toward the irregular rows of doors at the north end of the fort.

Nathaniel scowled at the governor's back and hurried to catch up with him. "Governor, this is unscrupulous. I could easily be looking at the ore as it comes in. If I can't do that, I might as well go back to Denver."

"On your own?"

"I'll hire someone to ride with me."

"Suit yourself, Nathaniel. But you've come this far. Don't risk everything now."

"You think I'm going to stay here with nothing to do while you're out there doing who knows what? It's your usual deception. I'll talk to the other men. They will agree that I come."

"They're all in my pay. That means they will agree with me."

Nathaniel fumed. It was clear Gilpin had planned all along to leave him behind. His suspicion about the governor's lack of integrity was being confirmed. The governor had backed him into a corner with his bluff about returning to Denver. Like all schemers, Gilpin had a sixth sense about a prey. It would be difficult for Nathaniel to hire escorts to Denver unless he went back to the fort where they had stopped at the previous night. Nathaniel had become too entwined in the outcome to turn back now, and he knew that Gilpin knew that too.

They walked on in silence. As they passed by the near edge of the campground, they could hear the high-spirited joking of the explorers. Some of the men called out a loud halloo when they noticed Nathaniel and the governor walking toward their own lodging.

"Our last taste of town," the cook called out to the other explorers. "Don't waste it."

"When *do* that fandango start?" A mule driver shouted back to him.

"As soon as I get washed up," the cook chortled. He lifted his knees high and thumped his boots, doing a mock jig in preparation for the evening festivities.

Gilpin turned to Nathaniel. "The men will restock and reorganize here in La Costilla before we move on. The guest rooms ahead are where travelers stay—hunters, trappers, prospectors. Before our party departs in the morning, we'll enjoy the local culture for a night. The town's residents will celebrate the arrival of so many gringos with a fandango. Wait till you see it. The colors will dazzle your eyes, and the music will send you singing—even in Spanish." Gilpin smirked mockingly and walked across the courtyard toward a row of rooms at the north end of the compound.

The idea of a fandango brought Nathaniel little cheer. He could only think of his plight for the next weeks. He glumly walked behind Gilpin to a narrow interior door where the governor left him, explaining that he had a business matter to take care of in another part of the fort.

In the room they would share for the night, Nathaniel brushed off the gritty layer of dust from his valise and pulled out a sheaf of thin writing paper. There was no official post office. Mail was picked up by infrequent passersby willing to take it on to Fort Garland, but no matter how long it would take to be sent, he needed to communicate with Alice . . . with civilization . . . with anyone other than the unreliable Gilpin.

The room had no writing table or chair, just two iron beds and a stand for the washbowl. After cleaning the travel grime off his hands and face, he sat in the middle of the drooping mattress, his legs crooked over the edge, feet touching the plank floor. He opened his inkwell with caution and put it by his right foot, where he could reach it while balancing his valise on his knees as a writing surface. His first thought was to explain to Alice the disconcerting news that he was going to be left behind with no way to communicate. He felt disconsolate about the distance between them, as well as with Gilpin's shenanigans, but he reconsidered. It was not fair to alarm her. Instead, he described the scenery and safe arrival. After half an hour of writing, the door banged open as he was carefully folding the filmy paper in thirds and then over again to write the address on the blank outer space. With a rapid scoop, Nathaniel lunged for the ink bottle before it tipped over.

"Are you ready for the fandango, Nathaniel?" Gilpin asked as he dropped a metal box on the floor with a clang. "Our mining boys are itching to go."

"Have you ever considered entering quietly, governor? I almost spilled the ink with all your commotion." Nathaniel leaned over and screwed the top on the bottle, trying to keep his anger in check.

"Sorry, Nathaniel, my hands were full and I had to kick open the door. Are you going to join us?"

"Is there anything else to do?" He spat out the words, putting his writing materials back in his valise. "I should probably learn about the culture of the people I'm going to be surrounded by while you're gone. It's a ridiculous position to be put in."

"They are mostly friendly people here."

"I may never know that since I can't communicate, and frankly, I'm wondering about your relationship with them." Nathaniel's lips were

strained into a thin line. "Tell me, governor, are we friends or ene-
mies of our hosts? You may end their way of life with your plans, but
tonight we're friends? I'm having trouble understanding the conflicting
concepts."

"Don't worry, Nathaniel, tonight we're all friends. So let's be on our
way."

Nathaniel put both hands on the bed's front rim and pulled himself
out of the depression in the straw mattress. "I have no idea what to
expect, but I guess I'm ready."

"Not quite yet. You need to be dressed appropriately." Gilpin pulled
two red calico bandannas from his satchel, gave one to Nathaniel, and
tied the other around his own sunburned neck and short collar. Nathaniel
watched what the governor did, removed his starched collar, and replicated tying his bandana around his own neck. He walked over to a small
tin-framed mirror hanging on the wall and turned from side to side to
assess the effect. "I look like a cowhand," he said disgustedly.

Gilpin looked him over, clearly straining to avoid laughing. "Your skin
is definitely darker that when we started our travels, but I don't think
you'll be mistaken for a vaquero. But before we leave, I should explain a
custom of the fandango. After the singing, there is a dance. The señoritas
will ask to dance with you—"

"You must be joking. I don't know any Spanish dances."

"Ah, it's easy. They twirl around you, and you just move your feet to
the beat of the music. The room is full of swinging skirts, so your steps
probably won't be closely observed. If you accept a dance, it is the tradition to take your partner to the refreshment table and treat her to food
afterward. It's only a few coins, but they expect it."

"Do I eat too?"

"By all means. You may enjoy the local cooking. It's nothing fancy, but
it is very flavorful. And it's a way for them to earn a little hard cash. Also,
Nathaniel, the traders will set up tables of trinkets: saucers, face powder, and other gewgaws. You're expected to buy your dancer a present."
Gilpin reopened the door he had recently burst through.

Nathaniel shook his head in a combination of disbelief and bewilderment as they left the room.

As they walked the half-mile from the fort to the squat adobe church where the festivities would take place, the sun was edging behind the mountains on the far horizon, coloring the wispy clouds with a pink glow. A mocha-skinned man paraded up and down the hard-packed dirt path outside the compound, his flute sending trills of music inviting people to the dance.

Gilpin gave his companion one more word of advice. "Let the ladies ask *you*. Husbands and sweethearts are very jealous. You don't want to choose the wrong partner."

"Don't worry, I've thought about it. I'll just watch from the shadows." They crossed the portico and entered the interior of the church. "I'm not going to put myself in any more danger."

Nathaniel surveyed the festivities with a vigilant eye. The room was full of people and music. The dancing took place on a raised platform, encompassing much of the space in the main room, which looked to be about forty feet by fifty feet. Twenty women, some Indio and some Mexican, danced in a line. Filmy white blouses clung to their dark skin, revealing the cleavage above their full, round breasts. Their cascading tiered skirts swung to the beat of the music. As the women danced, they whipped the lacy scarves from their heads, mixing them with the frenetic kaleidoscope of swirling skirts while they twirled with their partners to the music. Five musicians stood at the back. Like the women, their attire was traditional: loose-fitting white shirts, unfitted pants, and low-crowned, broad brimmed hats. Three played stringed instruments, one played a flute, and one alternated between thumping a small drum and clicking castanets to set the tempo.

Nathaniel was entranced by the rhythm and motion of the dancers. His groin warmed and hardened, enthralled by the women's sensuous movements, but he stayed cautiously at the edge of the crowd, resisting any invitation to join in the frenzy. Away from Alice for more than a month, he was afraid of what might happen if he joined the dance, even with women of another culture. Unlike him, the dancing explorers appeared to be unconcerned. Lust shone in their eyes as they bent and swayed across from their indigenous partners.

After he watched the dancers for almost an hour, Nathaniel became curious about the rest of the parish hall. He walked to the tables set up for vendors and inspected the items for sale, finally settling on a brown clay burro with black mane and tail. It was just bigger than the size of his thumb—small enough to carry in his luggage for Alice.

The sounds of the rhythmic music and laughter reverberated in his ears, growing louder with the increasing consumption of alcohol by the participants. Nathaniel wearied of the cacophony, and at ten o'clock, he decided that he had learned enough about the fandango. It was reminiscent of the sirens who lured sailors with their seductive music in Jason's search for the fleece of the golden-haired ram. Back in his room, sleep overtook his thoughts of siren songs. He was barely aware of Gilpin's return to the room and his collapse with a thud on the adjacent bunk.

In the morning, Nathaniel was up before many of the others, but not before the cook, Bevan McIlroy. McIlroy had a reputation for finding flour and beans where they did not seem to exist and getting the best riflemen to compete with one another on how many deer and bison they could bring to the cook wagon. He made Irish stew while entertaining the crew with jokes, singing ribald songs, and instigating never-ending pranks. On this morning, the fare was coffee, Mexican-style venison, and cornbread baked into thin cakes.

At the cook wagon, Nathaniel was joined by grumbling men who, he learned, had danced the fandango into the wee hours. The aroma of breakfast had roused them, and they moved groggily to fill plates and sit cross-legged on the dirt around the campfire. Nathaniel filled his own plate and joined them, sitting next to Gilpin. They ate silently for a time before Nathaniel spoke up. "I'm getting worried about the time."

Gilpin was working at the last bits of breakfast. "We have to search each of the three rivers carefully."

"If it takes too much time and I don't return to Providence for fall classes, I may be giving up all my opportunity."

"The time will be worth it. This might be our opportunity, Nathaniel—yours and mine."

"*I* have a family. Alice is fending on her own with two children. I came to do a survey for you and other businessmen. My investment is secondary. At the moment, it seems as if I'm risking everything, while you have little to lose."

"Ah, but I have money tied up in this project. There is plenty to lose. I owe Colonel Reynolds and others the funds they lent me to secure the land grant and pay for the expedition. My reputation is at stake. It's at low ebb at the moment. I need to find minerals to support myself. If you have noticed, I have no livelihood presently."

Nathaniel was startled by the frankness with which the governor made his points, but did not let that deter him from pressing on. "That's just the point. I do have a livelihood, and one that many men would covet: professor of applied chemistry at a prestigious university, a wife, children, and many friends in Providence. Some of my friends and colleagues thought this was a wild goose chase, and they may well be right."

Gilpin rose stiffly to return his empty plate to the cook. "Well, let's try to prove your well-heeled Eastern friends wrong."

After breakfast, Nathaniel walked across the open plaza to the corral to watch the prospecting party prepare to leave. They were unloading the equipment they had brought with them, including picks, sledgehammers, and other implements, to pack on a procession of burros. The animals seemed no bigger than a large dog to Nathaniel, but Gilpin told him that each was capable of carrying loads of up to three hundred pounds. His wax-covered chemicals and the dynamite for blasting were wrapped in waterproof tarps spread out among the burros. Bevan McIlroy's cooking provisions were loaded in a covered wagon to be pulled by two mules.

Nathaniel lingered at the corral gate in misery, watching the trailing plume of dust from the cavalcade of men and burros as they moved northeast toward the mountains to follow the streams up to their source. When they disappeared in the distance of the San Luis Valley, he returned to his room and sat down in a chair in front of a narrow table that he had badgered Gilpin to find him so he would not have to read and write on the sagging bed. Once again he felt the need to communicate with Alice in the only way he had, through writing a letter that would not reach her for weeks. Feelings of imprisonment squeezed his gut and crept up to his chest as he began to share his impressions with her.

La Costilla
July 9, 1864
My dear wife,

I am staying at the fort and trading post of Mr. Frederick Posthoff, a German who speaks both Spanish and German but only a few words of English. He is the major storekeeper in La Costilla. I was introduced to him last night.

I estimate this extensive compound to be on two hundred acres of land contained by four adobe walls just adjacent to the village of houses. Adobe, by the way, is like mud-colored stucco. There is only one entrance from the outside and no exterior windows. All the doors and windows are on the inside of the fort. It was built a few years ago when they worried about hostile Indians.

The interior space contains rows of rooms on the west, north, and east for visitors. Posthoff's trading post occupies some of the space, as well as a kitchen and communal dining room, which are near his personal rooms. On the south there is an open space by the well for camping. Under threat of attack, horses and cattle could be brought inside, but now they stay in a partially covered corral to the south. There are two lookout towers on the exterior walls with a ladder to get up to them to look out the windows facing each direction. To the south of the trading fort is the scattered village of La Costilla at the fluctuating border between Colorado and New Mexico territories.

The governor and his men have left the compound, but I remain here until they gather ore for me to inspect. They will then take me to the collection site. Much to my fury, I learned last night that the exploration party may be gone a month. The time worries me. Governor G always underestimates how long something will take. He is well educated, but he is also a dreamer. He is determined to find minerals in the three rivers, but what they will actually find is only speculation at this point. Whether they will turn out to be like placer finds of Central City and Black Hawk is a gamble. Now, like it or not, I'm part of that gamble.

In some ways I'm not unlike Gilpin. I'm betting our future on this. Not only will the stipend help, but, if we find gold, it will give us hard currency. All our property is in the form of greenbacks or their equivalent, and the value of our little bank account is fading away without my having the power to do anything about it. Everyone, including me, would rather replace greenbacks with gold. If Governor G's samples are void of precious minerals, it will affect all of us.

I should leave in six weeks at the most to be able to make it back by the time students return. There will be those working against me if my responsibilities with Governor Gilpin and his agent, Colonel Reynolds, slip into autumn. The possibility keeps me up at night.

My thoughts of you are constant. Take good care of yourself and the children.

Your devoted husband,
N. P. Hill

→ ←

Posthoff's trading post was the place where local residents, travelers, and indigenous people gathered to buy or trade goods and exchange information. Nathaniel learned that everyone trusted Frederick to give them a fair deal. The affable German communicated with words or sign language to all who came to his well-stocked store. At first Nathaniel hung back, feeling awkward with sign language. Reading the German language, as Nathaniel did in scientific texts, was far different than trying to speak it. But his hunger to communicate with someone, coupled with Posthoff's urging, broke down his inhibitions. Frederick would clap Nathaniel on the shoulder when he entered and begin pointing at items in his store, saying the Spanish words for them. Nathaniel wrote down the words when he returned to his room to memorize them. He wanted to remember everything to tell people back home, and learning was a mental exercise to fill his time. Strangely, he was learning Spanish from a German.

One afternoon, as he stepped into the courtyard on his way to the trading post to ask Frederick the meaning of a word, he saw a group of people in sombreros and serapes clustered outside the store's entry. Amidor Sanchez, the only local English speaker, beckoned him with a wave. Nathaniel quickened his pace, hoping for a real conversation.

Sanchez strode forward and placed a tentative hand on Nathaniel's shoulder. "Professor Hill, they come to see you."

"Me? I know no one here."

"Indios of the village heard that a professor had arrived at the store. They come here to be cured."

"Cured? Why would they come to me?"

"You are an educated man."

"That's not the same as being a doctor. Señor Sanchez, you have to explain." Nathaniel was alarmed that he would be required to perform cures or, even worse, minor surgery.

A squat, thick-waisted woman shuffled up to Nathaniel, holding out her arm. Near her wrist was an oozing sore, around which she had painted crosses in different colors. "It's Señora Reynaldo," Amidor Sanchez said. "She has had this wound for weeks." The others pressed close, their bodies redolent of sweat and dirt, their brown eyes guarded but hopeful. They were pointing to their maladies—all marked with crosses they had painted on in a futile attempt to relieve the infirmities.

"Señor Sanchez, I feel terrible about these poor souls. Where is the nearest doctor?"

"Fort Garland." Sanchez pointed north in the direction of the military fort where Gilpin, Nathaniel, and the prospectors had made their last stop before arriving in La Costilla. "He almost never comes here. We have little money." Sanchez turned toward the shabby, brown villagers, switching from English to Spanish to explain that Nathaniel could do nothing for them.

Nathaniel looked at them, desperately shook his head, and thumped his fingers on his chest, saying. "Not doctor. Not doctor."

They scuffed the dirt with thin, rope-soled huaraches but did not move away, refusing to give up. Remorse based on his belief that he could not help them kept Nathaniel rooted in place. Finally, he turned away, walking with slow steps to his room, where he fell prostrate on his drooping mattress to stare at the wood-beamed ceiling. The situation seemed helpless. What were these people to do? What was he supposed to do?

Never could Nathaniel remember feeling so spiritless. He felt isolated by the lack of conversation, bereft of anything meaningful to fill his time, and miserable about his inability to help anyone. Letter writing occupied his time until he ran out of both his own paper supply and all that Frederick had as well. After four days alone, he decided he had to get away from the compound whether there was danger or not. After breakfast, he passed through the gate without hesitation and walked down the main road, where he began to explore his surroundings. The plants he saw were not lush but managed to grow in the arid environment. In areas where there was water, purplish asters and an unfamiliar type of daisy— deep red and yellow with fringed edges—poked up from the ground. Sage was prevalent. He plucked a leaf and rolled it between his fingers, breathing in the warm, woody scent. His investigations lifted his spirits.

By the time he returned to the fort after two hours, he found Frederick frantic with concern. The storekeeper kept waving his arms at Nathaniel and the gate, exclaiming "Nein, nein, nein!" The man behaved as if he were responsible for Nathaniel's safety, but Nathaniel was unwilling to comply with his demands to stay inside the fort. From then on, he left the fort every morning in search of flora and fauna. At a nearby creek he saw bird species he did not recognize, and whenever close to the creek, his eyes scoured the rocks for glitter.

Back in his room, Nathaniel challenged himself to draw small depictions of plants and birds, accompanied by brief descriptions. He had to use the bottoms or edges of letters since he had run out of blank paper.

After his morning walks and noon dinner, he traded his suffocating, airless room for a shady corner of the adobe complex where he could sit in a chair tipped back against the wall to unobtrusively observe trading parties that came to Posthoff's store. Indians were frequent traders. Arapaho and Utes were the only tribes legally allowed to come to that part of the Colorado Territory, and Nathaniel was soon able to distinguish between them. The Arapaho tended to be scrawny and malnourished while the Utes had stronger physiques and were more self-assured when they traded with Posthoff. At first Nathaniel was on his guard. The stories he had heard crossing the Plains predisposed his perceptions, making all Indians look treacherous and mean.

"They must feel that their lives have been taken away from them. I feel trapped here after only a week, yet they spend their lives like this," Nathaniel said to Amidor Sanchez.

"The Arapaho and Apaches have been raiding white man's property, so the government has been harsh. It made them move. Many of the Apaches have already gone to Bosque Redondo in New Mexico." Sanchez rolled the words off his tongue so quickly that Nathaniel did not understand what he said and responded with a quizzical look. "It's a reservation and terrible. There is not even enough water to drink, much less to grow food."

Nathaniel straightened his chair to look at his leathery-skinned companion. "That's an awful situation. I witnessed thousands of settlers crossing the Plains for every reason you can imagine. Some are returning, but many are still coming in numbers that will bring conflict."

"There is already conflict."

"What can be done?" Nathaniel asked somberly.

"The contest for who will own the West will be settled with a high prize going to the winner," the short Spanish man said gravely. "But it will also have many costs."

TEN

ቶ

A pounding against the timbered door made Nathaniel's hand slip from his drawing. Because of the urgency of the sound, he dropped his pen and took two long strides to open the door to his temporary quarters. Frederick Posthoff stood there, short of breath and wildly pointing his knobby finger beyond the compound. Nathaniel stepped outside to see what was happening. Frederick beckoned him toward the two-story tower with its vantage point to observe the entire vista of the scrubby flatlands and blue peaks. Something had attracted his attention.

"What is it, Frederick? What are you pointing at? Is it an Indian attack after all?"

"Komm, komm!" The German kept waggling his finger toward the exterior of the fort.

Nathaniel rushed with Frederick across the courtyard to scramble up the rungs of one wooden ladder and then the next two to reach the fort's twenty-foot tower at the northeast corner. Four openings presented a view in each direction. Grabbing a cylindrical spyglass from a long, narrow table, Frederick tugged at Nathaniel's arm to direct him to the opening at the east. Once in front of it, Frederick thrust the telescope into his hand while continuing to point toward the horizon.

Through the small optical circle, Nathaniel could see a column of dust coiling above the ground far in the distance. There was no doubt. It was Oro and Silvy plodding toward the fort with Gilpin at the helm.

Relief engulfed him at first sight of the governor, but it was soon replaced by doubt. He returned the spy glass to Frederick and clambered down the three tiers of ladders to lope across Posthoff's plaza to the outside gates. Without considering why, he began trudging toward the cart, which was still more than a mile away. When he had gone far enough to be heard with a shout, he cupped his hand to his mouth and called out, "Hello, Governor. What's the news?"

"I'm coming to the fort," Gilpin called back. "Why are you walking?" When the cart came close, a visibly irritated Gilpin pulled on the harness straps to stop and said in disgust, "Come up and have a seat."

Nathaniel took the long step up to sit next to Gilpin. "What did you find? It's been only two weeks. Does that mean you have good news?" He scrutinized Gilpin's face.

"No news yet. I came to get you to look at what we found," Gilpin said in a growl. "Let me eat a good meal and get a night's sleep in a bed. We'll leave early in the morning to go examine the ore." Then he gave a *brrt brrt* to get his pony team going again.

Nathaniel grabbed the seat as the cart's sudden lurch nearly sent him off the edge. "You must have *some* information."

"I can tell you that we worked hard to get samples to the campsite, and I'm weary from traveling from the mountains." His hand smoothed his tangled brown beard. "Oro and Silvy have to be stabled."

Nathaniel turned to see if he could read anything in Gilpin's eyes. "What do the samples look like?"

"They are stacked in great mounds, but we don't know what they hold. There's a glimmer in some, but no one can really tell. It's time to do your job, Nathaniel. We hope you do it well."

"I can't do my job if I don't have anything to go on."

"There won't be any answers until you read the ore results to us. The men are all brooding about their futures. Their nerves are as dry as tinder and ready to go up in flames. You're the only one who can put everyone's minds at rest."

"If you had taken me along in the first place, it would have saved you this long journey back, and I would already have answers for you."

"Humph!" was Gilpin's only reply. Entering the gate, Gilpin pulled hard on the straps, stopping the cart to let Nathaniel get off.

"Shall we meet at the room, Governor G?"

"Fine, Nathaniel. But I'm going to nap, not talk." He ignored Nathaniel and slapped the reins to continue toward the stable.

The smell of spicy meat, beans, and rice greeted them as they entered the fort's dining room later that day. They walked through the compact room among the cheerful conversations of travelers who had stopped to trade and eat their supper. Nathaniel and the governor found a small table and sat across from each other, the air sizzling with tension. Without instructions, the waiter brought them two plates heaped with steaming food.

"I'll have coffee," barked Gilpin, much to Nathaniel's surprise. "I'm looking forward to having a conversation during supper," Nathaniel said, pulling his plate closer and putting butter on the steaming yellow cornbread. "For two weeks I've been alone for every meal except for a brief word with Amidor Sanchez and hand signals from Frederick."

Gilpin only nodded, occupied with his food and deep swallows of coffee.

"Let me tell you how I've filled my days while you were gone. To avoid complete boredom, I decided to document the local wildlife and architecture. Many of the plants are new to me, so I collected specimens and even drew small illustrations. When I get home, I'll write the descriptions and perhaps even teach a class about them." Nathaniel filled his fork with bites of meat and beans. He craved conversation but resented it being one-sided. And he resented Gilpin for telling him virtually nothing about what the expedition was finding. With effort, he kept his feelings and anger bottled inside.

"I'm glad you found something to do with your time," Gilpin said through a mouthful of food.

"I've made so many notes and drawings that I've run out of paper, but that isn't the point. I've been sitting here wondering what you have found. Now that you're here, I'd like you to tell me." Nathaniel stopped eating and fixed his dark eyes on Gilpin, subjecting the unreliable governor to a protracted scrutiny.

"I may have some extra paper back in the room," Gilpin replied without lifting his head.

Nathaniel's spirit plummeted as he observed his companion's glum demeanor. Usually animated, Gilpin was eating with his head bowed, his brow furrowed, and his eyes surrounded by creases. Life was aging him. Surely the former governor would have been in better spirits if he suspected success. "Gilpin, apparently you don't want to talk about the ore. But what's your plan if there is no precious metal?" Despair seeped into Nathaniel's voice.

"There are no other plans. This has got to work. Choices don't exist." His tone left no room for argument.

"But surely you've thought about the possibility—"

"No. What's the point of letting it grip my mind?"

"What if you have to consider something else?"

"A plan will occur to me, but it won't be necessary." Gilpin sponged up his gravy with a piece of bread.

"I've had little else to do but think for the last two weeks. You've been busy, but I've had time on my hands." Finished with his dinner, Nathaniel pushed his plate aside. "Now you're here and won't even talk to me. What else can I do but worry?"

"The problem is, you spend too much time thinking about details instead of the big picture."

Nathaniel glared at him. "I'm a scientist. That's why you hired me: to deal with details—or facts. Something for which you have little regard."

"It's possible to look at facts in different ways to achieve different results. They aren't always *yes* and *no*."

"Of course, but we use facts to come up with solutions, and sometimes it takes a long time to gather the right ones."

"I like the bigger scope of things: leading an army, running a state, and now investing in a million acres of land, speculating on sizable returns."

"Like you, Gilpin, I like enterprise. But it must have a factual basis, not be pure speculation. You can't spin gold out of straw. That's alchemy. Furthermore, if I get involved in something, the risk has to be commensurate with the reward. It can't be just fantasy." He drained the rest of his water glass in one gulp.

Gilpin stroked his beard. "There are few jackpots with certainties. The greater the gamble, the greater the rewards."

"And the greater the chance of losing everything."

"Don't fold your hand too soon, Nathaniel."

"I still have a stake in this game, a major one—my job and my family's future!" Other diners turned to look at him as Nathaniel's voice rose in frustration. "Unlike you, I'm not willing to risk everything to bet on an unknown, and at this point, everything is unknown because you're not telling me anything."

"We will both learn the results together."

Nathaniel moved his chair back. "I think I'll go to our room and make sure I have everything ready. When will we leave to see the samples?"

"Early tomorrow. We might as well get on with it."

In bed that night, Nathaniel could not quiet his mind. His arms and legs thrashed under the thin blanket, making the bed squeak as he repeatedly turned one way and then the other. His dreams were filled with images of barren ore stacked in piles at one moment and mounds of solid gold in the next. He finally gave up on sleep and lay under the covers waiting for the first morning sun to come through the calico curtains.

The sun was only partway up in the sky, reflecting pink off a string of wispy clouds when their cart pulled out of the corral. For most of the morning, Oro and Silvy ambled northeast along the valley floor toward the mountains and the miners' camp. Gilpin was still wordless, and Nathaniel had nothing to do except take in the scenery. With its spiny leaves and small pale flowers, greasewood, or chico brush as Gilpin called it, gave little color to the drab soil.

After nooning by a slim, silver creek, the scenery changed. The road steepened and stands of spruce and pine appeared in clusters as the horse cart ascended into the mountains. Bright orange Indian paintbrush and lavender columbine punctuated the forest's undergrowth. The constant rocking of the cart and lack of sleep made Nathaniel drowsy. Because his eyes were unfocused, he sensed before he saw something in the distance—a ropey rise of smoke.

"A fire, Governor. Look ahead. I think someone has a fire, but why? It's only afternoon."

"Mosquitoes," Gilpin mumbled.

"Beg your pardon?"

"It's our camp. The men have built a fire to get rid of the mosquitoes and flies, the unrelenting buggers."

"There were plenty of flies in La Costilla, but no mosquitoes."

Gilpin made no response. Nathaniel was beginning to dread examining the ore, fearing that after coming so far, they might fail in their quest.

The ponies clomped along on unbroken ground after the path ended, the cart bumping unevenly on the barely discernable rough trail. Close to camp now, Nathaniel could see a stream above that fed a mountain lake to the left of the campground. To the right was a low, rock-ringed fire and stacked tinder nearby to keep the fire stoked to a smoldering level. A dozen members of the mining crew sat downwind of the fire, backs turned to the ring to repel the insects without having to breathe the acrid fumes. They were keeping to themselves as they whittled sticks, tossed rocks, or fanned away the smoke when it blew too close to their faces. Now that their work was done, there was little for them to do but wait for Nathaniel's assessment.

When Gilpin's pitching cart got close enough for the men to notice, they rose uneasily, one by one.

"We're back," was all Gilpin said as he stopped the rig and took a long step down. One of the men offered to lead Oro and Silvy to water, and while it seemed to Nathaniel that the governor gave up the reins with reluctance, he finally released them, saying, "Thanks, Alex. Take good care of the girls."

"I'll treat 'em good, Gov'nr G."

"They're not getting any younger. Undo the cart and keep them far away from the burros. I'll check on them later. Nathaniel and I will find some water and get close to the smoke."

Nathaniel walked down the hill to the stream and filled his collapsible travel cup. Returning to the rock-rimmed fire, he greeted those standing close to the smoke. "Give me a recount of what you've been doing for the past two weeks. I'm interested in the details." Others began ambling over to find places to sit in a loose semicircle around him to explain their routine. Nathaniel lowered himself to sit cross-legged on a flat granite rock.

James Aborn, investor and exploration leader, described how they had proceeded. "We divided into three groups, one each for Culebra, Trinchera, and Costilla. Those are Spanish words for snake, trench, and rib, but they are also the names of mountain peaks." The jittery men rolled their eyes. "Just get on with it, James," Gilpin demanded in a tight voice.

James hurried on. "At any rate, the snow melts in the spring, loosens the rocks, and exposes any metals. We were careful to get different kinds of geology. Each of our groups had someone who knows something about rocks. Once we got the samples partway down, the burros hauled them back to camp, and we stacked them up over there." James stood up to gesture toward the obvious stacks of rocks the men had sorted from fist-sized pieces to boulders. Their futures lay exposed.

"Moving mountains would be a better word for it," Charles Sampson, one of the surveyors, groused. "No wagons 'cause weren't no paths. We just put tools on our backs and lugged 'em up hills so rocky and steep the burros couldn't manage. The sun's beating down on us, but the water's cold enough to make your blood freeze. Hot air don't mean nuthin'. There was no choice but to plunge into the icy drink to get samples. We got every kind of rock we could find. Some we broke open where we found 'em. We dynamited hillsides and did some panning."

"And tell him about the b'ars," interrupted Bevan McIlroy, slapping his thigh with a grunt and starting the story instead of waiting for Aborn or Sampson to do so. "Dick surprised a big brown sow with cubs, and she started moving toward him fast. Johnny got off a shot but missed her. The thunder of the rifle made her rear up, but instead of charging, she suddenly reeled around and high-tailed it into the woods with her cubs on her heels." He paused before adding, "I could've used some b'ar meat for my pot."

"If Dick hadn't gotten a'tween me and the old sow, I would'a got her," Johnny said defensively, his face flushed with embarrassment.

Having listened to the men's stories, Nathaniel went to inspect the lines of rocks. Lightning streaked through the pale sky, accompanied by a sudden clap of thunder and pouring rain. He jumped up and ran with the rest of them for their tents. They stayed inside until the pelting stopped and they heard the sound of Bevan clanging the iron triangle to signal supper. The group of explorers picked up their plates and reached into their pockets for their flasks. Unscrewing the top of the curved metal containers, they took deep slugs, keeping them close at hand. Stories of the past two weeks became edgy and pugnacious with the influence of spirits. Nathaniel leaned against a rock, plate balanced on his knees while he ate and listened.

The fireside chatter was about everything but what might be in the samples. Reckoning time would come soon enough. Apprehension seemed to dampen the conversation. One by one, the weary men returned their plates to the cook wagon, then went into the woods to relieve themselves before they turned in. Some slept in tents, but many just pulled out their bedrolls and crawled in to lie by the fire. Nathaniel found a tent and took his leave, exhausted from the day's events.

In the cool stillness of the following morning, Nathaniel untied his tent flap as the pink glow of sunrise tinged the mountains to the color of blood red that gave the range its name. He walked past the tethered burros to a small tent that protected his chemicals. Lifting the canvas, he examined each of the wrapped bundles, then returned to the campsite where Bevan had put coffee on the fire to percolate and was heating beans in a three-legged Dutch oven.

When breakfast was ready, the men ate in silence. Finished, they crowded toward the equipment tent, offering to carry packages for Nathaniel, who explained his coding system. They turned each box until the numbers and letters, inscribed in his meticulous handwriting, were visible. At the site, they arranged and rearranged them until they were in order. Nathaniel strolled along the line of parcels, counting them. They were all there. He gave the signal to remove the thick protective wax coating and put it in a pot to be melted and applied around any chemicals that would be left when he had finished his work.

Nathaniel set up a narrow folding table as the golden orb of the sun rose over the mountaintops. On the table he put his bottles of chemicals, an alcohol lamp, and a Bunsen burner. To the right of the burner he placed a grooved charcoal block the size of his palm and a mortar and pestle. Starting at the left of the long stack of rocks, he took a piece and crushed it with a blow of his iron hammer to pulverize enough for a sample. Putting that in the mortar, he clutched the pestle in his fist to grind his sample into powder and then mixed in nitric acid. He spread the paste in the grooves of the charcoal, blew a hot flame to melt it, let it cool, and then submerged it in a bucket of cool water. Silently, he made notations in a notebook he had packed with his equipment.

"What is it supposed to do if there is metal?" Gilpin asked, slapping a mosquito on his arm.

Not in a mood to talk to the man who'd refused to speak to him about the ore, Nathaniel ignored the question and fixed his attention on what he was doing, straightening up, moving the camp table forward, and squatting or kneeling beside another of the samples. After an hour, he stretched and rubbed his knees before continuing. The men milled around him, waving away mosquitoes and becoming irritable with their idleness.

Gilpin was stomping back and forth, occupying his hands by thrusting them in his rumpled trousers pockets and untying and re-tying his neckerchief. "Can I help you move things?"

"This is going to take time. You might as well get some coffee." Nathaniel replied, feeling a small sense of triumph as he continued to punish the governor for his withheld information.

Gilpin grudgingly left for the cook wagon. The men were getting testy, swearing at each other. Three of the younger men almost knocked the chemicals over with their roughhousing.

"Goldarn it! What's wrong with you? Get your asses out of here. Do something worthwhile and catch some trout for supper," James barked, red-faced with anger as the three men slunk off, cuffing each other as they went.

Towards late afternoon, Nathaniel washed off the chemicals and dried his hands on his trousers. He bent over to make the last notations on sheets of paper that were held secure against gentle breeze with rock paperweights. Groaning inaudibly as he straightened his sore back, he finally stood upright. "James," he said, "it's time to gather around."

Immediately, everyone stopped what they were doing. Puffs of dust from their boots mixed with the smoke as they sat down around the low fire.

Pressed together in a thin line, Nathaniel's lips revealed the story before his words. "It's discouraging news I have to tell you. Luck wasn't on our side this time." His shoulders drooped with the weight of the disappointing news.

Bevan McIlroy tossed his metal cup across the camp with a peppering clang. "That can't be right, Professor. We saw the glitter ourselves."

"He wants to keep it for himself," The mule driver said, his voice low and hoarse.

"I know all of you understand the term 'fool's gold.' These rocks are iron pyrite, which dissolves in sodium hydroxide. Gold does not. I'm afraid that's all we have. Most of you knew that if you were honest with yourselves."

In annoyance, a muleteer flung a stick across the fire ring, accidentally snagging the cheek of another man. The wounded man jumped up, one hand against the jagged, bloody tear on his face, the other menacing toward the perpetrator. They were all up now, agitated feet kicking rocks into the fire with showers of sparks, clenched fists ready to lash out with any provocation.

"Sit down and shut up or get out of here," James commanded, his body tensed to take on anyone who did not obey him. "Fighting's not going to solve anything."

They lowered themselves around the broken fire ring, bristling but silent. James sat down last, emphasizing his authority.

Nathaniel had stepped back, keeping his eyes alert for anyone reaching for a weapon. "I'm as disappointed as you are, but I can't fabricate what isn't there. You did your job well and collected different rocks to examine, but there is *no* gold or silver here." He started pacing back and forth in front of the downcast men who were reconciling the news and their futures.

"It's easy for you to say, Professor. You ain't got no money to lose." Bevan's tone was harsh and argumentative.

"Coming up empty is going to affect everyone: you, me, my wife, my Brown colleagues, investors . . ."

"We were counting on you, Professor. All that education? A waste of time," one of the muleteers barked.

"Even a chemist can't turn rocks into gold." Nathaniel refused to be scapegoated for the failure, but his voice sounded hollow, even to his own ears. "Believe me, I wish I could—for my sake as well as yours." He tried to catch their eyes as he attempted to absolve himself of guilt, but they would not look up. "My hopes got ahead of me, just like yours."

"Nathaniel, you've got to do something," one of the men pleaded.

"At the moment, there isn't anything I can do."

"Well, I know what I'm going to do," Gilpin growled as he stomped toward the row of specimens. "I'm going to put a few of these rocks in the cart and take them back Central City or Denver. Someone else will look at them."

"You can do that, Governor, but I'll stake my reputation that their answer won't be any different. They won't have any more chemicals than I had to test the ore and probably fewer."

"Well, it seems that all our reputations are at stake here, Nathaniel. And watch your back, my chemist-mineralogist-geologist-etcetera, or you'll have a knife in it." Gilpin turned and walked away toward his tent.

The others began dispersing too. They all looked raw, drained, and full of pain. Nathaniel suspected that their futures had been so connected to the rainbow of a bonanza that most hadn't planned beyond the illusory pot of gold at the end.

Nathaniel was drained too, his reserves empty. He had pretended to be prepared for the possibility that he would find neither gold nor silver, but he knew it had been self-delusion—just like believing in the glitter of fool's gold. Now that failure had actually happened, his mind was in disarray. He tried to think of what to do next. Should he stop in Central City and Black Hawk before leaving Colorado? Should he go directly to Providence?

As he walked back to the equipment tent to start preparing to wrap his chemicals and paraphernalia for their eventual return to Providence, Gilpin appeared through the flap of his tall canvas tent. "Nathaniel, there you are. I was just going to come looking for you."

"What is it, Governor? I'd like to leave first thing in the morning. We're finished here, and I want to get back to La Costilla as soon as possible." His body was stiff with resolve. Through with the site and fed up with Gilpin, he refused to tolerate any dithering that would have them leave late, risking the possibility of a thunderous downpour or travel after dark.

"The men will get everything packed up and come along with us in the morning," Gilpin assured him, his lips twisting into an ingratiating smile. "But I have something to say to you." He gestured for him to enter his tent, which was considered the camp headquarters. "Have a seat. The stumps are my chairs."

Nathaniel inhaled a strong waft of whiskey on Gilpin's breath as he reluctantly entered and took a seat on a crooked stump.

"What if we say that signs of gold are present in the area, that we just have to do a little more work?"

"How would you substantiate that? There's no evidence." Nathaniel stood up again and bent over to twist the stump to a straighter position so he would not list to the right.

"You could say there are chemical traces, but we have to research more of the land."

"You said that the three rivers were where gold would be found."

"But I didn't say it absolutely."

"There is a remote chance that gold may be found elsewhere in your grant, but it's doubtful. Searching a million acres will take months, if not years, of work."

"But if we just say there is good possibility of finding precious metals, the land will become valuable."

"Anyone with any sense would question that."

"You can have a big piece of the land, and we can both make money that way. People will flock here just for the prospect of finding gold on what will be their property."

"You can't sell the land on a false premise." Nathaniel bristled at the suggestion.

"False? It's not necessarily false. We won't make specific promises, just say it's realistic that one million acres of land has gold somewhere."

"What if it's never found?"

"You'll be back at Brown, and I will be on to other things. We will each have money in our pockets."

"What about our reputations?"

"We will be careful not to say anything definite." Gilpin paused, reached into his vest pocket for his flask, unscrewed it, and took a swig."

"That's not a game I want to play."

Gilpin held up his hand, waving it in protest. "Don't give me your answer now. Think it over."

"It will be the same answer tomorrow as it is today." Nathaniel got up from the wobbly perch to leave.

"No, no, no, Nathaniel. Don't say anything yet. You'll have a long time to think between La Costilla and Denver. This could solve things." Gilpin took another draw from his flask, his lips showing stained teeth behind his smile.

Nathaniel threw open the flap to stomp out. "And just what do you think these men will tell people? That we lied? Or do you plan to give them some land to keep them quiet. For that matter, why not just salt the land and get it over with." Nathaniel was incensed at the suggestion that he deceive people, angry that his reputation was on the line, and dispirited that he would return home empty-handed to face all the now-correct doubting Thomases. Most of all, he hated to face Alice and John Peirce as a failure.

That morning, Alice was sitting with Kate in the kitchen having tea while she read aloud Nathaniel's most recent letters about his arrival in the area where they would search for gold. His correspondence, written two weeks before, was full of cheer, describing Colorado Territory's mixed scenery of mountains and dry land as well as an amusing account of the fandango. She had read the letter to herself, but when she tried to read the part about the Mexican dance to Kate, she dissolved in laughter. The two of them broke down in a fit of giggles. Their laughter made Crawford clap his hands in merriment.

"Nathaniel sounds as if he had a good time at the fan . . . what did he call it?"

"Fandango," Alice read from the letter.

"He also sounds a little out of place." Kate took a sip of hot tea from the china cup that Alice had placed in front of her.

"He must have been, but he also sounds curious. He's like that. He always wants to experience something new to understand different kinds of things."

"You should be grateful that he tends to be straight-laced. Some wives would worry."

"No, there's no point in worrying. Sometimes I wish he could be content with what he has instead of always needing something new. That's my vexation, not distrust. And I do like to hear about what he's doing, no matter what it is."

"I like the way you and Nathaniel share your different worlds." Kate's smile dimpled her creamy cheeks. "You two are like a jigsaw puzzle fitting together."

"Speaking of puzzles, what did you think of the last YWCA meeting?" Alice asked, hurrying to talk while Crawford was still content in his play area and Isabel was asleep in her bassinet. "The organization impresses me, but I was a little surprised when they asked each of us to be a girl's sponsor. I thought we would only be teaching classes on hygiene and economics the way we have been."

"So did I, but I can see the point. The girls can take classes and meet others in the same situation, but it would be more helpful for them to learn how to navigate life here with someone to guide them—instruct them about how refined people live their lives."

Alice reached over to hand Crawford a cookie. "The girls who come to the association left Europe or our rural areas in desperation and with almost no resources."

"No resources and little hope," Kate mused. "I suspect we can't even imagine what their lives are really like."

"My mother thinks it's a mistake for us to actually mix with them," said Alice tentatively.

"Hmm. Do you think she's worried about our getting ideas from them rather than the other way around?"

"Maybe. She's always encouraged my education. Some mothers don't do that. On one hand, she thinks I should know as much about the world as I can, and at the same time, she wants me to be separated from anything she considers improper." Alice paused to ponder the contradiction. "Your mother was the same. You went to college and even graduated. Both our mothers influenced us. Most of our friends don't care about learning the way you and I do."

"At the moment, my parents are more concerned about finding a husband for me than being proud about my education," Kate said, laughing and rolling her eyes in mock despair. "They're worried that at twenty-four, I'm destined to become an old maid if I'm not careful."

"I admit I envy your independence, even though I adore being married."

"Mama, Mama, ball gone," Crawford cried. "My ball. I want . . . I want my ball."

Alice sighed, the conversation ended. "Kate, it's time for me to do some housework, but I think I'll say yes to meeting with one of the girls. It won't hurt to just meet with one of them."

"Me too. I'm so glad you're willing. They all seem so appreciative of anything we do for them."

"I'm not sure we can help someone's life by doing this, but I think we should at least try."

"All the girls will want to be like you, Alice," Kate said with affection. "Your life is perfect—just like you. I'll drop by the association and let them know our decision." She gave Alice a small, quick kiss on her cheek in parting, picking up her reticule as she moved with her usual jaunty step toward the front door.

Alice watched her go and wondered if she did consider her life perfect with Nat thousands of miles away, risking his life.

ELEVEN

A crescent moon shone golden in the glitter of stars by the time the twenty men arrived back at the fort. La Costilla residents had left their fields hours earlier for home. Frederick Posthoff and any visitors to the fort would be in their bunks now that it was dark. Nathaniel was relieved that he and the prospectors would not have to admit their failure to others until morning. They left their horses at the stable and went to the fort. With his gun at his side, the night sentry opened the gate for them to file through. In minutes, lanterns were lit in the interior campground, and tents sprouted like summer weeds. The men would stay overnight before dispersing to their next destinations and livelihoods. For now, they retreated to their tents.

In the morning, Nathaniel walked from the room he had occupied for over two weeks to the fort's interior campground to say good-bye to the men. He found them sullenly rousing themselves, having little idea of what lay ahead. Their only acknowledgment of Nathaniel was a nod of the head. He grumbled under his breath, "Blame the messenger, or worse, ask him to do something dishonest. It's much easier than accepting science." Shading his eyes from the rising sun, he strolled over to the men eating breakfast and broke their silence. "What are your plans now?"

Bevan raised his red head and looked over at him with a shrug. "I hear Montana is showing gold." He glanced at the others. "That's where I'm headed. I'd tolerate company."

One after another, the men mumbled their answers, scarcely raising their eyes from their food.

"I'm going to California. Maybe something's left there."

"Me and Jonesy'll go back to Denver with the equipment to get paid. Dunno what then."

"I'm done with this humbug. I'm a go-back—back to Missouri."

"No plans now, Professor."

They barely gave him a wave as he said good-bye and turned toward the stable. It would be faster if he rode the thirty-five miles to Fort Garland alone instead of waiting for the governor. Riding alone would give him solitary time to consider his own future. He was still seething at Gilpin's suggestion that he write the report to make it seem that gold or silver had been found or was there but not yet discovered.

The thought occurred to him that he might never see Gilpin again. His opinions about the man rolled over in his mind. In many ways, Gilpin was the very symbol of this new land filled with people searching for their fortune, however they might define it. The governor's personal style and integrity was contrary to his own, but, like Gilpin, the West's untested possibilities enticed Nathaniel. The potential fired his mind as nothing had since his laboratory innovation at Brown. Colorado had changed him forever, even in the face of failure—or maybe because of it. Like his mistakes at his childhood workbench in his father's barn, failure toughened him. The pain of not finding gold was raw and at the surface of his feelings, but failure would not stop him from risking disappointment again for a chance at success. And he was beginning to suspect that personal success was more likely in Colorado than in Providence.

Nathaniel was the first to leave Posthoff's enclave to ride north to Fort Garland. Gilpin and the one-time explorers were strung out well behind. The military fort where he and the twenty men had stayed overnight on the way south was a six-year-old cavalry outpost built to protect the San Luis Valley from hostile Indians. As Nathaniel approached Fort Garland, he realized how much his perspective of the fort and its soldiers had changed after his two-week experience in La Costilla. Posthoff's fort was for trading. It was a destination where cultures combined and bartered or paid for goods, while Fort Garland was one of a series of government forts built across the Plains as lines of defense against the hostility of clashing cultures. He was just beginning to understand the complexity of the West.

When the dinner bell clanged, he crossed the parade ground to go to the mess hall. He paused inside the door to see which of his party had arrived. After looking around, he carefully chose a seat away from Gilpin and the official expedition leader, James Aborn. Nathaniel had spent most of his time on the expedition with Gilpin and would not have minded conversing with Aborn, but he had no desire to take his dinner in Gilpin's company, which eliminated taking a seat next to the expedition leader.

The soldiers spent dinner quizzing the travelers for information. "I can't believe you came up empty-handed. I've lost a few coins over it," one mustachioed soldier laughed. "My bet was on a strike."

"Gold is a fickle mistress," another retorted.

Nathaniel could think of little other than returning to Denver and taking the stage for the first leg of his return trip to the East. Letting the conversation wash over him without participating, he overheard one of the officers farther down the table say, "I'm heading for Denver in the morning."

Nathaniel dropped his fork, stood up, and leaned across the table, pressing his jacket against him so it would not fall into the candle in the middle of the table.

"Captain, did I hear you say you're going directly to Denver?"

The uniformed soldier shifted his attention to Nathaniel. "I'm Captain William Van Vliet. You're the chemistry professor, aren't you? I arrived a few days ago and heard you had overnighted here before." His face was florid and full, and his thinning, acorn-brown hair was bisected with a center part. Matching brown sideburns reached below his ears. Otherwise, he was clean-shaven.

Nathaniel nodded in acknowledgment. "Yes, that's right. Nathaniel Hill from Providence."

"I'm leaving at daybreak with a wagon and four mounted cavalrymen. You're welcome to join me, either in the wagon or on horseback."

"That's good news, really good news." Nathaniel settled back in his chair with relief. "I'll be ready first thing in the morning. The horse I used from La Costilla is hired, so I'm without a mount. I'd like to join you in the wagon if I may. I'm really much obliged. I have too many things to do before I return to the East. Are four riders enough? So far, I haven't seen any trouble, just heard about it."

"We're soldiers, and we're all armed. We can get you safely to Denver City. But beyond that, there are no guarantees. It's a roll of the dice. As far as the military is concerned, there's no good Indian. There's murder in all their eyes."

"The Indians I saw coming to Posthoff's compound seemed to be little more than scavengers."

The captain brushed him off. "They murder each other, kill whites on sight, and take anybody they can for slaves. The West would be better off without them."

Nathaniel decided not to argue. "I'll leave that up to you military men, but I'm much obliged for an escort to Denver."

→ ←

The next morning, Nathaniel joined Captain Van Vliet in the wagon. Behind them trailed four soldiers armed with rifles and pistols. Van Vliet snapped the reins and the mule team lumbered forward. He turned his ruddy face to Nathaniel and mumbled, "I heard you were working for Gilpin, and I didn't want to say anything in front of him, but there's talk about Colonel Reynolds and his money."

Nathaniel sat bolt upright. The first communication he had received about the trip had been from Reynolds, and he knew that the colonel was heavily invested in cotton as a manufacturer of cotton textiles. "What kind of talk."

"The textile trade has taken a bloody drop from the war. Ninety percent of manufacturing is done in the North, but two-thirds of the world's cotton supply comes from the South—a supply that has been disrupted."

"And?"

"Some people are questioning whether the money to pay for part of the land grant was his or was conveniently borrowed from the government without its knowledge."

Nathaniel's eyes narrowed in doubt. "What's the proof?"

"There is none yet, just speculation about the colonel's ledger sheet."

"Maybe he saved money before the war."

"Maybe. His business is in desperate straits presently, so I suggest that you keep your ears to the ground."

"Can you give me a lead? Someone who knows something."

"No, no," he muttered. "It's just words in the air. I doubt anyone will come forward."

Trying to sound grateful instead of sarcastic, Nathaniel uttered his thanks.

That revelation seemed to be all Captain Van Vliet had to say. He became taciturn, sitting hunched over the rig's leather straps, the sun reflecting off his brass buttons and epaulets. His cocked army hat bobbed up and down, and he occasionally sent a spew of russet tobacco juice over the rump of the mule directly ahead.

The return trip from Fort Garland to Denver was monotonous. The two hundred miles gave Nathaniel too much time to think, and he was losing his ability to do that logically. Only in Providence was it reasonable to make any decisions about his future in academia. On the other hand, any intention of tackling Colorado's extraction problems should be done onsite. The distance between New England and the mountains put him at a disadvantage. The problem made him wish he could have one more conversation with Joe Watson. Joe was not a miner, but he had a canny knack for absorbing information from his customers. One thing Nathaniel did know was that he would have to start east very soon if he was going to meet the commitment he had made to the board and to John. If he did not, he would lose their confidence—and possibly even lose his job.

At the eastern base of the foothills, he cupped his hand to shield his eyes. In the far distance, he could see the structures of Denver taking form. It had taken them seven days to get there. Van Vliet's mules and the four soldiers riding behind the wagon quickened their pace. Nathaniel worked out a schedule in his mind of what he wanted to accomplish in the two days he planned to stay there before he left for Providence. During those two days, he could meet with some of the miners to see if there was any new information, and he could also say good-bye to Reverend Tom Potter. Having a conversation with Joe was problematic since Joe was in Central City, and Nathaniel didn't have time to get there and back before leaving.

Once they reached Denver, Van Vliet dropped Nathaniel off at the Pioneer Hotel. Nathaniel slapped the dust off his jacket, straightened his hat, and stepped down to the ground. He pulled his valise from the splashboard and hauled his satchel from the back before giving a half-salute to the soldiers, who were impatiently keeping their own mounts in check. "Good-bye, men. God speed."

They gave a tip of their caps in response.

"We got you through the easy part. Good luck on the rest of your journey." Van Vliet snapped his whip, and the mules and wagon moved on down the hard dirt road, the four mounted soldiers following behind.

Being back in Denver felt oddly like coming home. The town he had explored while waiting for Governor Gilpin now gave him a sense of familiarity instead of the foreignness he had felt on his arrival. He took the steps up to the hotel door slowly, his eyes gazing up and down the street. The door swung open and he was almost knocked over by someone exiting in a hurry. He struggled to keep his balance and looked up at the culprit. "Joe?"

"Sorry, I didn't mean to bump into you . . . Nathaniel?"

"Why are you in Denver?" he sputtered to Joe in astonishment.

"Did you just get back? Sorry to be in such a hurry. How did it go?" Joe was visibly distracted, ready to move on.

"It was a lot of work and nothing to show for it. But what are *you* doing in Denver?"

"I've been here getting supplies, and it's been one holdup after another. I was due back long before now." He stepped down on the dry, dirt street.

"This is an odd coincidence. I'd like to tell you what happened with Gilpin's property, but I would also like to hear if there is anything new with the mines. Do you have time for a brief talk? I promise to make it short."

"Sorry, Nathaniel, I've left my store with my clerk, and I've been gone much longer than I intended." Joe's words were rushed.

"You couldn't just spare half an hour to listen to some of what I've been thinking? I may never see you again."

"You've been on my mind for weeks. I'd like a talk, but I told the stable I'd be back an hour ago. My wagon will be loaded, and I've got to get going. We could talk on the way if you want to join me. There's room."

Nathaniel tried to hold Joe with his eyes. "I was just about ready to check into the hotel and make arrangements to go east. I have little time to spare."

"I wish I could wait, but I'm also in a bind."

Pausing to rethink his schedule, Nathaniel said, "If I go with you, I'll be cutting things even closer."

"Could we do it by letter?" Joe took another step forward with Nathaniel moving in tandem.

"They take too long." Nathaniel put his satchel on the dirt and shifted his valise in his other hand. "Okay. It might be possible to go to Central City. I'll hire a horse and turn right around to come back here."

"What's so burning?"

"The West has crawled under my skin like a tick. I'm torn between whether I should get more involved in Colorado mining or just be grateful to have the university job in Providence . . . or do both."

"Whew. I try to stay quiet on other men's life decisions. I'd be glad for your company, and I am willing to listen as we ride, but be quick about it." Impatient, Joe started walking with brisk steps down the street. Nathaniel jerked up his luggage and silently kept pace, his agitated mind churning about what to do. If he went to Central City, he would have to forego any time for the people in Denver. He looked back over his shoulder to the hotel where he should be checking in but kept walking beside Joe, trying to push away his desperate need to leave the West and meet his obligations in Providence.

At the stable, the head stable hand had already hitched Joe's two stout draft horses to a wagon fully loaded with supplies for the store. "You're ready to go, Mr. Watson. It's a heavy cargo. Drive careful." He handed Joe the straps with his calloused hands.

"Thanks. We'll get halfway before dark and be there tomorrow. I expected to leave this morning."

Nathaniel stopped and calculated again. Four days. If he rented a horse, it might be three. It still gave him time, but barely. He put his foot on the buckboard to step up, paused, and looked again down the street at the Pioneer Hotel as if it housed his tenuous future. "I might as well go with you," he said, sighing uneasily. He lifted his satchel and valise over the side to fit it under the canvas and stepped up to the spring-loaded seat. His decision had been more impulsive than consciously made, but now in the wagon, he was committed.

Joe swung himself up into the wagon. "Glad for the company. I want to hear about the old schemer and his land."

"You'll hear an earful from me about him and his accomplices."

Nathaniel felt the pull of the weight as the horses strained to get underway. "I'm all ears."

"I hope this reckless decision doesn't cause me more problems than I can handle."

"Sorry I can't make it easier, Nathaniel, but glad to have you. What did you find?"

"Nothing—no luck!" Articulating failure added to his nervousness. "The prospectors explored the most logical places with no sign of gold or silver. The governor and his partners own a lot more land than we explored, but it is probably unlikely to yield anything. He suspects the same, so he wanted me to shave the truth."

As the horses settled into a steady pace, Joe turned to Nathaniel. "Well, I can't say it surprises me. He was banking everything on his land grant and won't let anything, including the truth, stand in his way."

"I'll make sure my report is accurate and my investors know the truth about the results, but I can't do much about what *he* says. He and Reynolds are going to be in a bind. Now I hear there are questions about where Reynolds got the money to fund his part of the grant and expedition. Thankfully, that's not my business."

"It's bad news for the governor, but now what's next for you?"

Nathaniel twisted on the seat to look at Joe. "That is the question, and it's causing me no end of consternation. I'd like to take one more look at some of the mines. The problem of getting minerals out of the ore just has to have some solution."

Joe pulled his jacket collar up against his neck for protection against the midday sun before he spoke. "Every day, I hear some complaint about the unpredictable gods of gold. They shine on one man and pass over the next. There's little logic in who they choose to be rich and who they let go bust. I hear way too much misery from my customers."

"But maybe it doesn't have to be so random," Nathaniel said. "Maybe science could solve some of the puzzles."

"You're the scientist, Nathaniel, I'm not. Consider yourself lucky. You have a career to go back to. Most of the desperate people here gave up everything to take a chance. Now they're walking around like confused war-wounded, pondering what to do next. At least you have Brown University and a family. All you have to do is make it across the Plains."

"I don't know why this has gotten to me. I guess failure is never easy to take. I'm wondering how I can turn it around."

"Yeah, I've felt failure. Almost went under when I went from gold seeker to merchant. My first store was no instant success. Now that I have a bigger store and bigger costs, it's still risky. If everyone leaves, no one will want store goods. Everything's hard fought here."

"At the moment, mining is anything but sure, but what if I could accomplish what everyone thinks is insurmountable?" Nathaniel asked himself as much as Joe.

"If you can find answers for relieving the rocks of their metals, you will be considered a hero."

→ ←

Denver, Colorado Territory
August 9, 1864
My Dear Wife,

Yesterday I mailed from Central City a packet of letters that I wrote while in the southern part of the territory. I know receiving them will be a relief, and I'm sorry I couldn't send them sooner.

It would be my greatest pleasure if you could witness this majestic land yourself. It is beyond words. When the transcontinental railroad is built, thousands of people will flock in the summer months to the grand scenes of the Rocky Mountains. They will not only visit but settle here. There is even talk of railroads to Black Hawk and Central City, but so far that is a fairy tale.

I have just returned from a second visit to Joe Watson. Central City and its neighbor, Black Hawk, hold interest for me. I have made a momentous decision. I have taken the risk of purchasing a house for $1,800. The house has been rented by a local man for $56 a month and will bring us some income.

I have also put options on two mines, called the Bobtail and Fairfield, and have rejected a third, the Hesperus, with the intent of returning next summer to experiment with the ore. I believe it is possible that science can solve the problems, working for the greater good of mining and even the country. This prospect is one of the finest opportunities that has ever presented itself to me. If I am successful, it will add to my reputation and bring remuneration. I trust you will understand the opportunity for our family.

My arduous journey begins tomorrow. I will be back a few days before classes. During my journey, I will be sustained by the thought of returning to our pleasant home. Kiss Crawford and Isabel many times for me. What a frolic I will have with Crawford when I can take him in my arms. This last desire applies to his mother and sister also. Good-bye. God bless and guard you and the dear babies.

Your very affectionate and loving husband,
N. P. Hill

Postscript: Just as I was ready to turn in for the night, a knock came at my door. There has been an Indian uprising, and the stages will not travel for the next days. It is unknown when the first will leave. I know this delay will be as much a blow to you as it is to me. I will walk directly to the telegraph office to send you, President Sears, and John a wire to make sure you all know of my delay. What a frustration this whole thing is.

The despair over returning late to Brown made even eating unpalatable. The only salve to his aching soul was a packet of letters from Alice waiting for him at the Pioneer Hotel. She had written him regularly, and without any sure place to send them, had addressed them to Denver. Most contained attempts to remain cheerful, but she could not conceal her fear about Crawford's scarlet fever. Nathaniel's heart beat hard and fast when he read her terse description of the days doubting his recovery.

Not able to stand being cooped up in his hotel room any longer, Nathaniel decided to accomplish what he had earlier intended to do in Denver. He sent a message to Amos Sprague to arrange a meeting with the miners who had met his stage the morning of his arrival. They met at the hotel dining room at noon, eight of them sitting around two tables pulled together to make space. First, Nathaniel reported that he and Gilpin had found nothing in the Sangre de Cristo land grant.

The miners were despondent about the news. Amos Sprague lit a cigarette with his calloused hands and grimaced. "This is a punch in the gut. If the famous governor and a fancy professor can't figure it out, what's the hope for us ordinary chaps?" He blew out a puff of acrid cigarette smoke.

"Don't give up hope yet, Amos, nor the rest of you." He looked into each set of morose eyes. "As soon as the route is clear, I'm going to go back to Providence to see if I can figure out something to help."

The conversation went back and forth with little new, just a rehashing of the problems. Then the man sitting next to Amos Sprague said, "Professor Hill, I'm Aldwyn Brynmor, com'n from Wales. My cousin, Liam Bond, is newly in the country—in New York. Before he left Wales, he heard talk about a new process there."

"Can you describe it, Alden?" Nathaniel's eyes were alert with interest. "Wales you say?"

"It's Aldwyn, sir. Swansea, Wales. That's all I know. It's like a rumor without legs."

"I appreciate even that much." Nathaniel hesitated to let optimism trickle up through his misery. "I'll follow up on it." He looked around him at the other men. "Anything else? I'll be leaving soon."

The seven other men shook their heads as they tugged and scraped their chairs back to take their leave.

The next morning, an unseasonably cold August rain left the town dark and dreary. Nathaniel trudged through the downpour to the stage stop to check on schedules. No stages were coming or going. He turned away in despair and walked purposefully to minister Tom Potter's house, the umbrella he rarely used unfurled. It was early Saturday morning, and he knew Tom would be working on his Sunday sermon. He knocked on the door.

Within the time it took for Nathaniel to inhale three humid breaths, Tom opened the door. "Nathaniel? You're still in Denver. You should be gone by now."

Nathaniel removed his hat and stepped into the room at Tom's beckoning. "I'm afraid I've made a serious error in judgment." He hung his wet coat and umbrella on a hook and balanced his dripping hat on the hook next to them. "I took a side trip to Central City, cutting my time close, and now there's an Indian delay. Who knows when I'll leave. I may have to go through San Francisco and by boat if this continues."

"Why did you go back to Central City, and what happened down south? All I've heard are a few scurrilous comments."

"We didn't find anything valuable, and with no prospect there, I didn't want to leave without seeing the mines again in case I am never able to return."

"I hope that's not the case, but come have a seat. Do you have a little time?"

Nathaniel nodded and sat down on the familiar rawhide-cushioned chair. Tom went behind his desk and sat back down where he had been working on his sermon.

"When I get back, I need to write up my findings for Gilpin and Reynolds. I'll report empty results no matter what Gilpin would like me to say. I have little respect for either of them at this point."

"I'm sorry to hear about your results, but you and Gilpin aren't the first to come up empty-handed." He looked at Nathaniel's downcast expression. "Here now, I was so interested in what you had to say, I forgot to offer you something to drink. What about hot chocolate on a morning like this?"

"Thanks. That sounds good right now."

"Let me go get milk from the icebox. I'll be right back."

Nathaniel glanced out the window at the rain, missing the usual sunshine of the West.

Tom returned with a saucepan of milk to put on the cast-iron stove just on the other side of the door from his study. "Did you learn anything more about the land by going to Central City?"

"Not really, but I'm still optimistic about the future of mining. In fact, I've put some options on two mines for myself, as well as three others for my investors.

"So you now have a stake in the West."

"I've also decided to buy a house in Black Hawk. For the time being, it has a renter."

"A house in addition to mines, you say?"

"For better or worse."

Tom looked at Nathaniel intently. "I hope you don't mind a little philosophy from a preacher. Everything you do will have consequences. That counts double in a sparsely settled territory."

Nathaniel nodded in acknowledgement. "I'm already facing consequences. When I went back to Central City, it cut my time to get on a stage to the bare bone, and now the Indians have gone on one of their unrelenting uprisings. As you've heard, the stages have stopped."

"You might not get back in time for classes?"

"There's little chance. I've sent a telegram to Alice and another to my university colleagues. Heaven only knows what consternation my wife is experiencing."

"I've heard the wires are still working. That may be a piece of luck if it lasts."

"I'm worried about what the delay will do to my career. It will likely be seen as a brazen disregard for the university."

"Giving up teaching was always a vague thought in the back my mind," Nathaniel admitted. "Now I may have forced my hand, and it will impact other people."

The rattling of the saucepan lid interrupted their conversation for a moment. Tom stepped through the door to prepare the drink and returned, carefully handing the hot cup to Nathaniel. "It's rarely otherwise."

"Giving up teaching would be giving up my life. I'd be foregoing the day-to-day interaction with my students and, frankly, my identity. And I shouldn't leave out Alice. It's her life too."

"What's on the other side of the slate?" Tom asked, sipping his own coffee.

"I haven't sorted it out altogether, but I've come to understand that it is an advantage in coming early to an unsettled land. With a little initiative, you can influence history." Nathaniel inhaled the hot chocolate and took a tentative sip. "As much as influencing history, it's a way to test myself. That need seems to be part of my constitution."

Tom nodded sympathetically. "Not a bad trait."

"Giving up opportunity in the West would be sacrificing what I thrive on."

"You don't mind its roughness? It's often uncivilized here, even lawless. Some people wear guns on their hips here. It's a far cry from Providence."

"On the contrary, that's part of the appeal. So is the puzzle of getting gold or silver out of the hard rock. The challenge intrigues me. It's a lot like your sermon on Jason and the Argonauts. I like sailing off to unknown shores."

Tom shook his head in doubt. "Be careful what you wish for, Nathaniel. Men with good intentions fail here and give up more than they should. I see it every day. I've watched a lot of broken men go back, especially miners. And some never make it back."

"It's possible that science can help the West." Nathaniel stroked his jaw in thought. "I'd like to see what I can do. Maybe I can do something for Amos Sprague and others like him."

"I'm not as familiar as you are with science. I concentrate on the spiritual side of life."

"Both have their value," Nathaniel said with a sigh, "and to succeed at anything, you have to be passionate about it, even if the passion increases the consequences."

"Going about it honorably is also important."

Nathaniel nodded in agreement and took another sip of hot chocolate. "I guess I let my hopes run away with me about Gilpin's land, and now the West is pulling at me to try something else. What about you, Tom? You were going east around this time too?"

"I'm having problems of my own. The War of Secession makes raising money difficult. The most recent reports in the newspapers say the Union forces sank the Confederate fleet at Mobile Bay. Maybe that means the war might be winding down and everyone can go on with their lives—if they haven't died in the effort."

Nathaniel bowed and shook his head as he thought of all those killed on both sides. "I hope you're right about the war nearing an end. I thought it would end long ago."

"At any rate, I hope to go east next spring. With God's grace, that deadly confrontation will be over by then."

Tom got up to stoke the stove with chips of kindling and nodded toward the window. "It's starting to rain again. The sound of the rain always helps my thinking." He sat back in his chair. "I haven't designed the architecture for my new church yet. I would like the outside to reflect what will happen inside."

Nathaniel smiled gently. "Denver doesn't seem ready for a cathedral yet."

"No, I don't have a cathedral in mind. Rather, I'm thinking of something modest but also substantial, and with a spire that can be seen from far away, even as the town grows. It should beckon people to come and reflect on God's word in their lives." He reached for the pan to refill Nathaniel's cup. "A church is important. Without considering the soul, men can get off track and have other forces drive their actions."

"Your own inspiration will make your congregation grow in a new church, and, who knows, I may be one of them if I spend more time here."

"That would please me no end, but raising money takes a lot of effort. All of which takes time away from working with people—the very reason I'm here."

"I know you won't give up on a new building. Just don't become over-confident about turning everyone into God-seekers."

Tom shrugged. "I don't deny it's a lofty goal. I need to write to more potential sponsors in the East." He looked at Nathaniel with a good-natured smile. "It's a little like writing a sermon. Both are meant to persuade."

"You are a master of persuasion."

Tom smiled in response.

"I'd better leave you to your work. Anyway, I need to make sure I'm on the first stage out of Denver. Nothing in Providence is going to be smooth sailing, and I need to get there as fast as I can."

TWELVE

ꝗ

The calendar was a vexation for Alice. Mail from Colorado
to Rhode Island was often delayed, meaning weeks could
go by between the time Nathaniel wrote a letter and she
received it. At her kitchen table, she opened her daily
journal to make a checkmark on the corner of every date
she had received a letter from him. She thumbed the journal pages back to the day he had composed the letter to
remind her of what she had been doing at the same time.

His letters usually arrived in packets of five or six, bundled together for the stagecoach delivery across the Plains.
Her hands trembled with relief when the letters came.
She carefully sorted them by date, wanting to read them
in chronological order. This morning, the postman had
brought four letters. The most recent was written on August
9, 1864—a month ago. The month had been wretched.
She had received brief words, clicked out in Morse code
across the wires, telling her of his delay. After the telegram
arrived, she had fingered it until it was worn thin. It was
the only material link she had to his life. She scanned the
newspapers for information about the Indian uprising,

stoppage of mail, and downing of wires—information that was tucked in among the many words describing the War of Rebellion. Knowing the reasons why she had not heard from him was little consolation.

She settled down in her rocker, losing herself in Nathaniel's presence, if only on a page. His first letters were about the return journey from La Costilla. Reading so many letters all at once was like standing under a rushing waterfall and trying to stay upright. Just as she was absorbing Nathaniel's anguish that no gold had been found on Gilpin's land, she carefully unfolded the last letter to find that Nathaniel had returned to Central City and had purchased mines and a house in Black Hawk. She wondered what that would mean for her and the children. Tracing her finger over his fastidious cursive calmed her nerves. Everyone in Providence was acutely aware that Nathaniel would miss the beginning of Brown's fall semester. It was an egregious act. Nathaniel had also sent John Peirce a costly telegram asking him to either add Nathaniel's class responsibilities to his own or assign them to others. Only Alice knew from this batch of letters that there was more to his lateness than Indian restlessness. His vacillation about teaching and his interest in the West was now clear to her. She was already avoiding faculty members or their wives on the street, giving only perfunctory greetings and moving on quickly to avoid queries about Nathaniel.

She longed to share her concerns with her mother or best friend, Kate, but made a quick decision to keep them to herself. Until he returned, everyone could think his delay was simply transportation stoppage across the Plains and do their own wondering about why he had waited until the last minute to begin his month-long journey home.

She looked at the gold watch clipped to her waist. It was time to feed Crawford and Isabel and change their clothes. It was Tuesday, the day she took Crawford and Isabel to her mother's house for their naps. Today she was going to spend her free time at the Young Women's Christian Association. It occurred to her that she had more in common with those young women than she could have imagined because her future was uncertain too.

Once Alice had gotten the children settled with her mother, she left her mother's house and headed for her two o'clock appointment with Maggie. Thoughts swirled in her mind as she walked toward downtown Providence. Eighteen-year-old Maggie had emigrated from County Cork, Ireland, in early 1864 to live with an older cousin, Vinny. He was not a close relative, but he was the only one she knew in America, so she had no choice but to stay with him. Alice had volunteered, through the association, to help her find employment. Thus far, Maggie's job interviews had come up empty, and the young girl was close to giving up. Alice was still thinking of ways to reassure Maggie that she should continue looking for something better than cleaning her cousin's bar when she stepped up the stairs to open the front door.

The association waiting room was all wrong. It was decorated like a parlor to make immigrant girls feel at home, but the fancy room only intimidated Maggie. She had told Alice that in Ireland, she had lived in a two-room house with her parents, three brothers, and a sister. She had never been in a parlor.

Alice saw Maggie seated on the black horsehair sofa with her head down, staring at her clasped hands. Her auburn hair was twisted into a knot at the base of her head, with loose strands carefully pinned behind each ear. When Alice had first seen her, Maggie looked slightly tanned, but when she got closer, she saw that there were so many soft brown freckles covering her porcelain-white skin that they blended together at a distance. Maggie wore the same neatly ironed blue calico dress that she had on during the previous two visits. This time, she had draped a white sweater over her shoulders.

"How are you, Maggie? Thank you for being early. I don't think I'm late, am I?" Alice lifted her round gold watch at her waist to check the time.

"No, ma'am, you're early yourself."

"It's nice to see you again. Let's go to an empty office so we can talk."

Maggie's brown eyes darted up, but glanced quickly away as she obediently stood up and followed Alice, who led the way down a short corridor. Small rooms at the YWCA had been designated for meetings between volunteers and girls in need of help. Alice passed two closed doors, but the third was open.

"Here we are. This will do. Please have a seat." Alice pointed to a chair on one side of a table and pulled out another to sit across from her. "I want to know how you've been. Did you go to any interviews since our last appointment?"

"That I did, Mrs. Hill, but they'd already hired," she said in a nervous Irish brogue. "The jobs go so quick. It's not looking good for me." Maggie bent her head, brows furrowed.

"Don't get discouraged yet, Maggie. I know it seems like a long time, but I'll ask someone here if there are more names."

"Vinny, my cousin, is getting tired of me not helping enough with the rent and food. He has his little ones to feed. His money don't stretch so far."

"Can he wait a little bit longer? Surely the association will help us find something. We just need a little more time."

"He wants me to work cleanin' his pub full-time. It's the least I can do, he says. Hildy—that's Vinny's wife—is making it hard for him. She don't want me around the house no more. There's never a kind word for me, or even her babes. Those little tykes yowl all day."

"Oh, Maggie, I'm disheartened at the thought of you working in a bar. Then you'll never get a respectable job. What kind of people will you meet there?"

"Beggin' your pardon, Mrs. Hill, it's not a bar, it's a pub. The Irish come for a drink and to pass the time of day. It's like home."

"Is that what you want to do, Maggie?"

Maggie put her arms through her sweater sleeves as if a cold breeze had come in the room. "My father went to the pub after work, or at least when he had work. When he didn't, he idled the day away there. There was a lot of yelling between Mum and Dad."

"Wasn't that a reason you came to America—to escape that fate?" Alice idly opened her purse as if an answer would be inside.

"Some people have choices, ma'am. I thought maybe I would here, but it's not turning out that way. I'm grateful you tried for me." She placed her hands on the arms of the chair, ready to pull it back.

"Maggie, would you give me one more week to try to find a solution? I don't know if there is one, but would you be willing to meet with me again next week?"

Maggie stood up, her body enveloped in the oversized sweater. "I'll see what Vinny and Hildy say. I don't want to be where I'm not wanted."

Alice too stood up and gently put her other hand on Maggie's shoulder. Maggie's own arms hung loose, without response or promise. At the front door, Alice released her hand from Maggie's shoulder with reluctance as they left to go their separate ways. "I'll see you next week, Maggie. Please hold on until then."

→ ←

When Nathaniel arrived in Providence after almost a month of traveling, it was as if he were visiting the city for the first time. The long, Romanesque railroad station was palatial compared to the West's stage stops. A thick fog made Narragansett Bay monochromatic. The difference between the West and the civilized East collided against his consciousness. It took only a moment to find an available cab for hire. He breathed in the scenery with its familiar sites of church steeples and university buildings, and his nerves tingled in anticipation of being home. With a loud knock he entered his home.

When Alice answered the door, Nathaniel encircled her in his arms. Her familiar shape and scent made him feel as if he had only been away on an overnight journey. The passion he had kept in check for so long urgently pushed against her.

She was almost jumping out of her skin with joy. "Nat, it's really you! But you feel different. You're thinner . . . and your skin is so tan."

"I spent a lot of time outdoors in Colorado. But since then, I've been trapped in one conveyance or another heading east. It's good to be home."

The unnoticed hansom driver cleared his throat in embarrassment as he hesitantly put the satchel and valise inside the front door. Nathaniel reluctantly broke away from Alice and turned to the man. "Could you wait one more moment while I write a note for you to deliver?"

The driver nodded, hat in hand.

As Nathaniel strode down the hallway, his words trailed behind him. "I have so much to tell you. The scenery, the people—it's incredible. Colorado is such a different place, but I better talk to John to see where I stand with Brown." She caught up to him as he continued. "I need to send him a message that I want to meet early tomorrow morning. Let me get that done, and then I can have the evening to be with you and the children."

"Would you send my parents a note too?" Alice asked. "They expected your arrival soon, but they would be grateful to know that you're here in one piece."

He scratched out two notes, addressed them, attached his seal, and gave them to the driver. "I appreciate it. You're a good man. Here's an extra bit of pay." Nathaniel handed him coins and closed the door behind him.

"I'll just let the news spread by word of mouth, except for the university, which I have to face very quickly."

"Nathaniel, give me your coat and hat. Come see your children now that you've sent your messages. You can leave business until tomorrow morning."

Nathaniel laughed happily at Crawford's insistence for attention, while Isabel reached up responsively for toys, no longer the swaddled infant he had left.

When the children were in bed, Nathaniel and Alice had dinner together for the first time in months.

"I'm glad you're going to meet with John in the morning," Alice said. "I've been avoiding everyone at the university because I didn't know what to tell people."

"It will be relief to get that behind us. The university has also been weighing on my mind. He took a large forkful of fresh green beans. "I'm grateful to be eating your cooking. There wasn't anything like it out there." He smiled at her with appreciation.

"I'm so glad to have you home."

"After I settle things with Brown, I will write my report and be done with that."

"Doesn't Governor Gilpin already know the results?"

"He knows the results, but he wants me to write something different."

"What do you mean?" A frown creased her brow.

"He'd like me to say that there's great potential on his land."

"Is there?"

"I doubt it, but he wants to deny it. For him, what he wants justifies any means." Nathaniel carefully swallowed a spoonful of hot mashed potatoes. "I have my suspicions about Colonel Reynolds as well."

"Oh dear, what are you going to say in your report?"

"The truth. We found no valuable minerals near the source of the three rivers. They have no leverage over me because they have already paid me. How they are going to repay the money they borrowed to buy the land is not my concern."

"You didn't tell me anything about this side of Governor Gilpin in your letters." She looked at him quizzically.

"I didn't want to worry you any more than I already had." He gazed at her, grateful to finally be able to share his travails.

In the morning, Nathaniel strode along the familiar neighborhood toward campus to meet with his colleague. The gray sky he had been accustomed to before he left for Colorado now chilled him. It was so different in the West, where the cerulean sky was usually cloudless, except during the frequent, brief afternoon rains.

John had eagerly made time to meet before classes. Nathaniel stepped into the campus inn, welcomed by the steamy aroma of freshly brewed coffee and baked bread. The familiar din of student conversations made him feel as if he had never left. Two of his former students gave him welcoming waves. Nathaniel spotted John and threaded his way to greet him with a friendly embrace.

"Good to see you, Nathaniel, very good. Maybe even relieved to see you. Sometimes we feared you'd never return. The news makes the Indians sound as dangerous as the war on this side of the country."

They sat down at a small round table. The proprietor gave Nathaniel a hearty "Welcome back," with a hint of curiosity. Nathaniel thought for a moment and then ordered hot cocoa, letting the university ambiance sink in as he spoke. "I don't deny there's reason for worry. Out there, people are in constant fear for their lives. There is no relaxing. The gun is cocked most of the time."

"Were you ever attacked?"

"Not personally, but attacks and kidnapping were on the lips of each resident and every traveler. The fear makes people tense and combative."

John took a sip of his steaming coffee. "Always living in fear—that wouldn't be for me."

Nathaniel looked around distractedly to see if he recognized anyone else, enjoying the comfort of the congenial surroundings. "There's always another side to everything," he said as he turned back to John. "Indians have reasons for their anger. Settlers are threatening their very existence without giving them any say in where or how they live, or even if they do live. The white men are invading places Indians consider their own—even sacred places that define who they are. Their vulnerability makes them strike back any way they can."

"Aren't there armed forts to keep the peace?"

"There are, but they are few and far between, and this bloody North-South war is reducing what little military protection there was. Putting the natives in reservations may be best for both sides."

"Some say it's just empty land out there, nothing more than a waste-land," John said.

"That's the surprise. I had heard that, and I didn't know what to expect. But it's really not a desert as some people call it. There's a different kind of beauty there. The West is a different place altogether. It's a land ready to develop. People are going to the West for more reasons than you can imagine. Many are enterprising people trying to capitalize on the land.

"I was sorry to get the letter about your findings. I wish there had been better results."

"It was always a risk. I knew that. I turned down other offers, but this venture seemed to have more promise. There's disappointment all around, not only for Gilpin and me. I will have to be honest with my investors so they will trust me in the future. I'll also hand over the titles for property to Dyer, Harkness, and Caswell, and I will probably be badgered when they don't produce immediate results."

"I imagine you just let past successes sway you. Pikes Peak or bust, I guess," John mused.

"Many who went to Colorado did go bust. But, you know, here's what's interesting. I may have failed, but I'm not quite ready to give up on the territory. There *is* more gold there, at least in some of the mountains. They just don't know how to get the metal out. I want to learn more about that. There has to be a solution. I'm thinking about going back next summer, after classes are over. The best part is that solving it would be good for others, not just me."

John fingered the spoon on his saucer, averting his eyes from Nathaniel's before finally raising his head. "Nathaniel, although I questioned your decision, I was fine with taking over some of your classes, and some others didn't mind either. But those on the executive board, especially President Sears and Professor Harkness, might not have shared my sentiment. I have heard some things along the lines that professors should be focused on academics, not money-grubbing, and that you've let them down by not returning when you said you would. Classes started two weeks ago."

"I wonder what their feelings would be if I had found something and there was a chance for good investments."

"Point well taken, but they are more than disgruntled."

"They weren't disgruntled when we raised funds for the new laboratory. It didn't seem to be money-grubbing when Brown benefited."

"I know, I know. I understand your point." John kept his eyes down on his coffee cup rather than looking at Nathaniel. "I just don't want you to go into a meeting without understanding the mood."

Nathaniel paused to finish his hot chocolate. "That sounds like a warning." He took a deep breath. "I appreciate your raising the alarm."

"You're of an age where you should be settling down, Nathaniel. The world was your oyster."

Nathaniel's face darkened with resignation as he looked up at his mentor. "I was thinking of saying that all oysters don't have pearls, but that would sound glib, and I don't feel that way. I hope you don't think I'm not appreciative of all the extra work you took on so I could be away. Failure aside, it allowed me an opportunity I couldn't imagine not taking."

"I look forward to hearing about those opportunities at another time."

"I have a lot of thinking to do. In my letters, I told Alice about some of the changes that might come, but now I have to be more specific about what might happen at Brown. She's hoping for the best."

"Don't think too long. The sooner you get this matter behind you, the better for everyone." John's tone was foreboding.

"Do you want me to take over my classes this week?"

"Meet with the executive board first. You have to be realistic about your situation." The chair legs rubbed against the floor as he pushed it away from the table. John extended his hand. "Good luck. I hope we continue working together."

The word *hope* sent a jolt up Nathaniel's spine.

The conversation with John affirmed that his job was in danger. The meeting with the executive board was going to decide his fate. When he returned home, he opened the front door hesitantly. He had forewarned Alice about the consequences of his late return for university classes, but he wanted to avoid concerning her before he met with the executive board.

He was hanging up his coat when Crawford called to him. "Papa, Papa." Nathaniel scooped his young son up in his arms. "Play ball with me, Papa, play ball."

"Get the ball. I'd much rather play than think about other things."

Alice stepped into the hallway from the kitchen with Isabel balanced on her hip, her light brown hair neatly clasped above the nape of her neck. She leaned forward and gave him a lingering kiss. "How was John?"

"Full of news of the university, and I made an appointment with the board for the day after tomorrow." Giggles came from Crawford as he hurled the stitched leather ball along the corridor's planked floor. "By the way, is it tonight that we're going for dinner at your parents?"

"Yes. Mama asked us to come at six. They can't wait to put their hands on you to make sure you're not a ghost."

"That's fine, but I have to spend time at my desk before we leave."

"Oh, Nat, sometimes I think you are married to your desk."

He looked at her in surprise at the mild rebuke. "I need to see what you've put on my desk while I've been away," he replied, grinning at her. She had continued her habit of clipping articles that might interest him while he was in Colorado. "I know you're an avid collector."

"I tried to save the things you'd be interested in." She was partly placated.

Normally, he would relish seeing what Alice had saved for him, but now his mind was elsewhere. He was thinking about Brown University. The big metal spring of his desk chair made thrumming sounds as he swiveled. His mind darted from thoughts of the meeting with the executive board in two days to what he should do in Colorado. He wondered how to broach the subject with Alice—something he had not resolved even after hours of thinking about it during his travels.

THIRTEEN

ᚠ

Nathaniel went two blocks out of his way to walk along the bay and pass the ships on the dull, gray water. Frigid humidity enveloped Providence. Abandoning his usual brisk stride, he walked slowly home from his meeting at Brown. The longer route and his pace gave him time to consider what had happened. It took an hour before he sorted out his thoughts about his past and his future.

Reaching home, he quietly turned the brass knob, knowing that Crawford and Isabel would be napping. His shoes thumped softly as he walked down the hallway to the kitchen where he found Alice kneading bread dough. He kissed her cheek where a trace of flour remained from brushing back a wisp of hair with a floury hand. "Tastes good."

"How did the meeting go?" Alice asked as she slowed the rhythm of pushing the elastic lump with her knuckles. The oven, fired in preparation for baking, warmed the room.

"I submitted my resignation."

The dough dropped from her hands. "Oh, Nat, I thought you could make things right again. What did they say?"

"Let's sit down and talk about it," Nathaniel said cautiously. "I need to hang up my coat."

Alice wiped the flour away from her anxious hands. "I was afraid you were being unrealistic." She began following him into the hallway but then stopped. "Wait just a moment. I have to put in the bread for dinner while the oven is hot. I'll be right there."

He looked up as she joined him in his study, taking her place on the overstuffed chair across from his desk. "President Sears led the meeting. They told me, in no uncertain terms, how disappointed they were that I hadn't lived up to my agreement to return in time for classes." He avoided looking directly at her, his face crimped with gloom. "Oh, he was complimentary enough about my work. I went back and forth with him and the others about my consulting. Their desire is to have someone devoted to teaching and to Brown University rather than one interested in outside consulting or exploring the West."

Alice looked at him, the edges of her eyes growing moist. "What now?"

"They said that Brown University is an academic institution with a mission of education, not business." Nathaniel unbuttoned the two middle buttons of his jacket, trying to find something to do with his hands. "I wanted to remind them that I had been consulting with businesses for years and that those contacts had allowed us to raise funds to build the chemistry laboratory. Sometimes I suspect that my lucrative contracts reinforced what they already thought was a problem.

"You know, Alice, I really didn't have the heart to argue. I don't have much ground to stand on, and I just can't let go of the notion that there is some way to get gold out of the rock in Colorado. If there is a solution, it could bring rewards. I just have to—"

"But you thought going to the Sangre de Cristos might bring rewards." She had picked up her mending, which she had brought with her out of habit.

"We both knew it was a risk. Most of the time my consulting has been lucrative, but occasionally not."

"That was different. It wasn't a real risk as long as you had your position at Brown. Now you don't have that."

He watched her squint as she pushed thread through a needle's eye. "This has even greater potential than being a university professor—if I can figure it out. You should see the country there. Everything is new. There is an opportunity to influence the future in so many ways. I think I could do some good there."

"How long would it take to figure it out?" She started sewing a button onto a pair of Crawford's shorts.

"That's anyone's guess, but I've had a little luck. Just before I left Denver, I met a Welshman who spoke of a smelting process there. Other than the location of the plant, he didn't know much more than that. Maybe this Welsh process could be useful in Colorado for gold and silver. I can't tell until I find out more about it."

"It sounds like as much of a risk as the land grant," she replied. It might have sounded severe, but her voice was softer than the words.

"Yes, it will be more uncertainty." He had to be honest with her. Only truth would make his future credible. "Rewards seldom come without risk. Nothing came of Gilpin's venture, but this is different." He rolled his chair a little closer to her, wanting to take her hand, but she stayed preoccupied with her needle and thread.

"You'll be separated from me again . . . and our two babies," she murmured, her voice quavering.

"I need more information from everyone, but particularly what the Welsh process entails. I might have to return to Colorado Territory in a few months. Would you consider going with me? I'd like you to see the place."

"Join you?" Her shoulders turned rigid. "What about the children?"

"Believe me, Central City and Black Hawk are as safe as Providence. It's just getting there."

"We can't expose Crawford and Isabel to that peril. You told me the Indians sometimes kill the adult white travelers and kidnap the children. How can we put our children in danger of being murdered or growing up as Indians? And I'd be leaving my family." Tears made tracks through her flour-smudged cheek.

"Let me do more research on the new smelting process before we make any final decisions. I'm going to go to Boston to raise money and possibly hire men to manage the two mines I invested in."

"Nat, I'm afraid I may not see you again if you go to Colorado. What if something happens to you?"

Nathaniel got up to bend down and put his arm around her shoulder, pulling her toward him until her head rested on his chest. "Let me learn more about the situation before we make plans or worry."

Nathaniel pulled out the desk drawers, one by one. It had been over four months since he had been in his university office. He felt strangely dislocated. As he took items from the drawers to put in the wooden crates he had carried up the stairs, he felt his career draining from him like sand in an hourglass. The drawers of his desk now empty, he turned behind him to pull textbooks from the shelves and examined each cover like the face of an old friend. They all held memories of lectures to students or discussions with other faculty members.

The three crates now held more of his academic paraphernalia than remained. His desktop was empty except for an ashtray and a large steel bolt he used as a paperweight. He grasped the bolt in his fingers and then rolled the cool metal along the palm of his hand. The bolt was one he had taken from the old farm workbench after his father's death. Every time he placed it on papers to keep them from blowing, it reminded him of his family. He carefully put it in the corner of one of the boxes to pass along to Crawford, hoping it would mean something to his son someday. Three years had passed since his mother moved to Ohio to be with his brother James. He envied Alice's close family connections.

He rubbed his eyes and observed that the office no longer felt like a place where he belonged. In the future, someone else would meet with inquisitive students who'd come to talk over projects and review marks. For him, there would only be memories of conversations with enthusiastic undergraduates. Nathaniel walked to the window and looked at the college hill with its student-worn paths, the rectangle of buildings, and the bay in the distance, realizing how much he would miss the campus environment.

A knock on the oak door made him turn. John stuck his head in, his pipe protruding from his square jaw, his broad shoulders filling his tweed jacket.

"John, come in. Here, let me move the box off the chair. Sit down. We can at least share one last conversation."

"Class just ended and I saw your door ajar. For your information, this may be the last conversation in this room, but it won't be the last you see of the Peirces. We will stay in touch."

"I hope so," Nathaniel replied, his face lifeless. "You know, I've lived all my adult life here, either as a student or as an instructor. Teaching is the only job I've ever had other than outside contracts. Now that I'm leaving, I feel as if I'm losing my identity. Brown has been part of that identity for a decade. I'm not even sure how I should introduce myself to people now. Not having a job is somewhat of a disgrace."

"You're going to be missed by everyone around here, both students and faculty members, but I have no doubt that you'll find your next step." John's voice was reassuringly chipper. "I understand your uneasiness. This endless war makes everything unsettled. What are you thinking of doing next?"

"The first thing I have to do is make an official report about the Sangre de Cristo findings—or non-findings—to Governor Gilpin's agent, Colonel Reynolds." Nathaniel grimaced. "Did I tell you one of the army officers from Fort Garland questioned where Reynolds got the money to purchase the land grant? He had heard rumors the esteemed Colonel used federal money rather than his own. It seems he may be no better than Gilpin when it comes to scruples."

John shook his head and took a draw from his pipe. "What will Gilpin do with the land?"

"I suspect they will try to sell it. There will always be people gullible enough to take a chance, hoping it will be like the strikes in other mining camps." Nathaniel stood up and started distractedly taking the last books off the shelf and arranging them, spine up, in the cardboard box.

"What about your properties in Colorado?"

"They aren't worth much at the moment, but I'll hold onto them as long as I can manage financially. Now that I don't have a job, money weighs on me. After I finish my report, I'm going to inquire about different extraction methods. I think I told you that I met a Welshman just before I left Denver. He's heard of a process in Wales."

"Wales? You don't let dust gather, do you?"

"At this point, I have to follow every lead. At least I have one."

John stood up and walked over to tamp out his spent tobacco into the fireplace grate. "It looks like you're just about finished with your packing, and I have another class." He put his pipe in his pocket and came around the desk to clasp Nathaniel's hand. "It will be empty here without you. Let me know what you learn. I am interested." He paused before he went through the door. "Give my regards to Alice and the children."

Evening had fallen when Nathaniel returned home to Providence from Boston. Four months had passed since his return from his trip to Colorado. "I'm home." His voice cascaded down the hall.

Alice's voice echoed in return. "I'm in the kitchen."

The warmth enveloped him as he entered the room and leaned down to wrap his arms around Alice, who was seated in front of two highchairs with dishes of preserved vegetables in front of her.

"There are a couple of letters on your desk. I'm almost finished feeding the children, then I'll read them a story and get them in bed. It won't take too long—we can talk over dinner."

"Good, I'll go relax with the paper. It's been a long day."

In half an hour, Alice was back downstairs. They walked together into the dining room where Alice had lit the slender logs in the small tile fireplace to take the chill off the room. She fetched the platter from the oven while he sat down. "How did you do in Boston? Did you find the men you were looking for?"

He ladled the deep brown gravy on his pot roast and potatoes, his mouth watering in anticipation, and picked up his knife and fork. "The first meetings were successful. I found two good men to manage the mining companies. You'll like them both. David Barlow has children the same age as Isabel and Crawford. Edward Gould is a bachelor and has a lot of experience. He'll scrutinize every decimal of the finances." He swallowed a savory piece of meat and sighed. "This is just what I needed."

"What about raising money?" Alice stood up to refill Nathaniel's glass from a pitcher of water. "How did that go?"

"Not as well." Nathaniel didn't look up to meet her questioning face. "There aren't many men willing to invest in an unformulated extraction process. The long war is making everyone jittery. I came away with twenty-five thousand, but I was hoping for more. It came from an investor I had consulted for in the past. He had faith in me where others were skeptical and too short of cash."

"But what does it all mean for us?" Alice asked with a frown as she stopped eating.

"I'm not sure yet." He paused with a rueful glance at her. "I told you it may be prudent for me to return to Colorado and try mining my properties with existing mining practices. Maybe there's something the miners have overlooked. I'd be the only professional chemist out there. That should count for something."

"I appreciate that you asked me to go with you, but I can't believe that you're seriously thinking of risking your life, and even our lives, to go back there next summer. Isn't that why you're hiring men . . . Barlow . . . Gould . . . to do that work? Have you been deceiving me?" Her eyes looked angry.

"No, Alice, I'm not practicing deception." He shot back an icy stare. "I just refine my thinking as I talk to people and get new information."

Her tone slightly edgy, Alice retorted, "I thought you were going to look for another position in New England. Aren't we going back to academics?"

Nathaniel could tell that she was struggling to remain calm and rational. "Eventually, but no one will be interviewing for teaching positions until spring, and the war is upsetting hiring for jobs of any kind. I can rely on savings from my consulting for a while."

"Our savings won't last forever."

"So far, I haven't neglected our finances," he said brusquely.

"I know things are slow, but shouldn't you at least begin talking to people to show them you're interested?" she asked.

"The sooner I go to Colorado, the faster I can get the mining problems resolved and decide on my future. If I hurry, I should be able to get things ready to go next month, or March at the latest. One of the new men can go with me then, and the other can leave by summer."

"Next month? It's winter. Surely, you won't go in the winter?" Alice rested her elbows on the table and let her head drop into her palms.

"Things are changing." His voice was pleading. "The overland railroad is under construction. It won't be long before people can get all the way to California by train. It's as if the whole country is tipping west."

She leaned forward. "It sounds as if you have already decided to go and you're just informing me."

"I know how worried you get, but this is business. It's unavoidable."

Alice slumped back into her chair while Nathaniel busied himself cutting his meat. He stole a look at her, noting that she seemed to be trying to compose herself. Then she sat straight up and looked at him squarely.

"If you're going away again, I wonder if I could get some help."

"Help? What kind of help?"

"With housework."

"I thought you always liked to take care of things yourself."

"My life is changing too. The children are growing, and Isabel will be walking soon. I could use someone to do laundry and cleaning."

"I'm trying to economize. We're dipping into our reserves as it is." He paused, knowing he was on shaky ground. "I guess household help isn't that expensive, is it?"

Alice looked away from him and said nothing for a moment. Then she looked at him evenly. "Nathaniel, do you remember when I told you about my work at the Young Women's Christian Association?"

He nodded. "Vaguely."

"I wrote to you about what Kate and I are doing. There's an Irish girl I've met with there. I'm trying to teach her the ways of America. She's young and needs a friend. I can't be her friend exactly, but I can be her adviser—counsel her on the way things work here."

"What does that have to do with your getting household help?"

"She hasn't found a job yet. There seem to be more Irish girls coming than there are positions. She might be willing to do light housework."

"Don't you want someone with references? You are usually so thorough."

"She . . . she is currently helping her cousin . . . doing a bit of cleaning for him, and I've met with her several times, so I do know something about her. She wouldn't have gone to the YWCA had she not wanted to better herself."

Nathaniel raised his eyebrows, which seemed to have the effect of making Alice increase the tempo of her next words.

"She could stay in the attic room. I've always said that I wanted to fix it up. And it has a back stairs to the kitchen."

"I have to say, you've taken me by surprise. I'd like to think about it for a while."

"Would you be willing to let me ask her what she thinks of the idea, without making a commitment? I have one more appointment with her. I'm afraid that if she doesn't find something, she'll do something desperate."

"Desperate? What do you mean desperate? I don't want you dealing with desperate people."

"I don't know. I'm just afraid that if she doesn't find something soon, she'll take a wrong step. She seems so vulnerable."

"I don't begrudge you household help while I'm gone, but let's be sensible."

"Sensible! You're asking me to be sensible? What about you?"

"I can tell you that we're not going to take on a charity case, and I'm leery of the new Irish, but you can meet with her. We can discuss it after that. I'm not making a commitment."

"If she's interested, we could hire her before you leave." The space between her eyes scrunched into furrows. "What would happen to us if you didn't come back? Did you ever think of that?"

"I wish you didn't worry so much. I returned safely once, and I can do it again." He extended his hand to reach for hers. After a moment, she acquiesced and put her palm against his, entwining their fingers.

Alice spent the following week coming to grips with Nathaniel's plan to leave again. Maggie was another worry. She was not sure she would come to the meeting they had set. On the appointed day, Alice left Crawford and Isabel at her mother's house and walked to the Young Women's Christian Association ahead of time. Maggie was not there yet. The young immigrant was so close to resigning herself to a life in a bar, Alice shuddered to think what might come next. A brothel? Maggie rushed through the door exactly at two o'clock, and Alice stepped forward to touch her shoulder in relief.

"Mrs. Hill, I don't want you to be mad at me, but it's no use."

"Why would I be mad at you, Maggie? Come. Let's go back to an office so we can talk in private."

They entered an empty office and sat opposite each other.

"Mrs. Hill, Vinny's going to throw me out if'n I don't spend more time cleaning his pub," Maggie blurted out in fear. "It's that or be on the streets."

"Maggie, I have an idea. What if you kept house for me and my family? We have a small attic room with a bed where you could stay. My husband is going on a trip, and we've talked about getting some help—"

"Be your servant girl, Mrs. Hill?" The young woman's lower lip quivered. "You would do that for me?"

"Yes, Maggie. You would be helping me too. It's much better than a bar. Maybe you could take classes some nights."

"You'd hire an Irish girl, Mrs. Hill?" she asked with disbelieving eyes.

"I have to talk to Mr. Hill again, but we both want to know if you'd be interested."

"Oh, Mrs. Hill, I'd work hard, and I like to be around children, just not when there's so much screaming like at Vinny's." Maggie pulled a swatch of wrinkled linen from her sleeve and dabbed one eye and then the other in an unsuccessful effort to stanch the flow. She was trembling.

"It's not completely settled. Can you hold on another week?"

Maggie nodded, unable to choke out a response.

"I'll send word here on how you can get to our house and when you should come, but now I better start making preparations."

Alice pushed back her chair, and Maggie jumped up so fast that she almost knocked over her own chair.

"Mrs. Hill, I'm not going to get my hopes up. They'll just get dashed again. But I'm grateful to you. I just need a chance."

"Don't worry, Maggie. I will send for you as soon as I can." She turned to walk with rapid steps down the hall and out the door, thinking about all she had to do.

That night, Alice waited to talk to Nathaniel until the children were in bed and she and Nathaniel were finishing their dinner. As she placed her knife and fork on her empty plate, she said, "I saw Maggie this afternoon, and she's willing to work for us."

"Who is Maggie?" Nathaniel asked, looking up with a frown.

"You remember." Alice twisted her napkin through her fingers. "We talked about getting some household help."

"I didn't realize you meant so soon."

"You said you're going to leave in a few weeks. She can help with housework and take care of the children occasionally."

"Hmm, I've been too busy with work to think about it. Can't it wait? I don't plan to be in Colorado long."

"I think she is suitable," Alice said in a hopeful voice. "She would work hard."

"How much is she going to charge?"

"We haven't settled on that, but I can get her for little more than room and board. The attic is small, but it's better than . . . better than where she is now," Alice finished hastily.

"You better put away anything valuable. You know the new Irish."

Alice swallowed the words she wanted to say. "I'll be careful. I think she could come the day after tomorrow."

He gave her a conciliatory look. "I know this is important to you, so I agree." He put his napkin beside his empty plate and left the table for his study.

Nathaniel received two bits of news that made his spirits rise in February 1865. A letter came from London informing him that there was a smelting process in Swansea, Wales, that might be the one about which he had inquired. A company name and address was included, but no other details. He assumed it was the company his acquaintance, Aldwyn Brynmor, spoke about. Nathaniel wasted no time in writing to Vivian and Sons, hoping that they would respond despite his lack of references.

The second piece of spirit-lifting news was that his new employee, David Barlow, would be available to meet him in New York City. He'd written back, setting a specific date to go to Colorado the following month. David was approximately his own age and well educated, and Nathaniel had found him to be an interesting conversationalist during their interview. He would make a good traveling companion for the month-long trip.

FOURTEEN

ዋ

A heavy March snowstorm had made the trip difficult, and Nathaniel could tell that the burned-out stage stop had added to David Barlow's apprehension about traveling across the Plains. The two men sent telegrams to their wives when they stopped in Denver. Finally, tired and on edge, they arrived safely in Central City.

"We made it," Nathaniel said when the stage stopped across from Watson's Dry Goods.

Joe Watson was there to greet them, and Nathaniel shook his hand with a friendly clasp. As David joined them, Nathaniel made the introduction. "Joe, this is David Barlow, the new manager of one of my properties. He's here to get the mine producing again."

"Happy to meet you, Mr. Watson," David said, pumping the man's hand.

"Call me Joe."

Nathaniel watched David's face noticeably relax, as if he was finally released from the strain of the past six days.

"My God, what a snowstorm. And a burned-out stage stop," David said, suddenly becoming loquacious. "I really thought I was going to die, one way or another. Mr. Hill says you're an expert. I'd like to talk to you and meet others so I can get going with the business—"

Nathaniel cut him off, laughing. "Slow down, David. We have time for that later." He motioned to the driver to bring the luggage into Joe's store. "Let's go up to the café for some dinner and begin our conversation there."

"Where's the privy?" David asked, leaving his valise on the board walkway in his urgency.

"It's at the back. The fastest way is through there." Joe pointed to the narrow passageway between buildings.

When the luggage was hauled upstairs to the sleeping quarters above, the three left the store to go up the steep hill to the Thunder Café. Nathaniel and Joe were already in conversation about what had transpired in the past six months. At the café, most of the tables were filled, but the prominent round table in the back was empty. It did not escape Nathaniel's attention that the eyes of other diners followed them as they made their way to the table. The locals were, no doubt, curious about the man accompanying him.

A young waitress with green eyes and raven hair pulled tightly back in a bun stepped quickly toward them. "Afternoon, Joe. What can I get you folks to eat?"

Joe's smile widened and his face glowed as he greeted her. "Anything new on the menu, Emily?"

"Just the usual today: beef stew, roast pork, and chicken. They're all pretty fresh."

"Nathaniel and David, this is Emily O'Neil," Joe said. "She came from Missouri just after you left last fall, Nathaniel. She followed her sister and brother-in-law to Denver, but then ended up here."

To Nathaniel, Joe appeared to be smitten by the young woman. He could not seem to take his eyes off her.

"I thought they might be the visitors you were expecting," she said politely. "Did anything sound good enough to order, sir? And what to drink?"

They responded and Emily repeated the orders, almost under her breath, before retreating to the kitchen behind the bar. She was back in a few minutes with Nathaniel's water and with hot coffee for the other two. "I put cream in your coffee, Joe, instead of milk. It's a special treat." With a blush creeping up her cheeks, she turned to go back.

Nathaniel's eyebrows rose as he glanced sideways at Joe, who was attentively watching Emily's slim-waisted black skirt swish as she disappeared behind the bar. "Seems sweet on you."

"I don't know if sweet is the word for it, but I'm not complaining." Joe straightened his chair toward the table from where he had moved it an angle to talk to Emily. "How many women do you see around here?"

"No offense intended. Seems like you have your share: Claire Foster from Providence and now Emily. You better not be complaining."

"This really has nothing to do with Claire. Women are scarce here. I'm trying to find a a way for Emily to work in my store. She's too good to be working in a café that's little more than a bar. The problem is that I already have one clerk, and I can't quite afford more overhead yet."

"Sounds like Claire Foster from Providence may be a thing of the past?"

"Maybe, maybe not. But Claire is there and Emily is here." Joe shrugged his shoulders.

David changed the subject. "Now that we've made it here safely, I want to see what we can do to get the mines running—"

"I *need* to get the mines I bought producing again," Nathaniel interjected.

"Good luck. I hope your optimism is warranted." Joe's look turned serious. "I was sorry to hear you left Brown. I guess mining is now more than a side interest."

Nathaniel nodded. "It's definitely more than a side interest. When I was here before, I told you that the problem of metal extraction intrigued me. Now it's more than a curiosity to me. I need to find a solution. David and I—and Edward Gould, who you will meet soon—will be grateful for any help you can give us. Our livelihoods depend on finding an answer."

"So far, it's the same problems without anything new to report," Joe replied. "It's like one of our famous box canyons—no way out."

For two days, Nathaniel and David tramped up and down the hilly inclines of both Central City and Black Hawk looking for inexpensive office space for Nathaniel's two newly formed mining enterprises, The Hill Gold Mining Company and the Sterling Gold Mining Company. Although most miners were forsaking the profession, even the shoddiest property was overpriced. The owners had not made much profit from mining of late and expected to wring it out of their real estate.

Weary from searching, they stopped at the Thunder Café for lunch and to go over finances. David opened the ledger book he had brought along. There had been $2,500 from Gilpin, $1,800 of which had been spent on Nathaniel's house in Central City. Nathaniel explained that he had rented the house to a local man, but now that the lease was up, he was living there himself with nothing more than a cot, a table, and two chairs. David was staying in the bachelor quarters above Joe's dry goods store where Edward Gould would join him when he arrived.

"You still have the leftover of Mr. Merrill's twenty-five thousand dollars from your mine purchases," David pointed out as he looked at the ledger.

"Merrill gave me my first consulting job eight years ago and has given me recommendations since then. Fortunately for us, he is interested in Colorado."

"It is fortunate," David agreed. "Generous investors are scarce in wartime."

"Generous, yes, but he has reminded me more than once that he makes investments, not gifts. You can be sure he wants a return."

David gave an understanding nod. "From all the property we've seen, I think the south end of James Lyon's property is our best bet. The construction isn't perfect, but with four hundred square feet, three of us should be able to work there."

"It's also a good location, just off Main Street and only a mile from Central City," Nathaniel replied. "Let's draw up the papers and meet with Mr. Lyon."

Two days later, they closed the door to Lyon's office. "Well, we have a roof over our heads—that's progress." Nathaniel perfunctorily blew on the newly signed lease to make sure the ink was dry, folded it in thirds, and put it in his vest pocket. "I think I'll go have a sign fabricated to hang over the door. We might as well let everyone know we're operating as a viable company and are here to stay."

"While you're doing that, would you like me to scout around for furniture? I can ask Joe Watson for ideas about anything secondhand."

"Don't get too much," Nathaniel said with a chuckle. "When Edward comes, the three of us will be knocking elbows even without furniture."

Cast-off furniture was apparently easier to find at a good price than office space. People who had decided to leave were trying to rustle a little cash by selling their surplus goods. It only took David two days to accumulate the little they needed.

David was already moving furniture when Nathaniel came across the hill from his house to their new office in the crystalline early morning three days later. There was a mule cart full of furnishings tied up in front, and the driver was helping David jimmy a desk through the door at the far end of Lyon's building.

"Morning, Mr. Hill," David said as he wiped his brow with a rag, leaving a streak of dirt across his forehead. "I got a long table I think will work for Edward and me. We can work at opposite ends of it. The desk I bought has seen better days, but you'll have workspace of your own. I even found the kind of swivel chair you said you like—well broken in." He shrugged his shoulders and gave a wry smile. "Following instructions."

Nathaniel watched as David went back to the door to continue helping the cart driver shove the table through the narrow entry. When all the furniture was unloaded, David paid the deliveryman. Inside, they surveyed the furnishings. David leaned down to inspect the desk, pulling out the wide horizontal top drawer, which fell out of his hand instead of sliding. Grabbing it to keep it from hitting the ground, he laughed.

Nathaniel laughed with him. "You did follow orders—no wasted money on fancy furnishings."

David rolled the swivel chair up to Nathaniel's desk, then pulled the straight slatted chairs to the ends of the long table. "I found some clean boxes we can use for filing our papers."

"Great!" Nathaniel slapped David on the back. "Let's get to work. We have to make a plan for processing ore we take out of our two mines."

The only thing lacking was the sign outside, but it arrived and was hung before the day was up. "I'm sure the grapevine will have already spread the news that we are in the mining business, but it's good to make it official," Nathaniel said as he looked up at it with David.

In bold block letters, two business names were printed on the sign: Hill Gold Mining Company, which was at the top, and Sterling Gold Mining Company below that. In the wide space above the names was the figure of a ship.

David turned to look at Nathaniel questioningly. "A ship in the mountains?"

"I decided on it for a trademark," Nathaniel replied, lifting his hand to point at the sign as he explained. "It's Jason's Argo—from the old story about Jason and his Argonauts. You can see that it has a long, slender hull and shallow draft for speed and flexibility. It has full sails to use when the winds are favorable, but it also has rows of oars. When winds are still, the ship depends primarily on human exertion for propulsion."

David seemed to be listening attentively but his face reflected doubt.

Nathaniel's cheeks were flushed with enthusiasm as he continued. "Human strength gives it—us—freedom to move independently of winds and currents with great precision. This was a ship designed to sail across an unknown ocean to uncharted lands. Like Jason, we will hope for favorable winds, but we will count on human ingenuity."

David nodded. "I guess it doesn't matter that no one but us will understand the symbolism of the ship. But now that I understand it, I will keep my eye on those uncharted lands and hope, as you suggest, for favorable winds."

→ ←

They had an office, but little to do. Nathaniel had yet to receive a reply from Vivian and Sons with information about the Welsh smelting process. Without new information, they were stymied. By late spring they had used up all the ores in the upper crust of both their mines with some positive results, but below that crust they were coming empty. All the valuable metals were bound to the ore by the problematic sulfurets.

"We can't just sit around forever waiting for the Welshmen to respond," Nathaniel said with a sigh one day.

David looked up from a scientific equipment catalog Nathaniel suspected he had read a dozen times to fill the hours after the ore played out. "We're seven thousand miles away, so they may be having difficulty seeing any prospect for business. I guess there's little motivation on their part."

"We've got to do something to build credibility for our new enterprise, not only to earn our reputation here, but to preserve it with eastern investors," Nathaniel muttered. "I'm inclined to go ahead with stamp milling despite all the failures others here have had with it. We have just enough room to put a mill on the Sterling Mine property."

David appeared to hesitate before responding. "The sulfides in the ore seem resistant to all the methods that have been tried. That much I have learned." The sun shone through the office directly into his eyes, making him squint.

"That is the dilemma," Nathaniel admitted. "No one has discovered how to get the impurities out yet, but there must be a way. The Welsh have a smelting process that works to separate gold and silver from ore— at least from *their* ore."

David nodded. "From what I've heard, the ore here is different. Their method might not work out here."

"Their process is used mostly to extract copper, and there's not much copper here."

The two men had talked at length about stamp milling in lieu of the Welsh process. It had been tried by many others, but it had failed to release the metal from the ore no matter how fine the particle.

David had been exploring other possibilities. "If you are interested, I've been researching every possible process while we've been waiting to hear from Wales, and I've made a list of equipment for each one. We can get some of what we need for stamp milling locally, and I found an advertisement for other used equipment in St. Louis. Here, let me show you the list and costs." He pushed a tidy pile of paper with figures on them across the table.

Nathaniel scrutinized the numbers before replying. "I say, David, this is good work. I have been doing some research of my own, but some of your prices look even better. Let me compare the two. I can send a letter to Edward to have him order the equipment we decide on and pick it up on his way here."

"It will use some of your savings that you've tried so hard to spare, Mr. Hill."

"I realize that, but we have to get going." He put David's list on his desk and extracted his own. "Let me scout around and see what more I can find out about stamp milling equipment before we order. The war isn't going to make it easy to get equipment. Every time I think it's going to end, my hope is thrown back into my face."

The war had finally ended, but the country was in turmoil over the president's death when Nathaniel's second manager, Edward Gould, arrived in Black Hawk. There was additional disturbance in Colorado. The territory still reeled from the brutal murder by the militia of Cheyenne and Arapaho families at Sand Creek in southeastern Colorado. The massacre had taken place five month earlier, and the results were cataclysmic. Many of the dead had been innocent women and children, and the Indians smoldered with anger and hostility. They turned the Plains into a deadly ground of resentment and fury, and it was under these conditions that Edward Gould had traveled.

It took Nathaniel a moment to realize who it had to be when the pale, thin, bespectacled man stepped into the office. He had been dropped off by a Conestoga, which then continued on to the mines, where the driver would find men to help him unload their equipment. Nathaniel was startled by the looks of the man. His face and neck were covered in hives.

"Mr. Hill, I made it," he said as he stepped into the room.

"Edward, I'm glad you've arrived." He rose from his chair and extended his hand to his new employee for a warm handshake. "We were wondering when you'd get here. I'm sorry, David isn't here just now."

"I wondered if I really would get here," Edward said in a halting voice. "I had read reports about the crossing, but I had no idea the trip would be so . . . exposed."

"Here, let me take your coat and hat. Have a seat."

Edward explained that having spent all of his life up to that point in Boston and New York, he'd had only a fanciful idea of the West. The westward trip had begun for him in May when he'd taken a train to St. Louis. From that point on, he had crossed the country in a Conestoga wagon full of stamp mill equipment, with only a driver for protection. They had joined other wagon trains for company, but that did little to quell his fear.

"These broke out when we passed a burned-out stage stop," he said, running his left hand along the side of his face. "It was a chilling sight, only to be made worse when we went on to pass many a solitary stone grave marker along the way."

"I'm relieved you're safe. Did you send the equipment on to the mines as directed?"

"It's on its way, and I'm glad that I'm really still in once piece, Mr. Hill."

Edward paused as if collecting himself, then let out a deep sigh and continued. "I have to admit that I think I have made the worst decision of my life to change my career so drastically. Boston felt crowded and dirty, and I was keen to leave, but Colorado is too much the other extreme. It's nothing but wilderness."

Nathaniel laughed. "Give it a little time. I almost died of fright during my trip—and even my first days here—but I've settled in. Granted, I have no intention of letting my family cross for a while, but I've gotten used to the surroundings."

"Fear infused me every day and every hour of the trip. It was the worst month of my life."

Gould explained that his fear was heightened by his poor eyesight. Without his glasses, he was helpless, and he had been in such fear of losing them that he had spent money for two extra pairs to bring with him. Nathaniel could not blame him for his feelings. It took courage to leave the relative safety of the East for the West. As for the eyeglasses, Nathaniel assessed the extras as a wise decision. Lost or broken spectacles would have been an inconvenience for the man in Boston, but in Central City, they would be something of a disaster.

"I'd like to get cleaned up," Gould said. "There's dirt in every pore."

"You will bunk the same place David does, on the second floor of Joe Watson's dry goods store in Central City. It's too financially risky for either of you to buy housing of your own yet. I own a house here in Black Hawk. We'd normally walk from here to Joe Watson's store because it's just over a mile from Black Hawk to Central City, but with your baggage, let's rent a buckboard instead. I'll explain the area as we walk to the livery station and come back for your baggage."

Nathaniel put on his hat and coat and stepped out to the street, Edward in tow. Remembering how David had struggled on his first walk because of the altitude, he kept his pace slow. "This is all Gilpin County, named after the former governor who hired me in the first place."

"Looks like a lot of empty storefronts," Edward commented, breathing hard.

"There are. After gold was found, hordes of people came. From what I've been told, it was a rough place with frequent brawls and gunfights. At one time, there were thousands of people. Now there are only around six hundred in each town, and things are lot more peaceful."

They rented a buckboard at the stable and started for Central City. Nathaniel pointed to the butcher shop, hardware store, and bars as they drove to Watson's mercantile. Once at Watson's, Joe helped Edward unload his things and take them up to the second-floor bedrooms.

The next morning, Edward looked cleaner but still grim-faced. As he entered the office, he remarked that if it weren't for the thought of having to return over the relentless Plains, he'd leave as soon as possible and return to his old job.

Nathaniel pulled out a chair in welcome. "Have a seat, Edward. Let me show you some things about our two companies." He unrolled long sheets of paper and showed Edward the drawings for the new stamp mill they had already begun building. "I want both you and David to be involved in every aspect of the business. Better decisions are made if all three of us contribute to them."

"I don't know anything about mechanics," Edward admitted as he extracted a handkerchief from his vest pocket and cleaned each lens of his wire-rimmed glasses before settling them on the bridge of his nose.

"Maybe not, but you should be aware of what's happening." Nathaniel smoothed the set of drawings and tapped the paper with the round end of his pen. "It's pretty basic. Cams on a rotating axle lift the oversized steel hammers. Those are the stamps you brought. They will fall on a mixture of water and ore and smash it into gravel. The gravel is fed into a box beneath the stamps and then sorted for precious metals."

"What's the power source?" Edward asked with a hint of interest in his voice.

"Ours will be a small steam engine."

Edward leaned back in his chair. "Aren't there other stamp mills here that we could use instead of building a new one?"

"There are others in the area, but this gives us more control." Nathaniel did not change his expression, but he was pleased that Edward used the word *we* instead of *you*. "And we may earn revenue from stamping other miners' ore as well as our own."

Edward pulled the drawing toward him and peered at it closely. "When you interviewed me, you were looking for another process because stamp milling wasn't working in Colorado."

Nathaniel moved his chair sideways to sit closer to his newest manager. "At the moment, I haven't found anything new, so we're going to try this again and see what happens."

"Have you and David gone over the figures?" Edward asked. "How much is the mill going to cost, and how much do we have?"

He had said *we* again. Nathaniel smiled. "Here, take a look at the pro forma analysis David put together. We've tried to project the potential of our companies by reviewing any cost savings we can make—there aren't many—and assessing what changes can be made with a stamp mill. Technically, David oversees the Hill Mining Company and you the Sterling Gold Mining Company. But the stamp mill is for both." Nathaniel reached into his box of business papers. "You'll meet David this afternoon and get his take on things." Looking up at his unsure employee, he handed Edward a stack of papers lined with figures.

FIFTEEN

❦

By summer, Nathaniel, David and Edward could hear the rhythmic boom, boom, boom of the stamp mill from their office. The 750-pound cylindrical hammers crushed a ton of ore at a time. Water sizzled over the particles, blowing them onto a screen to separate the heavier, valuable minerals from the chaff, which began mounding around the site into amber-colored hills of dump. Because gold was soluble in mercury amalgam, the hired laborers used mercury on the crushed material to attract gold from the residue. After the mercury was used, it had to be burned off through a retort, filling the air with hazy vapor.

After so much waiting, activity at his mines made Nathaniel's optimism soar. He sat with his two managers around the long office table one Friday for their weekly meeting. "See, men, I knew there was a way to get the gold out."

"We're still pretty much at the upper crust. We'll soon have to go below that," David warned. "That's where the problems start."

"At least we have something compared to Gilpin's Sangre de Cristo grant. At this rate, the company might pay a twenty-five or even a thirty-five percent dividend the first year."

"We may have a little revenue coming in," Edward said, "but the money we spent on the stamp mill hasn't been recouped yet. Our income statement is still in red ink."

"But a profit isn't too far away," Nathaniel retorted. "Even the mines I located for my colleagues in the East are producing something through our stamp mills. What a relief." Nathaniel was puffed up like a bird in winter about his good judgment and hard work.

He, David, and Edward worked long hours. They began each day when the sun came up and quit only when there was no more light by which to see. The three men, who had all spent their careers behind desks, sometimes joined the laborers in shoveling ore and adjusting heavy machinery to save money. They were sunburned and gaining muscles. After dinner each evening, David and Edward climbed the stairs to Watson's second floor and collapsed into bed. Nathaniel did the same on his narrow canvas cot, too stiff and sore to notice his surroundings.

At their end-of-the-month Friday meeting, David and Edward sat at each end of the long table and Nathaniel at his desk. He asked his two managers for a report on the total output for the month of June 1865.

David spoke first. "Mr. Hill, we're on site every day, and I don't see any change in effort or tonnage processed, but the output of metal is declining." He pointed to a stack of papers next to him. "It's all here."

"The same can be said of the Sterling Gold Mine, sir," Edward added, straightening up and stretching his shoulders. "Our beginning results must have been still using the upper crust without sulfides—either that or we've had an out of the ordinary occurrence."

Nathaniel shook his head and rose from the table in frustration. He walked the length of the room as he thought. "I guess we've proved what I hoped we wouldn't. Stamp milling alone doesn't work on Colorado ores." As he jammed his hands into his pockets, his face fell in dejection. "We had to give it a try since we had nothing else."

"Have you had any response from your correspondence to Wales, sir?" David asked.

"Nothing yet." He walked the short distance to the other side of the room and back again.

"I suspect my lack of references is a barrier. The Welsh company has no real motivation to respond."

"And you've received nothing else from your other letters?" Edward asked respectfully.

"I've received some, but nothing useful." Nathaniel settled into his desk chair again. "I think it's time I have a conversation with our landlord, James Lyon." He paused as he contemplated the merit of such a meeting, slowly unbuttoning his jacket as he considered.

David broke the silence. "There are a lot of rumors about his business methods."

"I've heard plenty of those too. He's been working on a heating process to roast ores to get metals out of them for the past three years, but I don't think he's done anything to test it." Nathaniel debated what to do next. "It's probably unworkable, but our own problems are going to force me to listen. There's something about him that makes me uneasy. He has slap-dash ideas but not much follow-through, and there's something secretive about him." Nathaniel sighed with reluctance. "I'm going to be cautious, but I better see if he'll meet with me."

He left Lyon a note requesting a meeting and was surprised by how quickly he got a response. At the appointed time the next day, Nathaniel went to the opposite side of the building, tapped on the door, and was invited in.

They exchanged greetings as Nathaniel stepped into the space that had a mechanical contraption on every flat area—just as it had when he and David had come to sign the lease. James had a full gray beard and frizzled hair curling just above his ears. His smooth crown was covered with brown splotches from exposure to the sun. He stepped around a crate to shake Nathaniel's hand, then reached down to pull a crooked metal pipe off a chair to make a place to sit.

"It's funny that you asked for a meeting," Lyon said. "I was thinking of walking over to call on you."

"I wanted to ask you if you would be willing to explain the process you're working on? I've only heard bits and pieces."

"I'll tell you some of it, and since you're a chemist, you may grasp my exasperation faster than most. We've tried every which way to get the metal out of the rock, but the ore and metals here are just dagnabbed complicated."

"So I've learned, much to my regret."

James turned to his desk and rooted through the pile of papers on it. "Let me draw you a diagram." Mumbling to himself, he continued to sift through papers until he found a blank sheet.

Nathaniel watched the unkempt man, wondering how much veracity his words could possibly have. He was afraid James would only divulge what was already known: Sulfur was binding the metals to the ore.

James Lyon took a writing stand off his desk to make a flat place to draw and moved closer to Nathaniel. "Okay, once you get through the upper mantle of ore, you run into sulfurets." He began drawing. When he finished, James tapped his ragged fingernail on the paper. "See here, the sulfurets bind tightly to gold and silver, making them all but impossible to separate. Crushing the ore with a stamp mill at that point doesn't work." He thumped his knuckles to reinforce his point. "The amount of precious metals you can get out of the ore plummets, along with its value. But now look at this." He reached for the pen again and stroked some lines. "What might be possible is using extremely high heat to smelt the metals. If you use high heat, a base mineral like copper will attract gold and hold it. I'm sure of it. I've been working on this theory since 1862. High heat has been used on copper for centuries, but not so much on other metals in ores. A month ago, I shipped some samples to a test furnace in Staten Island, New York. I recovered about $250 in gold from every ton of ore."

Nathaniel tried not to show any reaction. "Who owns the furnace in New York?"

"Well, I'm the principal," James said as he jabbed the pen back into the inkstand, "although it's my investors who really own it. Since I'm a far piece from New York, I hired two metallurgists, the Johnson brothers, Frank and Charlie. They recently came over from Wales."

Nathaniel could not keep his fingers still. He buttoned and unbuttoned his jacket, waiting for what would come next. "Could a similar smelter work in Colorado if it works in New York or Britain?"

"It will take heat and different chemicals than in New York. The rocks are different here. I'm working on a furnace here in Black Hawk. I'll first use it with galena—"

"That's a lead mineral that often contains silver, right?" Nathaniel asked, his mind alert, estimating how James's system might produce results.

"Yes. Once I test that, then I'll try it on gold. I should know before long," James said. "Then you and the rest of the world can learn what I find out."

As the amount of silver and ore sold diminished from stamp milling, Nathaniel spent his time corresponding. He wrote more letters to Germany and England, but responses were a long time in coming. His tension from the waning results in Gilpin County spilled over into his letters to Alice.

> Black Hawk
> July 30, 1865
> My Dear Wife,
>
> I said that I would live or die with these investments. The first results with the stamp mill were splendid, but our recent samples have yielded fewer and fewer precious metals. My worry now is that the project will become an embarrassment and may defame my credibility. Future investors may lose their faith—maybe even Merrill and friends. Then my prospects for work will become problematic.

I wrote to you about James Lyon. Joe introduced him to me at the beginning, and I think I told you that we rent our office from him. He has a heating process he's been working on for three years, but he'd done little to really test it, so I considered it just one more wild mining scheme. Now I'm in conversation with him to get more information. My desperation has forced me to listen to any and every idea and let science be the judge.

Everything is quiet in the mining communities, so please don't worry about my safety. Our little house in Black Hawk, down the road from Central City, is bare but comfortable, waiting for you if you come. Joe's bachelor quarters above the store are still sufficient for David and Edward.

David, Edward, and I do little else but work. They are both proving to be good employees. When we have our meals, Joe is often at the café talking to a small, dark-haired girl named Emily who works there. She is cheerful and stays to herself in the evenings. Joe seems a little smitten with her.

I long for your company and the charming disturbances of Crawford and Isabel. Please kiss them each and help them remember their Papa.

Your affectionate husband,
N. P. Hill

For three weeks he had expected every knock on the door to be James Lyon coming from his office on the north side of the building, but instead of hearing any news from James, he read it in the newspaper one morning over flapjacks. It was in a headline on the front page: "Victory! The Day Is Ours!" The newspaper crowed about James Lyon's success in producing a single silver-lead ingot with his small Black Hawk smelter. After three years of dilly-dallying, he had some results and the potential for income.

Nathaniel read the article a second time. Shaking his head in disbelief that he was finding out the news second-hand, he retrieved his coat and hat and, with newspaper in hand, stomped out the door and headed for

James' office at the other end of the building. James opened the door with a flourish.

"Congratulation, James. Well deserved." He waved the newsprint. "I had hoped to hear about it from you personally."

"Sorry, sorry," James said as he piled a stack of papers on a table with a frenetic effort. "William Byers always likes a scoop, and I promised to let him be the first to know."

"The article said you just got your smelter up and running a day ago."

"And none too soon. My purse is almost spent." The distracted inventor began taking implements off his desk to stack in a corner. "Come in, Nathaniel, and have a seat."

Nathaniel sat down, trying to find a place for his feet among the pipes and motors. "What now, James? Do you think what you've done with a silver-lead ingot with your furnace can be replicated with gold?"

"You've asked the right question, Nathaniel. The gold still doesn't want to separate. I've already tried it and got nothing, but I feel like I'm close. It's going to be a more complex process than copper and even silver, but we should be able to figure it out." He drummed his stained fingers on the top of the desk nervously. "Nathaniel, I'm not sure how to proceed, and I've been thinking about it. I wonder if you'd consider working for me as a consultant for a while." James turned in his chair and looked at Nathaniel intently.

Staring back, Nathaniel tried to read motivation or conniving, but the cat eyes kept their secrets. He hesitated, wondering if he wanted to waste time on something he was only learning about. "I'm a chemist, not a metallurgist, James. What about the Welsh brothers you have working in New York? You said they were trained metallurgists."

"I need a scholar as much as anything, someone who has education and is inclined to look at all sides of a problem. I've heard you're willing to take on big problems—and you don't give up even when the contest is difficult."

"I'll take that as a compliment, James. I need this heat system to work just as much as you do, but I can't imagine how I can be of much help."

"You could look at all sides of things. And you could mix up a batch of chemicals."

"From what I've read, this is going to require high heat and many complicated steps. It's going to take more than chemicals. And anyway, chemicals aren't magic."

"Sometimes they are."

"Not often, but I suppose I can tinker around with you for a while. I hope it isn't just a waste of time for both of us."

"Just come to the smelter to watch what we're doing to see if you have anything to add. That's really all I'm asking."

"I'll do it as much for interest as for money. I definitely want to see the furnace in operation."

Nathaniel and James Lyon spent the next weeks at the smelter in Black Hawk with no positive results. Then the machinery broke down. By the end of that day, they had not solved the technical problems with the equipment, and the smelter was still inoperable.

Everyone on the project was at each other's throats from overwork and tension. News of the breakdown spread fast. After so much optimism over the silver ingot, the setback plunged Black Hawk and Central City into a fog of gloom. The towns' futures were dependent on James Lyon's.

After four months of trying every mechanical means he knew to separate the precious metals from the ore, Nathaniel finally came to the conclusion that he needed to travel back to New England and maybe even go to Europe in search of an answer.

His income from his mines was dwindling daily, and he feared his two managers would abandon him. To his relief, both men remained loyal. Not only did they promise to stay on and keep the business going, they also offered to post letters to keep him apprised of what was happening in Colorado. He assured them of his trust in them and told them to only post a letter if anything serious happened.

His relief was evident to him in the way his shoulders relaxed once he had their commitment to stay on. Unaware that he had been carrying what felt like the weight of the world on his shoulders, he was happy enough to let a bit go so he could focus on finding a solution to their smelting problems.

The first two days at home in Providence he frolicked with his children and caught up on the news with Alice. His heart pulled him two ways. There were sun-soaked skies of Colorado and proximity to his mines, but there was unrestrained pleasure in being home with his family. Now it was time to turn to the unsolved problem of smelting and his future income.

He spent the morning in his usual methodical way, reviewing all the technology he had heard or read about. Dipping his pen in the ink bottle, he wrote down reasons why they had failed in the West. At the end, one remained: the Swansea method from Wales—the one James Lyon had constructed experimentally; the one that had stopped working. Now he had to decide whether it was the system that was at fault or Lyon's usual slap-dash way of constructing things.

He needed to visit Vivian and Sons in Wales to see how the process worked, even though he had not received a response. To go, he had to raise money for the trip. But he also needed to raise money for construction if he found that the process was worthy. He knew the Welsh process was expensive. The additional process of refining would have to wait. He did not have enough funds to accomplish any of it.

After all his letter writing, he had been turned down by almost every investor. He began to doubt his ability to achieve success in mining. Word of Lyon's failure with his experimental furnace was becoming common knowledge. There was an air of pessimism about mining in the West despite its early riches. Other than Warren Merrill, investors were willing to give him only token grants that did not add up to the $200,000 needed to build a heat-based smelter.

Alice wandered into his study. Her happiness about his presence at home was obvious in her demeanor. Dropping into the reading chair, a smile of pleasure crossed her face. "We're all so glad you're home, Nat. It is pure happiness when we are all around the dinner table together . . . and when we're in bed," she teased. "Everything seems in its proper place when you're here."

He nodded cautiously, not wanting to burst her bubble of contentment.

"But you're still working on your smelter project, aren't you? How is it going? Any progress?"

"Yes and no." He twisted in his seat. "The Welsh smelter I told you about has possibilities, but I have to proceed carefully. I think James Lyon got impatient after experimenting for three years. He rushed into construction and buying other equipment. Now his project is stagnant, and he's built up debt. I don't want to risk that if I build a smelter."

She leaned toward the light from the window and opened her darning basket to pull out a black sock and threaded needle.

"I've been thinking, Alice. I probably should go to Wales to see first-hand how the Swansea plant works."

She sighed. "Somehow I thought you wouldn't be here for long." She guided the smooth wooden darning egg inside the sock, began taking stitches, and then paused. "When do you think we will all be together permanently? The children and I cherish our time with you, but it always slips away too quickly."

"We will be soon, Alice. I promise you. I just have to get this problem solved to have a future. Then we will all be together."

"Oh well, crossing the Atlantic will not be any more dangerous than the threat of Indians."

"Since I'm going to go all that way, I want to meet with British scientists to hear what they have to say, as well as seeing the smelter." Nathaniel got up from his desk chair and started walking the length of the room. The carpet showed wear from his frequent pacing.

Alice looked up from her mending. "Would you go on your own?"

"I'd like to see if John would be willing to go with me. It would give me an opportunity to spend time with my old colleague. He has such a level head. If I go just after the semester ends, he could come. The administration wouldn't have a problem with his going to Europe to talk to scientists, and having his impression of everything would make me surer of the information."

"Uhm hmm," Alice replied as she moistened the end of another piece of thread to pull through her needle. Nathaniel knew from experience that even though Alice seemed to be as focused on her darning as on what he was saying, she was listening intently.

Nathaniel walked across the room and then back again. "The problem is, I can't just call on Britain's top scientists. I need recommendations, and I also need a letter of reference to get in the door of Vivian and Sons." He stroked his clean-shaven jaw with his fingers. "I think John could help me with that, too, since he still has the prestige of an academic profession. I'm sort of a cast-about at the moment."

"Nonsense, Nat. No one really thinks that. How much time do you plan to spend there?

"Several days in London and, I think, the same in Swansea. We may add France at the end."

Alice admitted to being envious of his trip, seeing it as both a business trip and an adventure. But Nathaniel was more pragmatic and more than a little determined. He would do whatever it took to get answers to the mystery of the smelting process. Not only did his reputation depend on it, his family's future did too.

Nathaniel had avoided the Brown campus since clearing out his office over a year earlier. No longer part of the university, he now felt like an intruder in its hallowed academic halls. But he finally swallowed his pride to meet his trusted mentor.

Across from John Peirce, Nathaniel put a list of eminent scientists on the desk and rotated it with his fingertips so it faced his former colleague. "Do you have any ideas about how to meet with these scientists? Some are from universities here, but most are in Europe."

John looked down at the paper. "Do you ever ask anything reasonable?" he groaned, blowing a spiral of tobacco smoke toward the ceiling. "You need letters of reference to meet with the president of the Royal Society."

Nathaniel knew that he was referring to Sir Edward Sabin. "I need to meet with the top scientist for every field if I'm going to have a chance at figuring out Colorado's ores."

"The Royal Society of London wears its prestige like a crown. They don't waste time with anyone they consider commoners—and that would probably include you and me."

"You're making it sound like getting an appointment with Queen Victoria might be easier."

"It might," John replied. He seemed to be trying to maintain a solemn demeanor, but Nathaniel could see a gleam in his eye. "You know, another strategy to getting an appointment is to intrigue them with Colorado Territory. There's always fascination about the western frontier. Even better is the lure of gold. If they think you have first-hand information about the new Eldorado, it might be as beguiling as references."

"Hmm. Interesting. It's definitely worth considering." Nathaniel got up to pace. "Let me tell you about another idea I have." He walked the length of the office. "Even though it's going to cost me a small fortune, seven thousand dollars to be exact, I've decided to ship several tons of ore from Colorado across the Atlantic to go through the Swansea process."

"All the way to Wales! Impossible."

"It really isn't. Mule-team wagons will freight the ore across the Plains to Atchison, Kansas. Then it will be loaded onto steamers to go down the Missouri River. After that, it will go on to New Orleans. From there, it will go to the port of Swansea, Wales, for examination."

"Good grief, Nathaniel. I'd like to see that," John replied with a harrumph.

"Well, why don't you?"

"Why don't I what?" John asked, sitting upright in his chair, hastily brushing an ash that had spilled in the abrupt motion onto his jacket.

"I'm going to ask for appointments when scientists meet together in London in June. College is out of session then. You're a chemist. No one at Brown could argue against your meeting with the top scientists."

"Wait a minute, Nathaniel. I try to lead a *normal* life, the life of a dedicated scholar. Why do you always try to make my life as complicated as yours?" John's brow pinched into a frown. "Finding letters of reference for you is all the challenge I need."

"You can't deny that my projects interest you."

"I admit you've got me intrigued, although you have yet to snare Britain's finest minds with your far-fetched ideas."

"I'm glad you said 'yet.'"

"But not 'yes,' at least, not yet."

"You'd consider going, John?" An optimistic smile lit Nathaniel's face.

"Don't count on anything more than *consider*, Nathaniel."

"I know I'm always asking for something, but having someone like you with me to make sure all the right questions are asked could make the difference between success and failure. We could compare our perceptions."

John slid the list to the corner of his desk. "The first thing I'll have to ponder is how in the world I would broach Mary with this far-fetched idea. Furthermore, the university might just dissolve the chemistry department if one more of its professors has an extraordinary request."

Nathaniel smiled. Whether or not John was willing to admit it yet, he was on board, and Nathaniel knew it.

SIXTEEN

ቶ

"I don't know how you put all the pieces in place in six months, but you managed to do it," John said, from their lower berths on the ship *Europa* to London.

"It's good to have you along. Traveling alone is a bore."

"If you want to know the truth, I feel guilty. This is the first summer I've taken off. I'm so used to my academic routine, it's as if I'm playing hooky from school knowing that a truant officer is not far behind. At the same time, I'm feeling a bit free. I've never been to London, let alone Wales."

"If luck's with me, the trip will be worth the expense."

"Your ideas usually pan out, even though there always seem to be snags along the way."

"I have the letter with its gold seal from the Royal Society of London safely tucked in my valise. That's a bit of luck to start with."

"Sir Edward Sabin! Pretty good for an unemployed chemist," John replied.

Nathaniel grimaced. "Not funny, John. It would be nice if you didn't bring my joblessness up in London or Wales."

He looked closely at his friend. John seemed a bit pale. Nathaniel suspected he was having another bout of nausea. But before he could say another word, John looked up at him biliously and then ran from the room, heading for the deck.

Fortunately for both of them, John eventually adapted to the boat's rocking, his stomach settling down enough to not only prevent his dashes to the deck but allow him to eat.

On the other side of the ocean, the atmosphere was not unlike the one they had left. London's air was full of soft, heavy moisture ready to burst into rain at any moment. They carried their long, black, crook-handled umbrellas to every appointment. Their daily schedule of meetings had been set in advance through correspondence. Nathaniel and John met with royal fellows in mathematics, engineering, and natural sciences, and finally with Sir Edward Sabin. The day after they finished with the hallowed grounds of the Royal Academy, they met with Sir John Percy. The British scientists were reserved, leery of sharing information with the Americans.

"I thought Brown was stuffy," Nathaniel said, as they ate in the hotel's mahogany-paneled dining room, with floor-to-ceiling velvet draperies and crystal chandeliers. "I'm glad we don't have to refer to each other as 'sir' and bow."

"Superiority exudes from every pore. And the accents—I hardly feel I speak the same language."

Nathaniel laughed. "Did you notice how they tip their nose up when they say *America*?" I'm surprised they didn't slip and say 'colonists' when they spoke to us."

"They treat us like rebellious bumpkins."

"It's just a ruse. I sense an inkling of envy about those of us who live on the opposite side of the ocean," Nathaniel said with assurance.

"Sorry, Nathaniel, I disagree. I don't sense even a dram of envy. When you have the prestige of being at the top of a hierarchy, getting pleasure from looking down on people beneath you is a much more likely sentiment than envy."

"Hear me out." Nathaniel's brown eyes flickered as each thought presented itself in his mind. "People have been crossing from this side of the Atlantic for a myriad of reasons: famine, poverty, religion, stifling government. Many of them had no choice but to emigrate because life was so grim, but their risk-taking made them different."

"How so?" John asked as he took his curved briarwood pipe out of his pocket to light.

"The ones who left for America were the risk-takers," Nathaniel continued, "and they had to innovate to survive. Those who stayed behind remained in the regimented confines of tradition."

John exhaled a puff of smoke. "I suppose you have a point. These scientists seem to be a little more reluctant to test a new idea than on our side."

"Maybe something similar is happening in our own country. The West is beckoning the people who live more by passion than reason."

"And beckoning the reckless, I might add." John's mouth assumed a humorless line as he added, "And I suppose that says something about my staying on the safe side of the country?"

Nathaniel frowned. "I'm not making any judgments whether either mode is right or wrong, just noting the differences. Spending time in Rhode Island, then Colorado, and now England makes the dissimilarity among them as apparent as the similarity, that's all."

"I'm getting tired of listening to English pontification. I'm ready to leave tomorrow for Wales, where there is action, not just words," John said as they got up to go.

Morley's Hotel, London
Friday, June 26, 1866
My Dear Wife,

I felt lost in this tumultuous city at first because of its contrasts.
Striking architecture is everywhere. We have seen St. Paul's Cathedral,

which sits on London's highest hill. We have also seen the Tower of London, which looks like a fortress, Westminster Abbey with its clocks, and many other buildings from past centuries. In our walks, we have discovered that commerce dominates this city. Barges and every other kind of vessel fill the Thames as they rush on their way to load their cargoes onto ocean steamers for distribution to the rest of the world. The river is clogged with refuse that turns the water brown and foul-smelling. It is often all we can do to keep from retching.

Black and gilt carriages choke the streets. They roll by, while we are accosted for coins by jobless men in rags. It is the stuff of the Charles Dickens novels you read. At the other side of the economy are royal palaces that would interest you just as much. I jot down notes at the end of the day so I can remember to tell you more when I return.

We have used our time well since we reached London, making several business calls every day this week. The scientists here are more formal than in the United States. I'm feeling somewhat like a huckster selling my idea while trying to hide my dire need for information. I sense that their curiosity is piqued, in a guarded sort of way, even though they consider anything in the United States to be second class.

The far part of our country arouses their imaginations just as it does at home. The mystery of the West seems to be my trump card for not being discounted. John and I are trying to gain information, but it's hard not to be daunted by the best academic minds Great Britain has to offer.

I long to have you with me. If I ever come to London again, you shall come with me if it is possible. I yearn to hear from you. It seems longer already than the times I was in Colorado. I close with love to you and the most earnest hope that you and the children are well.

Your affectionate husband,
N. P. Hill

Nathaniel felt adrift without frequent letters from Alice. He had given up hope of receiving something from her before they went to Wales, but after finishing supper the evening before they were to leave London, the desk clerk handed him a letter.

Providence

July 13, 1866

My Dear Husband,

Your letter warmed me in your absence. I can only imagine what it must be like to see the architecture that symbolizes so much of what I have read about in my favorite area of the world.

I hope you will describe everything. At the same time, I worry that your life has become so broad and my life so narrow that you will find me a dull companion after your many adventures. I hope you will not consider leaving me out of business matters because you think I am ignorant after your grand tour.

Kate comes over frequently and, like Mama and Papa, wants to hear every word of what you and John are doing. They are much more at ease with Britain than Colorado. Our servant girl, Maggie, is a help around the house but no replacement for your entertaining conversation.

Crawford has had a cold, but both children are doing well. Isabel is happy being able to walk and run with her brother. Every morning, she comes trotting into our room to see if Papa came home in the night. Her little merry voice can be heard all day long, singing and playing. I am as eager for your return as she is.

Your affectionate wife,

Alice4

→ ←

In a slate-gray drizzle, they left London at nine o'clock the next morning, traveling directly west for 190 miles to Swansea in a first-class passenger train. Nathaniel and John observed the scenery through the smudged windows with curiosity as the train passed mills, factories, and the dingy low-slung hovels of poor housing—all clustered together because of the lack of transportation. In mid-afternoon they arrived at Swansea, a city about the size of Providence. And like Providence, it was situated on a bay at the end of a river, in this case the Tawe. Little else was similar about the two cities. Disembarking, they walked through the city with umbrellas unfurled. Idle people languished against soot-stained buildings. Even in the drizzling rain, acrid smoke filtered into their throats. The high hills around the city were denuded of vegetation. Anything herbaceous had been killed by the fumes from the numerous smelting works. Dank, narrow canals ferried material from the place of production to ocean transportation.

The two travelers crossed the street, avoiding puddles, as they went to their lodging. The half-timbered hotel with peaked roof was surrounded by narrow trash-strewn streets. They signed the logbook in an interior where everything looked gray and filmy. Even indoors, the chemical smell stung their nostrils. Their conversation was lackluster as they ate in a dining room with worn upholstery and scabrous brown walls. They had run out of words. The following day's meeting would decide everything for Nathaniel.

In the morning, they asked the hotel clerk to call for a hack to drive them to Vivian and Company, where an employee took them through the plant to explain the machinery. When he had answered all their questions, he escorted the two Americans to the general manager's office.

A short, round man in a shapeless black jacket stood up as the door opened. "Come in, gentlemen. I hope you enjoyed your tour of our plant." With a slight bow, the bald man introduced himself. "I'm Henry Vivian, one of the owners and general manager. Come have a seat." He gestured to a stained, rectangular mahogany table where the three sat.

"You received our samples, Mr. Vivian?" Nathaniel asked, rushing his words before the manager could speak.

Mr. Vivian cleared his phlegmy throat. "We made a thorough examination, I assure you. The samples were taken at random to get a true assessment." He stopped to cover his mouth with a gray handkerchief as he coughed.

Nathaniel's chest constricted with tenseness, making it hard to pull enough air into his own lungs.

"Even considering all the circumstances of labor and cost of transportation, we believe the ore from your mine in these samples is worth twenty thousand American dollars."

Nathaniel felt faint and slumped back to take a breath, trying to absorb Vivian's words.

John leaned forward. "You are saying that despite the cost of sending ores to Swansea, this will pay off?"

"It will do more than break even." Mr. Vivian looked at him with disdain at being doubted. "What it means, Mr. Peirce, is that we are prepared to make a contract for any amount of ore you send us for a period of one year."

"Did you say one year, Mr. Vivian?" John repeated.

"I did, Mr. Peirce." Mr. Vivian's sallow face revealed no emotion.

"What will happen after a year?" Nathaniel asked, uneasy about the limitation.

"We will take stock on both sides and renegotiate."

Nathaniel gathered his thoughts before replying, but it was John who responded. "Mr. Vivian, I don't know how things work here, but in the United States, other people sometimes invest money in a project to make it possible to proceed. Because the investment is not entirely Mr. Hill's, it would be better for him to discuss it with his investors before signing anything."

"We are familiar with investment methods on the other side of the Atlantic, you can be certain. But our offer is for today. I can't say what it will be by the time you return to the United States."

"Are those the legal agreements in the folder, Mr. Vivian?" John asked.

"They are, Mr. Peirce. The papers our solicitors have prepared are very specific. You may read through them before you sign them." He pushed the file forward.

Nathaniel felt trapped into making a decision so quickly, yet he was worried that the opportunity he had waited for years to materialize would slip through his fingers if he hesitated. "We would like to take them to read and return them overnight."

Mr. Vivian nodded in assent. "My assistant has executed a copy. So until tomorrow, gentlemen." He rose to dismiss the meeting. As the three shook hands, the clerk opened the heavy office door for them to exit.

When they were back on the street, in the slow rain and out of earshot from anyone at Vivian and Sons, Nathaniel looked at John and nearly shouted, "It worked, John. It worked. It's almost too good to be true."

"And indeed, it may be," John replied evenly. "I'm sure Mr. Vivian realizes what the good news means to you and will negotiate with that sentiment."

"My ore is also a benefit to Vivian and Company. He profits too."

"You're right. Let's not let him forget that."

I'm going to make sure at this time next year, Mr. Vivian will consider it an advantage to renew," Nathaniel said.

In the morning, Mr. Vivian took only half an hour to review all the stipulations verbally. Nathaniel hunched over the paper and watched his signature flow next to that of Henry Vivian's as if his hand were detached from the action.

Mr. Vivian handed Nathaniel a check for $20,000. He carefully blew on it and tucked it in his interior jacket pocket. His company would have to pay for transportation of ores to Wales, and Vivian and Sons would smelt it and pay him for the gold.

Nathaniel and John were soon at the congested Great Western Railway station on High Street with tickets for London. "The smell here is overbearing, John. My eyes are watering and my nose won't stop dripping. Even my handkerchief is gray. And the odor of fish makes me feel like gagging. The loading dock must be just outside."

"I guess it is all part of industry, but I'll be glad to leave Swansea. London is another matter. With all the sights we've seen and a signed contract, the trip has been gratifying. Congratulations, Nathaniel. You stuck with it even though many of us were doubters."

"Thank heavens for a signed contract! Now I can start building my own plant. Once that's done, there will be income for me and others in the region." He hesitated. "If I could build a refinery as well as a smelter, I could cut out the time and expense of shipping the mixture of copper and gold to New Orleans and across the vast Atlantic. That would be the real benefit, but it means raising more money—an oppressive thought."

"Your mind is never still, is it? You should give it a rest."

"No, I can't do that and make a success of smelting. The other thing I should do, for business reasons, is move to the West."

"Permanently? How would Alice feel about that?" John asked.

"After the deadly Sand Creek catastrophe? She will not allow Crawford and Isabel to cross the Plains."

"I can't imagine her leaving them behind." John unfolded the newspaper he had just purchased.

"I can't either, but parting from her is not something I want to do again."

In Providence, Alice opened the window to stir a breeze on a hot, humid July day in 1866. Kate had come for tea and to hear the latest news from Nathaniel. Alice sat on the horsehair sofa next to her friend.

"This is the most recent letter from Nat. His descriptions are so vivid, I feel like I'm there with him." Alice sighed. "I wish I were with him. I miss him, and England is the first place I'd like to go outside America. They have so much more history than we do."

Kate leaned over to stir in a crystalline square of sugar. "Didn't you say he was on his way to Paris? That's the place *I'd* like to visit. Everything seems so modern and showy there."

"Paris is just a brief stop before he comes home. I think he feels he should meet with everyone now that's he's spent the money to go to Europe. His travel sounds so glamorous, but he's betting so much on this trip. He tries to make his letters sound as if he's savoring his time, but underneath it all, he's worried that this may be his only chance for success with his mining property."

"I know it worries both of you." Kate put her half-full teacup on the tray. "How is Maggie? Is she working out?"

"She tries hard," Alice replied, "but I think she's overwhelmed by being in this country. I give her two nights off to take classes at the YWCA and Sunday afternoon to study."

"Two nights off? Don't you think you're spoiling her?"

"No, no, I don't think so," Alice said gently. "I just want to give her every opportunity to improve her life."

"What classes does she take?"

"That's just it. She keeps delaying starting classes."

"Then what does she do on her evenings off?"

"She visits her cousin."

"Her cousin?" Kate gave Alice a quizzical look. "I thought she didn't like being there."

"I think she's going to his bar—the pub, as she calls it. She doesn't really like it, but it's reminiscent of home for her. I think we're all that way. It's hard to untangle the past from our lives, whether its influence is for better or worse."

"What would Nathaniel think of having a woman living here who goes to a bar?"

Alice smoothed her skirt. "Not much. She hasn't done anything wrong, and she always comes home right on time. Sometimes she's flushed, so I know she's run to get here."

"Maybe she's seeing a man."

"Maybe. I know she's lonely for someone her own age and her own background. That's pretty natural."

"Alice, you better get this sorted out before Nathaniel returns."

"I know, Kate. I still have a little time, but you're right. I'm already starting to worry about what I'm going to do."

→ ←

Through the train window, Nathaniel and John could see Providence amid an extravaganza of summer flowers and green trees. Disembarking first, Nathaniel scanned the platform until he spotted Alice, holding the curved handle of Isabel's baby pram, Crawford at her side. He met her with a hug.

"We've missed you," she murmured as she folded into his arms.

John caught up to them, and Alice pulled him toward her to quickly kiss his check. "John, I told Mary I would take you home. We can all fit in, and I hired a carter to take the luggage and Isabel's pram."

Nathaniel tossed Crawford in the air to a cascade of shrieks. His ecstatic giggles blended with Nathaniel's low, throaty laughter. He kept Crawford in his arm and began pushing Isabel's pram while inner thoughts tormented him. It seemed that he was going to return only to leave again on business.

After dinner, when the children were in bed and the dishes done, Nathaniel and Alice went up to their bedroom. Alice sat on the edge of the bed as he unpacked his clothing and supplies. Their eyes connected more than once as he moved about.

"Nat, you still seem so concerned after your trip. I thought the news from Wales would make you happy. Your work and research paid off. I'm proud of you. What worries you now?"

"Unfortunately, Vivian and Sons gave me only a year contract." Nathaniel pushed his suitcase to the hall and set it below the pull-down stairs for return to the attic.

"Does that mean you have to get all your ore shipped in a year? That seems impossible."

"It is impossible. I think Mr. Vivian—he's the owner—wants to be cautious and optimize his own profits."

"Won't he give you another contract after this one expires?"

Alice got up to bring a basket for his soiled laundry.

"You would think so. How much money we will both make is uncertain at this point."

"So you shouldn't be worried."

"I want to make sure that we get him enough ore so that *he* will ask *us* to renew the contract rather than vice versa. After that, I should consider building a smelter and refinery of my own using the Swansea method."

"Can't your managers, Mr. Barlow and Mr. Gould, take care of business in Colorado? Isn't that why you hired them?"

"Yes, and they're good men, but I can't take any chances now. We're in striking distance of success."

They were also within striking distance of failure, but Nathaniel kept that thought to himself.

A frown crossed Alice's face. "What does that mean?"

"I'm not sure yet. Now that I'm home, I have to correspond with David and Edward."

"That will take time."

"And it will give me time to think." He tossed a shirt and collars into the basket. "But at last, I'm home. Enough of business. Let's go to bed now, and in the morning, I can tell you more about London and Paris."

He folded back the quilt and urgently pulled her down beside him.

SEVENTEEN

ቀ

When Nathaniel read Joe's letter about James Lyon, he shook his head in disbelief. The words were clear. If James Lyon's Scotch hearth version of the Swansea process was successful, Nathaniel's nascent plans for his own plant would never get off the ground. Investors would not be interested in duplication. His trip and all the money he had spent would come to naught. He sent a note to John asking to meet with him the next day. He needed to talk to him even before Alice.

Nathaniel had written Joe when he returned from his meetings with scientists in London and plant owners in Wales. He had asked Joe to keep track of what was going on in Central City and Black Hawk. Now he had his answer. James Lyon had been bragging about coming across something new to get his Black Hawk smelter going again. He intended on trying to replicate the Swansea process.

The following day, Nathaniel quickly thrust the letter in front of his former Brown colleague as he sat down on the opposite side of the desk. John rubbed the bowl of his pipe pensively as he read the letter. "Maybe, maybe not," he said when he finished.

"Just when I seem to be making headway, Lyon has gone to the Swansea process. It's the fourth time he has changed his system. How does a man driven by whim and fancy have so much luck?"

"Luck would be the word for him, both bad and good."

"He seems to have more good luck than I do."

"When you were his consultant, you said James wanted to get going without doing much planning."

"He always likes to move fast." Nathaniel slumped in discouragement.

"It seems to me it would have been more productive for him to sit at a desk and plot things out instead of rushing pell-mell into every project. His hands are always occupied instead of his head."

"You're right about that. His failed plant cost his investors over two hundred and twenty-five thousand dollars, to say nothing of his wasted time."

"My bet is that he's going to rush this project through to try to convince his investors not to abandon him."

Nathaniel gave a nervous sigh. "He's not the only one who needs money. I'm going to have to contact investors in Boston right away." He pushed his chair back and rose to pace off his anxiety. "They are going to be concerned that Lyon has preempted me."

"James apparently has good metallurgists in the Johnson brothers, but didn't you say he is too disorganized to manage anything? That he was always cutting corners?"

"Investors sometimes look past that. They want results no matter how they are achieved." Nathaniel rubbed his chin in agitation and sat back down in his chair. "They want to have money in their pockets instead of ideas on their desk."

"How close are you to having the money to build your own plant?"

"I have interest but no commitments. Now that I have results from Wales, I think Warren Merrill might come forward. As a chemical manufacturer, he is the most logical investor, but he won't go it alone. I figure I need two hundred thousand dollars, and he will probably give me half of that. Others may be interested, but they will also be worried about competition from James when the news gets out. And most potential investors are apprehensive anyway."

"You will have to make a solid case for what you plan to do. You have the experience to do that. Lyon does not, and he has failed his investors several times already.

Nathaniel groaned. "I feel like I'm crossing an ocean in a small boat without a map."

John smiled. "You've put too much work into this to have it fail now, old friend. I'm hooked, even though my interest is purely vicarious. And if I'm hooked, you will find investors willing to back you once they understand the potential as I now do."

When he came back from the meeting with John, he went to his study to begin writing solicitations to investors. That task had now become urgent. When Alice wandered into his study and sat down to talk, he told her about Joe's letter and his conversation with John. From the look on her face and the intensity with which she pursued her sewing as they talked, he sensed her frustration. She and the children had been quite content to have him back at home, and he was certain that she had wished, more than once, that he had stayed at Brown instead of pursuing the enticing possibility of solving the gold smelting problem in Colorado.

But he had put too much of himself into the project to simply let James Lyon have a monopoly on the Swansea process. His own chance for success would be defeated if that happened. If he could get the investors he needed, he would have to return to Colorado to oversee the building of the new plant. But he wanted to do more than that. He wanted to end the pull between his work and his family. He wanted Alice and the children to move with him to Colorado.

When he gently suggested the idea to her, she balked.

"What do you mean—move to Colorado? What about Crawford and Isabel, Nat? You know they're too young to make the trip, especially after that deplorable Sand Creek affair. Indians are murdering travelers *and* kidnapping children."

"Would you consider leaving them with your parents or with Kate for a while?"

"Give up my children? I'm a mother. They are my life."

Alice leaned back in the chair and closed her eyes. Nathaniel could tell that she was trying to absorb the kaleidoscope of information he had just given her. "I love my parents and I love Kate, but they can't take the place of a child's own mother."

"It would just be for a while. Everything will eventually get safer. Schools are starting. My friend Tom Potter has a congregation in Denver, and it's one of many. Even Black Hawk has churches. Before long, there will be little difference between Colorado and Rhode Island."

"The children are part of me, and so are my parents and friends, and my work in the community. I can't separate from them without losing part of who I am." Her fists clenched. "They are what give my life meaning and definition. What would I do there without them?"

"Not going would put my business in a difficult position—a position bound to fail. At the moment, that's what's defining *my* life."

"Nat, I do *not* want to go. You're asking something impossible of me. How can you do that?"

"I can't make you go. I know that. I also know that my life is never the same without you."

"You're making me choose between having a husband or my children. What does that say about our marriage? It is so unfair."

"Business isn't always fair. It's just a decision I have to make." With that, he swiveled his chair around to return to his desk.

"You always go back to your papers when you don't want to face something."

"There's nothing left to say. There are no options, unfortunately."

There was nothing more he could say, and he knew she would need time to absorb what he was suggesting.

That night, Alice buried her face in the pillow, trying not to cry. She had trouble breathing when she finally drifted off to sleep because she dreamed that she was suffocating. Her arms thrashed around wildly, searching for someone to save her, but no one was there. Sitting up with a start, Alice looked over to see if she had awakened Nat, but he was peacefully snoring. She lay back again, fitfully considering her alternatives. She felt like a heavy stone had been placed on her chest, and she found herself thinking that it must be like this to have a broken heart.

She felt the pressure of time. How could she decide so fast about her life—a life she felt was selfishly out of her control? She knew that living apart from Nathaniel indefinitely was impossible, but how could she give up her children, even temporarily? He had to go, without the children and without her if necessary. Her mind swung wildly, suddenly pausing. What kind of an example would she set for them if she abandoned their father? Again and again she went over what choice she should make: Colorado and Nat or Providence and her children? Her head split with pain. What kind of a mother would put her children at such peril by taking them across the Plains? With almost no sleep, she gave up arguing with herself. There was no choice but to go, and go without them, but she would tenaciously do everything possible to have the children join them as soon as it was safe.

She knew her decision would surprise her mother and Kate, but Maggie would be undone. Maggie was being transformed with kindness and stability. It had taken months for her to trust that living with the Hills would give her a chance to build a life in her adopted country. The trust was new and fragile and could disappear like dew in a desert. Moving would leave her scared and vulnerable again.

Alice had considered asking her mother to take Maggie, but an Irish girl would be too foreign for Harriet. And anyway, Mrs. Morrissey, who had taken care of Alice and her brothers, still worked for her parents. She had to speak to Maggie after breakfast, before the truth slipped out. She twisted her pillow again, trying to think of what words to use to cause the least amount of damage. Finally, giving up on sleep, she got out of bed.

Alice was shrouded with gloom as she slowly walked down the stairs. When she reached the kitchen, Maggie was laughing at Isabel's insistence on scooping her porridge into her mouth on her own, usually losing it back to the bowl or the floor. For an instant, Alice almost joined the morning ritual of friendly banter with Maggie and the children, but laughter would not come. Instead, she avoided eye contact with the Irish girl who had become cheerfully relaxed in the months she had lived with the Hills.

Nathaniel came down to join Alice for breakfast, and the unsuspecting Maggie continued feeding Crawford and Isabel porridge and fruit in the kitchen while Alice and Nathaniel ate their bacon and eggs in the dining room in tense silence. She would tell Nathaniel of her decision later. Her feelings were too raw to trust yet.

Finished with breakfast, Alice put Isabel and Crawford in their play area near the kitchen hearth. Maggie poured hot water from the kettle into the sink, rubbed lye soap on a cloth, and began to wash the dishes. When Alice quietly walked up behind Maggie and spoke her name, Maggie almost dropped the pot she was drying. She apologized to the girl for startling her and asked her to let the dishes wait while they talked for a moment.

Maggie had been devoted to the children, and Alice had been devoted to helping Maggie find her way as a stranger in a new country. She could not let the news of her impending move to Colorado wait. If she did, it would make it all the more difficult for the girl. The sooner she had the conversation with Maggie, the sooner she could go back to the Young Women's Christian Association and try to garner a new position for Maggie.

With a deep breath, she began sharing the news. She was spent and they were both in tears by the time she was done. It had been the most difficult conversation of her life.

When Nathaniel and Alice publicly announced they planned to sell their house in Providence and move to Black Hawk by March 1867, longtime friends stopped by the distinguished brick house to say regretful good-byes. With each conversation and parting hug, Nathaniel knew that Alice's heart broke a bit more with the thought of never again seeing the cherished companions with whom they had spent so much of their married life. She put on a positive face for their friends, but he could see that doing so was draining her.

Nathaniel was perplexed at his own dour mood. Preparing to leave was far different than the giddiness he felt in getting ready for his previous trips. Saying good-bye had too much finality. The words stuck in his throat as he attempted to make his decision sound rational to his former Brown colleagues. When he was conversing, he forged an indelible memory of their faces, knowing that he would not likely ever see them again. John was the most difficult.

"You've been my compass for well over a decade, John. I'm not sure I'll be able to find my way without you close by for consultation." Nathaniel offered a thin smile of forced humor. The two men sat surrounded by boxes for one last nostalgic chat in Nathaniel's study.

"It will be hard to pass this house and not be able to stop in to say hello to you and Alice," John replied as he lifted the hot cup of coffee that Alice had brought on a tray. His familiar pipe was resting in the ashtray.

Nathaniel was seated restlessly in his desk chair. "I'll miss this house, but not as much as your company. I don't know who will listen to my fledgling ideas now."

"You'll find wisdom in the West, but most likely in unpredictable places."

"But how will I know who to trust with ideas?"

John put the cup to his lips to take another sip of coffee. The aroma blended with the scent of tobacco. "That will come, but don't act on any advice unless you've proved it."

"I plan to be very cautious." The desk chair started thrumming with his motion, giving away his uneasiness. "If I am forced to return, it will be with my tail between my legs."

John chuckled. "I doubt if I'll ever see you in that position."

"Competition with James Lyon is going to be relentless, but I'm still going to move ahead. My one-year contract with Vivian and Sons means I'll be sending the matte of copper and gold to Wales for refining while I plan my own structure."

"It's a good approach, Nathaniel. I know you're anxious about the race with Lyon, but the operation with the most solid foundation is going to be the successful one, even if it takes longer."

"You're almost always right, and I hope that holds this time. James is ahead of me at the moment, and he'll be hard to catch."

John took a last drink of coffee and stood up from his chair, his lips bent up in an ironic smile. "I'll miss your inventiveness. Life may be downright boring without you."

"And I'll miss your wisdom and friendship."

They walked down the hall together, arms draped on each other's shoulders. Nathaniel opened the door, and they shook hands as John stepped through. "Maybe you and Mary could visit some summer . . . when things settle down."

"Never say never," John replied, laughing. "Traveling to Britain once seemed farfetched." He went down the steps quickly and reached the street before turning and giving a last wave.

The newness of the environment during their three-week trip west made Alice as much curious as fearful. There were whole hours when the scenery seemed not to change, then it subtly evolved into something different. She asked Nathaniel questions about anything different she noticed in the foliage and animals. Seeing wagon trains clustered together for protection brought her face close to the window to see if there were children. She mourned at the site of makeshift graves and burned stage stops, but only during fitful sleep did her mind truly sink with sadness. The stage was even bumpier than traveling on the uneven railroad beds during the first part of the trip.

She and Nathaniel had traveled from New York with a German metallurgist, Hermann Beeger, whom Nathaniel had hired to help build the new plant in Black Hawk. Beeger had studied at Europe's most renowned mining school, and beyond that, he had developed skills by working at smelters throughout Europe, including Swansea. He was unmarried, so he had little to prevent him from going west.

Alice sighed as she thought about her children in Providence and her household goods, which were traveling by oxcart, just as Nathaniel's equipment had done three years earlier. The longing for her children stabbed at her heart, and she hoped she would at least have the comfort of her dishes and other household things around her in Black Hawk. She feared that they might not arrive safely since spring storms were common.

The surroundings became more open and barren. Stops were infrequent and the food unappealing. Their only scare came when they breathlessly watched a long line of Indians peacefully proceeding to the Republican River with their families and household accoutrements.

When the stage finally arrived in Central City, Alice felt a surprising calm mixed with inquisitiveness about her new life.

Joe was on the board walkway to greet them, and Nathaniel made the introduction. "Alice, this is Joe. You may remember him from a long time ago."

Alice stepped forward, almost tripping because her legs were so cramped from sitting. Her natural warmth overcame the weariness and longing for her children, and she reached for his hand to squeeze it. "Joe, I met you when I shopped at your father's dry goods store years ago. I would recognize your red hair and freckles anywhere." The color of his hair was the same, but the boy had grown into a well-muscled young man.

Joe gave her a half bow. "Welcome to our fair town in the foothills of the Rocky Mountains, Mrs. Hill."

"Call me Alice, Joe. I know we're going to be friends. I'm looking forward to being here." He looked at her as if unconvinced. "I really am. It's just been such a long trip, and we came without our children."

Nathaniel stepped forward before her voice could waver, and she was thankful for it.

"Joe, this is Hermann Beeger, the metallurgist from Germany. You wrote that he could stay in the bachelor quarters above your store for a while."

"He's more than welcome. You didn't say where *you* would stay. Your house is still almost empty."

"Alice and I will stay at the Argenta Hotel in Black Hawk until our furnishings arrive." He kept an eye on the drivers to make sure their trunks were left on top and only Hermann's unloaded.

Joe nodded but said nothing for a moment. "Oh, by the way, Nathaniel," he finally said, "David and Edward sent word that they are eager to meet with you. James Lyon has been busy lately."

Joe turned to Hermann. "Come with me, Herr Beeger. It's nothing fancy, but I'm sure the room will meet your needs." Then he turned back to Alice and Nathaniel as they stepped up to reboard the stage. "Nice to meet you, Mrs. Hill . . . Alice. Nathaniel, I will be happy to show Hermann around Central City tomorrow and bring him to the office the day after next." He gave a wave to them as they bumped along the road to Black Hawk.

EIGHTEEN

ᛳ

At breakfast the next morning, Nathaniel followed Alice's gaze as she looked out the window of the Argenta Hotel. There was still snow on the ground wherever it had not been trammeled into the dirt by horse and pedestrian traffic. The two-story hotel was crowded in among the other buildings marching up the steep incline of Black Hawk's main street. The intense sunlight danced through the streaks of dirt on the windows and played against the mirror behind the bar. He smiled to himself as he realized that she had never seen a bar before she started traveling to the Colorado Territory.

"I'm famished," she said, turning to look at him, "but I'm almost too busy looking at everything to eat. You've already finished and I'm still picking at things."

She looked overtired to Nathaniel, even after a night's sleep in a bed.

"Sorry, I guess I gobbled my food down. I was hungry too," he replied. He'd been looking at the newspaper before catching his wife in the act of surveying her surroundings, and now he tossed it aside. "Not much news in the paper."

She seemed a bit distant to him, and he imagined that she was thinking of the children. He avoided inquiring about her thoughts because he knew that if he was right, to do so would only stir up her emotions and make him feel guilty. "Did you hear Joe say that David and Edward are anxious to see me?"

"Yes. What does it mean, Nat?"

"It could really mean anything." He wanted to jump up and walk down the street to his office to find out, but said to her, "It can wait until tomorrow. I had the clerk send them a message that we have arrived. Today I want to show you around the town." Nathaniel smiled and took out his handkerchief to carefully wipe the bushy mustache he had grown on the way out.

"Are we going to walk?"

"No, not this time. There is still quite a bit of snow. While you finish, I'll walk to the stable and rent a buggy."

Back at the hotel, he tied the buggy to the scarred hitching post and went in to get her. She was standing at the front door waiting. He crooked his right elbow for her hand, squeezing it close to him with pride as they went down the stairs toward the buggy. For three years he had wanted to show Alice his life in Black Hawk, and now it was her new home, even if their house was mostly empty.

Alice looked around. "The mountains are so high and rocky. Everything is so harsh compared to the trees and gentle hills of Providence. Even the smell is different. There's none of the salty sea breeze we get by the ocean."

"These mountains may seem high, but they're just the beginning. Here they call them hills—foothills—at the base of the real mountains just to the west of us. It's a different land here. I had the same reaction the first time I saw it. It grows on you." Nathaniel paused. "The sea can be harsh, too."

"I'm surprised people can survive here."

"People have to have a toughness that matches the mountains to survive. Mountains test men here just as the Atlantic does in New England."

"I do say. This *is* a land of surprises."

They were both tired by mid-afternoon when they returned to Black Hawk from Central City. She turned to him and said, "I don't want to sound like I'm complaining, but I haven't seen many women."

"Don't worry. There are some, and more will come in time—school-teachers, wives. Just your being here will give them courage." He turned and patted her leg. "Here's our house, Alice. What do you think?"

Alice looked at the varnished-wood bungalow crowded by others in a row of ungainly residences. Round posts supported the roof over the front porch, dividing the two stories. Sunlight streamed through the windows—four on the first floor on each side, above a stacked rock foundation, and four above in replication around the building.

"There's no paint, but I guess that's all right," Alice said slowly. "It's natural and seems to fit in. But, Nat, there aren't any trees here either."

"Unfortunately, they've used all the trees for the mines and to build houses."

"I think I'll start a garden right away," Alice said with determination. "Maybe I'll even plant new trees—but no one will be allowed to touch *my* trees. I'm also going to make a play yard for Crawford and Isabel."

Nathaniel put his hands on each side of her waist and boosted her down from the buggy, and she followed him up the steep, snowy walk to the house and peeked in one of the front windows. Her feet tingled with the cold. To Nathaniel it seemed as if she was trying to see her future before she stepped into her new home. He opened the door with a flourish. "Voilà, madam, your new home." He put his arms around her and kissed her lightly. "Alice, my life is never the same without you." He kissed her more fervently. "It's too bad there's no furniture. I could make use of more than a cot right now." He smiled down at her, and she melted into his arms.

⇥ ⇤

Their second morning at Black Hawk, Nathaniel was jittery to leave for his office while Alice was still eating her breakfast at a leisurely pace.

While showing Alice Black Hawk and Central City the previous day, he had been startled to see that the sign on Lyon's building had been removed. The windows were bare and the only occupied portion was the small end section he occupied.

The hotel clock chimed eight. It was time to be on his way, but he wanted to make sure Alice did not feel abandoned. He took the napkin from his lap and put it beside his empty plate. "Alice, I need to go to the office so I can introduce Hermann to David and Edward. It's going to take a while to get caught up, but I can take time to come back here for lunch. Will that suit you?"

"That's fine," she said sleepily. "I need to write Mama and Kate to let them know about our trip and ask about the children."

He could read no concern about his leaving in her tired blue eyes. "You don't have to stay inside."

"Don't worry, I won't. I might get out this afternoon and get to know the town better."

Nathaniel's muscles relaxed at her effort to appear confident. It was probably put on, like her smile, but he was grateful.

He got up and kissed the top of her head. "I'll be back around noon."

Once outside, he took long, rapid strides up the incline toward his office. Half a block away he could see Joe's empty supply cart pull up in front of the office to let Hermann step down onto the board walkway. Joe gave Nathaniel a cheerful wave as he slapped the reins to start back for Central City.

"Good morning, Hermann. Ready to go to work?" Nathaniel reached for the brass knob to enter. As they entered, his managers jumped to attention like two soldiers recognizing a returning general, one with a new, full mustache. "Good morning, David. Morning, Edward. I'm glad to be back." He put his hat on the shelf over the coat hooks and placed Hermann's squat felt crown hat next to it. "Let me introduce you to your new colleague, Hermann Beeger."

David and Edward bumped into each other in the tight space as they rushed to shake his hand. "Was your trip uneventful?" Edward asked.

"Nerve-wracking as always. There was snow along the way, but not the storms I feared. In fact, we saw many travelers braving the road. The good news is that we made it in one piece."

"How did Mrs. Hill fare?" David inquired.

"Mrs. Hill is fine, just tired. She is looking forward to meeting you and wonders if we all might have Sunday dinner together at the hotel. She sends an apology that she can't entertain you at our house until the furniture arrives."

He walked to his desk. "Take a seat, gentlemen. Get Hermann a chair and catch us up." The two managers sat at the narrow ends of the long table and put a chair for Hermann at the long side. Nathaniel pulled the wobbly swivel chair up to his desk and positioned it so he could see everyone.

David began. "You know James Lyon's history. He spent a fortune, mostly on procedures that weren't suitable to western ores. His last money went to his smelter, the one that broke down before you left."

"Most of the money went for construction—shoddy construction, if you ask me," Edward interjected.

"So my friend John Peirce was right," Nathaniel mused out loud. The three men looked at him quizzically. "James rushed instead of thinking things through."

Edward tapped the pencil as he spoke. "James had almost run out of money, but he received an infusion of new funds when he shifted to his modified version of the Swansea method."

"But even then, he wasn't a good manager," David said. "With high overhead, his profits were not enough to get the plant working again. He recently put it up for sale. He's more or less closed shop."

Nathaniel's eyebrows shot up. "Well, well, well, that's interesting news. It explains the empty building. I've been thinking about that since I drove by yesterday. Has his plant been sold?"

"We haven't heard of any offers—at least not yet," Edward said. "There aren't many buyers in these parts."

"That may be to our advantage. What if we take a look-see and figure out if it's worth buying? It would be a good idea to take Hermann over there with you this afternoon for his opinion."

David and Edward glanced at each other with barely perceptible smiles. Nathaniel suspected that they had been discussing the possibility of buying Lyon's interests while he was gone.

"In the meantime, I have some news for you. When I arrived at the hotel, there were letters waiting for me expressing interest in the Swansea method." Spreading them on his desk like four playing cards, Nathaniel explained, "Not only does Warren Merrill want to learn more about our plans, but so does Gardner Colby. Colby manufactures woolens and imports a variety of dry goods." He tapped the third letter. "Joseph Sawyer, also a woolen producer, is interested too. Three of his sons studied chemistry under me at Brown." Nathaniel touched the last letter. "This is from James Converse, a shoe manufacturer. Merrill persuaded him to join in as well. They are all interested in opportunities in the West, but they need to know more about what we are planning."

"Mr. Hill, before you go too far, you should know that most of Lyon's plant will have to be torn down. James built it too fast," David ruffled his papers looking for figures on the Lyon property. "That's going to add cost before we can even start building anything new."

"Land is in short supply in this hill-stacked town," Nathaniel pointed out, "and Lyon's property is the most practical piece available at the moment. If Hermann agrees that it is of value, we can save money by starting to tear some of it down ourselves. Later, we will have to hire workers to dismantle the bigger equipment. You're right. Buying the property will add expense, but there is little other choice."

"We can probably give you some cost figures on how much money it would take to disassemble his plant fairly quickly," Edward said.

His slightly sheepish look told Nathaniel that he had probably already begun to compile that information. "We will need to know the price of the property, how much it will cost to tear down the plant, and the cost to build our own version of a smelter. The figures will have to make an air-tight case to get investors on board."

"Would you like us to go from start to finish with the Hill companies' figures for Herr Beeger?" Edward asked, twisting open his inkwell to get ready.

Hermann nodded.

"That would suit me fine," Nathaniel said. "I'd also like a review."

David and Edward took turns relaying news about Gilpin County as well as Lyon's property. After looking at figures for over three hours, Nathaniel rubbed his eyes in weariness. They had good information about the cost of the Lyon property and the expense of tearing it down. Edward and David had been looking at options ever since James Lyon had moved out of the building, making a contest of it to see who could come up with the most solid possibilities. Nathaniel was grateful to have two managers with enough independence and foresight to work so effectively in his absence, but they still needed to build a convincing budget for their investors.

Now that Hermann Beeger had joined them, he could verify the veracity of their proposal. Whatever they did, Nathaniel was convinced that they needed to be thorough in creating their own adaptation of the Swansea process. James Lyon's tendency to be expeditious without being methodical and careful had no doubt led to his failure. Nathaniel would not make the same mistake.

The short, stout German with square jaw and ruddy complexion had been doing more listening than speaking as Nathaniel's managers filled them in. Now Nathaniel wanted his opinion. "Hermann, what do you think?"

"I want to take a careful look at what your men have put together, but I'm relieved to know there isn't immediate competition, and I need to understand what went wrong with Lyon's plant." Beeger stroked his gnarly gray beard before continuing. "I have worked in Swansea and have confidence in the process. But there is a difference. In Swansea, the purpose is to recover copper. Granted, they expanded it to collect silver and gold because copper holds those metals."

"And here it is the reverse," Nathaniel added. "We use copper to hold the silver and gold. There is little copper in Colorado, and it isn't an exportable product."

Hermann tilted his chin toward the four letters on the desk. "Mr. Hill, do you think those investors will be willing to commit? We can't construct anything without money."

"The failures of Lyon's company will make them wary. We will have to prove to them how our effort will be different. It has to be well built and well organized using our version of the Swansea system." Nathaniel's brown eyes gleamed with enthusiasm. "I believe we can do it . . . and help the economy in the process. Convincing others will be part of the challenge. I would like the three of you to put together the figures to demonstrate the possibilities so we can send them off as soon as we can."

They had enough money to buy Lyon's property, but that was it. They needed investors to sign on quickly. The good news was that James Lyon appeared to be desperate to sell his property. Nathaniel did not want to take advantage of him, but he did want to get the property at a good price. The managers had put together a fair offer, and Nathaniel hoped that James would accept it, even though his investors would suffer a loss. But Nathaniel knew that his crew would have to tear down his existing structures before they could make use of his four acres, and that would cost both time and money. If Lyon accepted the offer, Nathaniel would have Hermann draw up a schematic of what he was going to call the Hill Smelter and put figures to it.

He was excited about the plan and eager to share it with Alice over lunch.

⟶ ⟵

After breakfast, Alice had gone upstairs to their room and located her slant-topped lap desk among her baggage. She was keen to describe her journey to her mother and Kate.

Black Hawk
April 4, 1866
Dear Mama,

I am hoping for a letter from you shortly telling me stories of the dear little children. My fractured schedule has helped keep my mind from missing their sweet presence.

Our trip required six different railroad lines and one steamboat just to reach Atchison, Kansas. We encountered the necessity of many river crossings. We had to be careful with our connections because every railroad uses a different time. You may think a train left at 2:00, but that may not have been correct. Cleveland had twelve different time zones to contend with.

The rolling hills of Illinois and Missouri are pleasant and filled with cattle, pigs, and timberland. As we followed the Platte River for four hundred miles from Fort Kearney, the land became arid. For long stretches, the Plains were covered with dead grass, and then it changed to a blanket of white when a wet snow fell during one entire day. We were told that when the temperature warmed and the snow melted, the spring grass grew only to dry up again during the latter part of May. This dry grass is almost as nutritious as grain, and cattle are as fat as our best grain-fed cattle.

The road had many travelers. Sometimes we saw a hundred oxcarts in a day. We held our breath for two days as we watched a good number of Indians on their way south to the Republican River. They had their squaws and papooses with them and presented no danger. The drivers fear the bushwhackers, which are gangs from Kansas and Missouri that attack trains, stages, forts, and even family houses as much as they do the Indians.

We stopped in Denver only briefly because the town was in a state of anxiety over threats from both Indians and bushwhackers.

I will write again about our tour of Black Hawk and our new home, as well as Central City, which is only a mile to the west of Black Hawk.

My heart aches when I think how much I miss you, Kate, and most of all, our little children. Kiss them each for me and tell them stories so they will not forget their Mama.

Your loving daughter,
Alice

She folded the letter and addressed the outside. Her head bowed as she collected her emotions, then she lifted the flap of her writing box for another sheet of paper to write Kate.

Over a noon meal of fried pork chops and syrupy peaches, Nathaniel explained to Alice what he and his managers had decided that morning about buying James Lyon's property and what they would do with it. They would start with something much smaller than the plants he and John had seen in Wales. There would be two roasting furnaces and one smelting unit to produce a matte of gold and silver combined with copper. No refinery would be built initially. He wanted to prove that the smelter could operate first.

Alice was grateful to be in the role of confidant again, and while it all sounded risky to her, she knew that he would carefully think through and manage the project because that was the kind of man he was.

Nathaniel warned her that he would be spending many hours at the office for a couple of weeks but promised to take her to Denver once the proposals were sent to his investors. She was excited about the prospects of seeing Denver. They had barely stopped there on their way to Black Hawk, and she had not even had the opportunity to meet his friend Tom Potter.

A trip to Denver held the added benefit of giving her a chance to purchase things for the house that she could not get at Joe Watson's store. The furniture would be arriving soon, and she began making a list in her head of what be needed.

→ ←

They arrived in Denver early on a Friday afternoon in April. Nathaniel and Alice had rented a black carriage with a cover to protect them against inclement weather. Today, the town was dry, brown, and dusty. Residents had begun to dig the City Ditch to give relief to the barrenness, but it was a long way from being completed.

Nathaniel had made reservations for two nights at the Pioneer Hotel. Alice would shop in the afternoon and on Saturday morning when the stores were open. They planned to leave after church on Sunday.

It had been nearly three years since Nathaniel's first visit and nine years since Denver was founded. The town of 4,700 people still held inexplicable appeal to him. He and Alice passed the post office, hook and ladder company, and barbershop. There were more saloons than anything cultural and far more cattle than women. Nevertheless, Denver had more to offer than Black Hawk or Central City, and Nathaniel knew that Alice was happy for the change of scenery.

And he thought she looked beautiful that morning. She wore a wide-brimmed hat with a curving lavender plume at the crown. Her short mauve jacket covered the lace blouse tucked into her black, softly crenu-lated wool skirt. A black cape was wrapped around her shoulders to keep her warm. It was the first time she had worn her Sunday-best clothing since she arrived.

They dropped the horse and carriage at the livery stable to be tended to and walked down Arapahoe Street for two blocks. Nathaniel stopped in front of a one-story red brick house with a gabled metal roof. "Here is where Tom lives." The white trim of the four-paned windows matched the painted front door. "Let me introduce you, and then you can be on your way." He rapped on the door, and in a few moments, Tom swung it open.

"Tom, I've brought Alice to Denver to shop for our new house, and before she does that, I wanted to introduce you to her."

She extended her hand to the young man. "Reverend Potter, I've looked forward to meeting you ever since Nat described your conversations. It's a pleasure to finally meet you."

"Can you come in?" he asked. "I have tea in the cupboard and maybe even a few biscuits. Nothing fancy." He smiled, releasing her hand.

"Ordinarily, I would enjoy that, but I only have a little time to shop, so I need to get started." Her tone was light and cheerful. "We plan to attend your church service, so I will see you on Sunday."

"Then I look forward to talking after the service." Tom turned to Nathaniel. "Can you stay while Alice shops?"

"I don't want to interrupt."

"You won't be. I have a little extra time."

Nathaniel kissed Alice's cheek. "Take your time. I'll meet you back at our room at the Pioneer. You can go there whenever you're through."

"Reverend Potter, Nat has told me about your church service. I look forward to seeing you again Sunday." She waved good-bye, then walked down the step and to the street toward the dry goods store.

Nathaniel turned away from watching Alice depart. "Are you in the midst of your Sunday sermon?"

"I'm almost finished." He closed the door and took Nathaniel's coat. "I need something more for the conclusion. Making sure my parishioners leave with inspiration is an important part of a sermon—and one with which I frequently have difficulty."

Nathaniel shook his head in friendly disagreement. "From my experience, you have a clever knack about leaving your congregation with something to take home to mull over for the rest of the week . . . and enough curiosity to come back for more the following Sunday. I've spent many sheets of paper explaining your ideas to Alice in my letters to her."

"The messages are sometimes slow to come to me. Have a seat. Maybe a good conversation will loosen my ruminations." His engaging smile lit his face.

The sight of the familiar chair made Nathaniel's mind whir in anticipation of Tom's latest contemplations.

"I've acquired some chocolate from a parishioner. It's better than the powdered cocoa I usually offer you. What about some hot chocolate for you? I'll put the last of the coffee in *my* cup."

"Thanks. As a matter of fact, I often order hot cocoa since you introduced me to it." He followed Tom into the kitchen so he could watch the preparation of the drink. Tom got milk from the icebox and set a small saucepan on the Franklin stove just inside the kitchen door. Then he shaved off dark brown curls of chocolate with the knife and dropped them into the warming milk.

"It's from Mexico. I keep a supply in my cupboard. It promotes talking."

Nathaniel laughed. "Conversation needs little prompting with you."

When the milk was heated, he poured it into a metal cup, added a lump of sugar, and took a few steps to extend the curved handle for Nathaniel to grasp.

Nathaniel took a careful sip of the too-hot liquid, set the cup on the side table, and leaned back against the cushion, enjoying the surroundings.

"What's in store for the congregation Sunday? Alice will finally get to hear your words instead of my rambling on about them in ink."

Tom settled into his own chair. "To have Alice among the congregation will be a pleasure. We'll be discussing aspirations of the human soul."

Nathaniel blinked, trying to absorb the scope of the words. "You always elevate my thinking. When I'm mired down with disappointment in getting metal out of the ore, it is hard to think of something lofty." He picked his cup and sipped the rich concoction. "This chocolate is even better than the cocoa I remember, and so are your words. For a man still in his twenties, you sail in deep waters of thought." Admiration rang in his voice. "This lesson sounds as if it was designed for me, and yet, you didn't know I planned to attend church. I suspect most of the congregation will feel the same."

"Aren't aspirations a challenge for everyone? Most people spend too little time considering what they want from life, and only a few are scientific about their futures. The latter know what they want and go after it. For some, what constitutes a worthy aspiration is not clear."

Nathaniel nodded. "Yes, some people take things as they come, almost like a twig floating down a creek, while others try to change the course of the water. And you threw in science. Unfortunately, not everyone is guided by science. Sometimes I think most people would rather go through their lives ignoring facts and just deciding things on the basis of emotion."

"Well," Tom replied, "there needs to be a balance between relying on science, which is inherently materialistic, and reacting to emotions, which are the feelings that make us human. Both science and emotions are fallible, and both can lead to either moral or immoral behavior."

"But in many cases, science can make conditions better for everyone. Like the telegraph. It's making communication easier and faster. And that's just one example."

"Yes, but we must be careful that as science advances, our morals do the same. Like Jason and his Argonauts. Can a quest be considered worthy if it's simply achieving a goal or for material reward? Shouldn't honor and consideration for others play a part?"

Nathaniel paused to consider. "I think you are saying that the ends should not justify the means. I agree with that, but does every goal have to have a broader purpose?"

Tom raised his eyebrows. "Hmm. In my mind, the greater good should always be considered. Life is held together by finding the boundary between one's own desires and a larger purpose."

Nathaniel leaned back on the rawhide cushion and let Tom's views sink in like ink on a blotter. "I'd like to give it more thought before I decide if I agree or disagree with you. If science can provide a way to get valuable metals out of the ore, it will help the West's economy and provide jobs in many different occupations—as well as bring me income." He shook his head in respect. "As usual, you've given me ideas to ruminate about."

Nathaniel finished the last hot chocolate in his cup and pushed himself up from the chair. "I regret that I'm too far away in Black Hawk to come to your church every Sunday to listen to your philosophy, but Alice and I *will* be there this Sunday."

"They're God's words, and I regret not being able to test you on a weekly basis," Tom replied as he got up. "You're one of my best sounding boards."

"That reminds me. I forgot to ask you how much luck you've had in raising money for a new church building."

"It hasn't gone as fast as I hoped. I've had some success, but not quite enough to hire an architect yet. I suspect that religion and taking care of the poor are not the inducements that the potential for profit and the lure of expanding scientific knowledge are. Fortunately, the most faithful are always willing to help, and I am getting closer to my goal." His face dropped. "Raising money is humbling, and it takes time from what I should be doing."

Nathaniel took his hat from the hook and matched Tom's firm handshake with his own strong grip. "We're in complete agreement about the burden of raising money. It takes way too much time for me too."

NINETEEN

James Lyon's property was at a bargain price, but Nathaniel had to deplete his remaining business coffers and additional personal savings to buy it. Once the Hill companies owned the four-acre site, Nathaniel and his men were eager to look more closely at Lyon's failed smelter. They put on work clothes and took sledge hammers and pick axes to begin tearing down the interior walls and floor so they could better see the mechanics of the plant. Afterward, they would hire a construction crew to dismantle the building's mechanical equipment. After a morning of work, dirt mingled with the sweat on their faces and clung to their overalls and boots. A heap of dismantled bricks and splintered timber lay discarded in a pile outside.

Nathaniel's muscles stung with exertion, and he could see that he was not alone. His men seemed as exhausted as he felt when they began ripping up floorboards around the concave brick hearth. They worked from the center to the edge of the room, leaving two feet of boards at the perimeter on which to gingerly balance themselves.

Hermann Beeger was kneeling on the bricks of the defunct flooring when he leaned down with an iron lever in his right hand to begin wrenching away more of the flooring. He paused when the first boards came up, then he seemed to hesitate before stepping to the side and letting the sun shine into the foundation. He knelt down again, and stretched his arm through the hole. "Oh my Gott! Oh my Gott!" he called out as he began splintering the bricks in haste.

"What's wrong, Hermann? What's the matter?" Nathaniel stepped carefully down onto the floor next to his metallurgist, balancing on a remaining strip of boards. Hermann had removed the center section.

"Nein. Nothing's the matter at all. There's been a leak—a big leak." He stood up and carefully walked over to the iron machinery. "It must have from come here, from the hearth of the furnace where no one could see where it was going." The German let a smile crack his lips. "Vott does it mean? Look underneath. It is the finished matte of gold, silver, and copper—maybe tons of it. It slipped through the hearth into the foundation. It means that we will stop running at a loss for a time."

Nathaniel brushed the airborne debris off his jacket as he tried to digest the information. "You say it's matte, Hermann? It could be shipped to Swansea for refining without doing anything else?" He thrust his hands toward the ceiling in fatigue-delirious celebration. "We needed some luck, and for once, we got it."

All four men were now blistering their hands to rip up boards, leaving only edges big enough for the width of their shoes to stand on.

"Once we know how much there is, we have to make arrangements to ship it to Swansea," Hermann said heartily, beaming. "With this to bring in a little income, maybe we'll be out of the red—temporarily at least."

Nathaniel turned to his metallurgist. "James Lyon and his men could not have known about this, could they?"

"No one could have," Hermann replied as he stroked his whisker-grizzled chin. "It was an accident . . . maybe from going too fast."

Nathaniel turned sober. Looking at David, Edward, and Hermann, he said, "It's a lesson to us. We will pay the same price James did if we are not careful. We have to put everything we do under a microscope. If James had known about this, he might have made a profit and kept the Lyon smelter going. He'll be undone when he finds out."

Nathaniel regarded their weary, dirt-streaked faces. "We need to keep this to ourselves until we know how much there is." He shook each of their hands. "I think we've put in more than a day's work."

He believed that even more as he groaned with fatigue and aching muscles when he swung his legs over the side of the bed to get up the next morning. After breakfast at the Argenta with Alice, he walked stiffly up the hill to his office. For him, the first order of business was to write about finding the hidden matte to the men who had shown interest in investing in the West: Warren Merrill, James Converse, Gardner Colby, and Joseph Sawyer. He had sent letters weeks ago about the demise of competition in the area for smelting after purchasing Lyon's property. The news of the discovered matte would not make building a new smelter less risky, but it was one more bit of positive information.

Nathaniel was correct about the effect of the good news. In two weeks, a messenger delivered the strips of telegram tape pasted on a small piece of yellow paper from Warren Merrill. Nathaniel read it once, and then he read it again. David, Edward, and Hermann were looking at him curiously. Good news illumined his face. "Men, the plan we sent to Boston has been approved. Our investors have begun legal work to establish the Boston and Colorado Smelting Company with a capitalization of two hundred thousand dollars. They have asked me to be the company's agent and local manager, and all of you its employees."

The four of them stood beside the long table and shook hands all around, murmured enthusiasm mixed with relief. Even the understated German could not restrain a half-cast smile. The new smelter would be underway.

Alice felt revived with something to occupy her time when their furniture finally arrived in Black Hawk at the end of April. She had hoped having her own possessions would make her new house feel like home. Instead, they conjured up memories that disheartened her. When she first tried to position all her furnishings, she was dismayed. Everything looked out of place in the rustic house. Half of her belongings had been left behind, but even so, the heavy mahogany furniture crowded every room. The dining room table, inherited from her grandmother, left little space to pull out the chairs. Memories of evenings spent in conversation around it with other faculty members and their wives warmed her heart. She wondered if she would ever again have friends like that or conversations as rewarding as those on a university campus. It took weeks of work, but she finally managed to get everything to fit.

Nathaniel's new study was more an alcove than a room, and it was now connected to the kitchen rather than down the hall from it. His swivel chair sat in front of his already neatly arranged desk. The room was lined with shelf after shelf of his science books and her history books. She busied herself with sewing curtains once the house was arranged as she wanted. Anything needed for warmth or decoration had to be made by her, and provisions of any kind were difficult to get. She felt fortunate to have the gossamer white material she was using for the curtains.

Without the diversion of academia and care of their children, Alice's relationship with Nathaniel had taken on a close dependency. He had confided in her that he was having trouble getting the supplies he needed. The spring rains in the Midwest were holding up the equipment he had ordered, and they were going to have to get their fire brick from Golden because it was the only place they could find it. But Hermann was not happy with the quality of the Golden brick. Still, Nathaniel felt they were on the right track. The building process was underway. They just needed to keep their patience and avoid being reckless.

It was nearly June, and she had been in Colorado since March. She missed her children and finally broached the subject with Nathaniel. "Now that we are settled here and you're building your own smelter, can we bring the children here? I miss the sound of laughter as they run down the hall. I miss their giggling in the cold mornings as they get out of bed and I snuggle them into their clothes. I miss their soft kisses and endless questions. They have to say their prayers without me—"

"Alice, stop. Please don't torture yourself. Don't you think I miss them too?"

"Of course," she said softly, "but for me, our children are my life. I want to watch them grow and hold them when they need to be comforted."

"Crawford will definitely take to these mountains," Nathaniel replied, chuckling.

"We can't just talk about it in terms of someday or it will never happen. I want to make a plan for my life—like you did with your smelter."

"How in the world would they come? It's simply not possible with the danger of murder or kidnapping. Denver is under martial law every other week."

She refused to think any longer about all the things that might or might not happen as an excuse. "I've asked Kate to come for a visit every time I write to her. You know how she likes adventure." Alice picked up her sewing to stay calm.

"What does Kate have to do with Crawford and Isabel?"

"She could bring them. The weather may be bad for moving equipment, but not for travel. As you keep saying, despite the dangers, things are getting easier."

"That's absurd. Kate is a sheltered city girl ... and she has no children—"

"She has spent almost as much time with the children as Mama has. They adore her. She is also strong and brave. I would have no hesitation about having her bring them here. There are guards everywhere."

Nathaniel frowned at her. "This is a wild notion. Can't you wait until we can go back to retrieve them?"

"Your business always has demands, like getting equipment through the mud. Everyone depends on you. You can never leave."

"Let's wait until I get things on an even keel, at least."

"I'm not sure there will ever be an even keel," she challenged.

He glared at her, "I'll think about it."

"I want to set a date for when Kate comes. She can use the third bedroom when she's here. Most of all, I want to have Crawford and Isabel in their own room upstairs." She looked at him with determination.

"Alice, how do you come up with all these ideas about travel? You are just as concerned about the danger as I am."

"It is a chance we'll have to take. We won't have a true family until we are all together again. I understand that you could not give up your dreams, but the children are what I dream about. They give meaning and definition to my life. I can't live without them."

When he seemed to soften a little and promised again to think about it, she stopped talking. She knew she had said all she dared to for the time being.

→ ←

His was sitting at his second-hand desk in his office, mired in the endless mission of cutting costs while still maintaining quality, when a firm knock interrupted him. He looked up to see Joe Watson hesitantly open the office door and stick his head in. "Joe? What brings you from Central City so early? Come in."

"I had an early delivery so I thought I'd stop by. Mind if I have a word with you?"

"Not at all. Shut the door so you don't let in the flies."

"Could you come outside?" Joe's eyes made a rapid visual sweep of the office, glancing at Edward and David, who were looking curiously at him.

"Outside?"

Joe nodded.

"All right." Nathaniel slowly rose, reluctant to leave the distressing budget. Grabbing both his jacket and hat, he followed Joe out the door. By the time he stepped onto the sunny walkway, Joe was already far ahead of him, and he had to hurry to catch up. "Is something the matter?"

"I just received a letter."

"The stage came to Central City already this morning?"

"No, it came last night, but it was too late to come to Black Hawk. I don't think I had a moment of sleep all night thinking about it."

"Is it your family?"

Joe kicked a loose piece of dirt off the board walkway. "It's not my family. It's Claire."

"Claire? Has something happened to Claire?"

"No. Well . . . yes. Claire is on her way to Denver. She's going to be a teacher there so she can be closer to me in Central City."

Nathaniel was starting to laugh as he turned to face Joe, but he swallowed it when he saw Joe's stricken countenance. "Let's take a turn around the block instead of just standing here."

They stepped into the road to stay in the sun and began to walk.

"I'm in a predicament, Nathaniel. What am I going to tell Emily at the café? What am I going to tell Claire when she gets to Colorado?"

Nathaniel shook his head and paused in the middle of the street until a wagon demanded the right of way. "You have a dilemma all right."

"Claire doesn't know about Emily, and Emily doesn't know about Claire," Joe said in a strangled voice. "I'm not at fault. I haven't made promises to anyone. I've written letters to Claire and picnicked with Emily—nothing more."

"Sometimes women take a kind act too optimistically. It's part of their makeup."

"I don't know what to do. If Claire comes to Denver to teach and then visits Central City, Emily is going to know."

"Which one do you favor?"

Joe took a few paces before answering. "I guess it depends on who I'm thinking about at the time. Claire is the girl of my youth, and she feels as familiar as family. Reading her letters links me to my past. She is a wonderful, kind person."

"And Emily?"

"Emily is different from my family. She had the courage to move here. Can you imagine a young woman doing that? She followed her family, but it was still a brave thing to do. I like her pluck, and I love to hold her in my arms. It's more than that. There is a curiosity about her, especially about plants and flowers. Whenever we are together, she points things out to me that I never noticed before." He paused with a frown. "With her bright face and figure, every man is after her. They don't have her best interests in mind, and I don't want anything bad to happen to her." He hung his head. "I have romantic notions for both."

"That's not going to make anyone happy."

"Whenever I'm just about ready to make an offer to Emily, I get a letter from Claire, and it rekindles the warm feeling I had for her at home. In a way, she is just as brave as Emily in coming to the West on her own. If she comes all that way and finds I'm committed to someone else, she will be brokenhearted."

Nathaniel sighed. "You're in a pickle, Joe. I don't envy you. The only advice I can give is to be honest."

"Be honest? What does that mean? Talk to one about the other? How could I possibly do that?"

"It's better for them to find out from you than from someone else."

"You must think I'm a coward . . . or a cad," Joe looked up, dreading affirmation.

"Those are your words, not mine. Give it some time, Joe. Since Claire is moving to Denver, there is some separation. Any decision will have consequences, but the situation won't go away just because you ignore it." Nathaniel patted his friend's arm and turned to go back to his office.

The sun was making a fiery late summer exit, sending streaky flames of clouds across the sky when Nathaniel opened the varnished door of his home. He had barely closed it when Alice came down the short hallway between the dining room and the front room, her heels clicking with rapid strikes. She leaned up and brushed her lips tenderly across his.

"Nat, I know you haven't had time to settle, but I have to tell you my news." She took his jacket and hat and put them on a hook. "I got a letter from Kate today. She is hoping for your approval to make travel arrangements to bring the children to Black Hawk."

He squeezed his eyes shut and followed her into the kitchen. "I've been so preoccupied, I haven't had time to tell you what I plan to do," he said.

"Plan to do about the children?"

"In part. Warren Merrill wants to come to Colorado to see the new Boston and Colorado Smelting Company operations. I want to finish the smelter before he comes."

"He's been one of your longest supporters, hasn't he?" she asked, as she arranged sliced bread in a napkin-lined basket.

"He gave me my first consulting jobs and invested in the chemistry laboratory at Brown. Without him, I would not have made a name outside the university. I owe him a lot."

Alice took two bowls off the shelf. "What does Mr. Merrill have to do with Kate?"

"He can accompany Kate and the children on their cross-country trip. It is unreasonable to consider letting Crawford and Isabel travel without a man to protect them. No doubt there could be danger even with him along. The Plains are still in turmoil."

"Oh?" Alice stopped motionless with a pitcher of water in her hand. "That's an interesting notion. That's a long trip for Kate to be with someone she's never met before."

"An unmarried woman traveling alone puts the children in too much peril, Alice. I won't allow it."

She put the pitcher down, came over to him, and kissed him. "Thank you, Nat," she said in his ear. "Thank you. I'll let Kate know what you want her to do in my next letter. When have you arranged for Mr. Merrill to come?"

Nathaniel was still almost reeling from her sudden expression of affection, and it took a moment before he found his voice. "He can leave the first of September before there is much danger of snow. Do you think that will suit Kate?"

Alice nodded. "I think it will. Kate is the only friend I have from home who envied my move to Colorado. She wants to come . . . and the children. I get to see my children."

He watched her hands tremble as she scooped chunks of hot chicken and vegetables from the black cast-iron pot and put them into the bowls. Even though he had put a bit of a wrench in her plans, Alice exuded happiness. Not only did that please him, but so did the thought that his little family would soon all be together in Black Hawk.

As he washed his hands for dinner, Nathaniel told Alice about his earlier conversation with Joe, knowing that she would not only have a womanly perspective about the Emily-Claire dilemma, but she would also probably provide wise counsel on the matter.

In rhythmic movements, the hired workers stooped and lifted as they covered the wide basin-like depression with hundreds of neatly placed firebricks. The temperature was ninety degrees when the midday sun rose to its apex—hot for the end of June—scorching the laborers. They were failed miners whom Hermann Beeger had recruited to build a hearth for the new Boston and Colorado Smelting Company. Nicknamed Beeger's Army, they were in desperate need of cash because of their own hardships. They met his exacting demands to get paid, but at the end of the day, they groused bitterly about the hard work when they retreated to a bar. Nathaniel had been told that they referred to Beeger as a Teutonic martinet, and they often used even more vulgar terms.

The firebrick had finally come from Golden, but the equipment had yet to arrive from St. Louis. The men were restless, thanks to the heat and the wondering when the rest of the equipment would get there. Tension caused friction resulting in minor scuffles. The altercations were about nothing, but agitation was palpable.

Fortunately, by the beginning of July, the last of the equipment had arrived. Before that, Hermann's hired men had managed to complete much of the structure. Two twenty-foot brick smokestacks rose into the jagged gray hills, becoming landmarks in Gilpin County. Tin roofs stretched across the length of the ore house, blast furnace, and receiving sheds. Twelve open ore bins ran along the back side of the building.

Nathaniel made daily trips to the site to check on the progress, despite knowing that Hermann found his scrutiny annoying. He was sick of being asked when it would be done and once even snapped, "It will be done when it is damn good and ready, not before."

Afternoon downpours were leaving the ground soggy, often delaying the work.

The ceiling was of utmost importance. It had to have just the right curve to send the heat down over the hearth evenly. Nathaniel restrained his frustration with the endless testing being done, knowing that the consequences of going too fast could be devastating. Still, an uneasy foreboding neutralized any excitement he had about the building being so close to being done.

When the construction crew left at the end of each Friday, Hermann took a solitary inspection tour of the growing smelter before going down to the office. David kept both a logbook that noted weekly events and a list of what remained to be done. On Friday, August 15, Hermann came in and sat down in his usual chair in the middle of the table, with Edward and David on each side and Nathaniel across the room at his own desk.

"We can fire it up on Monday," he said casually.

Everything in the office stopped as if time itself had stopped.

Edward finally slid his glasses up the bridge of his nose. "You mean it's done?"

"What, are you foolish?" Hermann replied tersely. "Would I start it up if it wasn't finished? I told you the ceiling was the last piece, and we've done all the testing we can without actually firing up the furnace."

Nathaniel felt a gnawing in his gut. So much was at stake. It was not just the scaled-down model of the Welsh system that was on trial, but everything on which he had counted and gone into debt to achieve. He looked at his anxious employees, their faces cramped with tension. They had as much pride invested as he did. "Well, this is it. Monday we see if everything we have put into this pays off."

He unconsciously picked up the large steel bolt saved from his childhood workbench, now kept as a paperweight, and rolled its cool steel along his palm as if it represented the call to challenge that his father had instilled in him. He was apprehensive, but beneath that was a tinge of exhilaration. He had put himself on the line. Success or failure was near at hand. The thought that public failure might be the result was nauseating, but the chance of success kept him buoyed.

The men gathered before daybreak that Monday morning, joined by Joe Watson, who had ridden down from Central City for the event after having been filled in by Nathaniel.

Hermann carefully lit a fiery torch and touched his torch to his specially designed Gerstenhofer roasting furnace before joining Nathaniel and the others. It would take time to get it to the right temperature. The five of them stood silhouetted in the emerging light, their fate hanging.

"How hot does it have to get before you start, Hermann?" Joe asked.

"Fourteen hundred degrees centigrade," Hermann replied evenly, his calm tone belied by the way he was nervously fingering his grizzled beard.

Word had spread, and an expectant crowd began to trickle down to the site to watch, milling and murmuring. Jittery and apprehensive, they all waited for two hours.

Finally, Hermann approached Nathaniel. "It is good. I begin." Hermann's footsteps rang up the stairs until he reached the top. He would pull the level above the hearth to release the ore.

A booming crash told Nathaniel that the ore had been released. He unconsciously put his hands over his ears. The ground shook, and he felt as much as heard a continuous, earth-shattering crack.

"What is happening, Hermann?" Nathaniel shouted above the noise of the escaping gases.

Hermann rejoined the group. It took him some time to answer. "The firebrick did not withstand the heat. It was no good."

"What do you mean, it didn't withstand the heat?" Nathaniel asked. "That's what firebrick is made for."

"Not this time. The cheap bricks didn't work, and there were no others, no matter what we were willing to pay."

In anguish, Nathaniel squeezed his fists closed, fingernails biting into his palms. "What now? What happens now?" he demanded, while the increasing number of onlookers crowded closer to overhear the words between the chemist and metallurgist.

"I have to think about another design."

"Another design?" The two men's faces were less than a foot apart, and the spectators were murmuring among themselves.

Nathaniel thought he heard someone nearby say, "I told you so."

Nathaniel jammed both fists in his pockets. "How long will that take?"

"I don't know yet. It needs to cool."

Nathaniel lowered his voice to keep the assembled crowd from overhearing him as he talked to his men. "This just can't happen. The timing . . . the results. It could not be worse. My principal investor, Warren Merrill, is coming."

"Could you ask him to delay his trip?" David asked.

"He leaves in a few days to come with the children and Kate. They will be here in three weeks. It's too late to delay him." Nathaniel shook his head sullenly. "Who knows how long it will take to rebuild it . . . if we even can. This could be the end of our business."

He smacked his hat against his thigh in frustration. So much time and money had gone into the project. Was it salvageable? He didn't know the answer to that.

TWENTY

ᛆ

She knew she was early when she walked down the steep incline, but she would not consider being late, even though delays were frequent. Excitement, joy, and disbelief took turns swirling around inside her.

Alice stepped up on the wide planks of the walkway in front of the bakery on Main Street. It was a crisp, cool late September morning. The bell on the door gave a friendly tinkle when she pushed it open. Alice greeted the proprietor and breathed in the warm, yeasty aroma before buying six cinnamon buns and six iced cakes.

Outside again, she strolled down the board walkway, admiring the shimmering yellow and gold Aspens on the distant high hills. Alice tried to remember what it felt like to hold her children. Crawford was a lanky five-year-old boy with eyes and hair the color of chestnuts and the nervous energy of his father. And her daughter! When she left Providence, Isabel was a plump cherub with blond hair that sprang into curls above her blue eyes. Even at two, she had outpaced her brother in talkativeness.

The rumble of the stagecoach was evident before it was visible. It was more like a low vibration under her feet than a sound. She jumped up from the bench and ran to the bakery to ask Meg's son to get Nathaniel. Eleven-year-old Timmy galloped down the dusty street, then turned the corner at the end of the block.

When the rangy young driver opened the stage door with a flourish, Alice was beside him. She felt Nathaniel's shoulder next to hers.

Crawford was the first one down the steps, letting go of Kate's hand as he saw his parents standing in front of him. "Mama. Papa. Papa, I protected Izzie and Aunt Kate all the way."

Alice enclosed him with her arms, laughing and kissing both cheeks. "Welcome to your new home, Crawford. Mama is so happy to see you."

Nathaniel pressed her shoulder to take Crawford in his own arms.

She looked up to see her friend. She had forgotten how elegant Kate was and feared she looked like a plump country pumpkin to her. Eyes meeting, they rushed toward each other, arms entangling. Time apart disappeared.

"Mama, Mama," Isabel shrieked. Alice looked up to see a solid balding man in his fifties with kind hazel eyes carrying her blond daughter in his arms. Isabel almost tipped him over as she leaned down for her mother.

"You must be Mrs. Hill. I'm Warren Merrill, your husband's investor. Izzie and I have become friends." His dark fringed eyebrows waggled in an amused gesture. "She didn't seem to be afraid. As a matter of fact, she talked the whole way when she wasn't asleep."

Alice took her daughter from him. "Mr. Merrill, welcome. What a kindness you have done for us. Thank you."

Nathaniel reached around Crawford, still in his arms, to shake his investor's hand. "Good to see you, Warren. One more hug from my children and we will go to the office while the women get settled. I echo my wife's sentiments in gratitude." Turning to Kate with an embrace, he said, "Welcome to the West. Thank you for accompanying the children. We are all grateful for your bravery."

"I left the bravery to Mr. Merrill . . . and Crawford," Kate replied with a wink. "I simply took in all the new scenery along the way. It's vast, isn't it? Some of it is pretty and some could use some water."

Nathaniel gave his blue-eyed daughter another squeeze and disengaged her from his shoulder, passing her to her mother. "We look forward to showing you all of it. Alice is beside herself with joy to have you and the children."

"Come on, everyone. Let's go home," Alice said, taking Crawford's hand.

Kate turned to her. "I'm bursting with questions. It's all so different. How are you really adjusting?"

"Mama, why are all the houses so close together?" Crawford asked.

"I guess it's because it's so hilly. I've gotten used to it," she said, in answer to both Kate and Crawford. "You must be exhausted from traveling." She leaned close as they walked. "I'm enchanted with everyone being together."

Kate laughed melodically. "I can hardly wait to get clean and sit in a real chair."

Once home, Crawford and Isabel sat at the table, wide-eyed and quiet. "All right," Alice said. "Let's have something to eat and then take a bath. Wait till you see your room."

Their eyes flickered with wariness. Alice guessed that they understood it would not look at all like their room at either their home or their grandparents' house. If so, they were right. But she had made their rooms as inviting and cheerful as possible.

After a small bite to eat and their baths, Crawford and Isabel sat on one of the narrow beds in Crawford's room. They would share that room while Kate stayed in the one next to it. Alice pulled a book off the shelf, and they leaned next to her as she began to read through teary eyes. "Mama is not sad," she explained to them, wiping her eyes with her hanky. "It is pure happiness that you are here." They leaned closer into her.

By the third picture book, their eyes were fluttering closed. Gently, she picked up each small body and lovingly turned back the sheets and quilts, tucking them in their beds as she sang a familiar lullaby. When she was sure they were sound asleep, she tiptoed down the narrow staircase.

"They are already asleep," she told Kate. "They must be exhausted. Did you have a nice bath?"

"The water is nearly black from the three of us," she admitted. "I emptied the water on the garden." Hand in hand, they walked up the stairs. "Alice, how do you breathe here? I take a breath, but the air doesn't fill my lungs. I feel like I might faint."

Alice laughed. "Don't worry, Kate. You'll get used to it. I felt the same way. Now I can walk the mile from Black Hawk to Central City at a brisk pace. I expect you will be marching up and down the hills in no time. You're much more slender than I am. Come into the little room I made for Isabel."

The beds were covered with starched white linen spreads trimmed in lace that Alice had tatted. Framed embroideries of red and pink roses hung on the walls. A polished maple wardrobe filled the corner and, at the side, one needlepoint cushion sat on the rocker.

"Alice, I can see your handwork. Thank you, dear friend." Kate reached for the satchel she had brought upstairs. "Here, I have something for you." She retrieved a delicate stack of letters tied in a silk ribbon.

"Before you read these, I wanted to tell you that I'm working with an Irish girl at the Young Women's Christian Association."

Alice looked up, startled. "Not Maggie?"

"No, but she knows Maggie. She told me Maggie is pregnant."

"Pregnant?" Alice's hand flew to her mouth. "I didn't know she was married."

"I think she is, although I don't know the circumstances."

"Oh, Kate, I let her down. If we hadn't left, she might have done something different. Now she may end up like her cousin or parents."

Kate touched her arm sympathetically. "You don't know what would have happened if you had stayed—maybe the same thing. Now, look at your letters." She pulled the ribbon to untie the bow and patted the bed for them to sit down together. Hips and arms touching, Alice took the translucent paper and unfolded it.

"Oh, it's from Mama."

"She's going to miss the children . . . and, of course, you. She became quite accustomed to their company. I've brought letters from other friends of yours. They all wanted me to bring you messages from their hearts."

"Poor Mama. I've stolen her grandchildren and her only daughter to what she considers the wilderness. I feel wretched about that part."

"Alice, don't cry. You'll make the ink run and you'll never know what she said." Kate took her hand. "Thank you for lending me this room. It won't be for too long. After I stay with you a while, I want to go to Yosemite in California. Since I've come all this way, I have to see more of the West. At twenty-seven, I'm afraid I'm drifting into spinsterhood with all the plans I have. I'm lucky my grandmother left me a little money to live on, and even enough to travel if I pinch every single penny."

"Please don't leave too soon. I want you to meet the friends I've made. More families are coming all the time. A few—not many—have brought their children, and Crawford and Isabel will soon make friends." She exhaled unevenly at the thought of her children's futures. "I don't know how much they will suffer from not living in a cultured civilization. It seems we have made a commitment to be here no matter what happens."

"Don't worry, Alice. There are benefits to each way of growing up. With you and Nathaniel as parents, they will be special no matter where they are. You can count on that. When a train track is finally built to Denver, you can take them back to Providence for a vacation." She moved her satchel to the floor and yawned. "All the travel is catching up with me. Thank you for showing me my little room. Tomorrow I'll tackle unpacking my trunk and walking up and down the stairs in this altitude." She put her hand dramatically on her chest. They looked at each other and broke into a fit of giggles like schoolgirls.

→ ←

Alice had waited until the following day to serve a homecoming dinner. She cooked their favorite meal of pot roast, mashed potatoes with gravy, and applesauce—all hard to come by in the mountains. She would surprise them with the iced cakes from Meg's bakery for dessert.

She watched as Nathaniel reached to each side of the table to help cut the children's meat while he peppered them with questions about their trip.

"If you're good and let your mother get you in your night clothes," he told them, "I will read you stories. Would you like that? Then we can all say our prayers together."

After everyone had finished, Kate pushed her chair back and picked up a plate and glass to clear the table. "May I be excused? I'm going to do the dishes tonight while you tend to the children. I'm not long for the world. I can hardly wait for my second night in a real bed instead of a moving stagecoach."

When the children were asleep, Nathaniel and Alice sat together in his study, him at his desk and her in her overstuffed chair. "I'm not sure I'm long for the world either," he said, leaning back in his chair and rubbing his eyes.

"We haven't really had a chance to catch up since the children and Kate arrived," Alice said. "How did your time with Warren Merrill go? Was he furious about the firebrick?" She waited a bit nervously as her husband took a moment before answering.

"Perhaps underneath he was, but he was also willing to listen. After all, I've done work with him for a long time. We spent a couple of hours at the office going over figures. During the time that it took him to travel here, we've ordered more of the only available firebrick, and Hermann is working on a system to modify the structure so the weight is not so sudden on them. That means he will have to give up his famous Gerstenhofer roaster because we now know ore can't be dumped in from the top. Hermann hasn't figured out how to load it from the side yet—or if it is even possible. That will take time."

"Is Mr. Merrill going to take away some of his money?" she asked, concerned.

"There is no doubt that he is interested in returns on his investment. He expects us to work out a solution, but he will talk with the other investors and give us time."

She squeezed her eyes shut and momentarily leaned back in the soft chair. "Thank heavens. The smelter has been such a burden for you. How long will it take to change?"

"Hermann still won't commit to a time frame. He wants to be careful, and I want him to be too. We can't have another failure."

"I hope it's fast. We've had worry for too long."

"Warren wants me to show him around the area for a few days. He asked me as many questions about Colorado as he did about the smelter."

"That's nice of him. He really could have been mean-spirited."

He smiled at her. "Anyone who crosses the Plains with children as young as ours probably doesn't have many mean bones in his body. Actually, I think he may be interested in purchasing some land out here."

Her gaze met his. "One more thing," she said, then hesitated. "I wanted to be sure before I told you." She reached out for his hand. "We're going to have another baby . . . sometime next spring."

He stood up, taking her hands to help her up, and pulled her tightly against him, encircling her with his arms. "I'm very happy," he whispered in her ear.

Her face against the space between his shoulder and jaw, she murmured, "Crawford and Izzie will take a while to adjust to all the changes. They are discombobulated from being torn away from what they know. But this new little person will be of the West from the beginning." She sighed. "Our family is coming around a new bend of our lives."

TWENTY-ONE

A second version of the Hill smelter had to work. There was no room for another failure after Warren Merrill returned to Boston. Nathaniel knew that the burden of redesigning it mainly fell to the metallurgist, Hermann Beeger. He, David, and Edward kept themselves busy researching available equipment, mostly to avoid their apprehension about a new smelter.

Nathaniel had not seen much of Joe Watson of late, so he was happy to oblige when his men came to the office one morning bearing a message from Joe that he would like Nathaniel to meet him for the noon meal that day.

It took him twenty minutes to walk the mile east on Gregory Street to pick up Joe at his store. The air was crisp, but the sun warmed him. Together they walked up the hill, entered the Thunder Café, and sat at their favorite corner table. A man with thinning hair and an apron tied around his waist came through the swinging door to their table. "I'll take your order, gents."

After giving him their orders, Nathaniel looked around and asked Joe if it was Emily's day off.

Joe squirmed in his chair. "Didn't you hear? Emily's gone back to Missouri."

"Went back, you say? To visit?"

"I think for good." His freckles stood out on his pale face.

Nathaniel was taken aback. The young woman had been there for two years. He'd thought she had made Colorado her home. He looked at Joe quizzically.

Joe fidgeted a bit and sighed before answering Nathaniel's unspoken question. "An old beau had been writing Emily all along and finally implored her to return with promise of a ring."

Eyebrows raised in surprise, Nathaniel took a sip of the hot chocolate the waiter had brought. "How do you feel about it?"

"I couldn't believe it when she told me. With my desperation and her tears, it was a scene I never want to repeat. It's hard to understand. Emily and I went on picnics every week this summer. I was thinking about buying her a ring—once I had things settled with Claire. A houseful of red-haired children was beginning to fill my mind." He stirred cream in his coffee with a noisy clank of his spoon.

"I guess that makes your choice a little easier. Is that good news for Claire?"

"I don't think so," Joe said morosely. "Before I knew Emily was leaving, I thought I should meet Claire and tell her my feelings face-to-face. It's been so long since I've seen her." He closed his eyes for a moment. "Do you know what I remember about her? She always smelled like lavender. And there's more. She had perfect penmanship when she wrote on the blackboard, and I can still hear her voice reading stories to younger children. I have to admit, I was looking forward to seeing her again, to talk about home."

"What did Claire say?"

"That's the thing. She wrote back describing her life in Denver. She seems very popular there. The town apparently puts a New England teacher on a pedestal. Claire made no mention of setting a date to meet," Joe said helplessly.

"You seem to have gone from too many to too few, Joe. Any regrets?"

He grimaced. "I really don't want to go through life as a bachelor. When I see you with Alice, I know what's missing from my life, but whenever I got close to making a decision about Emily or Claire, it was like seeing a rattler in the scrub. I turned and backed away the way I came. There is a shortage of women here, and through my own dillydallying, I've lost the two best."

Nathaniel said nothing for a moment as he tried to think of words to console his friend. "It must be disappointing, but how old are you now, Joe?"

"Twenty-six," he replied. "Twenty-six and a bachelor. There aren't many available females in these parts, or at least ones I want to consider for the future."

"You still have time. If there is a next time, you should know that women need attention. You can't just put them on a shelf, pull them off when it's convenient, and forget them the rest of the time." Nathaniel shook his head knowingly. "I've been guilty of that myself."

"Do you think it's too late? I might have already spent all my powder."

"Well, you've learned a lesson the hard way. Maybe the most important is that if you really want something, you have to go after it. Life doesn't always come calling. That would be like asking a deer to fall at your feet as venison dinner instead of having to go hunting."

When they parted, Nathaniel trudged back to Black Hawk ruminating on his good fortune in having a wonderful wife and mother in Alice. If he could just have a bit of the same kind of good fortune with the smelter, he could prove himself a success and make her life a bit easier.

After the firebrick had failed in August, Nathaniel had watched Hermann spend many days at his desk, sketching designs. He took each finished scheme to the site to pace off the measurements. When he returned, he numbered the sketch and put the unsuccessful plan at the back of a notebook. Then he sat down and began again. When he had finally found one worth consideration, he had gone over every detail with Nathaniel, David, and Edward.

After weeks of deliberation, they began building a modified Swansea smelter. Then their construction crews spent months remaking the hearth and constructing charging doors along its long side, through which tons of ore and tailings could be pushed instead of dropping them from above. The technology of roasting both ores and tailings first to reduce the sulfur content and then smelting the products to obtain copper matte was complex and costly. Not until February was it ready to test.

The cold and pessimism kept all but Joe and the Boston and Colorado employees inside. After the last failure, residents were too skeptical to mill around the new site in the cold to see what would happen. Nathaniel tried to stay calm, but his heart pounded as he paced from one end of the site to the other to keep the blood flowing in his chilled feet.

Hermann had spent weeks preparing a mixture of ores and tailings that weighed two tons. When the temperature of the furnace had reached the desired temperature, he cautiously ordered his workmen to push the mixture into the hearth through the side charging doors.

Nathaniel waited for the loud cracking of failed firebrick. The sound did not come. Instead, Hermann raised his hand in jubilation, and Nathaniel's other managers joined him in the rush to embrace the elated German. Keeping their footing in the slippery surface was not easy as they thumped each other in elation and triumph. The long built-up tension was released with success. Nathaniel's first thought was to run home and tell Alice.

Word spread fast that the firebrick—as inferior as the first—held. Gilpin County residents began popping out of warm interiors like gophers in the spring.

⇥ ⇤

For the next week the smelter worked twenty-four hours a day. Billows of smoke came from the twenty-foot-high chimneys, darkening the sky.

Night seemed to fall in the middle of the day, sending black, glassy dirt from the slag to coat any flat surface. The taste of sulphur dioxide was on everyone's tongue, but it was considered a small price to pay for success. With the simple act of lighting the reverbatory furnace and shoving the ore mixture through the doors, the Colorado and Boston Smelting Company had sparked hope for the territory's economy.

Nathaniel had sent word to Tom Potter to join the celebration and spend the night with his family. Tom arrived late in the afternoon. The temperatures were below zero, the roads were hard-packed and ice-slicked, and the surrounding hills looked like pillows of frosted snow. But Black Hawk was warm with convivial celebration. The hoopla had gone on nonstop for a week.

After dinner, Nathaniel and Tom sat in the book-lined study. Alice had brought them cups of steaming dark coffee and milky hot chocolate before she cajoled Crawford and Isabel upstairs for bed. The low light of the lantern stretched against the walls as they talked.

"It's a pleasure to have you at my place for a change, although I have to confess that I miss your deep rawhide chair," Nathaniel said as they sipped their drinks. His friend seemed relaxed in Alice's overstuffed chair, and it occurred to Nathaniel that Tom had the poise and confidence of someone whose opinions evolved from considerable study and thought.

"Thanks for asking me. I'm glad to finally see Black Hawk. Even a brief look tells me you've made yourself known up here. I don't know what I expected, but the smelter dominates the town more than I even imagined."

"In reality, my plant is on a minor scale compared to the Welsh versions I visited in Swansea. But you're right. It does dominate the landscape, though that wasn't my intention. I just wanted something that would work. Even the mines I found for Dyer, Caswell, and Harkness are producing, and my own as well."

"How *does* it work?"

"It is very, very complicated, as we painfully learned. Hermann is the only one who can really explain it, and the crusty old German has gone mute with all the questioning." He laughed, thinking of his short-tempered metallurgist. "My simple explanation is that the heat from the furnace and hearth make the ore molten. After six hours, the ores separate like oil and vinegar. One is worthless and the other is not."

Tom broke into laughter at the simplified explanation. "Thanks. You grasped the level of my ability to understand perfectly. I'm glad it works. I give you great credit for your perseverance. Many people in Denver say you'll save the territory with your contraption."

Nathaniel was quiet for a while. "You know, this journey started a long, long time ago when I was a boy. My father convinced me that there was always a solution—sometimes unexpected. He set the metronome for the rhythm of my life."

"He must have also taught you how to tolerate adversity. There was a lot at stake. You already had two failures in Colorado."

"They were agonizing to go through, but I learned from them. They taught me respect for difficulties and how to benefit from them. And they gave me a big measure of humility."

"Give yourself credit. Lesser men would have let the obstacles stop them."

Nathaniel brushed off the compliment. "Challenge seems to drive me, but it's not the only thing. My family is just as important. Sometimes it's hard to keep a balance between the two. Gratefully, they seem to be in harmony at the moment. But you know about my life. I want to hear about yours. Tell me about your plans for a church in Denver. Where do they stand?"

"I am happy to report that I've raised enough money to hire an architect."

"That is great news. Did you bring the plans?" Nathaniel asked, tilting forward in expectation.

"I don't go anywhere without them." From his rough brown satchel, he withdrew a stiff notebook of folded drawings. He laid them across the desk for Nathaniel to look at.

"It looks to me as if your architect has captured what you dreamed of. It's unpretentious, but with a sky-high steeple to summon people to come."

"About the height of your chimneys and, hopefully, as effective in its own way. I guess we both have symbols that reach to the sky for what we believe in."

"How close are you to having enough money for construction?"

"The cost will be twenty-five thousand dollars, and I have almost half that."

"That's quite a bit of progress. You should feel good about that. And now that my business is off the rocky shoals, I'd like to contribute something."

"I didn't mean to solicit."

"I know you didn't, and I would be honored to contribute."

"Thank you. That is very kind. I know the rest will come if I have faith." Tom folded the schematics and put them away. "It's not the only good news I have to tell you. I'm going to be married."

Nathaniel was surprised and pleased for his friend at the same time. Congratulations were offered and questions about the intended bride were asked. But if Nathaniel had been surprised by the news of Tom's impending marriage, it was as nothing compared to the revelation of who the bride was: Claire Foster. In hearing that, he felt almost as sad for Joe Watson as he was happy for Tom Potter.

"She came from Providence last year to be a teacher in Denver, and she became a member of my congregation," Tom explained. "Being a preacher's wife isn't always easy, but I think she's well suited. She is patient and thoughtful. As a teacher, she likes to help people learn, and her personality naturally responds to everyone. That's important for what I do. The ministry will of necessity be her calling too. She seems eager to accept that." He looked expectantly at Nathaniel. "We plan to be married in June. I hope you and Alice will come to the wedding."

"I assure you we would not miss it. I can hardly wait to tell Alice the news."

"It has been almost four years since we first met when you came to Colorado Territory," Tom said.

"Does it seem longer than that to you?"

"At times, and at others as if it was just yesterday." Tom set his cup to the side. "The West brought us both here—same place but for different reasons."

The room became quiet as Nathaniel reflected. "Our journeys may be different, but we both have a passion to accomplish something," he finally said.

"I like that idea," Tom said. "Whatever our dreams, we should hold fast to them. At the same time, the journey has to be more important than the dream of accomplishment." He took a moment to reconsider what he had just said. "Journeys and dreams are connected. A great journey depends on having a passionate dream."

Nathaniel rolled Tom's words around in his head. "There is not a time I meet with you that you don't make me think or add some relevance to my life. Someone like me who is in business must take charge of the journey. It's like sailing a ship. You can't just let a business run adrift. You have to steer it if you want to succeed."

"That's one of the ways our professions differ, Nathaniel. My job is to lead people so they can find the insight within themselves. Your line of work is to direct men to do what is necessary to meet a goal."

"I concur," Nathaniel replied. "We are sailing different oceans and have each captured a Golden Fleece—me with my smelter and you with your plans for a church."

"Speaking of that," Nathaniel said, "tomorrow when we tour the smelter, I want you to see my trademark. It is the graceful yet sturdy Argo." He laughed. "My employees questioned a ship in the mountains, but I've kept it."

Tom's face lit up. "The Argo is a trademark worthy of what you are doing. You risked everything you had—your career, your prestige, your income, and your family—to solve a problem by bringing the best technology of the world to Colorado."

"Thank you. I should feel satisfied, but according to your sermon, we have the second half of the journey remaining—the most treacherous part as you described it?"

Tom nodded. "Yes. Perhaps the second part of the journey is about the effect of our decisions on others. It's as much what we leave behind as where we are going."

"Our legacy, you mean?"

Tom nodded again.

"It sounds as if you're telling me that we have to consider our death as much as our life. The consequence of every decision lives on, and a legacy is forever."

"Agreed." Tom stretched wearily. "With that I think I've done enough philosophizing for an evening. I need to go to bed."

They both rose, reluctant to leave the conversation behind. Once Tom had left, Nathaniel settled back down at his desk and slid the newspaper off the top shelf as he twisted the light up higher. After reading a few paragraphs, he heard a rustling on the stairs, and Alice pattered into his study in her slippered feet. Her pregnancy was far enough along that the sheer size of her growing belly had made sleep difficult.

She awkwardly took a seat in the chair that had just been abandoned by Tom. "It's been quite a week of celebration, hasn't it?"

"It has, and I have to admit, there were times when I wondered if it would ever come." He smiled gently. "Really, though, it has been five months of celebration—ever since Crawford and Isabel came. That's when life began again." He inched his chair closer to hers.

"I never want to be without them for that long again, though I know I will have to let them spread their wings someday. It's good to think of what has passed and where we are because of what you achieved with the smelter."

"I've managed to capture my Golden Fleece, like Jason in the myth I've often recounted. But what lies ahead may have as many challenges as the unknown sea," Nathaniel said gently. "My success will be the envy of others who will be determined to blow me off course. And now that the territory has potential for solid economic footing, we should work to make Colorado a state." He paused for a moment and looked up. Then he smiled at Alice and laughed. "That will not be smooth sailing."

"There is so much promise here, especially for our children." His eyes gleamed with optimism. "I envy that they will have the opportunity to be raised on the frontier, near the mountains. They may be tested in ways that they would not have been in Providence, but the hardships will make them stronger—as they will continue to strengthen the two of us. This voyage will change all our lives, and it is one I'm glad we're taking together."

AUTHOR'S NOTE

ᚠ

Many years ago, when I was a volunteer in the archives of the Colorado State Historical Society (now History Colorado), I was asked to process the collection of letters and diaries of Alice Hale Hill. One of her journals contained her handwritten copies of letters received from her husband, Nathaniel Peter Hill, on his trips to Colorado Territory in the mid-1860s. The letters about a new territory were captivating. I promised myself that someday I would revisit them. Much had already been written about Hill, particularly Jay Fell's fine book, *Ores to Metals.* I decided that their lives demanded a bigger scope, one requiring more imagination than fact.

When the time came in my own life to return to the Hill family, I decided on a novel. The story that takes place over five years has an underlying foundation of historical fact derived from letters, diaries, and newspapers. Nevertheless, *Hill's Gold* is a work of fiction. The characters' motivations and actions come purely from the author's imagination. In some cases, I have diverged from historical detail to create a better story.

After the time period in which the novel ends, Nathaniel decided that to be successful in business, he needed to pursue public office. In 1871, he was elected mayor of Black Hawk, and in 1872–1873 he was a member of the Territorial Council. When Jerome Chaffee declined to run for a second term, Nathaniel was elected as a Republican to the United States Senate in 1879. He stayed there until 1885.

He moved his company and his family to Denver in 1878 and built the Argo Smelter in the Swansea neighborhood north of Denver. His business interests expanded in Colorado and elsewhere until his death in 1900.

When Alice and her family moved to Denver, she helped found the Young Women's Christian Association there to promote a safe haven at an affordable rate for women away from their own homes and families. As president, she led the effort to raise money for a building, which was completed in 1901.

Railroads finally linked Denver to the Transcontinental Railroad in 1870. Alice and her children used it to return to Providence twice a year for extended visits with her parents.

When Nathaniel became a US Senator and they moved to Washington, Alice became a member of the Mt. Vernon Ladies Association and was in charge of caring for George Washington's home. She served on the association until she died twenty-two years later, in 1908. Alice was also part of the movement to establish the free kindergarten movement, which was later adopted by public schools.

William Gilpin spent the rest of his life in land speculation that included promoting and selling pieces of the Sangre de Cristo Land grant. He never married. He died in 1894 when he was run over by a carriage at the age of eighty-one.

ACKNOWLEDGMENTS

Writing *Hill's Gold* has been like riding a magic carpet, never knowing where it would take me. I had the pleasure of meeting many talented people and discovering information I never expected to find. I am grateful to the amazing number of people who helped me along the way.

Barry Webb and Kim Barton in Arizona read and re-read drafts as I was just beginning to imagine a story from the Hills' letters and journals. Sheila Bender from Port Townsend, Washington, made invaluable suggestions about an early draft. John Kingman from Australia read a later version from front to back, offering insights on history and writing. Stan Dempsey in Denver explained the details of mining techniques used in the 1860s.

When the novel began to take shape, my late-in-life friend, Cotheal Linnell from New Gloucester, Maine and Tucson, Arizona, copyedited two iterations, eliminating chafe, streamlining sentences, and questioning assumptions. The DAC writers critiqued various versions, and Jay Fell generously allowed me to use what he had learned about Nathaniel Hill from researching *Ores to Metals.* As my historical fiction was nearing its final stages, Luther Wilson kindly advised me about the publishing process.

I was able to put together a dynamite team in Denver of editor Melanie Mulhall, designer Pratt Brothers Composition, and marketing master Mary Walewski. Cartographer Jay Kenney created two detailed maps: one of Hill's journey west and the other of his Colorado trip. *Hill's Gold* would not have come to life without them, and I sincerely appreciate their expertise. They made a world of difference.

Nathaniel Hill passionately sought a way to get gold out of ore. My passion was to write historical fiction about Nathaniel and Alice Hill, whom I grew to admire through their letters and journals. Thank you to everyone who came along with me as I created their story.

CPSIA information can be obtained
at www.ICGtesting.com
Printed in the USA
FFOW02n1039300618
47233242-50048FF